More Acclaim for Violet of a Deeper Blue

"Rick Malone is a courageous writer. His honest and compassionate portrait of a young man caught between where he was going and where he has been will open up conversation and move readers of all backgrounds."

—David Haynes, author of *All American Dream Dolls* and *Live at Five*

■ ■ ■

"Powerful...profound...a penetrating and unapologetically bold look at the race problem in America... *Violet of a Deeper Blue* is destined to join the ranks of such classics as Richard Wright's *Native Son*."

—Emmanuel Lewis, actor and star of the hit television show *Webster*

■ ■ ■

"Rick Malone writes with an emotional intensity and uncompromising honesty rarely found among today's writers...In this debut novel, he at once establishes himself as one of the foremost voices in African-American literature today."

—Gary Yates, Professor of Speech and Theater, Clark Atlanta University

Violet of a Deeper Blue

a novel by
Rick Malone

Grateful acknowledgment is made to the following for permission to reprint previously published material:

TRO and Ludlow Music, Inc. for excerpts from lyrics of "We Shall Overcome" by Zilphia Horton, Frank Hamilton, Guy Carawan and Pete Seeger. Inspired by African American Gospel Singing, members of the Food & Tobacco Workers Union, Charleston, SC, and the southern Civil Rights Movement. TRO © Copyright 1960 (Renewed) and 1963 (Renewed) Ludlow Music, Inc., New York, International Copyright Secured. All rights reserved including public performance for profit. Reprinted by permission of Ludlow Music, Inc. and TRO.

Bud John Songs, Inc. for excerpts from lyrics of "Can't Nobody Do Me Like Jesus" by Andrae Crouch. © Copyright 1982 Bud John Songs, Inc. All rights reserved. Used by permission of Bud John Songs, Inc.

Warner Bros. Publications U.S. Inc. for excerpts from lyrics of "Someone to Watch Over Me" by George Gershwin and Ira Gershwin. © Copyright 1926 (Renewed) WB Music Corp. All rights reserved. Used by permission of Warner Bros. Publications U.S. Inc.

Edward B. Marks Music Company for excerpts from lyrics of "God Bless the Child" by Arthur Herzog Jr. and Billie Holiday. © Copyright 1941 Edward B. Marks Music Company. Copyright renewed. All rights reserved. Used by permission of Edward B. Marks Music Company.

Rick Malone for excerpts from lyrics of "I Thought You Knew" by Rick Malone. © Copyright 1997. All rights reserved. Used by permission of Rick Malone.

Library of Congress Cataloging-in-Publication
(Provided by Quality Books, Inc.)

Malone, Rick.
    Violet of a deeper blue : a novel / by Rick Malone. -- 1st ed.
        p. cm.
    Preassigned LCCN: 98-71433
    ISBN: 0-9663926-0-4
        1. Racism--United States--Fiction.   2. Afro-Americans--Social conditions--1975--Fiction.
3. United States--Race relations--Fiction.   4. Discrimination in employment--Fiction.
    I. Title.
    PS3563.A427V56 1998

                                                                    813'.54
                                                                    QBI98-817

Published in the United States by Azure Publishing, Chanhassen, MN.

First Printing: January 1999
Printed in the United States of America
        02   01   00   99   7   6   5   4   3   2   1

This is a work of fiction. Names, characters, places and incidents either are the product of the author's imagination or are used fictitiously, and any resemblance to actual persons, living or dead, events, or locales is entirely coincidental.

To my parents, Douglas and Azalee Malone,
and to the memory of my late grandparents,
Van Risby and Annie Jones

When I was a child, I spake as a child, I understood as a child, I thought as a child: but when I became a man, I put away childish things.

I Corinthians 13:11

Acknowledgements

I would like to gratefully acknowledge the contributions of the following people, without whom this book would not have been possible: my editor, *Scott Edelstein,* for his brilliant developmental editing; my parents, *Douglas and Azalee Malone,* for their encouragement, support, and prayers along the way and for always believing in me and sharing with me in my dream of seeing this book one day published; my brother, *Dr. Douglas Malone, Jr.,* for advice on pharmacological and general medical procedures; *Jillian McAdams, senior marketing research analyst,* for advice on marketing and business-related matters; *Vivien Purmort,* for proofreading, cheerleading and being a sounding board; *Marv Truhler, computer and networking consultant,* for computer-related information; *the fine ladies in the Training Department at Shady Grove Hospital in Gaithersburg, MD* (whose names, regrettably, escape me now), for information on emergency medical procedures; my father, the *Reverend Douglas Malone, Sr.,* for advice on constructing the church scenes; my uncle, the erudite *Dr. L. C. Risby,* for helping nurture my inquisitive and analytical nature throughout my maturation years and beyond, which proved indispensable in the writing of this book; my sister-in-law, *Aurora Malone,* for her constant encouragement; and most of all to *God,* for blessing me with the vision for this book and the sustaining passion to see it through to fruition. To Him be the glory. And to the countless others far too numerous to name, who offered a word of encouragement or shared a tidbit of wisdom somewhere along the way, thank you, too.

One

Rrrriiiiiinng! Rrrriiiiiinng! The intrusive peal shattered the stillness of the night, interrupting his sleep. *Rrrriiiiiinng! Rrrriiiiiinng!* He stuck out an arm from under the covers and blindly felt about on the night stand for the telephone. *Rrrriiiiiinng! Rrrriiiiiinng!* After nearly knocking over the lamp, he found it and picked up.

"Hello?"

"Is this Brandon Northcross?" The voice was muffled, like someone trying to disguise his voice.

"What?"

"Is this Brandon Northcross?"

"Yeah. Who's this?" He peered at the glowing orange readout of the digital clock. 3:17 am.

"Never mind who this is. You just listen up, 'cause I ain't gon say this but once."

"What?" He wiped the sleep from his eyes. "Who is this?"

"If you know what's good for you, you'll stay the hell away from CSU in the morning, 'cause we don't want anymore of you blacks working here."

"Say *what?* Curt, I know it's you, man," he said, laughing, as he stifled a yawn. "You're not fooling any—"

"This ain't no gag," the voice said. "You better listen to what I'm saying."

"Curt, you wait 'til I get back home. I'm gonna—"

"Your composite score on the GMAT was 710. Your graduate GPA at Dartmouth was 3.65. Your date of birth is 11/5/65. Your social security number is 416-87-3462. Your blood type is B. You still think this is a joke?"

Bolting upright, Brandon blurted out, "How'd you know—"

"Don't worry 'bout that. All you need to know is this. You bring your black ass in here tomorrow, boy, you gon be real sorry!" The line went dead.

"Hello? Hello?"

Slowly placing the receiver back down in the cradle, he sat there for a long while, trembling, sweat dripping from his armpits, as he tried to figure out what he ought to do. Should he call the police? But what would they be able to do about it? They wouldn't know who had called anymore than he knew. He got up, went to the window, and carefully peered out through the blinds at the courtyard below, half expecting to see a bogeyman lurking about. There was no one there. Unable to get back to sleep, he lay awake until morning.

■ ■ ■

Sccccrrrrrreeeeeeeeeeeecch! As his connecting train groaned into the subway station, Brandon bounded down the escalator to the lower level. He could feel the platform vibrating and see bits and pieces of paper swirling up from the tracks. Already running late, he could not afford to miss this train. Although it was a typically hot, muggy, early-August morning out on the streets of Washington, D.C., it was pleasantly cool inside the station, the air rushing past his face crisp and invigorating.

Brandon managed to make his way aboard the train just as the doors were closing. With all the seats taken, he found a place to stand just beyond the door. With his free hand, he gripped one of the overhead chrome railings. In his other hand was his black, leather briefcase, monogrammed with his initials. The train operator's monotone voice droned over the PA system. "Blue Line train to Van Dorn Street. Next station, McPherson Square."

As the train proceeded through the darkened tunnel, he warily scanned the faces of the people in the car around him, wondering if one of them was the caller from the night before. Almost immediately he dismissed the thought. No, whoever it was had somehow managed to get a hold of his personnel records and was simply playing a prank on him. It was probably just a hazing kind of thing, sort of an initiation rite, they did with new employees. Whoever it was would probably reveal himself to him later and explain that it had all just been a joke.

The train pulled into the next station. Two teenage girls carrying school books bounded into the train car. They squeezed their way just beyond the threshold of the door to where Brandon was standing and quickly started up a stream of chatter between themselves, interspersed with frequent snickers and giggles. One was a brunette; the other was a blonde. Both were nice looking, but the blonde was by far the more attractive of the two. Tall and curvy, her skin was warmly aglow with a deep, brown tan. Her straw yellow hair was pulled back into a ponytail that fell midway her back. Her bare-midriff, candy-cane striped blouse stretched taut across her ample bust. Standing with her back to him, she was doing most of the talking.

"I wish I had been there to see the look on his face," she said, giggling.

"Oh, I almost forgot," the brunette said. "How was the Riviera?"

"Beautiful! You've got to go with us next time. I mean, the food, the music, the bars, the—"

"But what about the beaches? I can see by your tan that you caught some serious rays."

"Oh, honey, this is nothing," the blonde said, glancing down at her arms with a dismissive nod of her head. "You should have seen me when I first got back. I was so dark you wouldn't have recognized me. All I needed was a good perm and I could have easily passed for—"

The sudden, wide-eyed expression that fell over the face of the brunette and the almost reflexive motion of her hand up to her mouth halted the blonde in mid-sentence, as if the hand had come up to cover her own mouth. The brunette leaned forward and whispered something to her friend. Glancing over at the window, the blonde caught a glimpse of Brandon's reflection, then did a quick double take. Brandon smiled at her. She smiled back, then turned and looked directly at him. Turning toward her friend, she whispered something in her ear.

The operator announced the next stop. At the sudden lurching of the train as it braked, the blonde, in one deft motion that couldn't have been more skillfully executed had it been choreographed, did a half-turn and fell back flush into him, throwing both her arms tightly around his neck. In the process, her books tumbled to the floor. It took nearly all his strength to maintain his grip on the railing so they both wouldn't go down.

"I'm so sorry, falling into you like that," the girl exclaimed, slowly releasing her arms from around him once the train finally came to a stop. "It was so clumsy of me. I don't know what happened. I usually have a much better sense of balance."

"No problem," he said, stooping to pick up her books. He couldn't help but smile to himself at how contrived her little act had been.

"Oh, thanks," she said, accepting the books from him.

"It's really hard keeping your balance on these trains sometimes, the way they bounce you around," he said, playing along with her little game.

As passengers streamed in and out, Brandon happened to notice a big man in a dark, ill-fitting suit get on and squeeze in behind him, but paid no further attention to him.

"So, where're you headed?" the blonde asked, brightly. "To work?"

"Yeah. As a matter of fact, it's my first day at this new job I'm starting."

"Oh, cool, then!" she said. "What do you do?"

"I'll be working as a marketing research analyst."

"Sounds neat," she said. "Where at?"

"CSU."

"Awesome! Are you from here?"

"No, I'm from New Hampshire. What about you?"

"Yeah, I'm from the area. I live in Chevy Chase."

"Are you on your way to school?" Brandon asked.

"Yeah, I'm a sophomore at George Mason. By the way, I'm Heather." She offered him her hand.

"Hi, I'm Brandon," he said, shaking hands with her.

"And this is Paula," she said, motioning toward her friend. But Paula appeared nearly transfixed by something behind Brandon. Turning to see what it was, Brandon came nearly face to face with the big man in the shabby suit. He was glaring at the girls with a hard, penetrating hatred. Then, almost as if in slow motion, the man spat out the words, *"nigger-loving sluts!"* Though only loud enough to be heard by those standing closest to the man, the loathsome words seemed to fill the entire train car. The man then shifted his menacing glare to Brandon. For what seemed like forever, Brandon stood there, holding the man's gaze, but more out of shock than any desire to try to stare him down.

The train made another stop. As soon as the doors opened, the girls wasted no time getting off. As passengers shifted all around him, Brandon lost sight of the man. The doors closed and the train started in motion again. There was no longer any sign of the big man. But a lurid afterimage of his face, contorted in a spasm of hate, continued to burn through Brandon's brain. Suddenly, a terrifying thought slammed into his head like a two-by-four. Was he the one, the one who had made the threatening phone call?! Or was he just some bigot from a bygone era who resented seeing two white women talking to a black man? But why couldn't he be the one who had called? On the other hand, how would he have known which car he'd be riding in? All sorts of thoughts, sinister thoughts, began to race through Brandon's head, like pinballs ricocheting inside a pinball machine. He had to get a grip. His imagination was getting the best of him.

The operator's voice blared through the car again. "Crystal City. Doors open on your right." Crystal City! He had missed his stop. Pentagon City was where he had intended to get off. He exited as soon as the doors opened. Signs along the platform indicated various exits to the street. He studied them to get his bearings. The doors closed and the train began to pull away. Standing just feet from the tracks, he casually glanced over at the departing train. Terror leaped out at him. The big man was peering at him from inside the train, his face pressed up against the glass, distorting his features into a hideous, grotesque mask. Although the man was quickly whisked from view, his image, as before, stayed with Brandon, haunting him. After checking his watch, he hurried for the escalators.

A wall of thick, humid air greeted him when he emerged from the station. Five to six blocks away, the CSU highrise gleamed under the intense morning sun, dwarfing the other office buildings around it. An empty taxi meandered by, the driver appearing to be looking for fares. Brandon stepped off the curb to hail it.

"Taxi!" he yelled, flailing his arms. The taxi slowed. But not for him. Instead, it continued past him to pick up someone a half block ahead. Brandon tried again with another taxi, nearly leaping out at it to make sure he got the driver's attention. This one, too, continued past. Why neither taxi had stopped for him, he didn't know. But whatever the reason, he didn't have time to sort it out right now. He had to get to work. He decided to walk. It would do him good, help dissipate some of his tension.

Two

A glinting, black marble slab engraved with the wording *Computer Systems Unlimited, Inc.* sat just inside the office park. Surrounding it was a decorative bed of pink and yellow tulips. As Brandon hurried up the walk, he was forced to shield his eyes against the sun that glared cruelly off the mirrored glass of the lofty structure.

The lobby was refreshingly cool, a welcome relief from the stifling heat outside. Sunlight filtered down upon the checkerboard marble floor through an overhead skylight. The receptionist, a pleasant-looking woman with librarian eyeglasses dangling from around her neck, looked up as he approached.

"How may I help you?" she asked.

"I'm here for the new employee orientation," he gasped, out of breath from having practically run all the way.

"And your name, please?"

"Brandon Northcross." Bringing her glasses up to her face, she scanned a notebook lying open before her.

"Ah, yes, Brandon Northcross," she said, peering back up at him over her glasses. "Your orientation is being held in Room 308." She wrote the room number on a slip of paper and handed it to him, along with a plastic clip-on badge. "Use this temporary badge for now. You'll be given a permanent one at your orientation. Be sure to return this one at the end of the day. Now, to get to 308, go right through that door using your badge," she said, indicating a door across the lobby. "The elevator will be just to your left. Take the elevator up to three. When you get off, take a right. 308 will be toward the end of the hall on your left."

■ ■ ■

The orientation lasted close to an hour and a half. When it was over, Brandon headed to meet his second-line manager, Bob Tomasino, whose office was on the 24th floor. As he rode the elevator up, he felt an irrepressible effervescence. All of the weekend study sessions, the late-night cramming, the crummy cafeteria food, and the overall meager existence of a college student was finally paying off. He had gotten his foot in the door of corporate America and nothing was going to stand in his way of going to the top, the very top. *Ping!* The doors opened onto his floor. A glass-encased directory was ensconced on the wall straight ahead. Stepping from the elevator, his attention focused on the directory, he narrowly missed colliding with an intense-looking, bird-faced man who was hurrying past, an over-stuffed satchel cradled in his arms like a football.

"Excuse me," Brandon said, quickly stepping out of the way. But in the process he backed into a woman headed in the other direction. "Sorry." He nearly collided with several other people, too. Finally managing to extricate himself from the rush hour-like traffic in the hall, he stood to the side and observed the people for a moment. Everyone seemed in a big hurry. They reminded him of roaches scurrying for cover from the sudden onslaught of a bright light. After checking the register, Brandon started on his way. All along the plush corridor, glass-walled offices and meeting rooms teemed with beehive-like activity. Yes, this was where it all happened. CSU. Big Red. The big time.

A name plate outside the office read, *Bob Tomasino,* and underneath, *Manager Sales Marketing Research.* A petite woman with shoulder-length, straight blonde hair was seated at a desk just outside the office. She had her back to him and was busy searching through a file cabinet, while at the same time carrying on a conversation with someone on the phone. Through the partially opened door Brandon saw a man leaning over the front of a big mahogany desk talking with a shiny haired man seated behind it. Brandon tapped lightly on the door to get their attention. Neither man gave any indication he had heard him knock and continued their discussion. He tapped again, a little harder. This time they both looked up.

"Excuse me, but I'm Brandon Northcross, the new marketing research analyst, and I'm supposed to report to a Mr. Bob Tomasino," he said, nervously glancing down at his acceptance letter, "in the Sales Marketing Research Department." Neither man said anything, but just continued to look at him, as if they hadn't understood a word he'd said. Maybe he had the wrong office, he thought. "This *is* Mr. Tomasino's office, isn't it?" he asked, leaning back to double-check the name plate outside the door.

"Oh, oh, yes...I'm Bob Tomasino," the man behind the desk finally said, getting up from his chair and motioning him into the office. The bewildered look on the man's face told Brandon that he had not been expecting him and that now that he was here, he wasn't sure how he felt about it. "I'm sorry, but we were so wrapped up in these reports here," he said, sweeping his hand over the papers spread out on his desk.

"I didn't mean to barge in like this, Mr. Tomasino, but—"

"Oh, no...no problem. And call me Bob," the man said, coming around the desk and extending his hand. "And your name again?"

"Brandon. Brandon Northcross," he replied, shaking hands with the man. Bob was short, thick-bodied and a little pudgy around the waist. The sleeves of his white dress shirt were rolled mid-way up his hairy forearms. Cigarette butts overflowed the ashtray on his desk. Bob gestured toward the other man. "This is Peter McDaniel. Peter's one of my staff people."

"Nice to meet you," the man said, extending him his hand along with a cordial smile.

"Nice to meet you, too," Brandon said.

"You wanna pick this up later, Bob, like maybe after lunch sometime?" Peter said.

"Yeah, let's get back together then. I'll give you a call."

Peter excused himself from the room and Bob offered Brandon a seat in one of the comfortably padded chairs in front of his desk. Through the wide, ceiling-high windows that ran the length of the spacious corner office, Brandon could see the buildings of downtown D.C., the sun glinting off the tops of them.

Seated behind his desk, Bob tapped out a cigarette from a pack on his desk and lit up. He pulled the smoke from the cigarette deep into his lungs, then gave off a hacking cough. "Gotta give these things up someday," he said, removing a manila folder from inside his desk. "So, you were hired as a research analyst with our group. That right?"

"Yes, that's right," Brandon said.

"Ah, who'd you interview with? I see you're a new-college hire, right?"

"Yes, I graduated this past December '87. I interviewed with Nelson Ostowski. Does he still work here, by the way?"

"No, he retired about a month ago." Bob opened the folder. "It says here that you went to Dartmouth."

"Yes."

"Ivy league, huh? It says you have a B.S. in economics and an MBA, both from Dartmouth. That's a pretty rigorous MBA program they've got there, I hear."

"Yeah, it was pretty tough sometimes," Brandon said.

"You mind if I ask you a couple of questions, just to sort of get a feel for your knowledge base?" Bob said. "I do this with all new-hires."

"No, go right ahead," Brandon said, even though he did find it a little odd that the man would want to quiz him.

"You're familiar with corporate structure design, right?"

"Corporate structure design? Yes, I'm familiar with it."

"Good. So, describe for me a functional design." Brandon thought for a moment.

"Well, a functional design would be basically where, under the president or CEO, you had HR, Finance, Control, Production, Marketing and Sales."

"And in what sort of environment would you most likely use such a design?"

"To my understanding, you would use the functional design in a company that's operating in a fairly stable market with a single product or limited product line in which there are only infrequent product changes. The advantage of this type of design is that it encourages centralized decision making. One of the disadvantages of it is that it makes it difficult to meet rapidly changing customer needs, in addition to poor coordination across functional lines."

"What about a divisional design?"

"Well, if I'm not mistaken," Brandon said, "a divisional design is more apt to be used in a company with a more complicated product line and/or distribution network. One of the advantages of this design is that it allows decisions to be made relatively quickly. The downside of this design is that it can increase overhead and erode profit margins. Would you like to hear about the matrix design?"

"No, that's okay," Bob said, giving Brandon a paper-thin smile. "Good answers. Good answers. But let me ask you something a little more specific, something more in line with marketing."

"Sure."

"I'm sure you're aware that when making any marketing analysis, it's necessary to check the validity of certain financial concepts. You would agree with that, right?"

"Yes, I would," Brandon said.

"Can you tell me what those financial concepts are?"

"I'd say fixed costs, for starters, then variable costs, revenue, unit contribution and…break-even volume." Bob fidgeted nervously in his chair.

"How do you calculate the weighted average cost of capital?" Bob asked, leaning forward now, an unmistakable gleam in his eyes like that of a hunter moving in for the kill.

"The weighted average cost of capital?"

"Yeah." The questions were getting absurd. He was there to report for work, not to be interviewed all over again. Brandon considered telling Bob just that, but then decided to go along on this one last question. After taking a moment to collect his thoughts, he gave his answer.

"To calculate the weighted average cost of capital, you multiply percent of long-term debt in optimal capital structure times after-tax cost of long-term debt. Then you add that to percent of equity in optimal capital structure multiplied by after-tax cost of equity."

"Not bad," Bob said, slumping back in his chair, the gleam gone from his eyes. "Not bad at all. But knowing principles and formulas is one thing. Knowing how to apply them is quite another. That only comes from experience, real-world experience. And speaking of experience, do you have any?" That flicker had returned to Bob's eyes.

"Yes, I took off a semester and did an internship at one of the leading investment firms in Hanover. They offered me a position, but I declined it to finish up at Dartmouth." Bob managed a weak smile, leaned back in his chair again and took a pull on his cigarette, before casually placing it in the ashtray. A wavy column of pale, bluish smoke spiraled into the air, illuminated by a shaft of sunlight cutting diagonally across the desk. Bob cleared his throat.

"I'm going to say something that I hope you don't take the wrong way, young man," he began, hunched over his desk now, his hands clasped in front of him. "Now, I want you to know up front that I'm not a bigot or anything. I want to see blacks and other minorities get ahead just as much as anybody. But the fact is, blacks, in my experience—and this is just my personal experience—they usually don't do that well in marketing. I don't know why. Now, in other fields, blacks seem to do as well as anybody, but not in marketing, for some reason." Lifting his hands, palms outward, to stave off the rebuttal he obviously felt Brandon would be offering, Bob quickly added, "I know, I know. It doesn't mean you can't make the grade. Personally, I think you're a very bright young man with a lot of potential. But I just thought I'd tell you that, just in case you maybe wanted to reconsider, 'cause there are certainly other areas here at CSU where you could work, especially with that MBA. Before Brandon could manage to get a word in, Bob pressed ahead.

"As I'm sure you know, CSU prides itself on being a cut above other companies. We hire only the best candidates, who we then mold into CSU material. And we reward those employees who make the grade very generously. We offer probably the highest starting salaries and pay out the most lucrative bonuses of any company in the industry. Our employee stock option plan is second to none. We don't have layoffs. Never have. Never will. And if you have what it takes, we put you on the fast track, where you can go as high as your dreams and abilities will take you. But in return, we expect exceptional performance. And loyalty. Like I said, you're a very bright young man, but I'm concerned you might be getting in just a little over your head." For a moment, Brandon felt as if he'd just been hit with a sucker punch. But he quickly regained his footing.

"Well, I've given a lot of thought to working in marketing," Brandon said. "It's where my interest is, and I think I can do the job." He tried to say it in a way that he sounded confident, without coming across as overly defensive. Actually, Sales was where he wanted to be, eventually. That's where the real money was. But his long-range plans dictated that he first get a solid footing in Marketing.

"Well, okay, then," Bob said, conceding. "We're definitely committed to equal opportunity here at CSU. That's another thing that we're known for. We give everybody—regardless of race, creed or color—an equal chance. And if this is where you've got your heart set on working, then so be it." Bob picked up Brandon's folder again. "Is New Hampshire your home?"

"Yes, New Hampshire's my home. Manchester, New Hampshire."

"Lived there all your life?"

"Yes, I've never lived anywhere else."

"Your family, parents…they all back there?"

"For the most part, yes."

"So, you're not afraid you'll get homesick, being so far away from home and all?" Before Brandon could answer, the intercom on the desk buzzed. "Excuse me," Bob said, then pressed a button on the unit. "Yes, Cheryl?"

"Bob, I just wanted to remind you of your ten-thirty department meeting," a woman said. Bob glanced at his watch.

"Oh, damn! Thanks for the reminder, Cheryl. I'd forgotten all about it." Pressing the button again, Bob rose and stubbed out his cigarette. "We'll talk some more later," he said, rolling down his sleeves and grabbing his coat from the back of his chair. "Right now, come along with me." Brandon grabbed his briefcase and followed Bob out the door.

■ ■ ■

When they arrived at the conference room where the meeting was taking place, a curly haired man with a thick mustache, late-twenties was making a presentation using a flip chart. The rest of those present were seated around an oak table. Bob took a seat at the head of the table and motioned for Brandon to sit wherever he liked. Brandon grabbed a vacant seat toward the other end of the table.

Just as the man was finishing up his presentation, an attractive blonde, dressed in a close-fitting, tailored business suit that showed plenty of leg, entered the room. Somewhere in her mid to late thirties, she had the kind of body that could stop men in their tracks. And by the way she carried herself, it was obvious that she knew it, as she exuded what could best be described as a highly potent mixture of haughtiness and raw sensuality. Her heavy makeup made her look like a Las Vegas showgirl out of costume. She took a seat on the side of the table across from Brandon. Bob cleared his throat.

"Morning, everyone," he said. "Sorry for missing most of the presentation." Bob then shifted in his chair and looked directly at Brandon for the first time. "I want to introduce to you now the newest member of our department. This is Brandon Northcross. Brandon's joining us right out of college as a research analyst." Brandon nodded. "Okay. Now that you know who he is, let me introduce each of you to him. Starting to my right," Bob began, motioning to the heavyset, bearded man, "this is Norm Pollack. Norm is a senior advanced economist for us, but lately has been helping out on the statistics end as well." The man looked around at Brandon and welcomed him with a slight nod. He had a tired, spent look about him, his eyes crouched behind his silver-rimmed glasses. Seated next to Norm was a fortyish, elegantly dressed woman. Bob introduced her next. "And beside Norm is Francine Cohen, Fran for short. Fran heads up our Zeta team. A real sharp lady." She turned and extended her hand.

"Nice to meet you."

"Same here," he replied, shaking her hand. Next to be introduced was Terri Barbosa, attractive, early twenties, full-figured with dark Mediterranean features. Then came Sean Henkel, a narrow-shouldered, almost frail man with small, delicate-looking hands, in his early thirties. After Sean, came the sultry blonde. She was busy writing something in a legal pad. Her name was Layla Moran. She looked up at Brandon, smiled, then turned her attention back to her writing.

"And seated next to Layla is Tim Carvelas," Bob said, referring to the man who had made the presentation. "Tim is also one of our team leaders." Tim glanced at Brandon, frowned, then looked away. "Next to Tim is Allan Olson, the department's main statistician." The man's thick eyeglasses and braces gave him a decidedly nerdy look. The faint shadow of a mustache was about the only thing that saved him from looking altogether like an eighteen-year-old.

"Okay, any other business, anyone?" Bob asked. There was none. "Good. Oh, and Brandon, meet with me in my office around, say," he said, pausing to check his watch, "1 o'clock. We'll go over some things and get you started." Rising from his chair, Bob added, "Thanks again, folks, for coming—"

"Ah, wait a second, Bob," Tim cut in. "Whose team is he gonna be on?" Tim looked at Brandon with an air of concern, then back at Bob. Bob paused for a moment to consider the question. When he answered, it was almost apologetically.

"Well, your team, Tim. That's where we need the help, isn't it?" Tim threw up his hands in an exaggerated show of exasperation.

"Well, there goes the ball game." Surprised and a bit shocked by Tim's remark, Brandon looked at Bob to see how he would respond. Bob simply lowered his gaze and cleared his throat.

"Okay, folks, that's all for now. Let's break for lunch."

As people started to file out of the room, Sean was the first one over to greet him.

"Hi, Brandon," he said. "Welcome."

"Thanks," Brandon said, getting up from his chair to shake hands with him.

"Brandon, we're really happy about you joining the department," Fran said. "Would you like to join us for lunch? The three of us—myself, Sean and Norm—usually go down to the cafeteria."

"Yeah. Sure."

■ ■ ■

The cafeteria was rapidly filling with people when they arrived. Along one wall were sliding glass doors that opened out onto a patio filled with umbrella-shaded tables, where those who didn't mind the heat were going. The four of them found a table near the back wall.

"So, think you're gonna like working here at Big Red?" Fran said to Brandon.

"Or, perhaps, a better question is whether you think you're up to the challenge," Sean said. "CSU is a great company to work for. No doubt about that. But, man, do they try to get their money's worth out of you. If you're not careful, this place can become almost your life."

"Well, I certainly hope I'm up to the challenge," Brandon said. "I'm not sure yet exactly what I'll be doing, but I'm looking forward to it."

"Oh, you'll do well," Fran said. "And by the way, don't let Tim's attitude get to you. Just try to pay him no mind."

"Thanks."

"So, where'd you go to school?" Fran asked.

"Dartmouth."

"MBA?"

"Yeah."

"Great," Fran said. "At least you've got that going for you."

"How about you guys?" Brandon asked.

"MBA from Wharton," Fran said.

"MBA from University of Chicago," Sean said.

"Econ degree from RPI," Norm said.

"What about Allan and Tim?" Brandon asked.

"Tim just got his MBA not long ago," Fran said. "It was from some school in the area. And as far as Allan, he's got a degree in mathematics from MIT."

"Pretty big-name schools," Brandon said.

"Yeah, CSU likes the big names," Fran said. "No doubt about that."

"What does Layla have?" Sean said. "I know she doesn't have an MBA."

"Seems like I remember her saying she had a business degree from somewhere," Norm said.

"Yeah, that's right," Sean said. "And Terri's currently working toward her MBA."

"Tell me something," Brandon said. "Who's our first-line manager?"

"Well, at the moment, we don't have one," Sean replied. "She left a couple of months ago to take a position at our site up in Boston. Bob's just filling in until a new manager's named, whenever that is."

"I see," Brandon said. "Ah, something else I was wondering about. Where does Layla fit in with the department? Is she staff like Peter?"

"You mean Ms. Layla Moran?" Fran said, letting the first syllable of *Layla* roll slowly off her tongue.

"Layla's a senior analyst," Sean said.

"Among other things, which I won't go into at this time," Fran quickly added.

"Now, c'mon, Fran," Sean said. "Be fair. Just because she went from associate analyst to senior analyst in little more than a year, and stole other people's ideas to get there, that's no reason to dislike her. Or just because someone else usually ends up doing her grunt work for her because she has to be away on personal business." Sarcasm was thick in

Sean's voice. "Hey, I think she's just a perfect example of someone who's pulled themselves up by their own bootstraps."

"Yeah, right," Fran said. "More like someone who's pulled themselves up by their own bedposts, if you ask me."

"You know," Norm said, "I hate to say it, but I think someone should have looked into that situation a long time ago."

"It's politics, Norm," Sean said. "You know how things work around here and probably everywhere else. You scratch my back; I'll scratch yours. And Layla's been scratching the backs of some pretty big boys upstairs. I mean *way* up. You think she could afford that brand new Jag, those diamond necklaces, and that fancy townhouse over in Foggy Bottom just on what she's making here at CSU?"

"Oh, don't I know it," Norm said. "I know it all too well."

"The woman gets away with damn near murder," Sean continued.

"But Layla's no dummy, now," Norm said. "She can be pretty sharp sometimes."

"Yeah, I agree," Sean said. "In fact, she can be very sharp sometimes. But she can also be very devious."

"In street parlance, Layla's what you call a get-over artist," Fran said. "She does whatever it takes."

"And she gets over big-time, too," Sean said. "She comes to work when she wants. She leaves when she wants. She cuts under-the-table deals with managers for projects left and right. If you ask me, it's part of the reason Marci finally left. I mean, you know how it was. If Marci told Layla to do something and she didn't want to do it, she would just say 'screw this' and go over Marci's head."

"Marci was our first-line, Brandon," Norm explained.

"There're certain people that seem to be able to do whatever the hell they want and get away with it," Fran said. "Then there're others that, no matter how hard they work or how much they produce, they just don't want them around. And when they decide they don't want you here, buddy, they just go about weeding you out, one way or another. You remember what happened to Jarrett Knowles, don't you? The black guy that worked up in Accounting. Tall, good-looking guy, always dressed real nice."

"Yeah, I remember him," Norm said. "He was sort of high up there, mid-level, I believe, and rising."

"No one can tell me that what happened to him wasn't politics," Fran said.

"Wasn't he forced to resign over that whole incident?" Sean said.

"Forced to resign?" Fran said. "Ha! He was fired right there on the spot, from what I heard. And after fourteen years with the company. Let go without a pension, severance or anything. And her royal highness, Ms. Moran, was hardly given a slap on the wrist for her part in it."

"It's called being well-connected," Sean said.

"What happened?" Brandon asked.

"Well, Layla was Jarret Knowles' secretary at the time," Fran said. "Anyway, he and Layla were caught getting it on up in his office. When they walked in on them, Layla claimed he had coerced her into it, like it was sexual harassment or something. Gimme a break. People that didn't even work up there knew about them and how she'd been practically throwing herself at him for the longest."

"It was a real curious situation, what happened there," Norm said. "Some people tend to think that the whole thing with Layla was just a facade."

"What do you mean?" Sean said.

"Well, basically, that they were looking for a reason to get him," Norm said. "They say he had a reputation for being pushy, outspoken, and that he had rubbed a lot of people the wrong way."

"Aw, that's just a bunch of crap," Fran said. "You don't get to his level without being at least a little pushy."

"I know," Norm said. "But that's just what I heard. Personally, I think it was just a case of them being out to hang him and, unfortunately, he finally gave them the rope to do it with."

"The rope being his fling with Layla, huh?" Fran said.

"Yep."

■ ■ ■

Brandon met with Bob after lunch as scheduled, where he gave him a run-down of his new job. Eventually, it would involve designing surveys and questionnaires, drafting reports, preparing statistical analyses, making presentations and occasional travel to collect data and offer product samples to assess consumer preferences. And if he continued to progress, he might be placed in charge of his own projects. He would then be responsible for formulating marketing strategies and tactics, recommending pricing actions, and working with advertising sales managers and account executives to develop advertising proposals, sales presentations and business plans. However, as an entry-level analyst, he would initially be consigned more to performing some of the much-needed administrative functions, like copying, collating and tabulating survey results.

As Bob had announced at the department meeting, he would be a member of Tim's team, which included Layla and Allan. This meant that his job evaluations would depend to a large extent on input from Tim, who would be his immediate superior. Peter would also be working with Tim's team. As an entry-level analyst, Bob explained, he would have six months to qualify for promotion to the next level. Although not a requirement, the successful completion and presentation of a Beginning Product Proposal, BPP for short, was generally considered a definite plus in qualifying.

After his meeting with Bob, Sean gave him a tour of the floor, then took him around to meet some of the key personnel in the areas Marketing worked closely with. After the tour, Brandon retreated to the library for the remainder of the day to pour through the company and marketing literature he'd been given.

Three

It was late evening when Brandon finally left for home. With his coat tossed over his shoulder and collar open, he bounced along to the subway station. As he passed a row of neatly trimmed hedges lining the manicured parkway, the sweet, invigorating fragrance of the wild roses leapt out at him through the warm summertime air, propelling him along in a euphoric-like haze. The tension that had plagued him earlier in the day was gone. All he felt now was a marvelously rich high that he wished would go on forever. He was determined not to allow the crank caller, the bigoted man on the train, or Tim spoil this day for him.

Suddenly, he felt like running, just for the heck of it. He hurdled a low hedge that bordered a small park, stirring a flock of white doves grazing peacefully on the lush, green lawn. The gracefulness of their snowy wings in flight created a breathtakingly beautiful aerial display, as they rose high up over the treetops into the filtering dusk. Crossing a playground, he came upon a group of young boys playing soccer, their lengthening, late-evening shadows running with them as they jostled each other to get at the ball. Watching them brought back memories of his high school days when he had played on the school's soccer team. An errant kick sent the boys' ball careening out of their field of play toward him. With his briefcase still in one hand and his coat in the other, he deftly stopped the ball with his foot, then sent it back their way with a high, lofty kick that carried it sailing over their heads and into the net. Impressed by his kick, the boys sent up a cheer for him. He waved to them, before continuing on his way.

He thought of how proud his mother would be if she could see him now. He would give her a call later to let her know how his first day at work had gone. But what he really wished was that his father could see him, and know that he had made good. For once, perhaps, he would be proud of him. Maybe if his father had known that one day he would succeed, he wouldn't have left. He knew he never really measured up to his father's standards. His father had always wanted him to plan for a career in the military, to follow in his footsteps. In his father's words, it would make a real man out of him. Instead, he had had his own ideas about what he wanted to do with his life, and they definitely didn't include the regimented lifestyle of the military. He was a freshman in college the last time he'd seen or talked to his father.

His mind now wandered back over the events that had led up to him landing his job at CSU. It had all started during the final months preceding his graduation that past December. He had attended a half-dozen or so on-campus interviews, the same as had his classmates in the MBA program. But while many of them had received offers, he had received none. Bewildered as to why he was having such difficulty landing employment, he had enrolled in a mini-course on job interviewing, thinking that there must be something wrong in how he was coming across to interviewers. There could be no other plausible explanation, he reasoned. He then wrote to another half-dozen companies, four of which called him in for interviews. But to his dismay, he received rejection letters from these companies as well. Nearly all of his classmates, on the other hand, had all landed jobs by this time, mostly through campus interviews. It was mid-March now and he was still without even the slightest prospect of a job. Actually, he had received several job offers, but they were for positions well beneath what a Dartmouth MBA graduate was qualified for. Then, on the advice of his college advisor, he returned to campus to try his hand at interviewing with the upcoming Spring graduates. A little over a week later, he had been able to arrange interviews with several companies. One of them was the computer giant CSU.

He arrived for the interview dressed in his best suit, his shoes buffed to a glossy shine and his grooming immaculate. As he knocked at the door of the interview room, he felt confident, having committed to memory a host of facts about the company.

"Come in," a man said. Brandon entered the small room, which was sparsely furnished with just a desk and a couple of chairs. Seated behind the narrow desk was a slight, gray-haired gentlemen who looked to be in his mid sixties. He motioned for Brandon to have a seat, and then finished up what he was writing. The man then looked up and greeted him with a warm smile and a friendly handshake, introducing himself as Nelson Ostowski.

The interview went smoothly, the man asking mostly opened-ended questions about his career aspirations, internship experience, and how he might conduct himself in certain job situations. As Brandon talked, the man would make an occasional notation in his tablet. Brandon had come expecting to be quizzed on technical matters and his knowledge of the company, which is how his other interviews had gone.

At the end of the interview, the man put down his pen and said, "I've reviewed your transcripts. And I consider your grades and test scores quite exemplary. And based on them, your internship experience, and what I've just heard today, I see no reason why CSU wouldn't most likely be able to use someone of your caliber. You should be hearing from us within the next several weeks." The news was like a long-awaited breath of fresh air, just what he'd been waiting to hear. But as they shook hands at the door, the man said something that surprised him. "Young man," he said, looking Brandon squarely in the eye, "always remember that you have the ability to do just as well as or better than any white person you compete with. Don't ever let anyone convince you otherwise." The man then bade him farewell and left.

Afterwards, Brandon thought about what Ostowski had said. Why had he felt the need to bring race into the picture? There was nothing in his experience that had caused him to doubt his abilities or to think that others would doubt them solely based on his race. And even though he had been the only black person in most of his classes, he had never detected any prejudice toward him, from either his teachers or his classmates. He had always been taught by his parents, especially his mother, to never use race as an excuse for failure, to always look at things in a colorblind fashion. It was simply a crutch, they had taught him, a crutch used by blacks who simply didn't want to work hard enough and were looking for someone else to blame for their own failures. If you prepared yourself and worked just as hard as whites, there was no reason why you wouldn't succeed. And if some whites did still harbor biased attitudes toward blacks, it was only because of the negative image that far too many blacks presented to whites. But as soon as they discovered that you weren't like those blacks, you would be readily accepted.

Growing up in suburban Manchester, there had been only a handful of other black families in his community. Consequently, most of the kids he had grown up with and gone to school with, from elementary through high school, had been white. This remained the case throughout college. But he had never felt the least discriminated against. His childhood playmates had welcomed him into their homes with no regard to his race. Blackness for him as a child was never an issue one way or the other. Yes, he knew he was black. And he was proud of it. But it didn't define who he was as a person. Neither did he see where it limited his opportunities in any way. For him, blackness was something he could put on and take off at will, like a change of clothes. During his college days, he had never felt the need to join black organizations, for he believed that such organizations only called attention to race unnecessarily and that race only became an issue when you made it an issue.

A few weeks later, just as Nelson Ostowski had promised, Brandon heard from CSU. It was a job offer at their headquarters in Pentagon City, just outside Washington, D.C. He promptly responded, accepting the offer.

Four

Brandon arrived early for work the next day. He had decided that the first thing he would do to ensure that he got off on the right foot would be to be prompt. No, he'd be more than prompt. He'd get to work earlier than he had to and stay later than he had to. Few other people in the department had arrived yet, so he took the opportunity to make more headway with the mound of reading material staring back at him from his desk. Sean arrived a little later.

"Well, you're here all bright and early," Sean said.

"Yeah, thought I'd get in a little early to try and get a jump on some of my reading."

"Aw, don't knock yourself out trying to read all that stuff. You'll pick up a lot of it as you go along."

After getting a quick rundown of some general things from Sean, Brandon spent the early part of the morning getting his computer set up and running. Later, Tim came by to tell him of a copying job that was waiting for him in the copy room. When Brandon got there, Terri was there doing some copying herself.

"Hi," he said.

"Oh, hi," she said. "Your name's Brandon, right?"

"Yeah, and you're Terri, right?"

"Yeah," she said, reaching over to shake his hand. "They have you copying, too, huh?"

"Yeah, Tim said he had a job here waiting for me."

"Oh, that must be it over there," she said, pointing to a stack with a green cover sheet on top. After getting his job started, he came back over.

"You spend a lot of time doing this sort of stuff?"

"Too much time," she said. "I guess they told you that as an entry-level analyst, you get to do a lot of what they call their paper work."

"Yeah."

"Actually, being a gopher is basically what it is, until you qualify," she said. "In addition to doing your own research assignments, you get the privilege of acting as administrative support for everyone else. *Terri, would you make a copy of this? Terri, would you run these slides over to Repro? Terri, would you give me the breakdown on the results from this survey, and by tomorrow morning?'* Drives me up the freakin' walls sometimes. I feel like saying sometimes, hey, that's what we've got secretaries and interns for. It's like initiation into a college fraternity or sorority, but with one exception. You get paid for it. And paid pretty well, too."

"So, how long have you worked here?"

"Oh, about six months now."

"That means you should be qualifying soon, then, right?"

"I certainly hope so," Terri said. "But there're no guarantees. If I already had my MBA, I probably wouldn't have to worry about qualifying. But that won't be for another year now."

"You mean if you already had your MBA you'd already be associate?"

"Yeah," she said. "Most likely. Are you planning on going back for yours soon?"

"My MBA, you mean?"

"Yeah."

"I already have my MBA," Brandon said. "I finished this past December." Terri abruptly stopped what she was doing and looked over at him.

"You already have your MBA and you were hired in at entry level?"

"I guess so," he said. "I thought that was the level all new-college hires came in at, whether they had an MBA or not."

"Well, I don't know about that," she said. "Nearly everyone I know of that's started here with an MBA was automatically hired in above entry level. Where'd you get yours from, what school?"

"Dartmouth."

"You mean you have an MBA from an Ivy League school and you came in at entry level? That doesn't add up. I'd go talk to Bob about it, if I were you."

"Yeah, I'll have to do that," he said, debating in his mind if that would really be the right move at the moment.

For lunch, he and Terri went and grabbed a bite at a nearby deli. As they talked, Brandon became so engrossed in their conversation that he completely forgot about the time and that he had a team meeting at 1 o'clock. Just by chance he happened to glance at his watch.

"Oh, no!" he said.

"What?"

"It's a quarter after one and I had a team meeting at 1 o'clock!"

"We'd better get back."

When they reached the conference room where the meeting was being held, Brandon said a quick goodbye to Terri, then ducked inside. The conversation immediately halted. He felt like game that had suddenly been illuminated in the darkened underbrush by the probing beam of a hunter's searchlight.

"Hope we didn't cut your little luncheon date short, Brandon," Tim said.

"Sorry I'm late," Brandon said, quickly taking a seat. This was the last thing he wanted, to be late for his very first team meeting. The meeting resumed.

■ ■ ■

Later that day, Brandon ran into Tim and Allan in the restroom. The two of them were washing their hands at the sink.

"Welcome to the department, Brandon," Allan said, drying off, then turning and extending his hand to Brandon.

"Thanks, Allan," Brandon said.

"Why do you wanna shake his hand, Allan?" Tim said. "I bet the only reason they hired him is he's black, just to fill some quota." Allan looked away, obviously embarrassed by Tim's remark.

"Look, I'm not a token," Brandon said, turning to face Tim. "It just so happens I was hired for the same reason you were, because I'm qualified."

"Oh, is that a fact?" Tim said, taking a step toward Brandon. "Well, that's not the way I see it. I say the only reason you're here is to fill some affirmative action quota, just because we didn't have any blacks in our department. I'll bet there were white applicants more qualified than you that were passed over just so they could fill their quota. And I'm not the only one around here that thinks that, either."

"Hey, cut the guy some slack, Tim," Allan said. "I mean, really, you don't know that that was why they hired him. Personally, I don't think they would've given him the job if he wasn't qualified."

"Oh, yeah?" Tim said. "Just goes to show how much you know about what's going on these days, Allan. They're taking jobs from deserving whites and giving them to under-qualified blacks, just because of this affirmative action crap. I got a uncle back home in Queens that's a fireman. They passed him over for promotion last month, a promotion he had been waiting for for years, to promote a black, just because the city said there was this history of blacks not being promoted up through the ranks. That's the kinda bullshit that's going on today, man."

"Look, I'm sorry about what happened to your uncle," Brandon said. "But I know why I was hired, and it wasn't to fill some quota. My work will speak for itself."

"Well, we'll see," Tim said. "I'll be watching. You can count on that." Tim then turned and started out.

"Hey, don't let him get to you, man," Allan said. "I don't know what's eating him."

Brandon stood there, teeth clenched, as he watched the door close behind Allan. Why was Tim so convinced that he had been hired just to fill some quota and not because of his merit? Was it simply because of what had happened to his uncle? Or was it really true what Tim said, about deserving whites being passed over in favor of under-qualified blacks?

■ ■ ■

As Brandon headed for the copy room one day, he came upon Terri. She was struggling with a huge stack of papers. It was obviously too much for her to manage, for some of the papers were already threatening to spill onto the floor. He went over to help.

"Here, let me give you a hand, Terri," he said, reaching to remove the top layer of papers from the stack.

"That's okay," she said. "I can manage." But when she tried to take another step, the pile became even more unsteady in her arms. He stood by looking on as she grappled with the papers, trying her best to get a handle on them. Nothing seemed to be working, however. It was clear that she couldn't manage it by herself and that the pile was about to slip from her grasp at any moment. Brandon reached in again to help.

"Terri, you really should let me give—"

"No!" she said tersely, jerking away. But the abrupt motion caused her to lose her grip, scattering the papers all over the floor.

"Sorry, Terri," he quickly apologized. "I didn't mean to—"

"Look!" she said in a low but angry voice. "I told you I don't need your help! So will you please just—" A man passing by looked over at them. Terri froze. After nervously glancing one way along the hallway and then the other, she turned back to Brandon, like she wanted to say something. Instead, she just stooped and began gathering up the errant papers. Dumbfounded, Brandon could only stand by and watch before finally just walking away.

The explanation for Terri's peculiar behavior came the following evening. It was well past quitting time and most people had already left for the day. Brandon was still around because he wanted to get a head start on a copy job that was due the next day. The copier he was using needed toner, so he headed for the supply room down the hall. As he drew near to the room, he heard voices coming from inside, voices of a man and a woman. The woman sounded agitated. Brandon stepped behind a column so they wouldn't see him.

"And I definitely don't appreciate you going around telling people I'm dating this new guy in my department. Because it's not true. We went to lunch together. That's all. Now, can I get by, please?" It was Terri. He couldn't see her that well because the man she was talking to was standing between her and the doorway, his back to him. But he could see that every time she tried to go around him, he'd step over in front of her to block her way.

"Well, that's not what I heard," the man said. "See, I heard you had a thing for this black guy. What's wrong? White men not good enough for you anymore?"

"What?!" Terri said. "Look, I don't have time for this garbage. Okay? Now, if you don't get out of my way, I'm gonna report you to HR!" This time the man made no attempt to impede Terri's progress, as she brushed past him and out the door. Just as the man was about to turn around, Brandon heard footsteps approaching from around the corner behind him. So as not to look suspicious, he turned and pretended to be reading a bulletin that was posted on the wall. When the person had passed, Brandon quickly looked back toward the supply room, but the man was already gone.

■ ■ ■

Later that evening, Brandon leaned against the railing of his balcony, watching as the sun sank slowly in the faraway western skies. Bright orange like a hot stove top coil, it set the horizon aflame with fiery bands of an iridescent red and gold. The pale bluish light of televisions flickered from the high-rise apartment building across the way. Those that were tuned to the same station flashed in synchrony, like bulbs on a neon sign. Even now, as the intermittent phosphorescent glow of fireflies lit the darkening air, his mind kept going back to what had happened earlier with Terri. Did people at work really believe that something was going on between him and Terri, simply because they had gone to lunch together? And, if they did, were they as threatened by it as the guy who had harassed Terri evidently was? Were some white men really that insecure?

He watched as the streaking, white lights of a metro train shot swiftly by on the overhead trestle just beyond the thicket of trees, before going back inside. On his way to the elevator, he happened to come across an envelope laying in the hallway. He picked it up. It was addressed to someone who lived down the hall from him. He decided to go slide it under their door.

The TV game show *Jeopardy* blared from inside the apartment through the partially opened door. Sitting on a worn-out sofa was a man who was talking on the phone, an unlit cigarette between his fingers. It sounded like he was arguing with someone. The man didn't see him.

"Every time, we end up having this same conversation and—" The man picked up a cigarette lighter from the coffee table and was about to light his cigarette when he suddenly jerked forward, apparently reacting to something just said to him over the phone. "Look, Ann, it's not like I'm making a whole lotta money right now, myself, you know?" Maybe he ought to just lay the envelope by the door. But just as he was about to do so, the man noticed him and motioned him inside. "Just sit that stuff on the floor," he said, his hand cupped over the mouthpiece, as he nodded to an upholstered end chair that was piled high with photography magazines. The chair looked even more worn and frazzled than the sofa. Brandon placed the magazines neatly on the floor and sat down.

In the middle of the floor in front of the TV, a little girl, about four years old, was playing with a toy car. "Whadaya mean, you can't keep supporting her off what you make?... For crying out loud, Ann, she's over here half the time... What?" The man covered his ear, as he strained to hear. "Wait a minute." He then got up and went over to the TV. "Honey," he said to the little girl, "keep the TV down when Daddy's on the phone." He turned the volume all the way down, reducing the actors to pantomime, then came back to the sofa and resumed his conversation. "Look, Ann, we'll have to continue this some other time. I've got to go...Okay," he said, then hung up. "Man!" He looked over at Brandon. "I'm beginning to think divorce is worst than marriage." He let out a big sigh. "So, what can I do for you?"

"Oh," Brandon said, standing up, "I just stopped by to bring you this letter. It has your address on it. I found it out in the hall."

"Oh, I must've dropped it earlier. Thanks," the man said, taking the letter from him. "By the way, Gill Howard's the name." He stood up and put out his hand. The man's handshake was firm. Somewhere in his mid thirties, he had a rugged, craggy look about him, like he had been doing outdoor work all his life.

"Brandon Northcross," he said. "I live at the other end of the hall. I just moved in a little over a week ago from New Hampshire."

"Are you the man at the pet store with the talking bird?" the little girl asked.

"No, honey," Gill said. "Brandon just moved here from New Hampshire. He's one of our new neighbors from down the hall. She's talking about this guy that works at this pet shop we visit sometimes where they have this parakeet."

"Oh," Brandon said, smiling.

"This is Lisa, my daughter. Say hello to Brandon, Lisa."

"Hello," she said.

"Hi, Lisa."

"Listen," Gill said, "we were just about to pay a little visit on a neighbor that lives over in the next building. I've got to do a little repair work on her TV. Her name's Sarah and she's real friendly. Wanna come along?"

"Well, okay, but just as long as I won't be imposing," Brandon said.

"Don't worry. You won't be imposing. Let me just go grab my tools and I'll be ready to go," Gill said, heading to the back. The little girl, having grown tired of her toy car, jumped up from the floor and grabbed a little toy camera from off the sofa and came over to Brandon.

"When I grow up, I'm gonna take pictures just like my daddy," she said. "Can I take your picture?" She aimed the camera at Brandon.

"Now don't go worrying our guest, Lisa," Gill said, re-emerging with his tool box.

"Oh, she's not bothering me," Brandon said. "I don't mind. How do you want me to pose? Like this?" He made a silly face. The little girl giggled. "Or maybe like this?" He made a scary face. She screamed, then giggled even more.

"Yeah, like that!" she said.

"Say 'hold it!'" Gill instructed her.

"Hold it!" she shouted. Brandon held the pose and she snapped the button on her little camera. A little light flickered on top of it, imitating the flash of a real camera. She giggled. "Here," she said, handing Brandon her camera. "Now, take a picture of me!" He lifted the camera and focused. "Wait! I want my friend Demby in the picture with me." She ran over and picked up a little teddy bear from the floor. "Okay, I'm ready now!" She cuddled the little bear in her arms and smiled.

"Okay, gimme a big smile, Lisa." She stretched her dimpled cheeks into an even bigger smile. He pressed the button on the little camera.

"I know! I know!" she screamed. "Get one of me and my Daddy." She went over to her father, who had taken a seat back on the sofa, and climbed up into his lap with her teddy bear. Brandon focused and snapped. She giggled with delight. He was having just as much fun as she was. Even Gill, who he was sure had been through this little play-acting routine with her many times before, seemed to be enjoying it.

"Lisa, why don't you take a picture with Brandon?" Gill suggested, lifting her from his lap. "I'll take a picture of you all with my camera."

"Okay!" She ran over and stood with her little bear between Brandon's legs. Gill picked up one of several cameras laying on the coffee table in front of him and focused.

"Hold it!" A flash lit up the room. "Okay," Gill said, getting to his feet, "we'd better be heading over, Lisa, or Sarah's gonna think we're not coming."

"Okay."

■ ■ ■

"It's down this way, Brandon," Lisa said, pulling Brandon with her from the elevator. "You'll like Sarah. She's nice."

A pale, slightly haggard-looking woman, early sixties, answered the door. She was dressed in a long house coat and slippers, her hair pulled back into a bun.

"Hi, Sarah!" Lisa greeted her.

"Well, hi, there!" the woman said in a thick southern drawl, as she leaned over to give Lisa a big hug. "And how's my little girl, today?"

"Just fine."

"Hello, Gill."

"Hi, Sarah."

"And who's your friend you brought with you, Lisa?"

"Oh, this is Brandon," Lisa said, still holding Brandon's hand.

"Brandon Northcross," Brandon said.

"It's nice to meet you, Brandon. I'm Sarah Ramsey."

"Nice to meet you, too," he said.

"He just moved in down the hall from us," Gill added.

"Well, great," she said. "Please. Come in."

Flowering plants of all shapes and sizes seemed to be virtually everywhere inside the apartment, from lemon-yellow tulips, to flaming reddish-orange gladiolus, to bright red chrysanthemums. There were also daffodils, roses, begonias, dahlias, gardenias and other plants of all different hues. It was like an explosion of colors and scents.

"This is amazing," Brandon said. "It's like a florist's shop."

"Thank you," Sarah said.

"How do you do it, I mean, take care of all these plants?"

"Oh, once you get the hang of it, it's not so hard, provided you know what you're doing to begin with," Sarah said.

"Sarah's just being modest," Gill said. "She knows more about flowers than anyone I've ever met."

"Oh, you're much too kind, Gill," she remarked. "But would you like me to give you a little tour, Brandon?"

"Oh, would you?"

"Well, while you all are doing that," Gill said, "I'll go take a look at your TV."

"Okay," Sarah said, as Gill headed toward the bedroom with his tool box. "Why don't we start over here," she said, motioning to a group of shrubs with bright pink, yellow and orange blossoms. "These are my azaleas." The plants themselves were about four-feet high. "As you can see, they come in a variety of colors. In addition to the colors you see here, they can also be red, purple and white. Their maximum height is just slightly taller than these. That's for the indoor variety. The outdoor variety, on the other hand, can grow to be twelve feet tall or more."

"Is that taller than my daddy?" Lisa asked.

"I think so, Lisa," Sarah chuckled, smiling down at her. A fluffy white cat appeared from behind the sofa and began rubbing up against Sarah's leg. Lisa stooped to pet it. The cat purred as it arched its back into a ball. "Kitty's just like a little baby," Sarah said, as she reached down and picked it up, cradling it in her arms. It fastened its gaze on Brandon, its big green eyes like deep reflecting pools. "She always wants to be picked up and held." Sarah stroked its little head with her fingers.

"What kinds of plants are those out there?" Brandon asked, looking out at the balcony through the sliding glass door.

"Out there I keep my orchids and violets. Would you like to get a closer look at them?"

"Could I?"

The steady hum of a humidifier permeated the humid air out on the enclosed balcony.

"This looks like a miniature greenhouse," Brandon said.

"That's basically what I've tried to create here," Sarah said, closing the door behind them. "I had the balcony customized with these louvered tinted panes so I can adjust them to control the amount of light that comes in."

As Brandon looked at the various plants, he came upon one that, unlike the others, was encased inside a glass container. The plant was purplish-blue with big, overlapping petals. The blossoms, nearly five inches or so in diameter, had a smooth, velvety texture. The inner part of the blossom was of a darker hue than the rest of it and exuded an almost human-like countenance.

"Sarah, what kind of plant is this?" Brandon asked.

"It's a pansy, which is a type of violet."

"Why's it under the jar?" Lisa asked, her face up to the glass to get a better look. "Won't it not be able to breathe?"

"No, honey," Sarah assured Lisa. "It gets plenty of fresh air, better than even we get, through the little tube you see connected to the side of the glass. This little tube is connected to an air filtration unit. It's the little machine you see underneath the table."

"It's different from any flower I've ever seen," Brandon said.

"Yes, of all the violets, the pansy is the one most known for its distinctive beauty," Sarah said. "And it's easily recognizable by its color, which is always of a deeper blue than any other violet. But it's not an easy plant to grow. It requires the most attentiveness of perhaps any plant. This includes special soil and nutrients. It's also unique in that, during its early maturation, it must be grown in almost complete darkness. The beauty you see now came only after months away from the light."

"It has such huge blossoms," Brandon said.

"They may get even larger than they are now," Sarah said.

"What's the life span of a plant like this?"

"That's the only sad thing about the pansy," Sarah said. "Even with the best of care, it rarely has more than one flowering season. But, oh, what magnificence it attains in such a short life span. And as you can see, it has that rare ability to brighten a room all by itself, which makes all the caring for it worthwhile."

Five

Over the next several weeks, Brandon began to settle more and more into his job. Besides working on his own assignments, he was also providing support for the other team members, just as Terri had said. He always made it a point to get the work back ahead of schedule, if possible. He wanted to make sure that whatever fault anyone found with him, it wouldn't be with his work. But with each passing day, he grew increasingly frustrated at being relegated to the mostly clerical work he was doing. At weekly team meetings, where they worked on various marketing campaigns that the department was involved with, he was never called on for his input. When he did offer his opinions, he felt that they were hardly ever seriously considered. Representatives from Sales, Finance and Product Development were often at these meetings. He didn't want people from these groups to get the idea that he had nothing of value to offer. All he wanted was simply the chance to prove that he had what it took to do the job for which he had been hired.

His working relationship with Tim continued to be a sore spot. Their little run-ins were becoming more and more frequent. It seemed that Tim intentionally did little things to try to irk him. Sometimes, after he had completed a job according to the way Tim had asked him to, Tim would then change his mind and have him do it all over again in a different way. Brandon continued to remind himself that Tim was simply trying to provoke him into doing something that would jeopardize his chances for qualifying. He was determined not to let that happen. He considered going to Bob and telling him what was going on. But he decided against it. Bob would only think he was a whiner and it would confirm his initial suspicion that he couldn't cut it. Perhaps the best thing to do would be just to tough it out.

The closest Brandon got to doing anything that was even remotely creative, besides recording meeting minutes, was one day when he was asked to compose the terms for on-site customer visits for the new release of an existing product. These terms were to be included in the warranty. Actually, the contents of the terms had already been decided. All he had to do was flesh out the information, mostly by using boilerplate text from existing warranties. Susan Burgett was the corporate attorney whose approval signature he needed on the terms. He had called ahead, so she was expecting him when he arrived at her office.

"Come right in," she said, waving him inside. "I'm Susan Burgett."

"Brandon Northcross."

"Have a seat, Brandon." He pulled up a chair.

"So, you're new here at CSU, huh?"

"Yeah. Just started a few weeks ago."

"Where're you from?"

"New Hampshire."

"Really? It's funny, but for some reason I never pictured blacks living in such an out-of-the-way place like New Hampshire."

"Well, there certainly weren't many of us where I grew up," Brandon said. "That's for sure."

"How do you like it here so far, the D.C. area, I mean?" she asked.

"It's okay. I'm getting used to it."

"A lot more black people here than you're used to seeing back home, I'll bet."

"That's true."

"This is a good area," she said. "The cost of living is a little steep. And the traffic can be a pain. And there's the crime element, of course. But overall, the area boasts a pretty high standard of living. One advantage for you of living here is the number of black professionals. I used to meet quite a few blacks at the law firm I worked for before coming to CSU. One of our clients was Robbie Bowman, the former star running back for the Redskins. He was the nicest guy and, boy, was he funny. He had us in stitches all the time with his jokes. I remember one time, when somebody asked how he got to be so fast, he said it was because, as a kid, he'd have to make quick getaways with the watermelons he and his buddies would steal. Boy, he was so funny. I'm sure you must have heard of him."

"I'm afraid not," Brandon said, wishing the woman would simply get to the business of why he was there.

"You mean you're not a pro football fan?"

"Not really."

"I just love football," she said. "That's one thing you'd better get used to. People are Redskins fanatics around here. Well, enough of me running my mouth. So, you have some warranty information for me to approve?"

"Yes, some terms for the new release of Aspen," he said, removing the single page from his folder and handing it to her.

"So, how's Tim these days?" she said, as she casually skimmed the page. "I haven't talked to him in a while now. He writes up more of these for me to approve than practically anybody in the company."

"Tim's fine. But he didn't write this one. I did."

"Oh?" she said, pausing. She leaned back in her chair and began to slowly read line by line.

"I proofread it already," Brandon said.

"Yes, I'm sure you did," she said, reaching for a red pen on her desk.

"Also, it's almost exclusively boilerplate from other warranties I believe you've already signed off on," he added.

Brandon waited patiently as the woman continued her check. Occasionally, she would circle something.

"You've got a misspelling here." She leaned forward to point it out to him. "How do you spell expediter? I believe it's spelled *or*, not *er*."

"I always thought it could be spelled either way, unless there's a preferred spelling," Brandon said.

"Let's check the dictionary," she said, swiveling around to a large dictionary resting on a cabinet behind her. She looked up the word. "Well, what do you know. It does say it can be spelled either way." She closed the dictionary and resumed her review. "You missed a comma here. And here, too. And this, I believe, is a split infinitive. Do you know what a split infinitive is?"

"Look, I think I know correct grammar," he said, unwilling to mask his rage any longer. "I happened to have minored in English in college."

"Hey, you don't have to get an attitude about it," she said, with a look of bewilderment tinged with fear. Brandon took a deep breath and let it out slowly. "Tell you what. Go back and proofread it again. Then bring it back." She pushed the page to the edge of her desk. Brandon hesitated for a moment then picked it up and headed for the door. "Bye."

Back at his desk, Brandon looked over the terms and even had Sean look them over. They found very few of Susan Burgett's comments to be valid. Of the ones that were, they were so trivial that they hardly justified mentioning. Upon checking warranty information that Tim had submitted to Susan Burgett in the past for signature, Brandon found both punctuation and grammatical errors. But these errors had apparently been either overlooked or ignored. When he had made the necessary corrections, Brandon returned the warranty terms to Susan Burgett and obtained her signature. It was clear, he decided, that he would just have to accept the fact that his work would be more closely scrutinized than that of others.

■ ■ ■

"Excuse me. Do you have the time?" Brandon looked up from his newspaper in the food court to find an exceptionally attractive black woman standing over him. With lovely full features, exquisitely coiffured hair and warm carmel skin, she appeared to be in her mid twenties. Everything about her, from her single-breasted, charcoal-grey skirt suit to her precise news anchor diction, said professional. Unable to speak, he could only stare at her. A puzzled look on her face, the woman repeated her question. "Excuse me. But do you have the time?"

"What?"

"The time," she said. "Can you tell me the time?"

"Oh! The time," he said, quickly looking at his watch. "It's about a quarter past twelve."

"Thank you," the woman said. Brandon continued to stare. "Are you alright?" She was looking at him now with a sense of concern.

"Me?"

"Yes. You keep staring."

"Oh, I'm sorry," he said, snapping out it. "I didn't mean to stare. It's just that…well…I can't remember the last time I've seen anybody quite as attractive as you." The woman threw back her head and let out a hearty laugh.

"What's wrong?"

"You brothers are too much," she said, smiling. "I mean, you all don't miss a beat."

"No, I'm serious," he said. "You really are. I wasn't trying to shoot you a line."

"Well, thank you for the compliment. Gotta run, though. Bye." She gave him a killer smile and turned to go.

"Wait!" Brandon said. "Would you join me?" He indicated the chair across from him. "Just for a minute?"

"Well…okay. I guess I can talk for a moment. But then I have to get going." She took a seat.

"I'm Brandon Northcross," he said, extending his hand.

"Nice to meet you," she said, shaking his hand. "I'm Rachel Toney."

"You work around here?" he asked.

"No, I work for a pharmaceutical company up in Silver Spring. What about you?"

"I work up the street at CSU."

"Big Red, huh?"

"Yeah."

"What do you do there?"

"I'm a marketing research analyst. I just started a few weeks ago. And you?"

"I'm a sales rep," she said. "That's why I'm down here. I was checking on one of my accounts."

"I had a feeling you might be in sales," Brandon said.

"Why's that?"

"Oh, I don't know," he said. "It's probably the way you present yourself, I guess. How long have you been in sales?"

"Just a little over two years now," she said.

"What did you do before then?"

"I was in college before then," she said. "A poor college student out at Bowie State."

"I can definitely relate to that."

"So, how do you like working at CSU so far?"

"Well, as far as CSU goes, I think it's definitely a great company to work for. And I think I've got a good position, one where I think I can really move up the ladder, but..."

"But what?"

"Well, there's this guy—he's my supervisor—I think he's got it in for me. Actually, I know he does."

"Why do you think he has it in for you?"

"Well, he thinks I'm a token, that I was hired just because of affirmative action."

"Oh. So, he's a white man who thinks blacks are now getting all the opportunities. And at his expense."

"Something like that," Brandon said. "He keeps doing little things to annoy me. I think he's trying to make me quit or do something that could jeopardize my chances of qualifying."

"Have you considered going to management about it?"

"You mean my immediate manager?"

"Yeah, for starters," she said. "But if for some reason you don't think your immediate manager would be receptive, I'm sure a company as progressive-minded as CSU is reputed to be has an Open Door policy, where you can take grievances to upper management. Or you can always go to HR."

"I think I can tough it out," he said. "As soon as he sees that I'm not the token he thinks I am, he'll come around."

"Well, I hope you're right," she said. "But don't count on it. Personally, I don't think most white people let reality get in the way of their biased attitudes toward us. And there's always that extra scrutiny. I learned that real quick."

"Yeah, I found that out, too."

"As a matter of fact, my older sister, who's a network manager at DB&T, says you've often got to work twice as hard to get half the recognition of your white peers."

"That wouldn't surprise me."

"Are there any other blacks in your department?" Rachel asked.

"No. I'm the only one. And I think the first, too."

"Well, you might want to try networking with other black people at CSU," she said. "The last thing you want is to be totally isolated. I know I wouldn't want to be."

"I'll be alright," Brandon said. "Actually, I don't like to talk about it. But, changing the subject for a moment, can I ask you something?"

"Sure."

"Are you usually busy in the evening?"

"Not all the time," she said. "Why?"

"Well, I just thought if you weren't busy some evening that...well..."

"Are you asking me out?"

"Well...yeah," he said, bashfully. "Are you dating someone?"

"No, not really," she said.

"So, how about it? Would you like to go out sometime?"

"Yeah, I guess we can hook up sometime."

"How about one day next week?"

"Tell you what," she said. "Let me check my calendar when I get back to the office and I'll call you and we'll set something up."

"Okay."

"Do you have a business card?"

"Yeah." Brandon took out one of his business cards and handed it to her.

"Well, I guess I better get going," Rachel said, rising from her chair. "But it was nice meeting you."

"It was nice meeting you, too," Brandon said, standing. "Hope to hear from you soon."

"You will," she said, flashing him that high-voltage smile of hers again. "Bye."

"Bye."

As he watched Rachel Toney disappear into the lunch-hour throng, Brandon was already thinking about where he'd take her on their first date.

■ ■ ■

To Brandon's disappointment, Rachel Toney never called. Hoping he might run into her again, he made it a point to have lunch several times a week at the food court where they'd met. But he never saw her.

Over the following week or so, Brandon attended several company-sponsored classes. There were four different classes, all offered through the company's Education department. The last one was a customer survey class. It was taught by Turner Adair, whose old-fashioned crew cut combined with his khakis, starched white shirt and scruffy brown wingtips made him look more like a drill sergeant than a teacher.

As the lecture proceeded that first day, Adair said something that wasn't entirely clear to Brandon. So when Adair paused for questions, Brandon raised his hand. Adair glanced over his way, but instead of calling on him, resumed his lecture, as though he hadn't seen Brandon's hand. Seated on the second row slightly toward the right of the middle aisle, Brandon didn't think it was possible that Adair could've missed his hand. A few minutes later when Adair paused again for questions, Brandon anxiously raised his hand. When Adair looked over his way, Brandon poised to ask his question.

"Yes, you have a question, Ms. Croft?" With his mouth open to speak, Brandon realized that he hadn't been recognized, after all. Instead, the woman seated several seats over from him had been called on. She must have had her hand up also, he figured. Brandon waited patiently while the woman's question was answered, then raised his hand again. Adair looked directly at him this time, then turned to the other side of the room to take a question.

For the next few moments, Brandon's hand remained frozen in the air, like a limp flag stuck atop a flag pole on a still, breezeless day. Then, slowly, he brought his hand down, as he tried to deal with what had just happened. There was no longer any question in his mind that the slight had been intentional. Neither was there any doubt in his mind as to why. It couldn't have been any more apparent had Adair screamed the N-word aloud. Yes, *nigger* is what Adair had shouted at him without uttering a sound. Suddenly, Brandon became very conscious of everyone around him. He was black; they were all white. He kept his eyes fixed straight ahead, certain that they, like Adair, were inwardly mocking him. He wanted to get up right then and leave the room or, better still, to somehow just disappear down through the floor beneath him.

From that point on, he felt estranged from the class, as if he were merely a spectator watching from behind an opaque glass pane, from which he could see and hear, but no one could see or hear him. He took notes and participated in the class exercises, but never again raised his hand to ask a question.

Later, when he had had time to reflect on the incident, he wondered if Adair's slight had really been because he was black. Maybe it had had nothing to do with race at all. He chided himself for having allowed himself to fall into the same paranoid thinking about white racism that he had so often been critical of other blacks for engaging in.

■ ■ ■

"You know you want that last slice of watermelon," a voice behind Brandon said, as he served himself at the cafeteria salad bar.

"What?" He turned to see a black man, about thirty, grinning at him. "Oh, yeah," Brandon said, smiling, quickly picking up on the joke. "Actually, I thought I'd save it for you."

"I'm not touching it," the man said. "They always seem to save that last piece for one of us." They laughed. "Roosevelt Aikens," the man said putting out his hand.

"Brandon Northcross."

"Look, if you're not with anyone, you're more than welcome to join us." The man motioned to a table across the way where several other black people were sitting. He had planned to wait for Sean or Fran. But he could have lunch with them anytime.

"Sure. I'd be happy to."

At the table, Roosevelt introduced him first to the woman. "Brandon, this is Candace Sesley." In her late twenties, she gave him a warm, sisterly smile.

"Hi," she said.

"Hello."

"And this is Sherman Green," Roosevelt said, introducing the man at the table.

"What's up now?" the man said, wiping his hand on a napkin, then shaking Brandon's hand.

"How you doing?" Brandon and Roosevelt took a seat.

"I came across Brandon as he was eyeing that last slice of watermelon up at the salad bar," Roosevelt said, grinning.

"But I see neither of you took it," Candace said. "You realize, of course, that they were nice enough to leave it for us. Now, they're going to think we're not appreciative of their thoughtfulness. 'Cause everybody knows how much we love watermelon." Sarcasm dripped from every word.

"And don't forget the fried chicken," Sherman said.

"And the ribs," Candace said.

"And the collard greens," Sherman added.

"Y'all making me hungry now," Roosevelt said, digging into his food. They laughed.

"Are you new here at CSU?" Sherman asked.

"Yeah, I just started back in August," Brandon said.

"What do you do?"

"I'm a marketing research analyst. What about you guys?" Candace was a software engineer with six years in at the company. Roosevelt was in his tenth year with CSU as a computer programmer. And Sherman, a buyer, had been with the company for just over two years.

"How do you like it over in Marketing?" Roosevelt said. "I've heard there're not a lot of us over there."

"You heard right," Brandon said. "I'm the only one."

"I bet that's partly because they don't want any of us," Candace said.

"Well, let's just say that I wasn't exactly received with open arms by everyone when I joined the department," Brandon said."

"I'd even venture to say that some of them probably think you were hired just to fill a quota," Roosevelt said.

"One person actually told me that to my face."

"I'm not surprised," Candace said. "I think a lot of white people here feel that way. Oh, they'll smile in your face and tell you how they don't have a racist bone in their bodies and all, but I don't buy a lot of it. I pay attention to what they do, rather than what they say."

"And they say there's no longer any need for affirmative action," Sherman said. "Sounds to me like we need more of it, not less."

"Candace, you know Barbara that works in HR, right?" Roosevelt said.

"Yeah."

"She told me those people in HR have been foot-dragging with meeting the company's mandated affirmative action hiring goals since day one. She said they do just enough to meet the bare minimum requirements."

"So, where did CSU get its reputation for being so open to minorities, then?" Brandon said.

"It's not the company, per se," Roosevelt said. "It's the people. The company has some really good hiring policies in place, as far as hiring women and minorities. It's the people put in charge of implementing them that's the problem."

"But doesn't CSU have a pretty good track record for recruiting blacks out of college?" Brandon said.

"Sure they do," Roosevelt said. "And that's where they meet their hiring goals, with entry level positions. But how many of those blacks are still around four or five years later? And when a management or senior level position opens up, why is it that they can never seem to find any qualified minority applicants?"

"Could that possibly be it, that they really can't find any qualified black applicants for these positions?" Brandon said.

"No, the truth of the matter is that they don't *look* for any qualified black applicants," Roosevelt said. "And when blacks do manage to get in for interviews, they hardly ever get hired. But the thing about it is, CSU wasn't always this way. It's changed. It's not like it used to be when I hired on. Again, it's the people."

"I've had to deal with HR on just two occasions since being here at CSU," Candace said. "And both times it was with a white person: a woman, one time; a man, the other. Both times I came away thinking, man, these people do not want us here."

"Sounds to me like they've got some serious problems in HR," Sherman said.

"But, actually, it's really not that much different anywhere else these days," Roosevelt said. "From what I've been hearing, most of corporate America nowadays has become almost hostile toward blacks."

"Why do you think that is?" Sherman said.

"Well, I think there's basically a backlash going on against blacks because of affirmative action, if you ask me," Roosevelt said.

"Also, with this conservative administration that's taken over in the White House," Candace said, "white people can feel comfortable being racist once again."

"So, in other words, black people are catching hell no matter where they work these days," Sheman said.

"But really, when you weigh everything together, CSU is still probably one of the better companies for a black person to be at these days," Roosevelt said.

"Man, now that's scary," Sherman said.

"Did any of you know a black guy that used to work here named Jarrett Knowles?" Brandon said. "I heard he was a mid-level manager in the Accounting area."

"Jarrett Knowles?" Candace said. "The name sounds familiar."

"I remember him," Roosevelt said. "I didn't know him, personally. But I knew of him."

"Who was he?" Sherman said.

"He was this brother up in Accounting that got booted out over an affair he was supposedly having with his white secretary."

"Oh, I remember now," Candace said. "Everybody was talking about that. The brother got caught knocking boots with Snow White. What was he, a third-line manager?"

"At least, " Roosevelt said. "Maybe higher."

"What was his name again?" Sherman said.

"I don't think you had started here yet, Sherman," Roosevelt said. "But his name was Jarrett Knowles. A very together brother, from what I heard. He seemed to be on his way up the ladder."

"But something happened on his way up that ladder," Candace said, shaking her head. "The brother came down with a deadly case of the white fever."

"It'll get you every time," Roosevelt said.

"That was the talk of CSU for a good little while," Candace said.

A lanky black man, his collar open and neck tie dangling, strutted up to the table. He was towing a computer device strapped to a little two-wheeler.

"Whassup, my folks?" the man said, setting his lunch tray down and collapsing in a chair.

"What's hap-pe-ning, Morris Geeter?" Roosevelt said, slapping fives with the man. "Now you know Big Red is not gon tolerate its CEs going around with their collars all open like that."

"Big Red can kiss it where the sun don't shine, as hard as I been working today," Morris said, starting in on his lunch. "Shee-it! They lucky I don't take this tie off all together. And the way my feet hurting from walking all over D.C., I might just kick my shoes off and stretch 'em out in one of these chairs." They laughed.

"Morris, this is Brandon," Roosevelt said. "Brandon's new with the company."

"Nice to meet you, man," Morris said, putting down his fork and reaching over to shake Brandon's hand.

"Same here," Brandon said.

"Where you work at?" Morris asked.

"Marketing Research."

"Boy, I bet you lonely over there," Morris said.

"He's the only one," Roosevelt said.

"Hey, but sometime I wish I could get away from y'all black folks, myself," Morris said, bringing laughter from the table. "Get tired of being 'round y'all loud-talking black folk all the time. Need some peace and quiet sometime. Tell me something, Candace. When you gon hook me up with the new girl in your department?"

"You mean Karen?"

"Yeh."

"Morris, I'm not doing any more matchmaking for you. If you want to meet Karen, you're gonna have to either get somebody else to introduce you or step up on your own, 'cause, homeboy, you got a reputation." The laughter started up again.

"Whatchu' mean, I got a reputation?" Morris put his knife and fork down and leaned back in his chair.

"I mean, women know about you, Morris," Candace said. "I'd probably be hard pressed to find a black woman here at CSU under 30 that you haven't tried to hit on."

"She knows you, Morris," Roosevelt said.

"They say you're a player, Morris," Candace said.

"Why they say that about me?" Morris said, trying his best to muster a look of innocence.

"Because of the way you are," Candace said. "For example, what happened between you and Allison?"

"Allison?"

"The girl I introduced you to at the Christmas party last year."

"Aw, yeah, Allison. Well…we went out a couple of times."

"And?"

"Well…it just didn't seem to be the right chemistry between us for some reason. I don't know."

"Allison tells a slightly different story, Morris, something along the lines of 'three's a crowd.' Does that ring a bell by any chance?"

"Word's out on you, Morris," Sherman said, laughing along with the others.

"Now, that whole thing was simply a big misunderstanding," Morris said. "It wasn't like she thought it was."

"Sure, Morris," Candace said.

"Okay. So, what you're saying, Candace, is I need to rehabilitate my reputation a little, before you introduce me to any other women, huh?"

"Rehabilitate?" Candace said. "Try major surgery." Morris let out a sigh.

"See, you just can't win with the sistas," Morris said, looking to the guys at the table for sympathy. "But it's just as well, 'cause I ain't got time to date nobody no way. Roosevelt, man, they got a brother hustling, working like it's going outta style. You know those commercials with O.J., where he's running through the airport to catch his flight? Well, that's me all day, man. They got me jumping over chairs, desks, tables, everything, running to my next service call. CSU oughta put me in one of them commercials showing me swimming across the Potomac to make it to a service call on time."

"Morris, will you quit it?" Candace said, laughing so hard she could barely eat her lunch.

"I ain't lying," Morris said. "Candace, you see these shoes here?" Morris stuck a foot out for her to examine. "This the second time I done had to get 'em resoled. And that's just in the last month. And I done worn out eight pairs of socks, too. I must've walked damn near 50 miles just in the last week. Shee-it! And I barely get time to eat lunch some days. Don't tell me slavery is over. I'm still waiting to be freed. Abraham Lincoln must've forgot about me when he signed that Emancipation Proclamation or whatever it was." Everyone at the table was rolling with laughter.

"Morris, you are so crazy," Candace said.

"I ain't lying," Morris said. "They work a brother hard out there in the field. When CSU says they provide customer support, they don't be messing around."

"But look on the bright side, Morris," Roosevelt said. "It's keeping you out of trouble."

"You ain't lying 'bout that, 'cause at the end of the day, I don't feel like doing nothing but going home and crawling in the bed. I can't even remember the last time I went out on a date."

"You'll survive, Morris," Candace said. "By the way, Brandon, do you know about the black social calendar that goes around?"

"No, what is it?"

"It's just a listing of all the social events catered toward black professionals for each month in the D.C. area," Candace said. "I usually get an issue each month, but for some reason I didn't get it this time."

"I got this month's," Roosevelt said. "I can send you a copy, if you like, Brandon. Just give me a call and I'll shoot it over to you through internal mail."

"Thanks," Brandon said. "I'll do that."

■ ■ ■

As Brandon worked late at his desk one evening, the sound of squeaking wheels broke the quiet of the near-deserted floor. The sound grew progressively louder, until it stopped abruptly just outside his cube. He looked around to see a black man in overalls with gray-streaked hair peering in at him. He was pushing a trash barrel.

"Working kinda late tonight, ain't you, young man?"

"Decided to stay and try to get some things done before tomorrow," Brandon replied, swiveling around in his chair to face the man.

"Well, it sure ain't nothing wrong with that," the man said. "You keep up that attitude, son, and you'll go a long way in life. Yes, ain't nothing wrong with hard work. That's what I tried to instill in my kids when I was bringing 'em up. With hard work and discipline, you can do just about anything you put your mind to."

"That's exactly what my parents taught me, too," Brandon said.

"See, when I was coming up, because of segregation and all, it wasn't but so many things they let a black person do," the man said. "But nowadays, you young people got so many opportunities that my generation and generations before never even dreamed of. I got a daughter 'bout your age," he said, reaching into his back pocket for his wallet, "or maybe a little bit older. She's a engineer for some big chemical company out in Colorado where she and her husband live." He pulled out a picture of his daughter and showed it to Brandon.

"You must be quite proud of her."

"Oh, I am," the man said, admiring the picture, before slipping it back in his wallet. "Sent her and my other two kids through college working two jobs, working for the city during the day and driving a taxi at night."

"That must've really been some sacrifice," Brandon said.

"Sure it was," he said. "There was a lot of things that me and my wife did without so we could make sure they got a college education. But when I see what they been able to make of themselves, and I see young men like yourself doing well, I don't regret it at all." The man was silent for a moment, his eyes not really focusing on anything in particular, as he seemed to reflect on what he had just said. "Hmmph." A broad smile stretched across his face. "Yes, if I had it to do all over again, I would. But tell me something, if you don't mind me being nosy for a minute," he said, emerging from his reverie. "Where do you go to get your hair cut?"

"Actually, no one place in particular, just here and there," Brandon said. Actually, he had been going to a particular barber, but lately hadn't been very satisfied with the results. Anyway, it was about time for him to get his hair cut again.

"Tell you what, if you want to get one of the best haircuts anywhere around, go down to Nathan's Barbershop on Georgia Avenue, not far from Howard. The owner and head barber is a good friend of mine, a guy by the name of Baxter. We go back a long way together. Tell him Reuben Harris sent you. That's me. You get him to cut your hair. All the barbers are good, but Baxter's the best. That's Nathan's Barbershop, now, across from Mr. Bill's TV Repair, right there in the 1600 block."

"Okay, I'll go by and check it out sometime," Brandon said, jotting down the information.

"Well, I guess I'd better be moving on," the man said, glancing at his watch. "Be seeing you, now."

"Okay. It was nice talking with you."

"Same here, young man."

Six

The friction between Brandon and Tim continued to mount, as nothing he did was hardly ever to Tim's satisfaction. And with the appraisals he was certain Tim was giving Bob, his chances for qualifying didn't look good. And not to qualify, he reminded himself, would almost certainly mean losing his job.

The weekly team meetings, which had up to that point been moving at a fairly moderate pace, now shifted into high gear. The difference was that, whereas they had been working on mostly existing marketing campaigns whose products were already out on the market, they now were embarking on getting a marketing strategy off the ground for an entirely new product line. In addition to the regular team members, also present was Sean, Kyle from Finance and Hal from Sales. Sean was brought in because of the scope of the project.

"Okay, folks, this is it," Tim said, entering the room and distributing handouts to everyone. "This is the stuff we live for. I don't need to tell you that this is a big project, one of the biggest that's come along in a while." He went to the white board and wrote across the top *CSU Universal Machine/A™ (UM/A™)*. "As you can see from your handouts, the UM/A is going to be one of the most versatile personal computers to ever hit the market, period. With its specialized micro channel architecture and individualized operating system called the OA/4, it's going to revolutionize the way PCs are built. Plus, it comes with the new state-of-the-art color monitor built with DGO graphics, which is going to make everything else obsolete almost overnight. It's even backward compatible. Also, the UM/A comes with a whopping 40 mg of hard drive capacity and 2 mg of RAM, expandable to 8 mg."

"This may sound like a dumb question, but why is CSU going with this OA/4 operating system, when the rest of the industry is going with

EOS?" Sean said. "I mean, shouldn't we be sticking with EOS, which is what nearly everybody else is using?"

"Believe me, Sean, once people see what OA/4 is capable of, they'll never want to use a machine loaded with EOS again," Tim said. "I saw a demo of it the other day and it just blew me away. It's that awesome. Once the rest of the industry sees how quickly OA/4 catches on, they'll be lining up to buy it from us."

"What's the clock speed on it?" Allan said.

"20 MHz," Tim said, "which is faster than anything out there at the moment."

"That's certainly fast enough, in my opinion," Hal said. "I can't imagine why anybody would ever need anything faster."

"Is anyone else developing anything similar to the UM/A, as far as we know?" Sean asked.

"The word out is that Spartacus Computers is coming out with a 386 that does a lot of what the UM/A is supposed to do, but they're using the same architecture as everyone else," Tim said. "The UM/A, on the other hand, is the future. It's gonna leave everybody else in the dust. Besides, theirs won't be out until late first quarter '89 at the earliest."

"If Spartacus is working on pretty much the same thing, or even something close to it, why don't we let them get theirs out first?" Sean said. "Let them get clobbered with doing all the fixes for bugs and incompatibilities that are sure to crop up in a system like this. We could then roll ours out, having benefited from their mistakes. Why set ourselves up for the chopping block by being first? Instead of going for speed to market, I think we should wait and play for number two. We can then hit the market with a polished product that we know there's a market for and one that has all the bugs ironed out."

"I appreciate what you're saying, Sean," Peter said. "If this was maybe a year ago, I'd be right with you on it. But if we go that route today, I guarantee you there are half a dozen little startup companies out there that have just sprung up in the past year or so just waiting to pounce on this. Whatever's hot, they can sniff it out. If we wait around, they'll hit the market with their version of the UM/A in half the time or less it would take for a company our size to do it. I know we've got this reputation for having the best tech support in the industry. But we need to begin to think a little differently. The market's changing. And we'd better start changing with it, if we expect to survive in the long haul."

"I think Peter's right, Sean," Tim said. "We can't afford to lay back in the tall grass and play wait and see like in the past. Not on this one. Speed to market. Better to be first and have to do the fixes than second or third and risk being left in the dust."

"Okay," Sean said. "But let's not rush in so hastily that we put out such a shoddy product that even an army of CEs can't keep afloat."

"Good point," Tim said. "And I say not only do we beat everyone else to market," Layla said, "but we go with the turbo feature and throw in a math co-processor, for those number crunchers like Allan. With turbo and the math co-processor we prove that we're on the cutting edge. And that garners market share."

"Now we're talking," Allan said, rubbing his hands together. "Heck, you might just get me to buy one now."

"Adding those kinds of features is expensive," Kyle said. "That's a big investment."

"I never said it'd be cheap," Layla said. "You've got to invest money to make money. PowerHouse went with turbo in their new PHX/1. And last I checked, their numbers in the market were looking pretty impressive. I'm convinced that this is something that's going to catch on. And we need to be on board with it, rather than being in a position where we're having to play catch-up."

"Okay, let's say we make the investment to add these new as-of-yet unproven features and they bomb," Hal said. "Then what? Or, say, somebody comes out with something new that captures the public's fancy and this turbo is suddenly old hat. What we've got then is a repeat of the Pendulum line, which turned out to be CSU's Edsel, if you recall. The Pendulum is probably now inhabiting some dusty corner in the garage or attic of its once-proud owners."

"Hey, I still make good use of my Pendulum," Kyle said. "As a boat anchor."

"And that's about all it's good for, too," Hal said, chuckling. "But seriously, turbo or no turbo, speed to market, or wait and see, how the hell do we make this delivery date? This is a very aggressive delivery date, people. So, I guess I'm kind of hearkening back to Sean's position. I'm afraid we're just too big to operate like one of these little fly-by-the-seat-of-your-pants companies that you talked about, Peter. And, furthermore, I'm not convinced we ought to even be trying to. Why not stick with what got us here? That's the Big Red philosophy. You don't switch horses in the middle of the stream. And the same goes for this movement away from the mainframe. It's sheer nonsense, this talk about how we ought to focus most of our resources toward the PC side of the business, because that's what everybody else is doing now. Mainframes are what made CSU the giant it is today. They're the big money makers and always will be. This new PC technology that everybody's pushing, there're no real profit margins with it. But nobody in the world matches CSU in its mainframe capability. I've been with this company for going on twenty-eight years now, and I know the computer industry inside and out. New technology is fine, but let's not kill the goose that lays the golden egg just because of what somebody else is doing. We're the leaders. We don't follow trends; we set trends. Okay, I'm off my soapbox now," he said, with a chuckle.

"Amen, brother, and pass the offering plate," Kyle said, grinning.

"That's right," Hal said. "I'm preaching trying to win the lost sheep back to the fold, Kyle."

"With all due respect, Hal, to your nearly twenty-eight years with the company," Peter said, "that philosophy that's worked so well for us in the past may not work for too much longer. That's the problem, I'm afraid. That's why we're starting to see these reorganizations all over the place. People are slowly starting to realize that we can't keep doing things the way we've been doing them. Those features that Layla just talked about that you seem to find so extravagant are well worth considering, if you ask me. I just hope we can turn this big freighter around before we hit that iceberg that's looming just up ahead."

"So, you're saying we're the Titanic, now, Peter?" Hal said, a smirk on his face. "And we're headed for certain disaster, right?"

"If we don't change some things and change them in a hurry, yes," Peter said.

"Peter, that's simply hogwash," Hal said. "It's that kind of alarmist propaganda that's got people running scared around here, talking about how the sky's falling, when the reality is—"

"Hal, when was the last time you took a look at where our stock is?"

"I know where our stock is," Hal said, turning red in the face. "I don't need you to remind me—"

"Evidently you do, Hal, because it's people like you who are so stuck in the past, that—"

"Okay, time out, guys!" Tim said, indicating the time-out sign with his hands. "Time out. Let's try to remember that the enemy is out there, not in here. Okay?" Hal and Peter both settled back in their chairs.

"Alright," Hal said, more calmly now. "Let's just say we accept what Peter is saying. My question again is how do we make this delivery date? Marketing and Sales are already stretched paper thin as it is. We're pretty near the point of reaching what I call critical mass. Anybody want to speak to that?"

"Well, as far as Marketing goes, I guess we put in 12- to 14-hour days, if we have to," Tim said. "And whatever we absolutely can't do, we farm out."

"But how long can we keep that up before we simply burn out?" Sean asked.

"For as long as it takes, I guess," Tim said. Then turning to Hal, Tim said, "And Hal, by pushing it, can you get your sales reps up to speed on the UM/A in time for roll-out?"

"In three months?" Hal said, paging through the thick specifications document in front of him. "With as much as there is to this product, including the multiple environments, it'll be tough. They're gonna need some extensive training. And like I said, we're already burning the candle at both ends just with current product coverage. Then there's Tech Support we've got to get trained and ready to go. And how about all the necessary market research that's needed? How can we do that and still make a 3-month delivery date?"

"We'll do a limited research," Layla said. "It's been done before."

"I know it's been done before," Hal said. "But I don't know how feasible that's going to be on a project of this magnitude, Layla."

"Yeah, I'm afraid I'm going to have to agree with Hal on this one, Layla," Peter said. "You're asking for trouble doing a limited research on a product like this."

"Anybody got any ideas?" Tim asked. The room was quiet. Brandon had been wanting to offer his opinion. Now was his chance. He cleared his throat.

"Ah, I have a suggestion that I think might work," Brandon said. All eyes locked in on him like radar. "What if we do this. We go with the speed-to-market scenario, putting in whatever time it takes to make it happen. We delay the turbo and math co-processor options, at least for this initial release. Maybe by the follow-on release we're in a better position to add them. Anyway, we get Sales to make the investment to get our sales reps staffed up and trained on the UM/A, along with the same commitment from Tech Support. And we provide 24-hour phone support."

"What!" Hal said. "We can't provide 24-hour phone support. Nobody in the industry provides that."

"Okay, maybe not 24-hour support," Brandon said, "but maybe extended hours to cover both coasts, and with a guaranteed response time. And, finally, to really provide an incentive, we offer upgrades to the next release of the UM/A at half the price of what we normally would charge. And with turbo and the math co-processor installed."

"We generally don't ask that much for upgrades as it is," Kyle said. "At half price, we'd be practically giving away the store. And with turbo, too?"

"Well, maybe not half-priced, but at a cut rate," Brandon said.

"Okay, Brandon," Peter said. "The incentives sound good in general. But how do we know that the competition isn't offering something similar?"

"Simple," Brandon said. "We do a competitors analysis."

"Only one problem with that," Peter said. "With the exception of Spartacus, we don't know who our competitors are going to be. Remember?"

"True," Brandon said. "But we can do a projected analysis that's built on a statistical model of who they're likely to be."

"Look, Brandon, the beefing up the phone support is a possibility," Tim said. "The cut-rate turbo upgrade with the math co-processor, there may be something there, too. We'll have to look into it. But this projected competitors analysis thing, it doesn't work in the real world. We go on some projected competitors analysis and we can get killed in the market. It's like operating in fantasyland."

"Wait, he may have something there with this projected analysis thing," Kyle said. "I've heard of this approach being used before."

"And why are you so convinced it couldn't work, Tim?" Sean said. "It does makes sense, theoretically."

"Because that's just what it is, Sean, theory, just a lot of hypothetical stuff he studied back in college," Tim said. "Brandon's got no real experience at this."

"Maybe not," Brandon said. "But we tackled a problem that wasn't that much different from this one in one of my classes at Dartmouth. And it wasn't just some hypothetical stuff, either. I don't see any reason why that same approach can't be applied here with success."

"I'll admit it does sound a little flaky what the young man's proposing, but it might be worth a look, Tim," Hal said. "We've got our backs up against the wall on this one."

"Okay," Tim said, conceding. "Allan you want to work with Brandon on setting up this projected competitors analysis?"

"Sure, why not?" Allan said.

"And in the meantime, we'll look into the feasibility of some of the other suggestions that were raised," Tim said. "Brandon, make sure everyone gets a copy of the minutes." Tim then adjourned the meeting. Layla came over to Brandon.

"Some pretty sharp ideas you offered today, Brandon," she said, sweeping her hair back from her eyes.

"Thanks," Brandon said. "You offered some pretty good ideas yourself."

"Thanks," she said. "I hope you weren't put off by the sniping. That's common. Actually, they went rather easy on you."

"Really?"

"Oh, it can get pretty nasty," Layla said. "Just wait until we pull a couple of sessions until 1 in the morning and we're all at each other's throats. You'll wish you had taken a course in debate back in college, or maybe even self-defense. Right, Tim?"

"The only thing he'll need to know right now is how to take good minutes," Tim said, derisively. "There's a lot to learn about marketing that you don't pick up overnight or get from a textbook." Brandon locked eyes with Tim, before Tim turned away to gather his things.

"Oooh! A bit touchy, aren't we?" Layla said. "He did offer some pretty good suggestions today, don't you think?"

"This is Big Red," Tim said. "You've got to crawl before you walk around here." Snatching his briefcase up from the table, Tim headed for the door.

"Hands and knees, Brandon!" Layla said, feigning fright.

■ ■ ■

One rainy October day as Brandon was leaving work, he noticed a young woman in a hooded cape in front of the building, struggling with an art portfolio. In addition to the portfolio, she was carrying a shoulder bag and an attaché case, and was trying to hold her umbrella over her head. She was having little success. As soon as she got her bag to stay up on her shoulder, the portfolio would slip from her grasp. And as soon as she got a grasp on the portfolio, either her bag would slip from her shoulder or something would happen with her attaché case or her umbrella. She looked like a circus juggler trying to juggle too many pins at once. With his own umbrella open, he went over to offer his assistance.

"Excuse me, but you look like you could use a little help."

"What?" she said, as she continued to grapple with her things.

"I said you look like you could use a little help," he repeated, a little louder.

"Oh! Ah, yeah. I suppose I could."

"I can take this if you like," he said, indicating the portfolio.

"Okay," she said, leaning it toward him.

"Where're you parked?"

"Near the back of the lot, I'm afraid," she said, motioning out toward the big lot on the left.

"No problem," he said. "Just lead on."

"Okay."

As they made their way out to her car, the headlights of cars emptying from the parking lot cut tunneling patterns of yellow light through the approaching darkness of the chilly, wet evening, illuminating the angling shafts of rain beating down upon the gray concrete. Wet faded leaves, swept by the wind and rain, were everywhere, on the ground and on the windows of cars. When they reached her car, a red Porsche, she put her things inside, then took the portfolio from him and placed it in the back.

"Well, thanks a lot," she said, turning to face him in the pouring rain. "I don't know what I would have done if you hadn't come along. I'd probably be soaking wet by now."

"Just glad I could help," he said, then turned and started away.

"Hey, wait!" she called out to him. "Let me give you a ride to your car. That's the least I can do. Where're you parked?"

"Oh, I'm not driving," he said. "I take the train."

"Well, let me give you a ride to the station."

"Thanks. But you don't have to go to the trouble. I can walk."

"No, but I want to," she insisted. "You certainly went out of your way to help me."

"Okay."

The Porsche's defogger, cranked up to maximum, labored to clear the condensation that had formed on the windows.

"You work for CSU?" she asked, as she pulled down the hood of her cape and began smoothing back her dark, wavy hair.

"Yeah. What about you?" he said, glancing over at her. Using the vanity mirror on the sun visor, she was applying a fresh coat of lipstick. She had a remarkably attractive face—high cheekbones, a cute, slightly upturned nose and sensuous lips that parted to expose an even set of pearly whites that sparkled even in the dim light of the car's interior dome lamp. More than just attractive, she was beautiful, but not in any artificially made-up way. She reminded him of Rachel Toney.

"No, I'm a consultant," she said, putting away her lipstick. "I do graphics consulting. I'm on a contract with Lazear and Schneider. Their offices are in the CSU tower." The windows were beginning to clear. She cut the interior light and defogger, put the car in gear and headed out of the parking lot for the street. "But," she continued, "I usually don't end up having to park so far away from the building. And I usually don't end up having so many things to carry all at once."

"Except—don't tell me—when it rains," he said.

"Yeah, that's right, except when it rains."

Because of the heavy rain, the rush-hour traffic was even more sluggish than normal, reducing speeds to little more than a crawl.

"This is a really cool car you've got here," he said, checking out the interior.

"Thanks. It was sort of a college graduation gift from my parents." Brandon noticed a theater guide on the dashboard.

"You into the theater?" he asked.

"A little? How about you?"

"I used to be back in college. We had an excellent theater department."

"Where'd you go?"

"Dartmouth."

"An Ivy Leaguer, huh?"

"Yep."

"You into any sports?" she said.

"Tennis was my game for awhile."

"You said *was.* You don't play anymore?"

"I've been on the court a couple of times since moving here, but not regularly like I would be back home," Brandon said.

"Where's home?"

"New Hampshire. What about you?"

"Minneapolis."

"Do you play tennis?"

"Occasionally," she said. "There's a tennis court near where I live. Or sometimes I go to this country club. My father's a member of an affiliated club back home. So, being his daughter, I get into the one here."

"That must be nice, being able to hang out at a country club," Brandon said.

"It's okay," she said. "But I think country clubs are kinda overrated. I mean, they're really nice and all, but a lot of the people who belong to them seem to be so into themselves."

"How do you mean?" he asked.

"Well, like putting on airs, always talking about what their family owns and who they know. I'm like, who really cares? I'm just here to work out."

"But it must be a good place to hook up with a guy with some cash," Brandon said, lightheartedly.

"Probably," she said. "But I've dated guys with money before. It doesn't fascinate me. I'd rather meet just a regular, down-to-earth kind of guy, someone who's dependable, who knows how to treat a lady, who'll be there for her, and who's fun to be around. I don't have time for the kind of egos that so often come with the money and the power." They were both quiet for a moment. Suddenly, Julie giggled, breaking the silence. "I was just thinking about the first time I visited my father's club alone," she said. "I was still in high school at the time. Anyway, there was this old guy there. He tried to pick me up. You should've heard what he said to me. First, he asked me my name and some other things, which was okay. Then, when he noticed the Star of David I was wearing, he said, 'Are you a Jap?'"

"A Jap?" Brandon said.

"Yeah, you know, Jewish American Princess," she explained.

"You're Jewish?"

"Yeah."

"I've never heard that term before, Jewish American Princess."

"It's supposed to be flattering," Julie said. "But, personally, I don't care for it. I think it just reinforces old stereotypes. Anyway, after I told him that I was, in fact, Jewish, which I really didn't think was any of his business one way or the other, he said, 'Well, look, maybe we can go back to my place for a drink sometimes. I've got a really nice place. Whadaya say? We could have a real nice time.'"

"So, what *did* you say?" Brandon asked.

"What did I say? I said no freaking way. He was old enough to be my grandfather."

"Yeah, I guess he was a little old for you," Brandon said. "Personally, though, I prefer older women, like at least in their sixties."

"What?" she said, eyeing him curiously. Then she saw the grin breaking out across his face. "You're full of it." They laughed.

"You know, I was just thinking," Brandon said. "Women have it so easy. They don't have to worry about coming up with pickup lines to get guys."

"You don't think so?"

"Do they?"

"Sometimes," she said. "They're just more subtle about it than men."

"Care to give me a sample of one?"

"Maybe I already have," she said, pulling up to the entrance to the station. "Well, here we are." She turned to him. "It was nice meeting you. And I've really enjoyed talking to you."

"I enjoyed talking to you, too." Brandon reached for the door handle. "Thanks for the ride."

"What's your name?" she said.

"Brandon. Brandon Northcross."

"It's nice to meet you, Brandon," she said, putting out her hand. "I'm Julie Stein."

"Nice to meet you, too." They shook hands. "Well, guess I'll be seeing you." He got out and headed for the station.

■ ■ ■

A few days later, Brandon received an unexpected call at work.

"CSU Marketing Research. Brandon Northcross."

"Hello, Brandon? This is Julie Stein," the voice on the other end said. "We met the other day out in the parking lot after work."

"Oh, yeah. How are you?"

"Fine," she said. "Listen, I know this is really short notice and all, but I was wondering, if you didn't already have plans this evening, if you might be interested in going with me to a musical. It's called *The World Begins Tomorrow.* It's playing at the Top Hat Dinner Theater in Georgetown and it's supposed to be really hilarious. And, well, to be frank, my date canceled out on me kind of unexpectedly. And from our conversation the other evening, you seemed to have some interest in the theater, so I—"

"Sure, I'd be happy to go with you," Brandon said.

"Great, then!"

■ ■ ■

When Brandon arrived at the theater that evening to meet Julie, a throng of people were milling about out in front.

"Hi!" Julie said, emerging from the crowd. She was wearing a carmine, satin-trim sheath with matching bolero jacket.

"Oh, hi!" he said. "You look really nice tonight."

"Thanks," she said, flashing a smile. "And so do you."

"What's going on?" he said, looking around at all the people mobbing the sidewalk.

"You're not gonna believe this, but they say the theater's flooded."

"The theater's flooded?"

"Yeah," she said. "So, they're postponing the show, of course. The manager says a pipe burst sometime last night and there's like water everywhere. But, hey! The evening doesn't have to be a total washout, so to speak. You ever been over to Georgetown?"

"Georgetown? I thought *this* was Georgetown," he said, looking around at the handful of bars and shops along the street.

"No, I mean the *real* Georgetown, the strip," Julie said.

"Guess not," he said, shrugging his shoulders.

"Wanna go?"

"Sure. Why not?"

"Believe me," she said, "you'll like it."

■ ■ ■

Awash in a sea of people, bright pulsating neon lights and music, the nine- to ten-block strip along lower M Street was a myriad of eating and drinking establishments and assorted shops and boutiques. Traffic crept along bumper to bumper. Brandon and Julie passed bar after bar crowded with people, their boisterous laughter and loud talk escaping through the open doors. For those who preferred to dine outside, there were a number of quaint little sidewalk cafes. Posh townhouses lined side streets that branched off from the main boulevard. At a novelty shop specializing in kinky sex toys, two little boys pressed their curious faces up against the glass to get an eyeful of the shapely, life-like mannequin dressed in a skimpy, see-through negligee. In the picture window of a discotheque called the *Kitty House,* two women and a man danced, their beautifully sculptured bodies sandwiched together, gyrating as one to the pounding beat of the music.

"Wanna go in?" Julie said.

"Sure."

Inside they squeezed their way through the throng of patrons—many dressed in '70's fashions, complete with big, bushy Afro wigs—to the bar, where they ordered drinks. On a catwalk high above the bar as well as on perches along the wall, women in skin-tight, cat-woman costumes danced seductively. After dancing to a couple of hot Donna Summer and Heat Wave hits from the disco era, they retreated back to the street.

Further up the strip, they came upon a blind man in a pair of dark sunglasses, standing in the dimly lit alcove of a storefront, strumming soulful, bluesy riffs on his electric guitar. They stopped to listen, joining a small but attentive audience that had formed around the man. A little man in a ragged shirt, sitting on an upturned soda pop box, his head bowed as if in active mourning, began to lay down a bouncy bass line accompaniment, giving a juke joint feel to the song. The blind man then reared back and let go in an earthy, field holler of a blues voice:

Them that's got shall get
Them that's not shall lose
So the bible said
And it still is news
Mama may have
Papa may have
But God bless the child that's got his own
That's got his own

As the man sang, his dark, rugged face gleaming under the light from the lone, naked bulb, it was as if he were finally emptying out of his soul all the pent-up pain and heartache that had been damned up inside of him his whole life.

Money, you got lots o' friends, crowdin' 'round the door
When you're gone and spendin' ends
They don't come no more

Rich relations give crust of bread and such
You can help yourself, but don't take too much
Mama may have
Papa may have
But God bless the child that's got his own
That's got his own

A worn-out guitar case, the latches broken and rusted, lay open in front of him. People in the crowd as well as passersby dropped money into it. When the man finished, there were no applause, only a reverent silence. After tossing in some change, Brandon and Julie moved on.

A few blocks up, they came upon a hot dog vendor set up by the curb and bought hot dogs. Across the street was a photo booth.

"Hey, look, Julie. There's a photo booth. Wanna go take a picture together?"

"You mean now?" she said, her mouth stuffed from having just taken a big bite of her hot dog.

"Yeah, right now." Grabbing her hand, he pulled her across the street with him. "But there's something else we need first," he said, scanning the street.

"Something else like what?" Nearby was a man who was selling all sorts of novelty items. "Wait here." When Brandon returned, he had with him two pairs of mouse ears.

"Wait a minute," Julie protested, laughing. "You're not suggesting we put these on, are you?"

"Sure, why not?" he said, pulling her inside the booth with him. "We'll look like twins."

"Oh, God. This has got to be the craziest thing," she said, unable to stop laughing.

"Here," he said, handing Julie her ears, "put your ears on." He slid some coins into the machine and pressed the button. A timer beeped off, giving them a few seconds to pose. "Here goes!" A flash went off, as the camera took their picture.

"What kind of face was that, Brandon?"

"Hey, you didn't pose."

"I was too busy laughing at you to pose."

"You've gotta pose, now," he said. "Those are the rules."

"Okay. Okay. How about this." Julie made a goofy face.

They took a number of pictures, making the zaniest faces they could think of. In one, they held their hands over their eyes. In another, they held their hands over their ears. And in yet another, they held their hands over each other's mouths. They left the booth only when they had finally run out of quarters.

"I can't remember when I've laughed so hard," Julie said. "You are too much."

"When I was little, we used to see how many of us could cram into one of these booths and take a picture," Brandon said. "We'd do some really crazy stuff."

"Hey, I've got an idea," Julie said. "Let's take a walk along the river. Sometimes, when the weather's nice, they have outdoor concerts down there. It's also usually not as busy as up here along the strip."

They headed down the hilly street to the waterfront, their footfalls echoing off the time-worn cobblestone. The lights from the Key Bridge stretching high above them glowed through the darkened night like strands of a pearl necklace laid against a black, velvety background. Headlights from cars inching across the span looked like glittery inner strands of the necklace being drawn slowly forward. At the bottom of the hill they passed under the vaunted stone archway entrance to the harbor. Across the top, and illuminated by lights, was the engraving *Washington Harbor.* To either side of the entrance were huge, marble gilt lions perched atop tall, concrete pedestals, keeping a watchful eye over those entering through its gates.

The Potomac stretched out before them like a shiny, black rippling tarmac. The lights from the boats moored along the pier shimmered softly on the surface of the water. From somewhere further up ahead drifted the faint strains of music, growing more distinct the closer they got.

The open-air complex was built in the shape of an amphitheater, with gradations of flagstone tiers leading down to a sunken courtyard where a band performed on a little circular island out in the middle of a pool. Underwater lighting colored the frothing water a cobalt blue. Along each tier were rows of tables filled with people dining as they enjoyed the live music. A hostess came over to greet them.

"Table for two?"

"Yes." She led them to a table on the upper deck directly overlooking the band.

"Your waiter will be with you shortly. Enjoy."

Torchlights placed along the deck lit the night, their flames, whipped by an occasional breeze off the river, reflecting in the translucent cubes of the building behind them like fire locked in ice.

"So, Brandon Northcross," Julie said, her elbows propped atop the table and her chin resting on her intertwined fingers, "what is it you do after work when you're not busy rescuing damsels in distress from torrential downpours? Do you also slay dragons?"

"A few pesky knights, maybe, but no dragons. My chivalry goes only so far." They smiled at their little shared witticism.

"Do you have a steady girlfriend?"

"Not at the moment. Actually, I haven't really dated anyone since moving here."

"Any particular reason why?"

"No, I guess I've just been mainly focusing on getting settled into my new job. I haven't really tried to get that much going socially yet."

"That's understandable," she said. "It takes time, getting used to a new job and a new city."

Their waiter appeared. "Hello. What can I get you to drink this evening?" The man took their drink orders and left.

"So, how about you?" Brandon asked. "You seeing anyone?"

"I was, up until just recently. We broke up not long ago."

"What happened? If you don't mind me asking."

"Well," Julie said, folding her hands in her lap and leaning back from the table, the gaiety now gone from her face, "it was one of those things where you try and try to make something work, but one day you finally throw up your hands and say, look, I don't need this anymore. I don't need the pain. I don't need the uncertainty. It's not working and it's never going to work."

"Was it a long-term kinda thing?"

"A little over three years. We lived together for a year. That turned out to be a royal disaster. When it came down to it, his business always came first." He watched as she toyed with the strap of her shoulder bag. "They're really good, aren't they, the band, I mean?" she said, re-emerging from her period of reflection. They were playing a funky, get-down number.

"Yeah, they really are," Brandon said. People were dancing in front of the bandstand. The saxophone player, sporting a beret tilted to the side, his gold-plated horn and its pearly keys gleaming under the bright lights pouring down from overhead, was grooving hard. When the song ended, the crowd showered the band with applause.

"Thank you, thank you," the singer said. "It's always a pleasure to play down here at the Esplanade. You're such a great audience."

"We love you!" someone in the audience shouted.

"We love you, too," she shouted back. "All of you wonderful people. We'd like to slow things down a bit now and do a ballad, give you a chance to cozy up a little. So, for all you romantics here tonight, this one's for you. We hope you like it. It's called *I Thought You Knew.*" The band opened, setting the stage for the singer's entrance. When she entered, she let go in a voice that seemed bigger than her slender body seemed capable of possessing.

> *I thought you knew that I had sworn off soft emotion*
> *That I'd buried deep within me love's very notion*

Couples from all over began making their way to the dance area. Brandon looked over at Julie, who was still gazing dreamy eyed over the banister at the band.

"Would you like to dance?" he said.

"Sure."

Down below they found a spot among the other couples. With his arms encircling her waist, he pulled her gently toward him. She in turn wrapped her arms around his neck.

> *I thought you knew all thoughts of you had swept to sea*
> *That I'd learned that only fools think love is meant to be*

As they danced, he felt her body gradually relax against his own, her head nestling into the cradle of his neck. Her scent swept up into his nostrils, giving birth to a passion that had all the hot, rhythmic urgency of a tiger on the verge of a long-awaited kill. Who was this girl in his arms that he suddenly felt such an irresistible attraction for? Did she feel as he did at that moment? His desire for her came to him with the sudden abruptness of a brisk, biting wind.

> *When you left you wiped love's smile from my heart's face*
> *But now I've finally found my heart a safer place*

I thought you knew the fire burning again for you would never start anew
But maybe that was just because I thought I knew

When the saxophonist got his turn, he picked up where the singer had left off, taking the song to an even higher level. Sticking the bell of the sax up into the mike, his eyes clamped shut, he began to rock back and forth, firing lightning-fast, gravely runs that plummeted the depths of the instrument from the middle register down, blanketing the air with thick sheets of molten sound. After building to a piercing wail, he gradually leveled off, like a plane descending from the clouds. Cheers and applause rang out from the audience.

"Mr. Marvin Speed Parrish on tenor sax," the singer announced. The sax player acknowledged the audience with a nod of his head, then resumed his interplay with the singer as she took over again.

When the song was over and the other couples had started back to their tables, he and Julie remained locked in their embrace. Then, as if magically awakened from a deep sleep, Julie lifted her head from his shoulder.

"That was nice. Thank you," she said, smiling, then gently squeezed his hand.

Back at their table, she sat quietly, sipping her wine, casually bouncing one leg over the other. Every now and then, he'd catch her glance over at him, then quickly look away. She continued with her little cat and mouse game for awhile. He wanted to say something, but she seemed to be trying to sort through something in her mind. Finally, he broke the silence.

"Wanna take a walk?" She nodded yes.

As they headed down the steps, Brandon noticed a woman standing under a light peddling roses. "Wait a second." He returned with a single, long-stem rose.

"Why, thank you," she said, sampling the rose's aroma. "This is sweet." She gave him a peck on the cheek. A chilly wind blew in off the water, bringing a slight shiver from Julie.

"Cold?"

"Just a little," she confessed.

"Here, take my coat." Brandon removed his blazer and draped it around her shoulders.

"You're sure you're not gonna be cold?"

"No, I'm fine," he said. She pulled the coat around her, leaving the sleeves hanging limply at her sides.

They continued along, leisurely taking in the night, the lights sparkling at them from across the river.

"Hey," Julie said, suddenly infused with life again, "what do you wanna bet I can walk this wall without falling?" A low concrete barrier ran along the inside of the boardwalk.

"Did you used to be a tightrope walker or something?"

"No, silly, but I used to be good at walking beams when I was a little girl. I was so good at it that my mother used to say I'd grow up to be a highwire performer in the circus."

"But instead, you grew up to be just a run-of-the-mill graphic artist," he said.

"Yeah, what a waste, huh? Here, help me up. But first," she said, pausing, "I'd better get out of these heels. Here." She handed him the rose. "You hold this." She removed her heels. "Now, I'm ready." He helped her atop the narrow wall.

"Okay, give me back the rose." With her arms extended out to her sides for balance, her shoes in one hand, the rose in the other, she started along the wall, one foot in front of the other, just like a tightrope walker.

"See," she said, "didn't I tell you I was a natural?" Julie was doing fine until she tried looking around. "Uh-oh!" She began to wobble slightly. "I think…I think…I'm about to lose it!"

"I've got you!" he said, quickly reaching up and grabbing her arm. Tumbling down from the wall, she wrapped her arms around him. When they both looked up, their faces were so close that they were almost touching. They remained that way for a long moment, gazing into each other's eyes as if entranced. Then, finally, they kissed. Startled by the sound of giggling, they turned to see two little girls peering at them from behind a tree. Seeing they'd been spotted, the girls, still giggling, hurried to catch up with their parents, who were walking further ahead.

"C'mon," Brandon said, taking Julie's hand and leading her over behind a gazebo, which was surrounded by wooden park benches and trees in the middle of a little grassy area. There they kissed passionately. Suddenly, Julie broke free of his embrace and backed away. Mischief danced in her eyes.

"If you want another kiss, you're gonna have to catch me to get it," she said, and took off running. Brandon immediately gave chase, pursuing Julie around the park benches and trees. Finally, she led him up the steps of the gazebo. Cornered, she backed into one of the support pillars. "Well, it looks like I'm trapped."

"That can only mean one thing," Brandon said, moving closer.

"What's that?"

"I win the prize." He took her in his arms and kissed her deeply. With her arms enfolding him, her shoes slipped from her grasp, first one, then the other, making a hollow, echoing sound on the concrete floor. When he released her, he noticed a tear trailing down her cheek. He reached out and gently wiped it away with his finger.

"Well," Julie said, laying the palms of her hands against his chest, "it's certainly been an interesting evening. Much more interesting than I ever counted on it being."

"For me, too."

"I have to admit, though," she continued, "and I hope I don't make you uncomfortable by saying this, but I never thought I'd be feeling what I'm feeling at this moment for a black man. I mean, before tonight I had never even danced with a black man before... And, yet, here I am...I'm sorry. I shouldn't have said that."

"No, it's okay. I understand."

"Would you hand me my shoes, please? They're right behind you."

As Julie drove him home, the only sound inside the Porsche was the purr of its finely tuned engine. It was as if they both somehow understood that to speak would mean to risk awakening from their beautiful dream and having it vanish forever. It had all happened so suddenly and unexpectedly that only now was Brandon's mind beginning to catch up to his emotions.

When they pulled up in front of his apartment building, Brandon turned to Julie to speak, but she silenced him with a finger over his lips.

"Shh!" she whispered. "Please, don't say anything." She then leaned over and planted a kiss on his lips. "I'll call you tomorrow."

"Okay."

Seven

Over the next week or so, not a day went by that Brandon and Julie didn't see each other or talk on the phone. They were like two addicts, their addictions one another. Occasionally, Brandon would catch himself just sitting at his desk daydreaming about Julie. When they were apart, all could seem to think about was when they would be together again.

■ ■ ■

"This must be your family," Brandon said, studying a picture resting on the fireplace mantle at Julie's place one night. The sunken living room was comfortably furnished with a large, oval-shaped sofa and matching love seats, with tasteful artwork adorning the walls. Recess-mounted floor lights provided a subdued lighting to the room.

"Yeah, that's the Stein clan," Julie said, entering the room with their drinks. She kissed him lightly on the back of the neck. He turned around, took her in his arms and kissed her.

"Wait a second," Julie said, slipping out of his grasp. She handed him his drink, then went over and put on some silky smooth Luther Vandross. Gazing at him from across the room, she beckoned him with her finger. He hesitated for a moment, making her wait, then put down his drink and slowly started toward her.

"May I have this dance?" she said, invitation glowing in her eyes.

"I thought you'd never ask."

As they slow-dragged to Luther's impassioned pleadings, *Baby, oooh, baby!* he began to kiss her neck, then her ear lobes, then her lips. Finally, his tongue found its way past her lips and into her eager mouth. They kissed hungrily, greedily. He began to feel her nipples stiffen and swell. At the same time, he became conscious of a slow fire beginning deep within his groin, a fire that had not been stoked for some time now. Her breathing quickened. He reached around and awkwardly tugged at the zipper of her dress. She helped him. Slipping her dress down over her hips, she let it fall to the floor, then stepped out of her heels. After unbuttoning his shirt, she unfastened her bra, allowing her heavy breasts to spill forth. Taking them in his hands, he began to caress them and knead them, then suckle them. She let out a whimper and fell into him, forcing them both back onto the sofa.

"Not here," she whispered, pulling herself up, her breathing even more labored now. Grabbing his hand, she quickly led him up the stairs to the master bedroom. There they hurriedly finished undressing, tossing their remaining clothing about the floor. Flinging back the covers, she climbed onto the bed and pulled him on top of her. With high fire raging, they rolled about in each other's arms on the huge water bed, her porcelain white skin aglow in the moonlight that shone in through the overhead skylight. Then laying back, she placed her hands on his strong, broad shoulders and gently guided him below.

"Oooh yes, Brandon!" she moaned, her hips rocking slowly from side to side beneath him, as she ran her hands through his hair. Her juices splashed over him, hot and salty. Finally, the tide sweeping over him surged so high that it began to pull him out to sea. He straddled her. Guided by her hand, he entered her in one swift, brutal motion. "Yes!" Slowly, he began to ride the angry waves "Yes!" Then gradually faster "Yes!" and faster "Yes!" She began to buck beneath him "Yes!" trying to get closer to it while, at the same time, trying to get away from it "Yes!" Soon, they were one rhythm, their bodies slick and sticky with sweat. As she thrashed about, her lustrous hair fanning wildly over the soft-pink, satin sheets, the blistering itch being carried upward by the roaring fire inside him threatened at any moment to engulf him "Yes!" Then just at the edge before the long fall, a shudder…a pause…then another shudder…and then…and then…WHAM!…a huge, high wall of water slammed into them "Oooooh!" and the steamy, hot molten lava that had been bubbling and churning inside of him came spewing out "YES! … Yes! … yes! …" and they drifted peacefully up on the sand. At that moment he felt an abiding deliverance, the turbulent darkness behind him. They lay there in each other's arms, their breathing harsh and shallow.

■ ■ ■

Brandon awoke the next morning bathed in a pool of sunlight pouring down through the skylight. Julie was curled up next to him, still asleep. He leaned over and kissed her gently on the cheek. She looked even more beautiful asleep than awake, her face colored with the innocence of a child. He got up quietly, so not to disturb her, threw on his pants and went out through the French doors onto the balcony. The chilly morning air brought him fully awake as he stood gazing out at the woods, which lay calm and serene in the distance. He heard Julie stir inside. Draped in her bathrobe, she came out and joined him.

"Morning," she said, snuggling up next to him. They kissed. "I have a confession to make."

"A confession?"

"I love you, Brandon Northcross," she said, laying her head on his shoulder.

"I love you, too, Julie Stein." He kissed her lightly on the forehead.

■ ■ ■

That Saturday, he and Julie went in search of the barbershop that the janitor at work had recommended. Julie drove. As they headed down Georgia Avenue into the heart of D.C., they passed block after block of mom and pop businesses, all jammed together, as well as stretches of abandoned buildings, many defaced with spray-painted graffiti. Painted on the side of one building was a large mural of famous blacks, with images of Martin Luther King and Malcolm X the two most prominent. Along the top of the mural was the message *A Legacy of Pride: Keep It Going.* Atop the building itself was a large billboard advertising a popular brand of cigarettes that showed a shapely blonde in a bathing suit stretched out on the beach and flashing an alluring smile, a cigarette daintily perched between her long, slender fingers. The caption read, *For Those Who Want Only the Best.*

A storefront church, one of many along the way, crouched between two taller buildings. In the plate glass window of the tiny church, a young boy was beating the drums and a man was playing an electric guitar. A woman in a long white robe was singing and slapping a tambourine. Just next door was one of the church's chief adversaries, a topless bar called *Club Utopia.* A flashing neon sign, some of the bulbs missing, advertised the name. In the tug-of-war for souls, the club appeared to be winning out at the moment, as several patrons entered through its red, vinyl-padded doors.

Further ahead, as they waited at an intersection for the light to change, a tall, statuesque, black girl, her skin so dark that it looked blue, crossed in front of them, swinging her hips like she owned the street. Her lips and nails screamed the same bright orange as her skin-tight skirt. A man crossing in the other direction was eyeing the girl so intently that he nearly walked into another pedestrian. The light changed and they moved on.

"We're in the 1600 block now," Julie said. "What was the name of the business it was across from?"

"A place called Mr. Bill's TV Repair." Several blocks up, Brandon spotted it. "There it is," he said, pointing to a building just ahead, the name painted on the door.

"Oh, yeah, I see it." Julie swung over to the curb. Outside the barbershop was an old-fashioned, striped barber pole, swirling slowly. Several pairs of curious eyes peered out through the shop's blinds at them.

"I'll be back in about an hour," Julie said. They kissed goodbye and she drove off.

Brandon opened the door of the shop and stepped inside. The buzzing of barber clippers permeated the air. Tufts of hair littered the yellowing linoleum floor around the four barber chairs. In the corner atop a metal locker sat a dusty little black-and-white television with a broken antenna, its picture drifting badly. But no one appeared to be watching it anyway. Nearly every seat was taken by those awaiting their turn with one of the barbers. In the corner by the window was a shoeshine stand, where several men were perched like lookouts.

"Can I help you?" the barber nearest Brandon asked, as he tended to the customer in his chair. He was a tall man with a pipe protruding from the corner of his mouth.

"Ah, yes. Are you the owner?"

"Yes, I'm the owner."

"A Mr. Reuben Harris recommended that I stop by and get a haircut from you and told me to tell you he sent me."

"Reuben Harris?" the man said, stopping and taking the pipe from his mouth. "Reuben's one of my oldest customers. Been coming here for years. Where'd you run into ol' Reuben at?"

"He works the evening shift over at CSU, where I work," Brandon said.

"Is that right? Well, I'll be. Now, as far as me being able to get to you today, young fellow," the barber said, resuming work on his customer, "it may be a wait, 'cause I usually take only by appointment. But I can probably work you in, 'cause somebody's bound to be late or cancel out. So, right now, after this man here," he stopped again, gesturing toward the man in his chair with the stem of his pipe, "I got, let me see, one, maybe two more before I can probably work you in."

"That's fine," Brandon said. "I can wait."

"Alright then," the man said. "Just take a seat then. There's a chair right behind you there by Goochi."

Brandon turned around to find a man with a big, comical mouth leaning on the back of a chair, studying him. Somewhere in his mid-forties, he was dressed in blue jeans, work shoes and a jacket, his shirt tail hanging out.

"Here, take this chair," the man said, turning the chair around for Brandon.

"Thanks," Brandon said, moving to take a seat. But before he could, an old, gray-haired man, one of the lookouts, bounded down from the shoeshine stand.

"How 'bout a shine today, suh?" he said in a slow half-mumbling, half-speaking way of talking. He was holding a fly swatter and had a wide grin stretched across his face. Brandon couldn't decide whether the man was grinning because of the prospect of some business or if that was just the way he normally looked.

"Taylor," Goochi cut in before Brandon could answer, "a shine? Can't you see the boy wearing hush puppies? And you wanna know if he want a shine? Have you lost yo' damn mind?" Everyone, customers and barbers alike, broke into laughter.

Taylor covered his face in embarrassment and mumbled, "You know, I didn't even look." He patted Brandon on the arm, then turned and climbed back up on the stand, shaking his head at his mistake.

"That's 'cause you so money hungry, Taylor," Goochi chided, bringing laughter from the shop again. "That's what's wrong with black folks today. They so money hungry. Always looking to make a buck any way they can off another black person." When the laughter died down, Goochi turned to Brandon. "Hey, college boy, was that yo' girlfriend, that white girl that dropped you off in that Porsche? What was it, a 911?"

"Yes, it was a 911 and, yes, she's my girlfriend."

"She's a cute something," Goochi said. "I'll give you that much. Look like she from some quality, too. And I bet her folks got some money, too, ain't they?"

"Well, I really wouldn't know about that," Brandon said. He was quickly becoming annoyed with the man.

"Yeh, look like she might be one of them blue bloods," Goochi persisted. "Tell me, do her folk know 'bout you? I mean, do they know you go with they daughter?"

"Goochi, why don't you quit bein' so nosy, gettin' all in the man's business?" a man seated next to the shoeshine stand said. He had on a windbreaker, khakis, and a pair of dirty, high-top sneakers. His wiry hair jutted out like wings from underneath a white beach cap.

"Aw, hush, Simms," Goochi retorted. "I was just askin' him a question. What's wrong with askin' the man a simple question?"

"You wasn't askin' the man no simple question," Simms insisted. "You gettin' all in the man's business."

"Look, I know if I was gettin' in the man's business or not. Matter fact, I'ma ask him if I was gettin' in his business." Goochi then turned back to Brandon. "Now, college boy, tell me, was I gettin' in yo' business? 'Cause if I was, just let me know." Brandon decided to just go along for the moment.

"No, it's okay," Brandon said. "It's cool."

"See there, Simms," Goochi said, looking over at Simms. "The man say I ain't gettin' in his business." Simms threw up his hands in exasperation. Then, like a trial lawyer just given the go-ahead to continue his line of questioning over the objections of his courtroom opponent, Goochi looked down at Brandon, a knowing smile on his face, and said, "I bet that white girl nice to you, ain't she?" Simms broke in once again to object.

"Goochi, ain't no different in a white woman and a black one. I don't know why you seem to think otherwise."

"I ain't sayin' a white woman no better than a black woman," Goochi said. "Personally, I don't prefer no white woman. I think a black woman is prettier than a white woman. I'm just goin' by what I heard, that white women, for the most part, they easier to get along with and that they treat you better. That's all I'm sayin'. I ain't even sayin' I know whether it's true or not."

"Well, take my word for it," Simms said. "White women ain't no different and show ain't no better. So, you oughta just leave it alone."

"Simms, what I want to know is this," Goochi said. "How the hell would you know? 'Cause you probably ain't been within ten feet of no white woman before in your life, and you know it."

"Who ain't?" Simms responded, indignantly.

"You ain't!" Goochi said.

"For yo' information, Goochi, I have dated a white woman before," Simms said.

"Now, Simms, you know Shirley be done whupped yo' big ass out them ol' run-down high-tops she catch you even thinkin' 'bout a white woman." The barbershop rocked with laughter.

"I'm talkin' 'bout before I started goin' with Shirley," Simms said, bristling.

"Aw, so you must be talkin' 'bout that big, fat white woman used to like you down at the laundromat," Goochi said. "Woman so big, Baxter, she had to turn sideways just to get through the door. And personally, I don't think the woman bathed too regularly, either, 'cause most times she was musty as the back of a garbage truck on pickup day. That's who you talkin' 'bout, Simms?" Waves of laughter rang out again.

"You kiss my naked ass, Goochi!" Simms said. "You know damn well I ain't talkin' 'bout that woman. I ain't never had nothin' to do with that woman. And you know it."

"Okay, so who *are* you talkin' 'bout, then?"

"It's my business who it was," Simms said.

"'My business who it was,'" Goochi said, mimicking Simms. "Simms, get the hell outta here with that ol' tired-ass shit."

"Goochi, you ain't got no sense," Simms said. "I ain't even gon' waste my time talkin' to you 'bout it no mo'." Simms folded his arms across his chest to make his point.

"Good!" Goochi said. "I don't know why I waste my time talkin' to you 'bout it, either. Now, somebody that probably know somethin' about white women is Chick over here. I remember back in high school when Chick, star on the basketball team and all, had him all kinda little gals, seem like a different one every other week. Bet you got to know some of them white women when you was stationed out on the coast and over there in Germany, didn't you, Chick?" The man Goochi was talking to, who was seated next to Taylor on the shoeshine stand, was tall with long sideburns. He had on a jogging outfit and a pair of house slippers.

"Yeah, I dated a few when I was stationed out in California and overseas in Germany," Chick said. "France was nice in that regard, too. I had a couple of buddies that even married white women that they met over there, brought 'em back to the states with 'em. Had some pretty little children with 'em, too."

"How they say them women treat 'em?" Goochi asked.

"Aw, they say they treat 'em pretty good, get along with 'em just fine, for the most part," Chick said.

"See, that's what I heard, that they easy to get along with, easier to get along with than a lot of black women," Goochi said. "'Cause you take the average black woman, she wanna argue with you all the time, always throwin' up in your face what you ain't got, always wanna know what you gon' do for 'em. But most white women, I heard, they don't get off on that kinda stuff. They wanna help a man, be nice to him, treat him good. I done run into too many black women, they always puttin' a black man down. You say good mornin' to some of 'em, and they near 'bout ready to cuss you out."

"You ain't tellin' nothin' but the truth," someone said.

"And, Goochi," one of the barbers, a short reddish man with a jerri curl, said, "some of 'em will even tell you to your face that you can't do for them what a white man can do. They don't want a black man. They want a white man. Like it's somethin' special 'bout a white man. Am I lyin'?"

"Walker Jay, I *know* you ain't lyin'," Goochi said. "You ain't said nothin' that ain't public information. It might as well be broadcast on the evenin' news."

"Some of these black women, especially these younger ones, I don't understand 'em," Walker Jay said. "You listen to 'em talk. They look at a man just as a meal ticket. If he can't give 'em what they want, financially, they don't want to give him the time of day. They define a man strictly based on what he can do for them. They just done gone crazy in the way they think."

"I know dat's right."

"But some of these white women, they can be a world of trouble, too, now," Chick said. "Don't fool yourself. They got their faults, too. But I know what you sayin'. I been there."

"Tell me, Chick," Goochi said, "these white women that them brothers was datin' out there on the coast, was some of 'em good lookin'?"

"Good lookin'?" Chick said, clearly taken aback by the question. "Man, those brothers out there on the coast was steppin' out with some foxes! No question. See, when a brother hooked up with a gray girl out there—and there was plenty of 'em that was into brothers—more than likely she was somethin' he didn't mind showcasin'. Yessir, some of 'em was even successful actresses and fashion models, that kinda action. It wasn't nothin' to see a black man walkin' down the street with some tough blue-eyed soul on his arm."

"See, now that's what I'm gettin' at," Goochi rushed to put in. "You see the average black man 'round here that's got a white woman on his arm, she usually so po' and homely that don't no white man want her. Shee-it! Ain't nothin' worst than a black man with a po', ugly white woman on his arm."

"Ain't dat the truth."

"Look out now."

"But you see a white man with one of our women, I betcha more than likely she's a fine somethin'," Goochi said. "Huh?" He stepped back and looked around, as if daring anyone in his right mind to dispute the truth of what he had just said.

"You right."

"You ain't doin' nothin' but shamin' the devil."

"And it's always been that way, too. Am I lyin'?" Goochi said.

"Naw, you talkin' the truth."

"So, I say if you gon' get you a white woman, get you a fine white woman," Goochi continued. "Don't be half-steppin' 'bout it."

"Yeh, you talkin' straight talk."

"Only thang 'bout it, though," Goochi said, more soberly now, "Mr. Charlie, he might give you a good job, might even let you move next door to him. But he catch you messin' with them blondes, them brunettes, and them redheads, he'll cut you down!"

"Aw, yes he will."

"Ain't dat the truth."

"You right. You right."

"I know I'm right," Goochi said. Everyone was quiet for a moment, as if to allow what Goochi had just said to sink in. Something passing outside the window caught Goochi's attention. "Damn! Look at that!" he said, lifting the blinds to get a better look out. "Now that's what you call a brickhouse there." Brandon peered out the window along with some of the others to see what it was that had gotten Goochi so excited. A woman with an hour-glass figure was going by. "Look at them big pretty legs," Goochi said, panting. "Now, that's a fine little brown gal there! Just one night with a young gal like that would take care of my back trouble for good." As Goochi continued to rave about the woman, and what he would do with her in bed, Baxter, having finished with his last customer, signaled to Brandon that it was his turn.

"Goochi, that young gal'll kill you," Simms finally said. "You wouldn't know what to do with all that."

"That's why I'd let you have her, Simms," Goochi said. "Can't you see Simms now, Chick, him and that young gal all wrapped up together?" Goochi began to dramatize how Simms would be carrying on in bed with the woman, thrusting his hips back and forth. "Look out now! Simms be done went through one of them Dr. Jekyll/Mr. Hyde changes, be done turned into super stud." Pretty soon the whole barbershop was rolling in laughter. As Goochi continued, the door to the shop swung open and a distinguished-looking man entered.

"Ah, hello, Reverend," Baxter said, in a surprised voice.

"Hello, Baxter."

Everyone, upon seeing the man, quickly quieted down. Goochi, however, who was standing with his back to the door, continued with his lewd talk.

"... yeh, Simms would be workin' his ass off, like it's goin' outta style. You wouldn't be able to tell that nigga shit!"

"How you doing, Reverend?" Baxter said, a lot louder, with special emphasis on *Reverend,* to make sure he got Goochi's attention this time. Goochi froze, then slowly turned around. "Aw, I'm sorry, Reverend," Goochi said, a pitiful look on his face, like a little child having been caught red-handed at some mischief by a parent. "I didn't see you come in."

"Sounds like you were putting in all the details there, Goochi," the man said.

"Yeh, you caught him, Reverend, with his filthy mouth," Simms said.

"How's everybody doing today?" the Reverend said, greeting barbers and customers alike.

"Just fine, Reverend."

"Hello, Reverend."

"Afternoon, Reverend."

"Goochi, I'm still looking for you one Sunday morning, like you promised," the Reverend said.

"That's right. Get on him, Reverend," Simms said, relishing the opportunity to rib Goochi without fear of reprisal.

"Ah, Reverend, I'm still comin'," Goochi said. "I just gotta get my good suit out the cleaners. You know, I wanna be lookin' right and all. But I'll be there one Sunday. You can count on it."

"Well, we'll keep a seat open for you."

"Thank you, Reverend," Goochi said. "Oh, by the way, Reverend, what time you got?"

"By my watch," the man said, checking his watch, "it's just after one."

"It is? Then we better be gettin' on, Simms," Goochi said, "if we gon catch that game. You still comin' with me?"

"Yeh, I'm still comin'," Simms said, getting up from his chair.

"How 'bout you, Chick? You comin'?"

"I wish I could, Goochi," Chick said, climbing down from the shoeshine stand, "but I promised Darlene I was gon take her two little boys to their Cub Scout meeting this afternoon."

"Chick, you just like a father to them little boys," Goochi said. "When you and Darlene gon get married?"

"I don't know. Maybe one day."

The three of them, Goochi, Simms and Chick, all said their goodbyes and left. Baxter turned his attention back to the Reverend.

"Stop by for a cut, Reverend? I think I can work you in."

"Thanks, Baxter, but, no. I just stopped by to let you know that I'm going to have to cancel my appointment for next week."

"Oh?"

"I'm going to be out of town for a few days. So, let's make it for the following week."

"Okay then, Reverend," Baxter said, picking up his appointment book. "I'll just make a note of it."

"I don't think I've met you before, young man," the Reverend said to Brandon, extending his hand. "I'm David Hollings." Brandon brought his hand out from underneath the sheet to shake the man's hand.

"It's nice to meet you," he replied. "I'm Brandon Northcross."

"Are you a college student here in the area?"

"No, I just finished college," Brandon said. "I work at CSU."

"Well, that's great."

"Where he works at, Reverend," Baxter said, "he ran into Reuben Harris. You remember ol' Reuben, don't you? Used to drive a cab."

"Reuben Harris?" the Reverend said. "Yeah, I haven't seen Reuben in I don't know when, since he and his wife moved out to Maryland. By the way," the man said, shifting his attention back to Brandon, "let me give you one of my cards." He took a business card from his coat pocket and handed it to Brandon. "Stop by and visit us some Sunday. We have two services: 7:45 and 10:45. We'll be happy to have you."

"Thanks. I certainly will," Brandon said, looking at the card, before putting it away.

"Baxter, I'm gonna run now. I'll see you," the Reverend said, opening the door to leave.

"Okay, Reverend. I'll see you in two weeks at your regular time."

"And I hope to see you soon, too, young man," Hollings said to Brandon, before letting the door close behind him.

■ ■ ■

The team's first late-night session took place the following week. It was past eleven and they still had work to do to stay on schedule. For dinner they had sent out for Chinese.

"I don't know about the rest of you, but I think I need a break," Allan said. "I'm so tired I can hardly see straight anymore. The numbers on my calculator readout keep growing closer and closer together with every passing minute."

"It's those mind-altering drugs you're doing, Allan," Layla said, getting a chuckle from the group.

"I could definitely use some about now," Allan said. "That's for sure."

"I think we all could use a break," Tim said. "It's about a quarter after by my watch. Let's take a really quick break and be back, say, around twenty-five after. We'll wrap things up and be out of here by midnight." People began heading for the door.

"How you doing, guy?" Sean asked, stifling a yawn.

"I'm hanging," Brandon said, getting up and stretching. "So, this is one of those marathon sessions Tim was talking about, huh?"

"Yeah, and it's only gonna get worst," Sean said. "Definitely not looking forward to it. But it's like they say, mind over matter, my friend. Look, I'm going down for coffee. Wanna join me?"

"Thanks, but I think I'll just chill out up here," Brandon said. "Besides, if I have another cup, I'll be wide awake 'til in the morning." Sean headed out. Everyone else had left, too, everyone except Layla. She was standing over by the window looking out at the twinkling city below. Brandon went and joined her.

"How's it going?" he said.

"Oh, hi," she said. "Okay, except for this splitting headache." She had a bottle of pills in her hand.

"What are you taking for it?"

"Just aspirin." She showed him the bottle. "I wish I had something stronger. So, how's it going with you? I guess it's not a lot of fun being stuck here at work this late, huh?"

"It's okay," he said. "It's all part of the job."

"Oh, God," Layla said, putting her hand to her temple. "There it goes again, that throbbing."

"Maybe you should just go home," Brandon said.

"No, I'll be alright. It'll pass in a minute. Would you be a doll and get me a glass of water? I'm gonna take a couple more of these."

"Sure." Brandon went over and poured a glass of water from the pitcher sitting on the table. "Here you are," he said, holding the glass out to Layla.

"Thanks. Let me just get this cap off." In her attempt to open the bottle, it slipped from her hands to the floor.

"I'll get it," Brandon said, stooping to retrieve the bottle.

"No, I'll get it," Layla said, also stooping and reaching for it. Their faces ended up so close together that he could feel her breath on his cheeks. Her hand, which was touching his, was warm. Their eyes were locked together in a kind of visual slow-drag. Brandon finally got a hold of himself and straightened up.

"Here's your water," he said, handing Layla the glass. His hand was trembling slightly.

"Thanks." Strangely, he felt both drawn to her and repelled by her at the same time. A heavy lump developed in his throat. Even as Layla popped the pills into her mouth and washed them down with the water, she kept her eyes glued to his. Slowly, very slowly, she ran the rim of the glass across her lips, leaving a smear of red lipstick. The lump in his throat had now doubled in size.

"Why fight it, man," she said, smoke rising from every word. "You're built for it." She blew him a kiss that seemed to take forever to leave her lips. Approaching voices broke the charged atmosphere in the room. He took a step back from Layla.

"Yeah, I'm the same way when it comes to gardening," Kyle said. "My wife's the one with the green thumb at my house." Peter was with him. Several others were also returning.

When the meeting resumed, Brandon could feel Layla's eyes on him, burning holes through his clothing. He remembered what Fran had said that day at lunch about Layla and Jarrett Knowles. Was this how she'd come on to him? One thing he knew. No matter how enticing Layla was, getting involved with her was the last thing he needed at this point.

Over the next week or so, Layla purposely went out of her way a number of times to make contact with Brandon, sometimes stopping by his cube to ask a question of him or Sean. Either through body language or a lingering glance, she made her intentions known. Once when he and Layla happened to arrive at a doorway at the same time, approaching from opposite directions, she intentionally brushed up against him, then turned to see his reaction, looking him up and down. Another time, when he had to go pick up some slides from Layla to deliver to Repro, he found her standing with her leg in her chair, adjusting her garter, her skirt pushed all the way back to her thigh. But Brandon refused each time to take the bait. Finally, Layla backed off.

Eight

The employee appreciation luncheon was held out on the lawn behind the CSU tower. From under a red canopy, caterers dished out generous helpings of barbecue and corn on the cob. A band set up on a makeshift stage filled the air with Motown hits from the '60s. A small but enthusiastic bunch danced near the stage. Most, however, were content to relax out on the lawn and enjoy the food and entertainment. With his plate and beverage in hand, Brandon scouted the crowd for someone he knew. Across the way he spotted Roosevelt and the others he'd met that day in the cafeteria. Brandon made his way over.

"Why is Al Schmidt out there making a damn fool of himself trying to dance?" Morris said, as Brandon approached. "And what song is he dancing to anyway? He's dancing more off the beat than on it." Those nearby laughed.

"Morris, will you leave that man alone," Candace said. "You're just jealous 'cause you can't hang with him."

"You ain't lyin' about that," Morris said. "Al's busting some moves I ain't never seen in my life. And probably won't ever see again, either."

"Hello, Brandon," Candace said, one of the first to notice him.

"Hey. What's up, everybody?" Brandon said.

"My man," Morris said, slapping fives with him.

"What's up?" Sherman greeted him.

"Pull up a chair," Roosevelt said.

"Thanks." In addition to Morris, Roosevelt, Sherman, and Candace, there were two other black women and a white guy.

"Brandon, this is Charisse," Candace said, indicating the woman closer to him.

"Hi," Brandon said.

"Hello," Charisse said.

"And this is Robin," Candace said, introducing the other woman. A near Whitney Houston double, she looked like she had stepped directly from a Paris runway. Everything about her was perfect, from her figure, to her nails, to her makeup, to her hair.

"What's up?" Robin said, in a cool, sexy voice, looking out from behind her Ralph Lauren shades.

"Hi," Brandon said.

"And please don't tell her how much she looks like Whitney Houston," Candace rushed to put in, "because she hears that all the time. Right, Robin?"

"Thank you, girlfriend," Robin said. "I don't think a day goes by that somebody isn't telling me I look like Whitney. But, hey, I'm cool with it. She's a good-looking girl."

"But not as good-looking as you, Robin," Morris said.

"This is true," Robin said, playfully. They laughed.

"And next to Robin is Todd," Candace said, indicating the white guy.

"What's happening?" Todd said, extending his hand.

"You got it," Brandon said, shaking hands with the man, who looked to be about his age.

"Did y'all see that?" Morris said, still focusing on the dancers. "Al Schmidt and this other uncoordinated guy just collided with each other. Why is it that the most non-dancing white people, no matter where you go, hafta' always run out on the dance floor, when they know they can't dance a tap, and ruin it for everybody else? I mean, I'll be trying to dance and I'll look over at some white guy that's dancing all off the beat and it'll throw me off. Why is that, Todd?"

"Man, I couldn't begin to tell you," Todd said. "But you looking at one white guy that just might run you off the floor."

"Say *what?*" Morris said.

"Uh-oh," Charrise said. "I think I hear a challenge coming on."

"You gon run *me* off the dance floor?" Morris said.

"You heard me," Todd said. "I've seen you in action before, Morris. You're pretty good. But I think I'm better."

"Hold up, now," Morris said. "Todd, you might be able to dance pretty good for a white guy, and I know you grew up around black people and all, but I don't think you could hang with me."

"Morris, where I grew up at back in Philly, I was the man at the parties. I mean, I was so smooth on the floor that the ladies would come ask *me* to dance. And that included sisters, too."

"I've seen him work, Morris," Robin said. "Saw him down at Escape one night. He can go."

"So, Robin, you know what I can do," Morris said. "You think Todd can run me off the floor?"

"I don't know if he can run you off the floor, but I think he could give you a run for the money."

"We gon hafta' get together sometime and settle this thing," Morris said.

"You can settle it tonight," Robin said. "It's ladies' night at Park Avenue. Me, Charrise and Toi, we'll be there."

"I can't make it tonight," Morris said. "I'm busy."

"I can't either," Todd said.

"But we'll hook up sometime," Morris said.

"Is Park Avenue a black nightclub?" Brandon said.

"About one of the only half-way decent ones around," Charrisse said.

"Why is it that somebody can't open a nice, upscale nightspot where black professionals can feel comfortable going?" Robin said. "I mean, Park Avenue and Escape are okay, but you got to always be dealing with the riffraff element, the brothers with no jobs and no class. If you wanna go somewhere really nice, you have to go to a white nightclub, where they hardly want to let you in the door to begin with a lot of times. And then, when you do get in, if too many blacks show up, they change the music on you. They go from playing something everybody likes—black people and white—and can dance to to some old hillbilly bullshit that they know black people don't like. I wanna know what's up with that."

"They don't want y'all black folks dirtying up their nice, white club," Morris said. *"That's* what's up with that. They like black folk's music, but they don't like being around black folk."

"They used to do that in Philly—changing up the music—all the time," Todd said. "Anytime a new club would open and blacks started showing up in numbers, they would switch the format. A buddy of mine who used to DJ said that the management at the white clubs he worked would tell him straight up that whenever the number of blacks reached a certain level, what they called a cutoff level, to basically whiten up the music. They felt that if too many blacks started coming, it would scare the whites away."

"Man, that's messed up," Sherman said.

"You wanna come with us to Park Avenue tonight, Brandon?" Robin said. "It's gon be plenty single ladies there."

"Thanks, but I don't think my girlfriend would be too cool about me going," Brandon said.

"I can understand that," Robin said. "I wouldn't want my boyfriend going to Park Avenue on ladies' night without me, either. As a matter of fact, he better check with me first, if he's planning on even being anywhere in the vicinity." They laughed.

"Sounds like you keep a close rein on that man of yours, Robin," Roosevelt said.

"You have to these days," Robin said. "These women will snatch your man right from under your nose, if you don't."

"Honey, I know that's right," Charrise said, high-fiving Robin. "Some of these women around here, you have to watch 'em. They'll get all chummy with you and everything and next thing you know they'll be trying to put the moves on your man, especially if they think he's got some money."

"Speaking of nice clubs, anybody been to The Preserve?" Brandon asked. "I hear it's really happening there."

"Morris, didn't you tell me you went there once?" Roosevelt said.

"Yeh, I went and checked it out one time, me and Craig," Morris said.

"Seems like I remember you had a pretty memorable time that night," Roosevelt said, grinning.

"Yeh, it was memorable, alright," Morris said. "Let me tell y'all what happened. After having to produce about eight forms of ID a piece, they finally let us in. Anyway, we step up in there. The music's slammin' and it's wall to wall women."

"White women, mainly?" Roosevelt said.

"Yeh, white women," Morris said. "It must've been ladies' night. Anyway, a lot of the women were just standing around, waiting for somebody to ask them to dance. You could tell they wanted to dance, by the way they were bopping and moving to the music, you know. But most of the white guys were just laying back, drinking beer, like they weren't even interested in the women. Anyway, me and Craig, we ready to take to the floor with somebody's daughter. So, we go to work. But to make a long story short, over the next three or four songs, we asked I don't know how many women to dance. And the answer was the same from every last one of 'em."

"You mean none of them would dance?" Brandon said.

"Nope."

"I think you and Craig were wearing the wrong skin color that night," Roosevelt said.

"You can say that again," Morris said. "At one point I felt like saying, look, I ain't asking you to go out with me. All I'm asking is for a dance. We ain't gotta get engaged."

"Weren't there any black women there you all could've danced with?" Charrise said.

"You could count the number of sistas that were there on one hand," Morris said. "We did step up to these two sistas. They turned us down, too, saying they weren't really in the mood for dancing. But the next thing we know, there're out on the dance floor with some white boys. Another sista shot me down, too."

"So, not only would the white women not dance with you, but the black women wouldn't either," Roosevelt said.

"Exactly," Morris said. "By this time, I'm ready to go ask for my money back."

"So, you and Craig found out the hard way why they call it The Preserve," Candace said.

"You ain't lyin' 'bout that," Morris said. "Everthing in a dress that night was preserved for white men. They might as well have hung a sign out front saying no black men need apply."

"It's like this," Roosevelt said. "If you're black and you wanna go somewhere at least marginally nice to party, somewhere you'll feel welcome, you got two options: Escape and Park Avenue. That's about it."

"Nolan and I went to a really nice club up in the Baltimore Harbor a few weeks ago," Robin said. "I forget the name of it. It was a mixed crowd and they were throwing down some serious jams. But it was for a private party. So, I don't know if that was the club's usual format."

"Probably not," Candace said. "They'd get too many of us up in there, if it was."

"Changing the subject for a moment, is Nolan still gonna ask to be traded, Robin?" Roosevelt said.

"If the Redskins don't renegotiate his contract to his satisfaction, he said he would," Robin said. "His agent is currently trying to work something out, from what I understand."

"Has he mentioned what teams he'd possibly like to go to if it doesn't work out with the Skins?"

"I think he said the Dolphins, the Chiefs and one other team, maybe the Eagles," Robin said. "Those would be his picks."

"Would you move with him, if he goes to another city?" Morris asked.

"I don't know," Robin said. "I'd have to think about it."

"Aren't you and Nolan engaged?" Candace said.

"We were, but I called it off," Robin said.

"What happened?" Candace said.

"Nothing really," Robin said. "It's just that I don't know if I'm ready for marriage."

"How's everyone doing?" a tall, middle-aged white man said, walking up, a plate of barbecue in hand.

"Hello, Art," Morris said. The others acknowledged the man, too. "You know, this is really nice. We need to do this more often."

"Well, actually that's something we've been looking into," Art said. "I think it's important that we get together from time to time, let our hair down a little. For some reason, we don't do it as much as we used to."

"You been hitting the greens any lately, Art?" Roosevelt asked. "I read in some magazine that you said you like to tee it up every now and then."

"Not nearly as much as I'd like to," Art said. "I'm just too busy these days. My wife got me a new set of clubs for my birthday back in April and I've probably used them maybe twice."

"You gotta make the time," Roosevelt said. "You know what they say about all work and no play."

"Yes, I certainly do," Art said. "But until they find a way to add a couple more hours to the day, I don't think I'm going to be able to do much about it. Are you a golfer?"

"I like to get out there with the fellows every now and then," Roosevelt said.

"I find it to be a very relaxing pastime, as I'm sure you do, too," Art said. "Well, you folks enjoy yourselves." The man smiled and moved on to greet another group of people.

"Wasn't that Art Hoffman?" Brandon said, when the man was out of earshot.

"Yep. Mr. Money Bags, himself," Candace said.

"I'd never seen him up close before," Brandon said. "He looks slimmer in person than in the pictures of him I've seen."

"That's what having a lot of money will do for you," Candace said. "It'll make you look fat and happy to the camera."

"If that's the case, I oughta look skinny as a rail in my pictures, as poor as I am," Morris said. They laughed. "How much you think Art Hoffman's worth, Roosevelt?"

"His base salary is reported to be right around a million a year, I believe," Roosevelt said. "But when you get through throwing in all the stock options and bonuses, he's probably taking home five to six times that much, at least."

"He's supposed to be one of the highest paid CEOs in America," Candace said.

"I heard he's got his own golf course on his estate," Todd said.

"Is his wife married?" Robin said, peering up over the top of her shades.

"Girlfriend, you oughta' quit," Charrise said, laughing with the others.

"What does a person do with that kind of money?" Sherman said. "I mean, isn't there a limit to how much you can buy?"

"It's not about buying stuff," Roosevelt said. "It's about acquiring wealth."

"I'd like to acquire just a li-it-tle bit of that wealth," Robin said. The band started in on another song, one that sounded more country western than Motown.

"I wonder if they take requests," Morris said. "'Cause if they do, I'd like to request that they take the rest of the afternoon off."

"They started out okay," Sherman said. "But this stuff they playing now ain't cutting it."

"Say, did you all hear about the black guy that got hassled at this clothing store because they claimed he was trying to leave wearing a shirt he hadn't paid for, when actually he had bought the shirt several days earlier?" Candace said.

"No," Robin said. "What happened?"

"They say the undercover security for the store stopped him as he was leaving and basically wrestled him to the floor, handcuffed him and held him for the police," Candace said. "When they finally checked things out, they found that the man had purchased the shirt just like he'd been saying all along."

"That's a damn shame," Roosevelt said. "Did they say what color the security personnel were?"

"They were both white," Candace said.

"And on top of that, the man is a school teacher and a deacon in his church," Candace said.

"I couldn't see them doing that to a white person," Morris said.

"I sure hope he sues," Charrise said.

"I know I would," Robin said. "I'd slap a lawsuit on that store so fast they wouldn't know what hit 'em. I almost did that with this jewelry store one time."

"What happened?" Candace said.

"I was out shopping around for a bracelet," Robin said, "and this particular store had some nice stuff showcased in their window. So, I decided to step inside and take a look. I'd come straight from work, so I was dressed, you know. Anyway, hardly any customers were in the store, so it wasn't like it was real busy. But these two white women that are working there, they're so preoccupied with their conversation with each other that they don't notice me. So, I just take my time browsing, just checking out the display cases. But not once did either of them ask if I needed any help. It was like I wasn't even there. I started to just walk out. But I really wanted to see this particular bracelet that had caught my eye. So, I go up to them and ask if I could see it. One of them looks at me and goes, 'Do you have credit here at the store?' I said, 'I beg your pardon?' Then she says, 'We don't do layaway here. And there are certain minimum requirements one must meet to qualify for credit.'

"I couldn't believe it. I said to that heifer, 'Look, for your information, I don't need credit here at this little five-and-dime to buy whatever you got for sale here. I can pay cash or I can put it on any one of my three gold cards.' I took one of them out and waved it in her face. 'Ah, ah, I'm sorry,' she said. 'I didn't mean to imply—' I said to her, 'Yes, you did. See, the fact of the matter is that you didn't think I could afford to shop here because I'm black. But you don't have to worry 'bout that ever again.' I then turned and walked out of there. I was so mad."

"It's really screwed up, what black people have to go through in this society," Todd said. "You should've got a lawyer and sued their prejudiced asses."

"Did these two incidents happen in some little hick towns somewhere?" Brandon said.

"Not unless you consider Rockville, Maryland a little hick town," Candace said. "That's where the incident I mentioned happened."

"This happened in Rockville?" Brandon said, astonished.

"And this jewelry store I was talking about is right here in D.C.," Robin said.

"Maybe it's me, but I never would have thought that this kind of backwards stuff would be happening in D.C., the nation's capital."

"Man, where you think we are?" Morris said. "In Canada or somewhere? That kinda stuff could happen anywhere in this country. And probably does."

"I never heard of it happening back in New Hampshire, where I'm from," Brandon said.

"Well, you ain't in New Hampshire no more, brother," Morris said. "You in the *real* U.S. of A."

"And below the Mason Dixon line, too," Candace said.

"But it's nowhere near as bad here as in the Deep South," Todd said. "You go right outside of Atlanta and you'd think you were back in the '50s, the way white people's attitudes are toward blacks."

"Tell me about it," Roosevelt said. "My brother used to work in this little town in Georgia, no more than about 30 or 40 miles outside of Atlanta. He said the racism was so bad that the white supervisors would crack racist jokes out in the open. And they wouldn't care if blacks heard them or not."

"You couldn't pay me enough money to work in one of those little redneck towns," Robin said. "But if you're gonna live in the south,

Atlanta's the place to be," Robin said. "It's happening there twenty-four seven. And the cost of living is so affordable, compared to here."

"I can't believe the prices of homes here in the D.C. area," Brandon said. "I don't know how single people ever afford to buy. With rent as high as it is, how do you save enough for a down payment?"

"I know that's right," Charrise said. "I would love to buy something, but when I get through paying my bills every month, especially my rent, I hardly have anything left."

"Honey, I've got friends down in Atlanta who've got two- and three-bedroom homes with swimming pools out back and big sprawling lawns that they didn't even pay a hundred grand for. Those same homes up here would run you two-hundred to two-hundred fifty grand, at least."

"Didn't you go to school down there?" Sherman said.

"Yep. Spelman."

"So, that's where you get those champagne tastes from," Morris said. "I bet I know what sorority you pledged, too."

"Don't even go there, Morris," Robin said, giving Morris the evil eye. "I don't wanna hear this stuff about this bourgeois mentality that Spelman women are supposed to be known for."

"Robin, you got me figured wrong," Morris said, feigning innocence. "I meant it in a good way."

"No you didn't," Robin said. "Don't even try it."

"But you did pledge, right?" Morris said.

"Yeah, I pledged."

"I knew it."

"You didn't know I pledged," Robin said, balling up a napkin and tossing it at Morris, who ducked it. "You just wanna mess with me."

■ ■ ■

"Knock. Knock." Brandon looked up from his desk.

"Oh, hi, Fran."

"Just stopped by to let you know I won't be around for a week or so," she said. "Simon and I are going away on a little vacation."

"Oh. That's nice. Where to?"

"Germany."

"Great," Brandon said. "I know you guys are gonna have a really nice time there."

"I hope so. Simon and I haven't really taken a vacation since the kids were little. I figure we deserve it."

"When do you leave?"

"Tomorrow morning," she said. "So, tell me. How are things, I mean, with Tim and all? Is it getting any better?"

"Not as far as I can see," Brandon said, shaking his head.

"Well, hang in there," Fran said. "It's bound to turn around. Just think of it as sort of an initiation you're going through. Believe me, you're not the first person to be tested this way."

"I'll try to."

"Things will work out," she said. "You wait and see. Well, gotta run. See you when I get back."

■ ■ ■

One evening, Brandon took Julie by to meet Sarah. After having heard him talk so much about her flowers, she had decided she wanted to see them for herself.

"Well, hello, Brandon," Sarah greeted him at the door.

"Hello, Sarah."

"Come in. This is certainly a pleasant surprise." He and Julie stepped inside.

"Sarah, this is Julie."

"Nice to meet you, Julie."

"It's nice to meet you, too, Sarah," Julie said. "Brandon's told me so much about your flowers. And now that I'm here," she said, looking all around her, "I must say they're as beautiful as he said they were."

"Why, thank you, dear. Please, have a seat." He and Julie took a seat on the sofa. Sarah took a seat across from them. "Can I get you all something to drink, ice tea or a pop, maybe?"

"Thank you, but I'm fine," Julie said.

"What about you, Brandon?" Sarah asked.

"I'm fine, too," Brandon said. "But thanks. We just came from dinner."

"So, Brandon, how's your job going?" Sarah asked.

"It's going good," he said. "But they're definitely getting their money's worth out of me."

"Have you found a nice girl to date yet?"

"Ah, yeah, I think so," he said, looking coyly at Julie.

"Julie, do you know who this girl is?" Sarah said, noticing the look he'd just given Julie. Julie hesitated, not certain just how to respond.

"Sarah, it's Julie," Brandon said, taking Julie's hand in his. A look of mild shock came over Sarah's face.

"You mean that—"

"Yeah, Julie's my girlfriend."

"Oh, I see…Okay." Sarah managed a smile. "Where'd you two meet?"

"At work," Brandon said. "Actually, outside in the parking lot, of all places."

"I see." Sarah's whole demeanor had changed toward them, even though she tried to hide it. It was clear to both of them that she didn't approve of their relationship. "Well, Brandon," Sarah said, suddenly rising from her chair, "I'm really glad you stopped by and brought Julie by so I could meet her." Picking up on her cue, he and Julie rose, too. "But I've got to get back to something I was just in the middle of."

"Oh, sure, I understand," Brandon said.

"It was nice meeting you, Sarah," Julie said.

"Yes, same here," Sarah said. "Do come back again." She let them out.

■ ■ ■

"So, what're you doing tomorrow after work, honey?" Julie said, as Brandon drove her home in his new car late one evening.

"I'm probably going to have to work late again, unfortunately. Why? What's happening?"

"Well, there's this art exhibit tomorrow at the Galleria. And it's only for one night. This guy—I can't remember his name offhand—is doing a showing of some of his work. He's been getting rave reviews everywhere he's exhibited. I forget what the type of painting he does is called. Anyway, I thought you might want to go with me to it. But I guess—"

"Julie, have you noticed that police car behind us?" Brandon said, as he looked in his rear view mirror.

"A police car?" Julie said, checking her side mirror. "No. What, you think they're following us or something?"

"I'm not sure. But I know they've been behind us now for awhile."

"They have?" she said, twisting around to get a better look at them. "Well, there's one way to find out. Turn off at this next street up ahead."

"Okay." Brandon turned at the street that Julie had indicated. The police car turned, too. "They're still behind us," he said.

"What do they want?" Julie said, more to herself than to Brandon.

"I wish they'd either stop us or go around," he said. "This is driving me up the wall."

The blue lights from the squad car flashed on. Brandon pulled over onto the shoulder of the road. It was dusk and the only lights were those from the headlights of the two cars and the revolving lights atop the police car. The police pulled in behind them. Brandon watched as the two policemen got out and started toward them, one coming along the driver's side, the other along the passenger's side. Their heavy boots made a hard, crunching sound on the loose gravel of the shoulder. Brandon rolled down his window. When the cop reached the door, he bent over and looked in at them, his flashlight in his hand.

"Good evening, officer," Brandon said. "Is something wrong?" The man ignored his question and, instead, clicked on his flashlight and pointed it in Brandon's face, then in Julie's. They shielded their eyes from the blinding beam.

"Well, look what we got ourselves here," the cop said, continuing to aim the flashlight alternatively at Brandon, then Julie. "A nigger and a white woman."

"Look, I really don't appreciate that," Julie said. "And I also don't appreciate you shining your flashlight in our faces like you're doing!"

"Oh, excuse me, ma'am," the cop said, in mock apology, but continuing to direct the light in their faces. "I suppose the polite term is interracial couple. Isn't that what they call 'em these days, Neil?"

"Yeah, I think so," the other cop said. Brandon could tell from the direction of the other officer's voice that he was standing back from the car at an angle. The cop clicked off his flashlight. Straightening up to his full height, he placed his flashlight back on his belt and removed his baton.

"Alright, boy, step out of the car," he ordered.

"Look, officer, I don't understand what this is all about and why you—"

"Boy, I told you to get out of that goddamn car! Now, if I have to tell you again, I ain't gon be so nice about it. Now move, boy!"

"Look, officer—" Julie started to say.

"It's okay, Julie," Brandon said, raising his hand to cut her off. He opened the door and stepped out. The cop immediately grabbed him, spun him around and shoved him roughly up against the car.

"Alright, spread 'em!" the cop commanded, pressing Brandon's head up against the car, while kicking his feet apart. He then frisked him, removing his wallet from his pocket.

"Why are you treating him like that?!" Julie demanded, jumping out of the car and pounding her fists on the roof for emphasis. "He hasn't done anything!"

"Don't worry about it, Julie," Brandon said. "I'll straighten this whole thing out." Brandon kept his voice even, though inside he was furious— and scared. The cop took Brandon's driver's license from his wallet and handed it to the other cop.

"Neil, run a check on this license." Neil retreated to the patrol car to run the check.

"Can I at least turn around while—" Brandon said, as he tried to turn to face the cop.

"You don't move 'til I tell you to, boy!" the cop said, forcing him back against the car.

"What is your damn problem, man?" Julie yelled. "You don't have to treat him like some common criminal! Is this how you get your kicks?"

"You'd best button that lip, girl, before I have to button it for you!" the cop said.

"You just try and—"

"Julie, please!" Brandon half shouted. "Let's just let them run the check and get it over with. Okay?"

They waited in silence as the license check was run. A few minutes later the cop returned.

"Ran it through. Nothing," the man said, handing the license back to his partner.

"Well, looks like you're clean," the cop said, finally allowing Brandon to turn around. He gave him back his license and wallet. "Been some break-ins in the area lately. You seemed to fit the general description of the suspect. But a word of advice. I'd be real careful where I drove at night and who I drove around with, if I were you. You get my drift, boy?"

"No, I'm afraid I don't," Brandon said, sternly, as he stuffed his wallet back in his pants. "I haven't done anything. And I'm obviously not the person you were looking for when you stopped us. So, why are you harassing us?"

"Well, let me see if I can't make it a little plainer for you then," the cop said, leaning in real close to Brandon. "I don't like your type riding around with our women. You understand what I'm saying now, boy?" Brandon didn't respond. Instead, he just bit his lip to try to hold back his anger. "Boy, didn't you hear me ask you a question?" The cop punctuated his last words with several stinging jabs of his baton into Brandon's ribs.

"Listen, man," Brandon said, pushing the baton aside, "if you're not gonna give me a ticket or arrest me for something, then I demand that you let us go. I know my rights!" The cop grabbed Brandon roughly around his collar and slammed him hard back against the car. He then drew back his baton in a threatening manner.

"Stop it!" Julie screamed, rushing around the car to try to get at the officer. But the other cop grabbed her before she could make it.

"Let me go, damnit!" she shouted, struggling to get free. "Let me go!"

"This boy says he knows his rights," the cop holding Brandon said.

"Yeah, I hear," Neil said, snickering.

"I guess one thing he don't know is I don't like no smart-assed niggers."

"Guess not."

"Boy, looks like I'm just gonna have to teach you some manners." He jabbed Brandon hard in the stomach with the baton, doubling him over. Brandon started to sink slowly to the ground, the wind nearly knocked out of him.

"Stop it, you bastard!" Julie screamed. The cop standing over Brandon then drew back his baton. But just as he was about to bring it down, a car rounded the curve, framing them in its headlights. The driver stopped to see what was going on. The distraction was just enough for Julie to break free and run to Brandon, where she knelt over him, shielding him from the cop.

"What the hell you people looking at?" the cop shouted at the people in the car. "This is police business. Move on!" The driver obeyed, continuing on.

"Come on, Manny," Neil said, as he took hold of his partner and began trying to lead him back to their squad car. "You made your point with the boy. Let's get out of here."

"Okay. Okay," Manny said, allowing himself to be led away. "But boy," he said, suddenly turning and rushing back over to Brandon and Julie, "you got off easy this time. Next time you might not be so lucky. You can count on that!"

"Come on, Manny," Neil said, restraining Manny. "Leave him alone. Let's go." The cops finally got into their squad car and pulled away.

"I'll have both your badges for this, you goddamn animals!" Julie shouted at them, as she helped Brandon to his feet. "Here, I'll drive. We're reporting this first thing in the morning. Those racist bastards! They're not getting away with this!"

The next morning he and Julie went down to police headquarters and filed a formal complaint against the officers. They were told, however, not to expect any immediate action, because such complaints usually took months to process, sometimes longer. In light of this, he and Julie decided it was best that he avoid visiting her place at night, at least until the matter could be investigated.

Chapter 9

Brandon arrived at work one morning to find a rather peculiar object in his chair. It was a toy gorilla. He picked it up. Who had put it there? There was no note or message attached to it. But the more he studied it, especially the exaggerated lips, the flared nostrils and the blackened face, the more he became convinced as to who had put it there and why. It was Tim. It had to have been. Apparently, this is what he thought of him, that he was a gorilla or a monkey, because he was black. The anger that he had somehow always managed to keep in check now boiled over. He stalked off to confront Tim. He didn't care who was around or even if it ended up costing him his job. All he could think of at that moment was having it out with him. He had taken all he was going to take.

When he got to Tim's cube, however, he wasn't there, only Allan was.

"Where's Tim?" Brandon demanded. Allan looked up from his desk, startled by Brandon's angry demeanor.

"What?"

"I said where's Tim!"

"Ah, I think he went to pick up some printouts in the copy room. Why? What's going on? Is something—" Before Allan could get the rest of his question out, Brandon had taken off for the copy room, the toy gorilla dangling from his hand.

When Brandon burst through the door, he found Tim waiting over by a printer.

"Here!" Brandon said, going over and holding the gorilla up to Tim's face. "I think this belongs to you!"

"What?" Tim said, slapping it away. "What the hell are you talking about?"

"I'm talking about your little sick idea of a joke that you left in my chair! Is this what you think I am, a monkey or something?!" Once again Brandon put the gorilla up to Tim's face. And again, Tim knocked it away. This time it fell to the floor.

"Listen, I told you I don't know what you're talking about," Tim said. "Okay? So why don't you just back off before you get yourself hurt!" The door to the copy room opened. It was Allan.

"Hey, what's going on between you guys?"

Ignoring Allan and standing toe-to-toe with Tim, Brandon countered, "You're lying! You've been riding me ever since I came here and I'm not taking it anymore!" He shoved Tim.

"Okay, goddamnit, you asked for it now!" Tim said, grabbing Brandon around the collar and throwing him up against one of the copiers. Brandon responded with a number of wild punches aimed at Tim's head, connecting a couple of times. Soon they were going at it full tilt, knocking over trash cans and banging up against machines. Stacks of papers, notebook binders and supplies spilled from shelves to the floor. They fought like this for several minutes, doing more wrestling than punching, until the door opened again and Allan and another man rushed over to separate them.

"Alright! Alright! You guys break it up! Break it up! Now!" Jerry, a second-line manager whose office was nearby, said, prying them apart. Brandon and Tim let go of each other and got to their feet. To Brandon's surprise, Tim had a black eye. He never even remembered landing the blow that did it. For his own part, Brandon had a busted lip and a torn shirt pocket.

"Somebody want to tell me just what the hell is going on here?" Jerry demanded, looking from Tim to Brandon. Neither volunteered anything. Jerry then looked to Allan. "You know anything about this, Allan?"

"Me?" Allan said, with raised eyebrows. "No. All I know is that Brandon came by looking for Tim, like he was real pissed about something. So, I followed him here to the copy room." People were now huddled at the door to see what was going on. Jerry turned to the onlookers.

"Okay, show's over folks. You can go about your business." He then focused on Brandon and Tim again. "So, neither of you guys want to tell me what this is about?" Again, Brandon and Tim were both tight-lipped. "Alright, since nobody knows anything, let me just make one thing clear. If you guys wanna fight, wait 'til after work and go duke it out across the street. You got that?" They both nodded that they understood. "Now, before lunch time, I want this room straightened up just like it was before.

And I mean put everything back the way it was—every printout, every piece of paper, every paper clip, ink pen and pencil. And if any of these machines are broken, the repair bill's coming out of both you guys' paychecks. Got that?" They nodded again. "Okay, then. You guys see if you can't get along like civilized human beings. There's no time for these kinds of shenanigans. This is Big Red. And you're professionals. Act like it. There's money to be made today. That's why we're here, gentleman. The only reason." Then he turned and started for the door. "Allan, you help them."

"What? Why should I—" Allan protested, as the door closed shut behind Jerry. The three of them spent the next hour or so straightening up the room. Luckily, there was no damage to any of the machines. Brandon and Tim said nothing to each other the whole time.

■ ■ ■

The next morning, Tim dropped by Brandon's cube. Allan was with him. A slight welt still showed beneath Tim's eye from their fight.

"Hey, look, man," Tim said. "I just stopped by to tell you that I'm willing to forget all about what happened yesterday, if you are. Bob doesn't have to know anything about it, unless Jerry tells him, which I doubt he'll do. Anyway, I know I've been riding you pretty hard, like you said, since you got here. I was wrong about you. You're alright. I guess I was just…," he said, searching for the right words. "Look, what I guess I'm trying to say is I'm sorry for all the grief I've been causing you." Tim then stuck out his hand. After hesitating for a moment, Brandon put his hand out and they shook. "But I want you to know—and this is the honest to God truth—I'm not the one that put that little monkey or whatever it was in your chair."

"He's telling the truth, Brandon," Allan said. "If he had done it, it's almost for certain I'd have known about it."

"Okay," Brandon said. "I accept your apology." He still wasn't sure if he believed Tim or not about the toy gorilla. Up until now, there had been absolutely no question in his mind that Tim had done it. Who, then, could it have been, if it wasn't Tim? He decided to just let it rest. What was much more important was that his feuding with Tim was over. And if Tim was really on the up and up about his change of attitude toward him, then a major hurdle to his qualifying had just been removed.

Later that day, Fran stopped by. "Hello, Brandon."

"Oh, hello, Fran. When did you get back?"

"We got back a couple of days ago."

"So, how was Germany?"

"Just great. We had a wonderful time. The weather was excellent the whole time."

"Glad to hear you had such a good time."

"Thanks. I should have the pictures back in a few days. So, how have you been? I hear there was a little excitement yesterday between you and your buddy Tim. What happened?"

"Oh, it was nothing, really," Brandon said. "I basically confronted him about something and it kind of got a little out of hand. But I think we've squared it away."

"Well, that's good. Maybe he'll quit riding you so much now."

"I think we might have turned that corner," Brandon said. "I'm keeping my fingers crossed."

"Well, if that's what it took, then so be it. Anyway, how'd you like the little furry gift I brought you back from my trip?"

"The little furry gift?"

"Yeah," Fran said. "The little gorilla I left in your chair the evening before. I got one for Sean and Norm, too. But because Sean's away, I didn't leave his. I picked them up at this really neat little gift shop in Cologne. Norm just loved his." Fran noticed the surprised look on Brandon's face. "So, what's up? What, did you think it was from a secret admirer maybe?"

"What? Oh, no," Brandon said, managing a chuckle.

"Well, listen, pal," Fran said. "Gotta run. You know how it is when you're out for awhile. The work piles up in triplicate, it seems, just waiting for you when you walk in the door. See you."

■ ■ ■

At home that evening, Brandon answered a knock at his door to find a little boy holding in front of him something in a paper bag.

"Are you Brandon?" the little boy asked.

"Yeah, I'm Brandon."

"Here," he said, handing him the package. "Mrs. Ramsey asked me to give this to you."

"Mrs. Ramsey?" Brandon said, looking inside to see what it was. It was a cake.

"Yeah, the lady over in the next building with all the flowers in her place."

"Oh, Sarah. *That* Mrs. Ramsey."

"Anyway, she told me to bring it to you," the boy said, and turned to leave.

"Thanks. Tell her I said thanks."

"Oh, I almost forgot," the boy said. "She says there's no hurry returning the plate."

"Okay. Thanks again." Inside the bag with the cake was a card. He opened it.

Dear Brandon,

Sometimes when you've been used to things being a certain way practically all your life, it's hard to change, even when the whole world, it seems, is changing all around you. Even more, you believe that the way things have been are the way they ought to stay, simply because they've been that way for so long. I know I'm not expressing this very well. I guess what I want to ask is that you be patient with me. Hope you enjoy the cake.

P.S. Please stop back by for a visit soon. And bring Julie along, too!

Sarah

Chapter 10

Things began to look up for Brandon when Bob called him to his office one day to compliment him on what a great job he was doing and to tell him that, to his delight, he had disproved his initial apprehensions about him joining the department. Furthermore, Bob added, he could expect to begin receiving much more interesting and challenging assignments and that he would soon be talking to him about his aspirations for getting on the management track. And sure enough, several days later, Tim stopped by to inform him of Bob's decision to allow him to try his hand at a BPP.

"This is for a really important project called the SE/2 that's currently on the drawing board," Tim said. "Personally, I'm a little surprised he'd give you one of this importance so soon. Usually, these go to only experienced analysts. But he obviously thinks you can handle it."

"I hope so," Brandon said.

"You'll do alright," Tim said. "There's a sample BPP on here," Tim said, handing him a diskette, "to give you a model of how a completed one should look. Use it as a template for yours. You took that proposal writing class, right?"

"Yeah."

"Okay, then," Tim said. "If you still have the course materials from that class, there ought to be some tips in it on how to do a BPP. That should be all you need. If you have any questions along the way, just ask me or Sean. Either one of us ought to be able to help you."

"Thanks, Tim."

Brandon could hardly believe it. He was finally getting the chance he had been longing for. He knew from talking with others that, in addition to helping one qualify, how well an analyst did on his first BPP could often make or break him as far as his long-term future. Yes, this could very well be his ticket to the fast track. He was determined not to make Bob regret having given him this chance.

■ ■ ■

To celebrate, he and Julie went out to dinner a few days later at the sumptuous Regency Plaza Hotel.

"I'd like to propose a toast," Julie said, hoisting her wine glass. "To Brandon. May this be the beginning of your first step up the corporate ladder on your way to the top." They clinked glasses.

"Now, *I'd* like to propose a toast," Brandon said, lifting his glass. "To Julie, a beautiful and really special lady who I wouldn't trade for all the money in the world." They toasted.

"Thank you," Julie said, leaning across the table to plant a kiss on Brandon's lips. With their palms touching and fingers interlaced, they gazed dreamily into each other's eyes. Nearby, the doors to a private banquet room swung open and a group of executive types began streaming out.

"Hey, look," Brandon said. "There's Perry Bingham, Executive Vice President of Finance at CSU. And Don Jacobs, Director of Overseas Commerce."

"I thought some of those faces looked familiar," Julie said. "Must have been quite a power meeting."

"Yeah, there're mostly mid- and upper-level managers at CSU," Brandon said.

"And one day, Brandon, you're going to be right there with them," Julie said. They kissed.

■ ■ ■

"How's it going, Brandon?" Peter said, dropping by one day.

"Okay, I guess," Brandon said. "What's up?"

"You know that template Tim gave you to use as a model for your BPP?"

"Yeah. I've got it loaded on my system."

"Well, maybe you should delete it."

"Delete it? Why? Is something wrong with it?"

"It's obsolete," Peter said. "Tim didn't know it when he gave it to you. This one's more current." Peter produced a diskette from his jacket pocket.

"Okay," Brandon said, accepting the diskette from Peter.

"Have you entered any data yet in the one you've got loaded?"

"No, not yet."

"Good. Go ahead and erase it from your system now," Peter said. "There's also a chance it might be infected with a virus that's been going around."

"Okay." Brandon entered the commands to erase the template.

"And while you're at it, give me back the diskette with it on it, too," Peter said. "We need to get it out of circulation."

"Sure." Brandon fished out the diskette from his drawer and gave it to Peter.

"Good," Peter said. "Now, load the template on this diskette on your system and you should have the latest."

"Thanks, Peter."

■ ■ ■

Brandon put in extra long hours on the SE/2 BPP, often coming in early and staying late into the night. Although he had nearly three weeks to finish it, once he'd added up all the work that had to go into it, he quickly found that it really wasn't that much time after all. During the day, he met with his list of contacts to gather the information he needed, while still completing his other assignments. The UM/A project was still taking up a significant amont of his time. In the evenings, he reviewed the information he'd gathered, made his assessments and entered the data into his report.

One night while still at work, Sean happened to stop by. "What's going on, Mr. Future Executive? Pulling an all-nighter?"

"Yeah, just about," Brandon said, checking his watch. It was nearly ten-thirty. He'd been so caught up in his work that he'd completely forgotten about the time. "What are you doing here?"

"I was on my way home from this function over at the Marquette when I saw your car out front," Sean said. "So, I thought I'd come up and see how things were going."

"Well, okay, I guess," Brandon said. "I'm just getting going really, though. Here, check it out," he said, leaning back and motioning for Sean to take a look at his computer. "I'm using this new template that Peter gave me. He said it was more up to date than the one Tim gave me originally."

"Hmmm," Sean said, after taking a minute to scroll through some of the screens. "Brandon, are you sure this is the one Peter gave you?"

"Yeah, why?"

"Well," Sean said, continuing to scroll through the screens, "unless I'm missing something, missing a lot, there are entire cost estimate fields missing. Like here, for instance."

"What?" Brandon said, pitching forward in his chair.

"As a matter of fact, I'm sure of it," Sean said.

"And another thing that's incomplete is the list of contacts for the key areas," Sean said, as he continued tiling through the template. "This is only maybe half the ones you're going to need."

"I wonder what happened?"

"I don't know," Sean said.

"Oh, I know," Brandon said. "Maybe this one got infected with the virus Peter said was going around. Anyway, I'll let Peter know about it tomorrow and maybe he can get me a corrected one."

"Tell you what," Sean said, going over to his desk and unlocking it. "I'm going to give you the BPP I did for the VyBase project last year. I know there's nothing missing in it. Plus, my contact list is much more complete than this one is, too. Sean handed him the diskette. "Make a copy of it to use as your template. It oughta get you pointed in the right direction."

"Thanks, Sean."

"No problem. See you tomorrow."

■ ■ ■

Finally, when everything was finished, Brandon did a dry run of his BPP for Sean. Except for a few minor rough spots here and there, things he could go back and change easily enough, Sean thought he was ready. Thanksgiving was right around the corner, and he and Julie were flying up to Minneapolis to spend the long holiday weekend with her family. His presentation was set for the following Monday.

■ ■ ■

He and Julie returned that Sunday night. When he arrived at his apartment, he found an envelope and a flower taped to his door. He opened the envelope.

Dear Brandon,

By the time you read this letter I will be well on my way to Arizona to live with my brother, Hastings, who I spoke to you about. He's been asking me for some time now to come out and live with him and his family, where he'd arrange for me to have my own nursery, like before. It all happened so terribly fast. It was only this past Friday that Hastings called to tell me that a friend of his would be passing through on his way back out to Arizona and that he had plenty of room in his camper for me, Kitty and most of my things, if I wanted to come along. The plants, of course, would have to be shipped. It's been a dream of mine for some time to get my own nursery again. And so, as much as I hated to leave, I couldn't pass up the opportunity.

Finally, I will miss you, just as I will miss Gill and Lisa. But I will forever hold in my heart fond memories of you and your wonderful smile. I wish the best to you and Julie. Send me an invitation if the two of you ever decide to get married! And if you're ever out this way, be sure and look me up.

Love,

Sarah

He unlocked his door and went inside. After placing the flower in a jar of water, he went out on the balcony and looked over at Sarah's old apartment. At night, there was always a light on inside. For the first time it was strangely dark. He stood there for a moment reflecting, before going back inside.

■ ■ ■

The presentation, which was held in one of the board rooms, started promptly at 9 o'clock the next morning. The entire department was there. Also present, of course, were the representatives from Planning Development, two men and a woman, whom his proposal would have to convince. One of them had flown in from Dallas, another from Phoenix.

"Good morning, everyone," he began. "I'm Brandon Northcross and I'll be presenting my BPP for the SE/2 project. This is my first BPP, so I apologize if I seem a little nervous." He cleared his throat, then proceeded.

The presentation lasted for the better part of an hour. When he finished, each member from Planning Development had a number of questions for him. He answered each of them completely and confidently. When there were no more questions, the Planning Development group convened among themselves briefly in an adjacent room. When they returned, the woman, who was the spokesperson for the group, said, "Brandon, speaking on behalf of my two colleagues, we like what we've heard this morning. Your cost estimates were particularly in-depth. At this point, what we'd like to do is take your proposal back to our respective groups and study it a little closer. But I think I can say with some degree of confidence that, barring any major discoveries, it looks like a go."

When the meeting was over, people came up to offer their congratulations.

"One of the better proposals I've heard, Brandon," one of the men in the Planning Development group said, shaking his hand.

"Thanks."

"Yes, very professional, very polished," the woman said, extending her hand. "I just know you've got a bright future with the company."

"Thank you," Brandon said, beaming.

"Good job, man," Tim said.

"Thanks, Tim." Fran, Norm and Sean then gathered around.

"Well, I think a star is born, guys," Fran said.

"Yeah," Sean said. "Great job, man."

"You're definitely on your way," Norm said.

"Thanks. But I couldn't have done it without you guys' encouragement and support."

As Brandon continued to greet other well-wishers, he looked around for Bob to thank him for having given him the opportunity, but he had already left.

Chapter 11

During the last couple of weeks leading up to Christmas, the Washington area got its first snowfall of the season. The snow came on a Thursday evening, closing schools and giving the kids a long weekend. He and Julie went to the park and built a snowman, outfitting it with an old hat and scarf they found in a nearby trash bin. Afterwards, they allowed themselves to get lured into a good, old-fashioned snowball free-for-all with some college kids. Around the same time, CSU held its annual Christmas party, a lavish, black-tie affair thrown at The Estate, one of the more exclusive country clubs in Northern Virginia. The cheer of Christmas was everywhere.

A few days before the Christmas break, however, that all changed when Brandon returned from a meeting to find Sean packing up his belongings.

"What're you doing, Sean? You moving to another cube?"

"They're forcing me out, Brandon," Sean said, plainly.

"What? Forcing you out? What do you mean?"

"Bob called me in this morning, told me they'd been watching me for sometime now and that I've been taking longer for my lunch breaks than allowed, which, in his words, was the same as falsifying my time cards and—"

"Wait a minute," Brandon said, unable to believe what he was hearing. "Just for supposedly stretching your lunch breaks?"

"Yeah. But that's not all. Get this. He also said I've been seen taking company property out of the building."

"Company property? *What* company property?"

"You won't believe this, but he's talking about the ink pens with the CSU logo on them, along with company stationery," Sean said.

"What?" Brandon said. "Ink pens? And paper? Everybody takes those home."

"Well, not according to Bob. Anyway, as a disciplinary measure, he told me that, basically, he had no choice but to demote me a level."

"Demote you a level?" Brandon said. "You've got to be kidding."

"And take a pay cut along with it."

"What!? A pay cut? What the hell's going on?"

"I can't prove it, but according to the little I've been able to uncover, he's getting back at me for helping you with your BPP," Sean said, trying to keep his voice low.

"For helping me with the BPP? But why would he object to you helping me? That doesn't make any—"

"I don't think you get it, Brandon," Sean said, carefully checking to see if anyone was around. "Bob, and who knows who else, meant for you to fail with that BPP, and fail badly. It was no accident that that database you were given was all screwed up. That wasn't the result of any virus. They were setting you up so they could fire you!"

"Fire me? Bob? But, why would—"

"Bob want to fire you?" Sean said, finishing the question for him.

"Yeah. I don't understand."

"Well, that, I'm afraid, I can't answer," Sean said. "But one thing that's clear is that the SE/2 was a major project. And you nearly single-handedly got it off the ground. People are impressed by what you did. It backfired on Bob. Don't you see?"

"But I still don't understand why Bob would want to fire me."

"Are you sure you don't have a clue as to why? I mean, looking back now, can you think of anything that you might have done or said that could have put you on Bob's bad side?"

"Not as far as I know, I didn't," Brandon said. Then he thought for a moment. "Wait. I do remember something. Julie and I were having dinner downtown at the Regency Plaza as a way to sort of celebrate me getting the SE/2 project. Anyway, a group of CSU managers passed through from one of the private meeting rooms. I guess they'd just had some kind of banquet or something. I think Bob might have been with them. In fact, I'm almost sure of it, now that I think back."

"So, you think Bob saw you and Julie together?"

"He had to have. There's no way he could've missed us. He had to have passed right by our table. Julie and I were sort of holding hands. Anyway, a couple of days later, Peter came by with that other template. But I remember something else. The very next day, when Bob saw me at work, he didn't speak when we passed. At the time, I didn't think much of it. I just thought he was maybe in a bad mood or something. But now…"

"Oh, shit," Sean said.

"You think that was it, that he had a problem with me being out with Julie?"

"It's hard to say for sure," Sean said. "But if Bob saw you out with Julie, it sure as hell didn't make him want to give you a raise the next day, especially if the two of you were holding hands. I remember once at this luncheon, the subject of interracial dating between blacks and whites came up. He said he found it disgusting and that he'd disown his daughter if she was to marry a black man. As a matter of fact, he said he'd almost rather see her with another woman than with a black man. So, it's not something he's crazy about. That much I know."

"Damn! I should've known something was up when Peter came by with that new template," Brandon said, slumping down on top of his desk.

"Hey, don't be so hard on yourself," Sean said. "You didn't know. By the way, did you ever talk to Bob about why you were hired in at entry level?"

"No, I never got around to it."

"Well, that's something else to think about."

"I know," Brandon said. "I should've brought it up way before now. But I'll definitely ask him about it now." Brandon took a moment to think. "So, obviously you've decided not to take the demotion."

"No, I'm just gonna go ahead and resign," Sean said. "I don't have time for this nonsense. I've been thinking about leaving for sometime now, anyway. Me and this friend, we've been thinking about starting up our own consulting business. So, the way I see it, this is as good a time as any to do it."

"Oh, well great, then," Brandon said. "I just hate that it had to come about like this."

"I'll be okay," Sean said. "It's you I'm worried about, Brandon."

"I'll just go in and talk to Bob and lay my cards out on the table and—"

"Brandon, if you want to go in and talk to Bob about this, fine," Sean said. "But he's only gonna snow you. He's not gonna be straight with you about this. Do you understand that? What you need to do—and the quicker the better—is make some contacts upstairs with someone who can help you, someone who's heard about what you did with the SE/2 project, was impressed, and would be interested in helping to further your career here at CSU, act as sort of a mentor to you."

"But Bob's already said he'd introduce me to people, help get me into Sales," Brandon said. "I mean, shouldn't I wait and give Bob a chance to—"

"Brandon, trust me," Sean said. "You don't have time."

"I respect your opinion, Sean," Brandon said. "But my review isn't for another two months. And there's no way Bob can give me a bad review after what I did with the SE/2 project, right? So, what can possibly happen?"

"What can happen?" Sean said. "I don't know. Maybe nothing. It's your call. But if I were you, I'd take with a grain of salt anything Bob told me. Don't trust him. You've got to look out for yourself, Brandon. You can't count on other people to do that for you. And something else. Try thinking beyond CSU."

"What do you mean, try thinking beyond CSU?" Brandon said. "Why?"

"I know you think, like most people do, that this is the greatest company to work for in the world and all and that job security here will always be pretty much a given. I thought that way for a long time, too. But I don't anymore. Look around at what's happening. Those early retirement incentives they've been quietly offering at some of the other divisions are just the beginning."

"Are you saying that you think there're going to be layoffs at CSU?" Brandon said.

"I don't know," Sean said. "But it could happen. It's possible. This company could change almost overnight." Sean paused. "Anyway, I've got to get out of here. If you need to talk, you know where to reach me."

"Thanks, Sean," Brandon said, as they shook hands. "I will."

■ ■ ■

"You want to see me, Brandon?" Bob said, pausing in the act of dialing, the receiver up to his ear.

"Yeah, but I can come back later," Brandon said, standing at the door of Bob's office.

"No, come on in," Bob said, placing the receiver back down. "Pull up a chair." Brandon took a seat. "So, what's on your mind?"

"Ah, well…it's about…" he said, looking down at the floor, unsure of just how to broach the subject.

"It's about Sean, isn't it?"

"Well, yeah," Brandon said, looking up now.

"Damn shame," Bob said. "That's what it was. A damn shame. Here, let me shut the door." Bob got up and closed the door, then came back to his desk. "I hated losing Sean. I really did. It was a tough decision. I know the two of you had become kind of close. But the guy really didn't give me much choice, under the circumstances. He could've stayed if he had wanted to, but he thought it best that he move on. Guess he talked to you about it before he left, huh?"

"Yeah, we talked," Brandon said.

"Guess he thought the punishment was a little harsh for the infractions, huh?" Brandon hesitated for a moment before speaking.

"He said he thought it didn't have anything to do with the reasons you gave him," Brandon said. "He said it was because you didn't like the fact that he had helped me with the BPP."

"What?" Bob said, in astonishment. "It had absolutely nothing to do with you, Brandon. Believe me. I don't know where Sean could have gotten that from. I really don't."

"He said you wanted me to fail with the BPP so you could terminate me."

"Terminate you?" Bob said. "Why that's ridiculous. Why would I want to get rid of you, Brandon? You did an outstanding job with that SE/2 BPP. Without the in-depth research that you put into that proposal and the way you then sold it to Planning Development, SE/2 wouldn't have stood a snowball's chance in hell of making it out of the starting blocks. You continue like you're doing and you're going places in this company. You mark my word. As a matter of fact, I was just on the phone to one of the Sales managers about you. I haven't forgotten my promise. I'm gonna personally see to it that you get the grooming necessary to realize your dreams here at CSU. You can bank on that."

"Something else," Brandon said. "Why, even though I already had my MBA, was I hired in at only entry level? Everyone I've talked to says I should have been brought in at associate."

"Brandon, I'm sure you've heard that. But in spite of what a lot of people think, that's just not how it works. It's not that simple. A lot of factors beside having an MBA go in to the decision to start somebody above entry level. Sure, maybe I could've started you off at associate. But the bottom line is this. You came in, you proved yourself, and in the process you earned my respect and everyone else's in the department. Now, when you get that promotion, no one can question it. You understand what I mean?" The phone rang. "Excuse me." Bob picked up. "Oh, hey, Marv! Listen, could you hold for a second?" He cupped his hand over the receiver. "I've gotta take this call, but like I said, Brandon, I don't know where Sean could've gotten such a cockamamie idea from. You just keep up the good work. Okay?"

"Okay," Brandon said, rising from his chair.

"We'll talk some more later." Bob gave him the OK sign and went back to his call. "Marv, baby, what's cooking out there on the coast?"

As Brandon left Bob's office, he was even more confused than before about what was really going on. Either Sean had been totally wrong about Bob, or Bob was lying through his teeth. He also began to wonder if Bob had really made the bigoted comments about interracial dating that Sean said he'd made. Maybe Sean had simply misunderstood him. Bob never appeared to him to be that bigoted. In any event, he decided to just try and forget about the whole thing. The last thing he needed was to become paranoid, thinking that people were out to get him. And he definitely didn't want to become like Roosevelt and Candace, believing that some kind of conspiracy existed among whites within the company to keep blacks down.

■ ■ ■

Christmas and New Year's came and went with the usual revelry. It wasn't really until the second week of the new year that everyone was back at work and things began to return to normal.

That Monday, Brandon got a call from someone named Fred down in Receiving. A package had arrived for him and he wanted Brandon to come down and pick it up. Brandon went to get it.

Just outside the Receiving dock, two men stood talking at the water cooler.

"Excuse me, but do you know if this is where you pick up packages from Receiving?" Brandon asked the men.

"Yeah, right through there," one of them said.

"Thanks." Brandon pushed through the swinging double doors. Strangely, the dock area was quiet, not a soul in sight. Where was everyone?

"Fred?" Brandon called out. There was no answer. He started along the aisles. "Anyone here?"

"Is that you, Brandon?" It was a woman's voice. Two aisles over, Brandon spotted Layla. She was midway down the aisle perched on a ladder. The lighting in that part of the room was slightly dimmed. What was she doing here?

"Do you know where Fred is?" he said. "I got a call from him saying there was a package down here for me."

"They're all on break," Layla said. "They should be back in a few minutes, I suspect. In the meantime, could you come and help me? There's this box I'm trying to get down. If you could come and be ready to catch it when I slide it off the shelf, I'd appreciate it." Brandon hesitated. Something about the whole situation made him uneasy. Something wasn't right. What was Layla up to? And where was Fred? "Please? It won't take but a second. I can't afford to wait until they get back. I need it now."

"Okay," he said, finally, going to her. "Look, I get can get it, if you want. It might be easier that way."

"No, I can manage, if you'd just be ready to catch it when I pull it off the shelf."

"Okay." She turned toward the shelf and seemed to fumbled with something, but he couldn't see what. Then she reached up and tugged at the box. But because it was slightly over from where she was, she lost her balance.

"Oops!" she said, slipping from the ladder.

"I've got you!" he said, grabbing her around the waist to break her fall. Her momentum knocked them both back against the shelf behind him. All of a sudden, she spun around and began kissing him all over his face. But before he had a chance to react, she backed off and began shrieking at the top of her lungs.

"Take your hands off me! Quit it! Stop it!" In the midst of the chaos, he noticed that her blouse was ripped down the front.

"What the hell are you doing?!" Brandon said. Then he heard the doors swing open and the sound of footsteps rushing in.

"What's going on back there?" It was the two men who'd been standing outside the door. Layla pulled her blouse together and rushed past the men and out the door. The men looked at him, then at each other, like they, too, were just as bewildered as to what was going on, then left.

Back at his desk, Brandon tried to sort out what had just happened. None of it made any sense. But something bad was going to happen. That much he knew. He could feel it. He decided to go get a drink of water, hoping it would help calm him. But just as he was about to get up from his chair, the phone rang. Startled, he looked at the phone as if it were a king cobra, just waiting to spring out and sink its sharp, venomous fangs into him once he reached out for it. He knew it was probably Bob. Maybe it was Security. Or maybe it had already gone through Security and the police were on their way to arrest him. The phone continued to ring. Droplets of sweat dripped from his armpits like water from a leaky bathroom facet. Finally, he reached over and picked up.

"Brandon Northcross."

"Brandon, this is Cheryl," the voice on the other end said. "Bob would like to see you in his office immediately."

"Okay. I'll be right there."

The door to Bob's office was closed when he got there. He knocked and heard Bob say to come in. Inside, Layla was seated in a chair in front of Bob's desk. She was dabbing her eyes with a handkerchief in one hand, while holding together her torn blouse with the other. One of the two men who had rushed into the Receiving area was sitting on the other side of her. Bob motioned for Brandon to take the other seat in front of his desk.

"Well, Brandon, I guess you know what this is all about, huh?" Bob asked, looking at him sternly.

"Yes, but I—" Bob cut him off with his hand.

"I just wanted to know if you knew why we were all here," Bob said. "You'll get your chance to tell your side of it in a minute. But first I want to give Layla a chance to tell her version again of what happened. Layla," Bob said, giving her the floor.

"Well, Bob, like I said, I was getting something down from a shelf down in Receiving, because—"

"You were by yourself?" Bob asked. "Nobody else there but you?"

"That's right."

"Okay, go on."

"Like I was saying, I was in Receiving, up on a ladder getting a package down that I needed, when, suddenly, I felt someone grab me from behind, around the waist kinda. It scared me so bad I nearly slipped from the ladder. When I turned around, it was him."

"Who, Brandon?"

"Yes," she said, drying her eyes again.

"What are you saying, that he sneaked up on you or something?"

"He must have," Layla said. "I never heard him come in."

"Wait a minute!" Brandon said. "That's not true and you know it!"

"Brandon, let Layla finish," Bob said. Brandon took a deep breath and tried to compose himself. "Okay, Layla, go ahead."

"So, I said to him, 'What are you doing? Are you crazy? Take your hands off me!' And he says that he's been watching me for a long time now and…"

"And what?"

"He said—and these were his exact words—'I've been watching you for a long time now and I know you want me just as much as I want you. So, why don't we quit beating around the bush?' Then he pulled me down from the ladder and started running his hands all over me and kissing me. I kept turning my head away so he couldn't kiss me on the mouth and trying to get him to let go of me. That's why my lipstick is smeared all over his face like it is," she said, glancing over at him. Out of reflex, Brandon reached up and touched his face. "But he wouldn't stop. At the same time, he kept pulling at my blouse."

"So, you're saying he was kissing you and trying to, what, tear your blouse off?"

"I guess so," Layla said. "I don't know. All I know is that he kept grabbing at me, putting his hands all inside my blouse, up under my skirt, just all over. And that's when I starting yelling. Dave and this other guy came running in. Oh, it was awful." Layla sniffled a little. Brandon thought he was going to be sick to his stomach right there in the room from all of Layla's lies. But what sickened him even more was that Bob seemed to be falling for them.

"C'mon now, Bob," Brandon protested. "You don't actually believe—"

"Hold on a second, Brandon," Bob said. "I want to hear from Dave, first. Then we'll hear your side. Dave, what did you see when you entered the dock area? Brandon, this is Dave Lorne. Dave works upstairs in Accounting."

"Well, like Layla just said," the man began, "I heard her scream, and so me and John Massey, who I was outside in the hall talking with, we ran inside to see what the devil was going on. That's when I saw Layla, her blouse all torn and all, with this guy back down near the other end of the aisle." Suddenly, something came to Brandon. He looked over at Dave Lorne. That voice. He was the one in the supply room with Terri that day!

"Okay, you guys can leave," Bob said, bringing Brandon's attention back to the more important issue at hand. Layla and Dave rose to leave.

"Wait a second!" Brandon said, half up out of his seat. "Don't I get a chance to defend myself? What is this?! I mean—"

"We don't need them here for that," Bob said, as Layla and Dave left the room, closing the door behind them. "Okay, now what's your side of it, Brandon?" He didn't really know where to begin, as he tried to collect his thoughts.

"This is what happened, Bob," Brandon said. "I got this call from this guy that works down in Receiving named Fred. He said there was a package down there for me and that I should come down and get it now."

"Wait a second," Bob said. "You say it was a guy named Fred?"

"Yeah. He said his name was Fred."

"I've never run into anyone down in Receiving named Fred," Bob said. "You sure he said his name was Fred?"

"Yeah. That's what he said, that his name was Fred."

"Just a second." Bob picked up the phone and dialed an internal number. "Hello, Lane? Bob Tomasino. Look, you got anyone down there in your group named Fred?…No? You sure?…. Okay. Thanks, Lane." Bob hung up. "They say there's nobody down there in Receiving named Fred."

"Nobody down there named Fred?" Brandon said, in disbelief. "Well, whoever called me said his name was Fred. That's all I know."

"Well, anyway, go on with your story," Bob said.

"Well, like I said, I got this call. So, I went down to pick up the package. When I got there, nobody was there, for some strange reason."

"About what time was it when you got down there?"

"What time was it?" Brandon said. "I guess it must've been somewhere around 2:15, 2:20, something like that. Why?"

"The Receiving people usually take their afternoon break between 2:15 and 2:30," Bob explained. "So, I can't understand why someone from down there would've asked you to come down during that time frame. If there's a pickup waiting for someone, they usually like to be there to sign it out. Layla was down there because a package had been stored there for our department. So, it was already signed for."

"Well, all I know is this guy who said his name was Fred asked me to come right down and pick up something that had come in for me," Brandon said.

"Okay. Go on. So, what happened once you got there?"

"Well, like I said, there was no one there. Layla heard me calling for someone to help me, and asked me if I would come help her get a package down from the shelves."

"She asked you to help her get a package down?"

"Well, no, not help her get it down, but just stand by the ladder to catch the package once she slid it off the shelf."

"Okay, then what?"

"Well, I stood by as she reached for the package. But she lost her balance on the ladder and fell back against me. Then all of a sudden she was all over me, kissing me. Then she started screaming, 'Take your hands off me! Stop it!' That's when Dave Lorne and the other guy came running in. It's like she just all of a sudden went berserk for some reason."

"So, that's how it really happened, huh?"

"I know it doesn't seem to add up, Bob," Brandon said. "But I'm telling you the honest-to-God truth. And something else. That's not the first time Layla's tried to come on to me."

"Look, Brandon, I want to help you, but you've got to be straight with me."

"But I *am* being straight with you, Bob," he pleaded. "I am."

"Okay," Bob said, leaning back in his chair. "I have to tell you that, based on what I've seen and heard, you could find yourself in some serious trouble over this whole thing."

"I know how it looks, Bob, but I promise you I didn't do it."

"I want to believe you. I really do. Maybe you just accidentally put your hand in the wrong place and Layla took it the wrong way."

"But I didn't touch her. I swear I didn't!"

"I hear you," Bob said. "Just calm down now. Tell you what I want you to do," Bob said, taking out a form from inside his desk. "I want you to sign this form here on the back." Bob placed it in front of him, his hand casually concealing most of the wording, leaving only the portion for his signature showing. "It's mostly just a lot of legal mumbo jumbo, something to cover my own rear end as your boss. What it says, basically, is that I've counseled you on the matter. It's just a formality for these types of incidents." Brandon signed his name. "Good." Bob took the form and placed it back inside his desk. "Now, I can see you're pretty upset about this whole thing, and I don't blame you. Hell, I guess I'd be crapping in my pants, too, if some woman went to my boss and claimed I had tried to practically rip her clothes off. Maybe you oughta take a few days off, try to relax, get this thing off your mind."

"Take a few days off?" Brandon said, finding the suggestion a little odd.

"Yeah, you won't be much good around here worrying over this thing," Bob said. "Plus, hopefully, it'll give Layla some time to get over it. Maybe it's just her time of the month. Who knows? Now, today's Monday." Bob checked his desk calendar. "Why don't you take off the next, say, two to three days, get yourself together, then come back all rested up on Friday. We'll call it management-directed time off. Besides, you've certainly earned it with all the overtime you put in on the SE/2 project. In the meantime, I'll see what I can do to try and resolve this whole situation," Bob said, rising from his chair. Brandon rose, too. "You're a good worker, Brandon. And as I've said before, you've got a promising future here at CSU. I'd hate to see something like this cast a dark cloud over it."

"Thanks, Bob."

"And by the way, I wouldn't mention any of this to anyone," Bob said. "It's best if it be kept just between the parties involved."

"Sure," Brandon said. "I understand."

Chapter 12

Friday morning, Brandon entered the CSU lobby and fell in line with other employees waiting to pass through the badge reader door leading to the offices. When his turn came, he ran his badge through the reader like he always did. This time, however, nothing happened. The reader light failed to come on, as did the door buzzer. He tried again and again. Still nothing happened. Aware of people waiting in line behind him, he stepped aside to let them go. Then he tried his badge again. Once again, the same results.

"Is there a problem with your badge, sir?" the security guard asked.

"I can't seem to get it to work," Brandon said. "I must have accidentally deactivated the magnetic strip somehow."

"Let me try it," the man said, coming around from behind his booth. He tried the badge several times, but with the same results. Back behind his booth, the man picked up a list and began browsing it.

"What's wrong?" Brandon asked, curious as to what the list was he was looking over. The man said nothing, as he continued his search. When he found what he'd been looking for, he looked up at Brandon.

"Sir, I'm afraid I'm going to have to confiscate this badge."

"What? Confiscate my badge? *Why?"*

"Just a minute, please," the man said, as he searched a drawer. What was going on? The man handed Brandon a sealed envelope addressed to him. "This should explain it."

"Explain what?" Brandon laid his briefcase on the counter and opened the letter. As he read it, a slow, sinking feeling began to come over him.

January 14, 1989

Prentiss Halifax
Director of Human Resources
Computer Systems Unlimited
446 Industrial Park Drive
Pentagon City, VA 20245

Dear Brandon Northcross:

This letter is to inform you that, due to your admission of guilt to the charge of sexual assault of Layla Moran on Monday, January 11, 1989 and the waiving of your rights to contest this charge in a formal hearing, and your subsequent unauthorized absences from work, January 12 through January 13, you are hereby terminated from further employment with CSU, effective immediately.

Sincerely,

Prentiss Halifax, Director
Human Resources

He felt as if a trap door had suddenly been opened beneath him and he was falling fast. There must be some mistake, he kept telling himself, as he continued to stare at the letter.

"You can use the phone over by the wall to call Personnel if you want to speak with someone," the security guard suggested. "Here's the number." The man wrote the number on a piece of paper and handed it to him. Brandon went over to the phone and dialed Personnel. After several rings, someone answered.

"Good morning. Personnel."

"Yes, my name's Brandon Northcross and I just had my badge confiscated. I'm out front in the lobby. The security guard just gave me a letter addressed to me telling me I've been terminated. I've been off work for the last several days, and I came back today and, well, I just don't understand what's going on."

"Well, I'm really not supposed to discuss personnel issues over the phone. What you can do is set up an appointment to come in to see one of the Personnel representatives and—"

"Yes, I understand that, but is there any way I could speak with somebody now? I mean, this doesn't make any sense. Like I said, I come back to work after taking a few days off, and I find that my badge doesn't work. The security guard checks this list and finds my name on it, then gives me this letter, which says I've been terminated, claiming it's because I took off these days without permission. First of all, that doesn't make any sense, because those days were approved by my manager. Then it says it's also because of this incident that I was involved in, where—"

"Tell you what, I'm really not supposed to do this, but you sound pretty upset," the woman said. "So, see if you can calm yourself and just tell me what it says in the letter you received." He read the letter to the woman.

"But, the thing is," he said, "I never signed any form waiving my rights to a hearing or admitting my guilt, like it says here. And secondly, I took those days off with my manager's permission. In fact, he's the one that suggested that I take them."

"Hold on a minute," the woman said. "Let me go get your personnel folder. That's Brandon Northcross, right?"

"Yes."

"And what's your employee number?"

"It's 642758."

"Okay. I'll be right back." She came back on the line a little while later. "Hello?"

"Yes, I'm here," he said.

"Well, young man, I see a waiver here that's signed by you, unless someone forged your signature."

"What? I never signed any waiver."

"Are you positive?"

"Well, at least not to my knowledge, I didn't."

"What do you mean?"

"Well, I signed a form, but my manager told me it was just something that said he'd counseled me on the incident. That's all."

"Did you read the form before you signed it?"

"Well, no, I didn't. He told me—"

"What you were signing, more than likely, was this waiver, which basically says that you admit guilt to the charge and that you agree to forfeit your rights to any hearing on the matter. Furthermore, while there is a form for managers to complete and sign to document that they've counseled an employee on a disciplinary infraction, there's no place on it for the employee's signature."

"What?"

"Yes, that's right," she said. "Secondly, you say your manager initiated the idea for you to take those days off?"

"Yes, that's right."

"Did he have you submit an RTO for it?"

"An RTO? What's that?"

"An RTO is a Request for Time Off form."

"No, he never told me anything about any RTO."

"Well," the woman said, sighing, "I hate to say it, but it sounds to me like there's very little you can do to be reinstated at this point. I really don't know what else to tell you." The reality of what had happened was just beginning to take form in Brandon's mind, like a gigantic puzzle that now had just enough of the pieces in place to start to form an image. "Hello? Are you still there?" The woman's voice seemed as if it was coming from miles away now.

"Yes."

"I'm sorry," she said.

"Thank you," he heard himself say.

Even after the woman had hung up, he continued to stand there holding the receiver to his ear. It was as if he were expecting the woman to come back on the line and tell him it had all been a big joke or a terrible mistake, that he really hadn't been fired after all. The recorded message of the operator stirred him from his mental paralysis. He looked at the receiver in his hand, then slowly placed it back in the cradle, silencing the squawking of the operator's voice. The next thing he knew, he was heading through the revolving doors on his way outside. He could faintly hear the security guard calling to him.

"Sir? Sir? Your letter. You dropped your letter. Sir, are you going to be alright?"

A cold, penetrating numbness came over him as he went out into the chilly, January morning and headed down the familiar walkway leading to the street. It was a numbness that dulled his body as well as his mind.

Minutes later, he found himself at the subway station. He descended the steps to the tracks and waited for the next train. He didn't care which train it was or where it was going, for he was going nowhere now and he had all the time in the world to get there. When the next train pulled into the station, he boarded and fell heavily into a seat by the window. Around him were men and women in business attire like he was. But he felt as if his suit and tie were now just part of a masquerade, that he no longer had any right to pretend to be one of them.

As the train pulled out of the station, part of him began struggling up from the wreckage to begin the painful task of reassembling the pieces of his life that lay before him. He picked up the first piece. It had been Bob who had done him in, with the help of Dave Lorne and Layla. Sean had tried to warn him that Bob was out to get him, but he hadn't wanted to believe it. Yes, Bob had been no better than the racist cops who had harassed him and Julie or the big man on the train that morning. It hadn't mattered to Bob that he had proven himself to be competent, honest and hardworking. On the contrary, all that had mattered was that he was black—which was all the big man on the train that morning had known—and that he had supposedly been after the white man's prized possession, his white women. What Goochi had said came back now to haunt him. *"Mr. Charlie, he might give you a good job, might even let you move next door to him. But he catch you messin' with them blondes, them brunettes, and them redheads, he'll cut you down!"* Perhaps the most ironic thing about it all was that he had never really wanted the white man's women. But had it not been the white women thing, it would have been something else. Maybe it would have been that he had an attitude or that he was too aggressive or that he was threatening. Yes, they would have found one reason or another to get rid of him. He was sure of it. And it wasn't just Bob, either. It was other whites, too, like Susan Burgett and Turner Adair.

Brandon thought now of the incident on the train and the one with the cops. At least they had been up front enough to come out and say how they felt toward him. Though each of them—Bob, Turner Adair, Susan Burgett, Layla, Dave Lorne, the bigoted cop, the man on the train—occupied very different stations in life, they all agreed on one thing, that he was an inferior, something less than they were. Yes, as dissimilar as they might be in their attitudes about almost anything else, they were in perfect agreement that, as far as they were concerned, he was a nigger and that was all he would ever be.

As he looked back over everything that had happened, to understand how it'd come to this, he found himself going further and further back, even to his childhood. At no time could he remember his parents imparting any sense of blackness to him—especially, what it meant to be a black man. Were not his parents, then, to blame, at least partly? Yes, he despised his parents and everyone else who had ever fed him the lie that he would be accepted by whites if only he measured up. Mr. Ostowski had tried to alert him to what he could expect. But he'd been too brainwashed with all the garbage he'd been fed his whole life, about how race was unimportant, to see it. If he did encounter racism, his parents had told him, once he had proved himself, white people would then accept him willingly. Well, he had proven himself, time and again. He had conformed in ways he probably wasn't even aware of, and still he hadn't been accepted. In the final analysis, the only person who'd been colorblind was him, blind to the fact that color—his color—made all the difference in the world.

Things that had happened to him over the last few months, things he had written off and tried his best to rationalize away, suddenly started to all add up, to make sense, like tumblers of a lock falling neatly into place. There were the times he'd been ignored by white sales clerks, or the times he'd been passed up by taxi drivers, or the times he had found out about parties and other get-togethers that white co-workers had thrown and not bothered to invite him to. And there were the instances when white women had cringed at the very sight of him whenever they had encountered him alone on an elevator or a stairway or had gripped their purses tighter. And why else, but race, could explain why most of his classmates back at school had gotten job offers, but not him? These and other countless incidents, some perhaps trivial in themselves, yet significant when all placed together, came rushing back to him now as eager witnesses. It was all coming together now. White racism, which before had been to him largely something that existed in the paranoid mind's of other blacks, now encircled him like a deep, impassable moat.

After riding the train into the afternoon hours, Brandon got off downtown. Climbing the stairs to the street, he fell in with the lunch-hour throng that was pouring out onto the sidewalk from the big department stores and office buildings. The temperature had risen slightly since the morning, but the sky was still the same pale, listless gray. The sidewalk was like a concrete treadmill moving beneath him, the scenery merely changing, giving the illusion of progress. Yes, life moved all around him. He could see it and feel it, but he was no longer a part of it. He felt that those whites around him, even those that came in contact with his body, didn't really see or feel him. Yes, they saw him as a face with two arms and two legs, but they didn't see him, his essence. To them, he may as well have been invisible.

Blocks and blocks passed as he continued on his treadmill. Eventually, he became aware, not of the sensation of fatigue, but of the knowledge that he ought to feel fatigue, after having walked for so long. He saw a movie theater up ahead and decided to go inside. It was at least somewhere that he could sit for awhile. The theater was a small, run-down affair, the kind that stayed open around the clock, featuring cheaply made foreign skin flicks. A fat man with a cigar stub embedded in the corner of his mouth and tired bloodshot eyes sat inside the ticket booth reading a newspaper. The man looked up over the top of the paper at him curiously, as if wondering why anyone would want to pay to see what was showing inside. Brandon bought a ticket and went in. The movie was already in progress. Only a few other patrons were in the theater. He took a seat near the back. The sound system was loud and blaring, and at times the sound slurred, as the tape dragged in the projector. The movie was in French with English subtitles.

His taut body began to relax as he watched the actors moving about on the screen. Like himself, he thought, they weren't really people, only flat, two-dimensional images being projected out into the air, having little or no free will of their own. And just like him, they had probably had little say about the parts they had played. In his case, the script had called for a court jester and he had been cast, unwittingly, for the role. All that had been missing was his own complicity in it. But perhaps the best clowns are those who don't know they are clowns. Yes, he had played the fool all too well.

As he became more and more relaxed, he began to drift off to sleep. Gradually, the images on the screen faded to mere flickering patterns of dull light and the voices to nothing more than white noise. Suddenly, he was back outside again, trudging through the streets. A big white church was just ahead. He went inside. A wedding was taking place. Everyone was white, except those up in the balcony. That was where all the black people were. Goochi, Simms, Baxter, the Reverend and all the others from the barbershop were there, as well as Ruben Harris, Rachel Toney, the black people he'd met at CSU and the blues singer from Georgetown. But instead of leading him up to the balcony, the ushers escorted him down to the altar to be the bridegroom. Perhaps the strangest part about the whole thing, however, was that all the bridesmaids looked like Layla and all the groomsmen looked like Bob. Because of the veil the bride was wearing, he couldn't see her face. But he could see that she had long, flowing blonde hair. The minister then told him he could now kiss the bride. They turned to each other, Brandon and his bride. Slowly, he lifted the veil. But the face underneath made him recoil in horror. The woman's face was old, sunken and wrinkled and covered with great big warts and moles, just like a witch. Her teeth were all rotted and saliva drooled from the corners of her mouth.

"But I thought this was what you wanted, boy, a white woman?" the preacher said. Turning to the preacher, Brandon saw that it was the big man he had encountered on the train that morning. The man was grinning at him. And to either side of him were the two white girls he'd met that morning, both dressed in the same attire they were wearing then. The blonde girl even had her school books in her arms. "You didn't think we were gonna let you have one of these pretty ones, now did you?" the man taunted him. Brandon became aware of laughter throughout the church. He turned to see that the laughter was directed at him. Up in the balcony, however, the black people were standing with their heads bowed in shame. He then remembered what Goochi had said. *"Ain't nothin' worst than a black man with a po', ugly white woman on his arm."*

A gurgling noise started up behind Brandon. He turned around. Greenish-yellow vomit had begun to spew from the mouth of the witch. At the same time, her face began to rot and decay right before his eyes. A fetid stench came off her, as worms crawled out of her nostrils, her ears and her eye sockets. The witch then reached out with one of her withered hands and grabbed hold of his. Her hand was cold and clammy, like death.

"No! No!" he screamed, as he struggled to break free.

"Don't you want to kiss me?" she said, trying to pull him closer.

"Let me go! Let me go!"

The next thing he knew, he was back outside again, running. The white people from the church were chasing him through a wooded area, with the ugly witch out in front. Ahead was a train trestle suspended high over a body of water. As he raced across the trestle, he took a quick glance back over his shoulder. A big white train was now bearing down on him. The white people from the church were hanging from the sides of it, still laughing. To keep the train from running him down, he had to reach the other side. He ran and ran, somehow barely keeping ahead of it. But it seemed that the further he ran, the further the other side moved away from him. Then, suddenly, he tripped and fell. When he tried to get up, he found that he couldn't. It was as if all the strength had drained from his body. Then someone appeared beside him. It was Nelson Ostowski.

"Come on, now," Ostowski said, nudging him. "You'd better get up before they get you."

"I'm trying!" Brandon cried, unable to get his body to respond. "But I can't! Help me! Please, don't let 'em get me!"

"I tried to warn you," Ostowski said, laughing at Brandon, too. "Rachel tried to warn you. Goochi tried to warn you. Roosevelt and Candace tried to warn you. Even Sean tried to warn you. But you wouldn't listen." Gripped with terror, Brandon watched as the train bore down on him, the laughter from the people growing louder and louder.

Then the train turned into a gigantic head. It was the ugly witches' head, and it was entirely consumed now by hundreds of big, slimy, hideous-looking two- and three-headed snakes. "Come on, now. You'd better get up," Ostowski kept saying, poking him in the shoulder. Just as the monstrous head was about to get him, Brandon let out a long, hard scream.

"Noooooo!"

Then he woke up. The man from the ticket booth was standing over him, nudging him in the shoulder. "Hey, mack. Hey, wake up." Startled, Brandon leapt to his feet, unsure at that moment just how much had been fantasy and how much reality. The laughter he'd been hearing was coming from the actors on the screen. The lights in the theater were turned up and the other patrons were all looking at him, as was a scrawny black man with a broom standing by the door. "Hey, everything's cool, man," the fat man said, backing away from Brandon as he eyed him cautiously. Brandon looked around at the movie still being projected on the screen, and at the other patrons, trying to collect himself, before brushing the man aside and racing for the exit.

Back outside, the grotesque images in his nightmare continued to plague him. White people couldn't be satisfied just to tyrannize him during his every waking moment. They also had to haunt him in his dreams as well. Damn them! Damn them all! He needed a drink. He noticed a bar across the street.

Except for the bartender and a man nursing a beer, the place was empty. Brandon grabbed a bar stool and ordered a shot of whiskey. He downed it in one gulp, the whiskey going down like dark, liquid fire, warming his insides. He ordered another and another. After awhile, the alcohol began to dull his pain. But at the same time, like kerosene poured on a flame, it fed his anger until it grew into an uncontrollable rage that kept growing more and more intense by the moment, feeding on itself.

He looked at his reflection in the mirror behind the bar. For the first time he was seeing himself as whites had always seen him—not as a man, but as a black man. This was more than just a knowledge of his racial heritage. Rather, it was a knowledge of the inferior status his race relegated him to in the minds of whites. To them he was not a person, at least not like they perceived themselves to be. Rather, it was a humanness that was on a scale below their own humanness, stranded on the ladder of evolution somewhere between a man and a monkey. Yes, he was at last seeing what they saw when they looked at him. He was a black. At least that's what was said in polite conversation. In not-so-polite conversation, he was a nigger, something that no white person, no matter how low he fell in society, no matter how poor or destitute, or how ignorant and unlearned, could ever descend to. For to be a nigger was to be something dirty, tarnished, inferior. And no matter how much education he might attain, or how well-cultured he might be, or even how successful he might one day become, he'd always be less than the least white person in the eyes of most whites. He wanted at that moment to hurl the empty shot glass he was holding and shatter the mirror for forcing upon him this painful realization that he couldn't escape. But it would be useless, for some other mirror would quickly be erected in front of him to remind him that he was a nigger.

Brandon looked at the shot glass in his hand and wished at that moment that it was a voodoo doll, so that whatever he did to the glass would happen to white people. If it was, then he'd squeeze it with all his might, squeeze it the same way they had squeezed the life out of him, until it splintered into little pieces. After staring at the glass for awhile, he sat it down on the counter, paid his tab and left.

Traffic had picked up, as people were getting off from work now. The sun, which had pushed the temperature up earlier, was now fading from the sky, allowing the thermometer to fall. The alcohol, however, insulated him from the cold. He had to walk or he would explode from the anger churning inside of him. Moving in a deliberate fashion, he pushed forward on the crowded sidewalk. He actually wanted some white person, any white person, to contest his right to the space he was carving out for himself. They had taken everything else, but at least he wasn't about to let them tell him where he could walk. He had never hated anything or anybody as much as he hated white people at that moment. While he conceded that some whites like Gill, Fran and Sean were not evil like those who had hurt him, he decided that it would just be a matter of time before they, too, betrayed him.

As he continued on, he looked hard into the passing white faces, trying to see if he could read in them the derision he knew they felt toward him. They were such good actors, he thought, when he couldn't see it. But he knew they were silently mocking him. Yes, he could hear them. "Hey, did you see that nigger in the suit with the briefcase? Ha! Ha! What a joke!" He had forgotten about the briefcase he was still carrying around. He looked at it. Suddenly, it became a symbol of white people's mockery. He had to get rid of it, somewhere that no one would ever find it and be able to retrieve it and bring it back to mock him with again. But where? A trash bin wouldn't do. Then he saw it. It was a bridge over a creek up ahead. He raced for the bridge. Standing in the middle of it, he flung the briefcase out over the murky water as far as he could. He watched as it sailed through the air, then hit the water with a plunking sound and disappeared under the surface. *Good,* he thought.

When he turned around, a well-dressed white woman was looking at him. He glared at her and she quickly moved along. A white policeman was up ahead in the direction the woman was going. Would she tell him what she'd seen, that he had tossed something into the creek? The cop might think he had been getting rid of something he'd stolen and come question him about it. That's what whites thought about black men, that they were all thieves. But let her report it, he decided. He didn't care. The cop could come and question him all he wanted. He'd get nothing out of him. Brandon turned and continued across the bridge.

A low-hanging billboard on the side of a building had a picture of a white, blonde-haired woman on it who reminded him of Layla. A revulsion like that of vomit heaved up from his insides. "White *bitch!"* he said, before spewing a glob of spit into the woman's face.

As he was crossing to the other side of the street, oblivious to the traffic, an oncoming car screeched to a halt to avoid hitting him. The driver rolled down his window and stuck his head out.

"Hey, buddy, what, you think you got goddamn bumpers for knee caps or something?!"

"Yeah, that's right!" Brandon shot back at the man as he planted himself directly in front of the car. "You wanna make something out of it, you white bastard?" Motorists behind the man leaned on their horns. After holding up traffic just long enough until he felt he'd made his point, Brandon moved aside, allowing the man to pass.

"Crazy son-of-a-bitch!" the man yelled, as he drove on. Others also shot Brandon angry looks as they went by. He glared back at them, before turning and going his way. He had reached the point now where the rage inside him had built so high that he was like a smoldering volcano just waiting to blow.

A dingy little tavern called *Dudgy's Bar and Grill* advertised half-priced drink specials during happy hour. Brandon ducked inside. The bouncer, a big, hulking man in a turtleneck, his hair pulled back into a ponytail, filled the doorway. The man looked at Brandon curiously for a moment, then waved him on in.

The blue-collar clientele crowded along the horseshoe-shaped bar and at tables. He was the only black person there. Some people turned to look at him as if he was lost and had stumbled into the bar by accident. Seemingly satisfied that he knew where he was, they went back to their conversations and their drinks. It didn't bother him that he was the only black person there. As a matter of fact, he dared anyone to challenge his right to be there. Never before had he felt the need to make such a statement, but now he did. Over in the corner was a pool table where two men were playing a game of nine ball. Others stood around watching. Brandon took a seat at a vacant table.

While waiting for the waitress to come over, he turned his attention to the dance floor. A woman in a cowgirl outfit was out on the floor dancing by herself. He wondered what she'd say if he asked to dance with her, not that he was really interested in dancing with her. If she said something racist, he'd give her a piece of his mind. He got up and walked over to her.

"Excuse me, but mind if I dance with you?" The woman continued to dance, looking straight ahead, as if she hadn't heard him. He tried again, this time louder. "I said, do you mind if I dance with you?" This time she abruptly turned her back to him. He hadn't counted on her ignoring him completely. This incensed him even more than anything she could have said to him. Brandon was vaguely aware of the attention he was drawing, but he didn't care. Who did these people think they were, that they could deny his very existence like that? He turned to two women sitting at a table nearby. "Excuse me, but would you care to dance?" One of the women smiled and shook her head no. The other woman also declined. He went over to a woman standing alone at the bar, her back to him.

"Would you like to dance?"

"Why, sure," she said, before looking around. But when she did, her smile quickly changed to a frown and she turned back to the bar without saying a word.

"What's wrong? You think you're too good to dance with a black man? Just because you're white doesn't make you better than me."

"Yeah, that's right," a man said, stepping between Brandon and the woman. "She don't care to dance with no nigger!" Except for the blaring music from the jukebox, the place quieted to a hush. "And that goes the same for the rest of these women here. So, why don't you just get the hell on out of here right now, boy!" A woman's startled gasp made Brandon instinctively turn to see what was going on. The pool cue was but a blur out of the corner of his eye before it slammed hard into the side of his skull. *Whack!* His legs began to give way beneath him and he started to go down, but almost as if in slow motion. At the same time, the room started to tilt, one way, then the other, then go into a spin. There was a loud ringing in his ears, like someone was clanging a giant bell just above his head. And then everything went blank.

The next thing he knew, he was being helped up off the floor into a chair. His head was throbbing.

"He seems to be comin' 'round now, looks like," he heard a woman say.

"Hey, you alright, man?" a man asked. His head was beginning to clear now, and the people around him began to come into focus. Brandon looked up at the man who had spoken. It was the bouncer. He was standing over him, his hand resting on his shoulder. One of the waitresses was applying a cold compress to his head. A sudden wave of panic overtook him. Springing up from the chair, he pushed their hands away.

"Leave me alone! Get the hell away from me!" Brandon backed away, then turned and fled from the bar.

He ran for several blocks before slowing. It was sleeting heavily now, and it was a cold, icy sleet. He touched his hand to his temple. There was a slight swelling, that was all. But he was still a little lightheaded from the blow as well as from all the liquor he had consumed earlier. He decided to go somewhere and sit for awhile. A small shopping mall was up ahead. Inside, he found a seat on one of the benches.

As he sat watching the people go by, he tried to deepen his hatred of whites. He glared at them. Yes, they were guilty, every last one of them, he decided. Devils, that's what they were, nothing but white devils. He tried to think of derogatory names he could call them. But of the few he could come up with, they all paled in comparison to that dreadful word they reserved for blacks. What word was there that even approximated the ugliness of *nigger?* Yes, they even took care that blacks wouldn't be able to have names to call them. He had never thought about it, but it was true. Nonetheless, he would hate them just the same.

He looked around to find a little white girl staring at him. She reminded him of Lisa. He looked away, hoping she would leave, but she didn't. He looked back at her, trying to muster the most hateful glare that he could. But instead of leaving to join her mother, who was just a few feet away browsing the window of a dress shop, the little girl bravely drew closer. Then she stuck out her hand. In it was a red lollipop wrapped in cellophane, a smile across the front of it. It was then that the tears began to slowly trickle down his face. He reached out and took the lollipop. He felt more ashamed of himself at that moment than he could ever remember having felt. But he was not ashamed for having wanted to hate those whites who were racist, but ashamed at having wanted to hate all whites. The little girl's mother came over. He kept his head down so she wouldn't see his face.

"Well, I see you've made a new friend, have you?" the woman said. "But, come along now." She reached down and took the little girl's hand. "We've got to be going. Say goodbye to your new friend."

"Bye," the little girl said, brightly. Brandon looked up at the little girl and gave her a smile.

If he couldn't hate whites, did that mean he had to love them? Was there not a middle ground, some neutral point? These were questions he'd have to sort out later.

Brandon got up and began to wander around the mall. He had been forced to give up the one last thing he could call his own, his hatred. Now that that was gone, his emptiness returned. Listlessly, he meandered along, unaware of the passing of time. Nothing meant anything to him anymore. He came upon a food court, where he bought a soda. He then took a seat at one of the tables. Sipping his drink, he tried not to think of anything at all. Instead, he just contented himself to watch the people as they hurried here and there and to listen to the soothing elevator music washing down over the mall. Everything seemed to slow. He nodded off.

He was stirred from his sleep by the announcement over the PA system.

"Attention shoppers, the mall will be closing in fifteen minutes," the voice said. "Please join us again when we reopen tomorrow morning at 9:30 am." He looked at his watch. 9:45. It was time he was getting home.

Chapter 13

The sleet had stopped and it didn't seem to have gotten any colder. Up ahead, a long stretch limousine pulled up to the canopied entrance of a nightclub. A bright, purplish neon sign across the front of the building advertised the name of the establishment, *Lush Life*. As Brandon drew nearer to the club, he could hear the music escape from inside each time the door swung open. It was jazz, hot jazz. Peering in through one of the big plate glass windows, he noticed that it was the same band that had performed down at the Esplanade the night he was there with Julie, but without the singer.

"Coming in, sir?" the doorman said, holding open the door.

"Yeah, I think I will."

The club was awash in soft teal lighting. Crossing patterns of light from spotlights placed at different angles high along the wall created the illusion of depth up on stage. A curtain of hazy smoke shimmered in the cones of light cutting down through the air. It was an upscale crowd and looked to be about two-thirds black, the rest white, with a sprinkling of Asians and Hispanics.

Brandon claimed a seat at the bar next to a man who was bobbing his head in time to the music. The band was thrilling the crowd with a fast, straight-ahead number. Featured on the tune were the two horn players, the saxophonist and the trumpeter, playing in unison. The saxophonist laid out and let the trumpeter have it to himself. The trumpeter, wearing a little black pork-pie hat, cut loose like a sprinter out of the starting blocks, exploding into a series of spectacular, angular runs, every note clear and distinct. He worked the melody, playing on top of it, underneath it, and then, it seemed, inside it, chiseling away at it like a diamond cutter chiseling away at a diamond to bring out just the right facets. The air quickly became crowded with the sheer volume and weight of the notes that were issuing from the luminous silver horn. Even when he rocketed several octaves up into the stratosphere, he kept up the same torrid pace.

When the trumpet player had said all he wanted to say, the saxophone player rejoined him, with them both restating the melody. The crowd burst into applause for the trumpeter. When they had played the melody through one last time, they ended with a little vamp. The applause rang out again. The saxophone player straightened his gooseneck mike.

"Mr. Wallace Redmond on trumpet. Mr. Wallace Redmond." There were more applause for the trumpeter, who doffed his hat to the audience. When the applause finally subsided, the saxophonist continued. "Ladies and gentlemen, I've just been informed that we have with us in the audience tonight a very special guest, someone widely respected throughout the jazz world. I'm talking about Washington's first lady of jazz, Ms. Shirley Horn. Maybe if we show her how much we love her, she'll come up and do a number for us." The entire club joined in applause with the band as the spotlight focused in on a woman sitting with several other people near the front by the stage. She signaled to the sax player that she didn't want to go up on stage.

"You can see they're not gonna take no for an answer, Shirley," the sax player said. The cheers then grew even louder. Finally, the woman gave in, rose from her table, and started up the steps to the stage. She was an elegant, stately looking black woman, who appeared to be somewhere in her mid to late sixties. The years, however, had been quite kind to her, as she possessed both a unique physical and inner beauty that radiated out from her. She came over to the mike, whereupon she received a kiss on the cheek from the sax player.

"Thank you," she said. "You are all so kind. I hadn't planned on performing this evening, but I hope you'll like the song I'm going to do. It's for a very dear friend who's recently fallen ill, someone who most of you know and who I affectionately call Dewey." Sighs went up from the crowd along with some murmured talk at the news she had just shared. The woman then turned and whispered something to the sax player, who in turn relayed it to the rest of the band. She went over to the piano, sat down, and with the slightest nod of her head brought in the rhythm section with her on the down beat. After playing a brief intro for herself, she began to sing.

There's a somebody I'm longing to see
I hope that he turns out to be
Someone to watch over me

Her voice was like flowing velvet, the enunciation precise and impeccable. As she sang, she caressed each word, shaping and molding it, then finally, after holding it in until what seemed like the last instance, releasing it into the air. Her voice was clear, but at the same time had a sensuously husky quality to it, especially in the lower register. And though often not much louder than a whisper, her voice seemed to carry with it its own volume, an emotional volume.

He may not be the man some girls think of as handsome
But to my heart he'll carry the key

The saxophonist, having traded his tenor for a smaller horn that looked like a brass-plated clarinet, weaved in tasteful counter melodies, but was careful not to get in the way of the singer. The horn had the poignant sound of a cross between a saxophone and an oboe.

Won't you tell him please to put on some speed
Follow my lead
Oh how I need
Someone to watch over me

The trumpet player then stepped to the mike, the spotlight now trained on him. A mute was affixed to the bell of the horn. He lifted the mute to the mike and began to blow, softly. The whole character of the instrument had changed. Instead of the big, bright sound that had come through on the previous song, it was now a brooding, almost mournful sound.

As the trumpeter sang out through the muted horn, it sounded like the distant pleading of someone crying to be saved from something bigger than they were. The pain that came through the horn was so profound that it made Brandon want to turn away, to get up and run from the club, for it matched his own pain. It was as if it was speaking to him personally, summoning up and giving life to all the sadness and bitter disappointment that now resided in him. The sound itself was difficult to characterize, for it was at once warm, yet cold; relaxed, yet tense; controlled, yet free.

"Damn! He sound just *like* Miles!" the man seated next to Brandon exclaimed in a low, excited voice to no one in particular.

"Who's Miles?" Brandon asked. But he got no response, as the man seemed too caught up in the music to be aware of anything or anyone else around him.

When the song was over and the singer had returned to her table, the saxophone player announced, "Ladies and gentleman, that's gonna do it for us tonight. We want to thank you all for coming out tonight and being with us on this very special day, the birthday of Dr. Martin Luther King, Jr., one of the greatest men who ever lived." He waited for the applause to subside, before continuing. "We want to give special thanks to Ms. Shirley Horn for being so gracious as to come up and do a number for us. So, I guess that's it. Peace, everybody!" He stepped back and joined in with the rest of the band on their little number to close out the set. When they finished, a white guy in a lavender dinner jacket rushed out to the mike.

"Let's hear it for Solar Eclipse and Ms. Shirley Horn!" he shouted, leading the audience in a big round of applause. "But don't go away now. The Harry Treybeck Quintet will be up next after a brief intermission." Brandon had never been so moved by a sound in his life. He had to find out who this Miles fellow was.

In the hallway leading to the dressing rooms, three attractive young women waited, fiddling with their hair and their makeup. Probably girlfriends of the band members, he thought, as he continued back to the dressing rooms. Standing in the doorway was the man in the lavender dinner jacket. He was talking to someone inside.

"Man, you guys were great tonight! Just keep packing 'em in. And Wallace, man, don't ever stop blowing. You got a gift, kid. A real gift."

"Thanks, Cal," someone inside said.

"Tell Harding I'll try to make it to the set later tonight, but I can't promise anything," Cal said. "You guys have a good time, though. You deserve it. Gotta run, now." The man turned and almost bumped into Brandon. "Sorry, friend." Brandon stepped up to the doorway and peered in.

"Excuse me," Brandon said to the trumpet player, who was standing nearest the door, "but I was out in the audience tonight and I really liked your playing."

"Thanks a lot, man," the trumpeter said.

"Oh, you're quite welcome," Brandon said. "Also, someone sitting near me commented, when you were playing on that last number, that you sounded like Miles."

"Oh, yeah? Well, that's quite a compliment, whoever said it."

"Well, could you tell me who Miles is?" Brandon asked, timidly.

"Tell you who *Miles* is?"

"Yo, what's up, man?" the piano player said, coming over. He was wearing a purple, silk neck scarf and a pair of hip, wire frame eyeglasses that rested on the bridge of his nose. "You mean you really don't know who Miles is?" The whole band had stopped what they were doing and were looking at Brandon curiously. Then some of them began snickering.

"Hey, cut it out now," the trumpeter said. "Don't be making fun of the brother. At least he's interested in knowing." He then turned back to Brandon. "Man, Miles Davis is like a god, as far as the trumpet goes, as far as jazz goes, really as far as any kind of music goes."

"That ain't no overstatement either," someone added.

"You see those pictures on the wall out there, what they call the Jazz Wall of Fame, just when you come in the club?" the trumpeter asked.

"Yeah, I saw them," Brandon said, recalling the black-and-white photos along the corridor leading into the club.

"Miles, he's out there with 'em."

"Yo, brother, where you from?" the piano player asked. "I don't mean that to be funny or nothing. I just noticed that you got sort of a northern accent that I can't really place. It sounds kinda like back home, but not exactly."

"New Hampshire," Brandon said.

"New Hampshire? No shit?" the man exclaimed. "I'm from Massachusetts, just west of Boston. We practically homeboys."

"Yeah, Redding," the sax player said, "you from so far out in no man's land that you glad to claim anybody as your homeboy." There was laughter from the others.

"Pay them no mind," Redding said. "But look, my brother, we got to get ready to hit it here in a minute. You coming back sometime?"

"Yeah, I'll probably be back sometime," Brandon said.

"Good. We'll hook up then. Just let me know you're here."

"Okay."

"Take it light, now," Redding said, clasping Brandon's hand.

As he passed the pictures on his way out, Brandon found the one of Miles. What stood out most about the man was his eyes. They were such sad eyes, the hurt in them impossible to miss. Brandon checked his watch. He decided to call it a night.

As he made his way up the street toward the station, a limousine pulled over to the curb. The rear side window rolled down.

"Hey, homeboy! Where you headed to?" It was Redding, the piano player.

"Oh, hey," Brandon said. "I was just on my way to catch the train home."

"You going home? This early?"

"Yeah. I guess so."

"Damn!" Redding said. "Sounds like slow motion to me. Well, listen, dude, we on our way to this party. You wanna hang?" He really was in no mood for a party. But what the heck. Anything was better than going home.

"Yeah, okay."

"Solid, then, my man." Redding opened the door and stepped out. Brandon climbed into the spacious interior of the limo. The rest of the band was there, along with the three girls who had been waiting outside the dressing room. Everyone had a glass of champagne. An uncorked bottle of the bubbly wine rested in a sterling ice bucket. Redding hopped back in, then tapped on the glass partition. The driver steered the limo back out into traffic.

"Yo, y'all remember my homeboy," Redding said.

"Yeh, what's up, man?" the trumpet player said, slapping fives with Brandon.

"Have some champagne," the sax player said, reaching for the bottle. "Give him a glass, Toots." The man handed Brandon a glass and the sax player poured him some champagne.

"Thanks," Brandon said. "Man, this is nice."

"Ain't it, though," the sax player said. "Even got us a French chauffeur."

"Yeah, we going in style, ain't we?" Redding said.

"What's your name, again?" the sax player asked.

"Brandon."

"Yeah, let me introduce you around to everybody," Redding said. "I'm Redding." Then turning to the girl sitting beside him, he said, "And this is Belinda, my pretty little thing." The girl blushed, as Redding planted a kiss on her cheek. "And that's Speed over there, with his main squeeze, Grazelle." He was talking about the sax player and his girl, an attractive light-skinned girl with short, wavy hair who Speed had his arm around. She smiled. Next to him was the drummer, who they called Toots. And seated beside him was Yogi, the bass player. The chocolate-complexioned girl, the prettiest of the three, with the trumpet player was Delores. Then, before Redding could continue, Speed jumped in.

"And that's Mr. Wallace Redmond, Wally for short, the best young trumpet player on the scene today, bar none." The other band members seconded Speed. The trumpet player blushed, raising his hands in modest denial.

"Naw, fellows, I'm just trying to pull my own weight," he said. "That's all."

"Hey, man. All this talk about Wally, what about me?" Redding demanded, in mock jealousy.

"What about you?" Speed said. "With ya one-note Samba-playing ass." Everyone laughed.

"Yo, wait a minute," Redding said. "What's this one-note Samba shit?"

"Redding, you got to be the only somebody I know can comp on one chord through half a damn song." The whole group, the girls included, split their sides laughing.

"You a damn lie, Speed," Redding protested. Speed turned to Wally for support.

"Wally? Wally?"

"Yeah, man?" Wally answered.

"Wally, you remember the other night when we was doing that Herbie Hancock number?" Speed said.

"Yeah, I remember."

"Didn't Redding stay with that same A-flat minor, or whatever it was, up through the whole damn bridge?" The group broke out laughing again.

"You know, y'all 'bout some dense somebodies!" Redding said. "It's obvious y'all don't understand advanced chord inversions." Speed finally stopped laughing long enough to respond.

"Yeah, we know all about advanced chord inversions, but not playing the same damn chord for twenty minutes," Speed said. "I know what you trying to do. You playing that modal shit. Just play the damn changes like everybody else, Redding."

"Yeah, I just thought he had got stuck or something, myself," Wally said. The laughter swelled again.

"See, that's why y'all ain't never going nowhere, 'cause y'all too afraid to try new forms," Redding said. "Coltrane wasn't afraid. And neither was Monk."

"Aw, so in your spare time you backing up the jazz masters now, huh?" Speed said. The laughter went even higher. "Redding, save your modal, or whatever you call it, for your own solos, not when you playing behind me. Okay?"

"That goes for me, too, Redding," Wally added. "Nothing personal."

"Alright, man," Redding conceded. "If that's what y'all want."

"But just one other thing, Redding," Wally said.

"Yeah, what's that?"

"You ain't gon wear that Liberace coat with them glow-in-the-dark shingles on it again are you?" Everyone fell out laughing again.

"Wally, yo mama!" Redding said.

"But seriously, though, Redding," Wally said, "those were some nice figures you were playing behind me tonight."

"Thanks, man," Redding said, slapping fives with Wally.

"Yeah, it was nice, man," Yogi joined in, also slapping fives with Redding.

"But, Redding," Wally continued, "just promise me you won't wear that loud-ass, sequin Liberace blazer no more, okay? It hurts my eyes, man."

"That's it! Come on!" Redding said, playfully jabbing at Wally, who cowered, covering up from the jabs.

"Hey, look," Yogi said. "Don't the L'Enfant Plaza look really weird-like in the fog tonight?" Brandon looked out the window. They were passing a long, cobblestone walkway in front of a big hotel, not far from the waterfront. A heavy fog had descended over the city, making the lamps glow eerily in the night.

"Yeah, don't it, though," Speed said. "Looks like high-stepping weather to me."

"What?" Redding said, in a disbelieving voice.

"Yo, Wally? Don't it look like high-stepping weather?" Speed said.

"Yeah, looks like it to me."

"Yo, man, wait a minute," Redding protested. "It's too cold for that shit tonight."

"What are you and Speed talking about, Wally?" Delores asked, looking first to Wally, then to Speed.

"Yeah, what are you guys talking about?" Grazelle said, echoing Delores' curiosity.

"I'd like to know, too," Belinda joined in. None of the guys bothered to answer. Brandon wondered, too. Redding obviously knew, but he was too busy trying to talk Speed and Wally out of it to tell anyone.

"Whatcha' say, Toots? Yogi?" Speed asked, ignoring the girls' questions.

"Yeah, let's do it, man."

"I'm game."

"Come on, now, fellows," Redding continued to protest. "It's too cold, okay? And on top of that, my corns hurt, man." Speed tapped on the window to get the driver's attention.

"Chauffeur?"

"Oui, monsieur?" the driver answered. Speed turned to Grazelle.

"Quick, how you say 'pull over' in French, baby?"

"Aw, shit, man!" Redding said, in disgust.

"I'm pretty sure he speaks English, honey," Grazelle said.

"I know, but I wanna do this right."

"Okay, you say, *Arrest, sil vous plait,"* Grazelle said.

"Arrest, sil vous plait," Speed said, rehearsing it to himself. Then turning back to the driver, he repeated it. *"Arrest, sil vous plait."*

"Oui, monsieur," the driver replied, and pulled the limo over to the curb.

"Alright, everybody out," Speed said. Wally opened the door and allowed the ladies out first.

"I wish somebody would tell us what's going on here," Delores said, grabbing her coat and climbing out, followed by the others.

"You'll see in a minute," Speed promised.

When they were all out of the limo, Speed placed a whistle around his neck, turned to the guys and, like a drill sergeant, barked out, "Band! Atteeeen, hut!" The guys snapped to attention. "Single file!" They fell in line, one behind the other, in order of height. Toots, who was the shortest, was at the front, with Redding behind him, then Yogi and Wally.

"What are they doing?" one of the girls asked.

"Shhhh!" Speed admonished the girls. "No talking." Then turning back to the band, he called out, "Band!"

"Yeh!"

"I said band!"

"Yeh!"

"Posiiiiiition!" Toots brought his drum sticks up in position. Speed then blew one long beep, then four short ones. They all started marching in place, with Toots keeping time with his drum sticks. To complete the cadence, they all vocalized the part of the bass drum. Speed blew one long beep again, then the four short ones and, like a supercharged drum major, whirled around and led the guys up the sidewalk. They were doing the most outlandish steps. The girls, who obviously had never seen them do this little routine before, began shouting their encouragement. Speed turned and yelled back at them, "Y'all come on and fall in!" The girls ran and joined them, falling in behind Wally. When Speed

discovered that Brandon was still back at the limo, he summoned him. "Yo, Brandon! Come on, man. No stragglers allowed in this crowd."

"Yeah, come on!" the others yelled. What the heck, he thought, then ran to catch up with them.

"Band!" Speed yelled.

"Yeh!"

"When I signal, we gon rip!" One of the girls began to ask Speed what he meant, but before she could, Speed blew four really quick beeps. Suddenly, the guys began stepping twice as fast as before, while at the same time scrambling around in a seemingly disorganized fashion, doing twirls and other gyrations. They kept this up for several minutes, until everyone fell out either from laughter or exhaustion or both. The girls were especially funny, because of their difficulty keeping up in their high heels.

"Just like old times, ain't it, Wally?" Speed said, coming over to Wally and slapping fives. Both of them were bowed at the waist, trying to catch their breath.

"Yeah, except we were in a lot better shape back then," Wally said. They laughed.

"Yeah, man, those were the days. TSU, the aristocrat of bands. Southern, Texas Southern, FAMU, Jackson State, Grambling—couldn't none of 'em touch us, man. We was the deal!" Speed exclaimed.

"Wait a minute, now, Speed," Wally said. "I don't know 'bout Grambling. Those were some fast-stepping brothers down there in that Louisiana bayou. If you ask me, they kicked our ass more than once." Speed reconsidered.

"Yeah, you right, Wally…all except for Grambling." They laughed. Then turning to the girls, Speed began to chide them. "And you girls supposed to be so nimble and everything. Y'all look all tired and worn out."

"You try doing this with heels on, man, and you'll see," Grazelle said.

"Baby, I saw you," Speed said, as he and Gazelle fell into each other. "You were so funny." The sound of a bottle shattering just yards away from them startled everyone.

"What the hell!?" someone gasped. Screeching tires from the cross street cut through the night air, as a jeep carrying three college-aged white guys sped away.

"Go back to Africa, you niggers!" one of them shouted. Stunned, they watched as the jeep faded into the misty night.

"The bastards!" Speed said, his dark face contorted into a mask of rage. "They never let you forget. They never let you forget."

"Forget it, baby," Grazelle said, trying to console him. "Don't let 'em get to you. They're just a bunch of idiots." Everyone was quiet.

"Come on, everybody," Wally finally said. "Let's get the hell outta here."

"Yeah, let's go," Yogi said. Wally signaled for the chauffeur.

When the limo arrived, they piled back in. The mood remained rather subdued until Speed snapped everyone out of it.

"Hey, what is this?" Speed said. "We going to a party or a funeral? We gon let the rest of that champagne go to waste?

"You ain't said nothing but a word, my brother," Redding said, coming to life. "Pass that champagne 'round this way, Yogi."

"Coming at you," Yogi said, pouring himself a glass before passing the bottle on.

"Everybody drink up," Speed said.

A few minutes later they pulled up in front of a posh, two-story in Arlington, just across the Potomac. After tipping the driver, Speed led them up the driveway to the house.

"Wow! This is nice!" one of the girls said. "So, this is Harding's place?"

"Yep," Speed said. "This is it."

Inside, the party was already in full swing. The band and their dates fanned out through the chic crowd. A curvy, honey-skinned black woman in a leopard costume complete with tail was getting a number of appreciative glances from the men. One eye-catching pair consisted of a Grace Jones look-a-like attired in a red leather suit, and her escort, a white guy in a Zoro outfit. Two shapely waitresses in micro-minis and stiletto heels moved throughout the room serving cocktails. Brandon went over and helped himself to some hors d'oeuvres and a cup of punch, then found a seat on the sofa.

"Attention, everyone!" The music and conversation stopped, as a full-figured black woman with reddish-blonde hair entered the room on the arm of a heavy-set black man in a chartreuse, double-breasted blazer, a flower pinned to the lapel. "I present to you the guest of honor, Mr. Harding Phillips!" As everyone applauded, a giant birthday cake was wheeled out from the kitchen and placed in the middle of the room. A girl in a bikini suddenly popped out and began leading the crowd in singing happy birthday to Harding. After a brief thank-you speech from Harding, the music resumed and the waitresses began serving chilled champagne to everyone.

Glancing around the room, Brandon's eyes met with those of a tall, stunning black girl who was standing along the wall sipping champagne.

She and her friend, who was even taller, looked like fashion models. The girl smiled coyly when their eyes met, then casually looked away.

"Yo, homeboy! What's happenin', man?" Brandon looked up to see Redding, who had a glass of champagne in one hand and a bottle of it in the other.

"Not much, man," Brandon said. "Just taking it easy."

"Yeh, I heard that," Redding said. "Here, let me pour some more of this good stuff in your glass." Brandon held his glass up so Redding could refill it. "But listen up, now. Don't go nowhere, 'cause as soon as these squares pull out, we gon do some serious partying up in here. So, just hang loose. I'll be back in a little bit." Redding weaved his way back through the crowd.

Once again, Brandon made eye contact with the girl along the wall. She smiled. He smiled back. After saying something to her friend, she started over.

"Mind if I join you?" she said, standing in front of him now.

"No. Please do," Brandon said, indicating the place next to him on the sofa.

"I'm Adrienne," she said, daintily planting herself beside him.

"Hi, I'm Brandon."

"You looked a little lonesome sitting over here all by yourself."

"Oh, I'm okay. I'm just chilling. It's been a long day for me."

"Are you a musician?" she asked.

"No, I'm just here with the band. What about you?"

"My friend and I, we know Harding through a mutual friend." Redding appeared once again.

"Hey, man, I see you found yourself some company," he said, casting an appreciative glance down at Adrienne.

"Redding, this is Adrienne," Brandon said. "Adrienne, this is Redding."

"Nice to meet you," she said.

"Nice to meet you, too," Redding said, taking her bejeweled hand and planting a kiss on it. "You are definitely one pretty lady."

"Why thank you," she said, smiling.

"Hey, check it out now," Redding said, removing several marijuana cigarettes from his shirt pocket. "I got some of the best Mary Jane here you done ever had in your life." After lighting one and taking a pull on it, Redding placed it and two more in the ashtray in front of them. "Y'all enjoy. And remember. There's more where that came from."

The lighting in the room suddenly dimmed and the music slowed. Couples began dancing close up. Adrienne picked up the lit joint, took several pulls on it, then offered it to Brandon. He hesitated for a moment, then accepted it. After taking several pulls himself, he passed it back to Adrienne. When they finished that first joint, they lit up and smoked another. Gradually, the weed began to relax him more and more. Adrienne leaned over and began to run her tongue inside Brandon's ear. The warm moistness of her tongue felt good, but he didn't respond. It wasn't that he didn't find her desirable. On the contrary, he found her quite desirable. But he just wasn't in the mood. Plus, he wasn't about to cheat on Julie. Actually, what he really felt like doing was curling up and going to sleep right there on the sofa. After several failed attempts at trying to seduce him, Adrienne stopped and got up from the sofa. He thought she was about to leave.

"I'll be right back," she said, then headed in the direction Redding had gone. A few minutes later she returned. "C'mon," she said, taking his hand. "Let's go upstairs."

"Okay."

She led him up the winding staircase and down the plush carpeted hallway. Along the way they passed several couples who were necking. Finally, Adrienne stopped at one of the rooms and knocked at the door. When there was no answer, she pushed open the door and they went inside. She flipped on a light switch. A florescent floor lamp came on. Closing the door, she led him over to the bed where they sat down. From her purse, she took out a cellophane wrapper of cocaine along with a little compact mirror. He watched as she carefully shook some of the white powder out onto the mirror, then arranged it into a neat line using a nail file. She then sucked it up into her nostril. Sitting back on the bed now, she closed her eyes. Slowly, her head tilted forward, like she was falling asleep. Then she straightened up and opened her eyes wide, a bright, dreamy look now coloring her face. She put some more of the cocaine on the mirror, just as she had done before, and offered it to Brandon. "Wanna try some?"

"I don't know," he said. "I've never done coke before."

"It'll be okay, baby," she said. "I promise. It'll make you feel really good. It won't get you hooked or anything, if that's what you're worried about. It's just a little. C'mon. It'll help you loosen up." She was right. What harm could just a little do? Besides, it was a party, wasn't it?

"Okay," he said, taking the compact from her. He snorted the line of snowy powder just as he'd seen her do. Almost instantly the room seemed to dim around him, then come back into focus more vivid than before, like someone had turned up the lights in the room. He had a slight burning sensation in his nostrils as well as a feeling of numbness in his teeth. And his whole face tingled. They did a couple more lines each.

After awhile, he didn't feel the need for sleep anymore. It was like he'd just been re-energized. The next thing he knew, Adrienne was kissing him. What had he gotten himself into? He should never have come up here with her. But at the same time, he couldn't deny that he was becoming aroused. She drew back. Thank God, he thought, catching his breath. He didn't want it to go any further.

"It's getting a little hot in here," she said, rising from the bed. "Mind if I take off my dress?"

"Take off your dress? No, go ahead." Reaching behind her, she slowly unzipped her dress and let it fall to the floor. To his amazement, she was stark naked, not a stitch of clothing on underneath. Stepping out of her heels, she pushed him down on the bed. "Ah, wait," he said, sitting back up and gently pushing her away. "Look, I don't think we ought to be doing this."

"Why? What's wrong, baby? Don't you like this?" she said, rubbing his groin through his pants. He grabbed her hand to still it.

"Yeah, sure I like it, but—"

"But what?" She flicked her tongue in his ear. Her tongue felt even hotter than before. He moved his head away.

"I have a girlfriend."

"Okay," she said. "I understand. But she doesn't have to know. Does she?"

"Well, of course not. But it's still—"

"I can keep a secret. Can't you?" Her hand was free again. That familiar hunger began to rage. He wanted to tell her that the last thing he wanted to do was to cheat on Julie, that it was all a mistake, him coming up to the room with her. But the hunger was too strong to fight. All he could think of at that moment was satisfying it. "Just lay back, baby," she said, gently coaxing him back down on the bed. "Let Adrienne do all the work." After helping him out of his clothes, she climbed up on the bed and straddled him. The heat inside her was incredible, her juices like scalding liquid. She started slowly, grinding her hips against him. The pace picked up little by little until, finally, she was riding him full throttle. As their bodies blended into one long, continuous rhythm, the cocaine began to really kick in. He now felt as though he could go on like that all night. It was a feeling of almost invincibility, like there was nothing he couldn't do.

With the fire continuing to grow, a tiny purplish light began to flicker inside his head, slowly at first. Gradually, over time—what seemed like hours—the light began to grow bigger and brighter, and flicker faster and faster, like a strobe light being set at increasingly higher speeds. As the light continued to grow, it began to make a whirring sound. Soon the light became so dense, and the whirring became so loud, that it pushed everything, including his thoughts, from his head, leaving only these thick, mounting waves of intensely bright, pulsating light and this deafening whir inside his head. When the screaming light could expand no further, it began to pound against the insides of his skull, like someone beating against it with a pair of sledgehammers. It kept pounding and pounding until, finally, there was this blinding, cataclysmic explosion, sending shards of hot, jagged light flying out in all directions, like shrapnel from an exploded grenade. When the aftershocks had subsided, it became quiet inside his head again. The girl, herself spent, collapsed on top of him.

The next morning, Brandon was awakened by someone calling to him.

"Homeboy? Hey, homeboy?" He lifted his head from the pillow and opened his eyes, then quickly threw up his hand to shield them from the overhead light. Squinting at the figure standing in the doorway, he saw that it was Redding. He was already dressed. "Aw, sorry 'bout the light, man," Redding said, quickly turning it off. "Man, you must've had yourself quite a night! But listen up. We gon be running people home in a little while. So, you might wanna go ahead and get ready, so you can catch a ride."

"Yeah, okay," Brandon mumbled, as he looked around for the girl. She was gone. Redding closed the door, then quickly reopened it.

"Oh, and there's a little continental breakfast downstairs, if you wanna grab a bite before we leave." He pulled the door shut again. Brandon sat up and gripped his head, which was throbbing with a dull ache. After wiping the sleep from his eyes, he got up and went over to the window and opened the curtains. Looking out on the morning, he saw things through a haze, which let him know that he still had not come down completely from the cocaine and marijuana. What time was it? He looked at his watch. It was nearly noon.

Brandon relaxed in the comfort of the supple leather back seat of Harding's BMW as Redding navigated through the streets on the way to his place. Belinda rode up front with Redding. When they neared his neighborhood, Brandon noticed a record shop at the corner. He remembered that he wanted to pick up some recordings of Miles.

"Redding, you can let me off over at that record shop," he said. "I wanna pick up something. I can walk from here."

"Okay, then," Redding said, pulling up in front of the record store. "Well, I guess this is it, my man. It's been real. We gon have to do it again sometime."

"Yeah, really," Brandon said, exchanging fives with Redding. "I appreciate you inviting me along."

"No sweat, man. You good people. Be cool now."

"You, too," Brandon said, stepping from the car.

Inside the little record store, a slender black man with a pepper-gray beard, sporting a pair of cool, horn-rimmed shades, was standing behind the cash register, preparing to cue up an LP on one of two turntables in front of him.

"My man," he greeted Brandon. "What can I do you for today?"

"You carry any jazz?"

"Carry any *jazz?*" the man said, looking at Brandon like he had just asked the dumbest question he had ever heard. "Man, that's practically *all* we carry here. Just let me put this record on and I'll be right with you. You definitely in the right place." The man started the record, then stepped from around the counter. The mellow tones of a quintet, featuring a trombone out in front, poured from the speakers mounted on the walls. "Now, any particular artist you interested in?"

"Miles Davis," Brandon said.

"Miles, huh? Come on back this way with me." The man led him into an adjacent room. Around the walls were posters and album covers of jazz artists. "CD or LP?"

"CD," Brandon said.

"Any particular era?"

"Era?"

"Yeah, there was the bop era, the cool era, and then, I guess you'd call it the electronic era, you know, when he did the thing with the amplified horn," the man explained.

"Oh, I see," Brandon said. "I guess I really don't know. I'm not that up on jazz. See, I heard this trumpet player down at the Lush Life last night. I liked him a lot and someone seemed to think he sounded a lot like Miles."

"Was he playing with a band called Solar Eclipse?"

"Yeah, that's the band."

"That must've been Wallace Redmond," the man said. "Everybody calls him Wally for short."

"Yeah, that's him."

"Hmmm," the man said, running his hand down his face, "I think I have a pretty good idea of what you're looking for now." He picked out a half-dozen Miles Davis CDs and laid them out along the window sill. "Look through these, my man. You oughta be able to find something to your liking among them. Take your time. I'll be back in a second, soon as I check on my man over here," he said, motioning to another customer who was browsing. Brandon looked the CDs over, reading the liner notes on the back. The names of the tunes and the artists meant little to him, however. All he knew was that if Miles sounded anything like Wally did the night before, then he wouldn't be disappointed with any of them. The man came back over.

"Well, see anything you like?"

"I'll take all six," Brandon said.

"All six?" the man said, somewhat surprised. "My, my, my. You really are serious about your jazz, aren't you, young man? But let me tell you something. You couldn't make a wiser investment, 'cause this is classic stuff you're getting. It's like gold. It'll never go out of style. Come on up to the register and we'll get you all squared away." Brandon followed the man back to the register, where he rang up his purchase.

"By the way," the man said, extending his hand, "I'm Lee."

"Brandon," he replied, shaking hands with him.

"Pleasure to know you, Brandon."

"Yeah, same here, Lee. But tell me something. Who's that playing right now?"

"Oh, that's trombonist Curtis Fuller and his quintet."

"He's good," Brandon said.

"One of the best," Lee said. "I put him right up there with J. J. Johnson."

"You really seem to know your jazz, Lee."

"Well, I know a little about it. But one thing I definitely know is that it's the most original music ever created. And, if I may quote the great drummer/band leader Art Blakey, to play it demands the highest execution on any instrument. That's to play it right, mind you. And on top of that, it was created by our people, black people. Makes me proud just thinking about it. Black folks the ones who created this music, the most beautiful music in the world. Well, listen, my brother," Lee said, handing him his purchase, "you enjoy your music and come back soon."

"Thanks. I will."

As he walked to his apartment, it puzzled him that the emptiness that had come over him the day before had yet to return. Could it be that he'd gotten past it? No, he thought. Even though he couldn't see or feel the pain at that moment, he knew it was just up ahead, waiting for him. It would bide its time, wait for the effects of the drugs to wear off, then pounce on him, like a tiger pouncing on its prey.

By the time he reached his place, fatigue had set in, so he went straight to bed. He awoke sometime later in the dead quiet of the night in a cold sweat. The drug-induced fog that had run interference for him since the night before had burned away. And all the painful revelation that had torn at him the day before had returned, but with redoubled strength. As he gazed out the window at the lonely courtyard below, he became deeply aware of his solitude. A dense shroud of sorrow had descended all around him, like the darkness that had descended on the world outside. He noticed the CDs he had purchased laying still unwrapped on his dresser. After loading them in his CD player, he went back and curled up on his bed. The same sad, probing sound that had enraptured him the night before came drifting out to him again, only more refined, like cold, liquid crystal. It reached so deep inside him that it made his river of pain overflow its banks.

Chapter 14

Over the next few days, his life fell into a predictable pattern of monotonous wakefulness, then sleep, as he rode an ever-descending spiral into an abyss of nothingness. Each morning he would get up, after having lain awake for most of the night, go to the window, and look out at the people trudging off to work with their briefcases. Only a little while ago, he had been one of them, and had been secure in the knowledge that he was moving up in the world, that he was going somewhere. Now, all that seemed like something from another life, like it had been someone else, not him. Yes, it had all been just a charade, a cruel hoax that he had believed to be real. Now that the charade was over, he wondered if he had ever known life as it really was or if he had merely been like someone wandering through a house of mirrors, unable to distinguish reality from fiction.

Whenever Julie called, and she called often, he would just sit and stare vacantly at the answering machine from across the room, listening to her voice, insistent and pleading.

Ring. Ring. Ring. Ring.

"Brandon? It's me again. Where are you? I've been trying you at work, been leaving messages for you. Did you like disappear into thin air or something? Or did you take that vacation without me to the Caribbean we'd been planning? If you did, you'd better not bring back any of those scantily clad women I know you're going to run into down there. Well, when you get this message, give me a call. Love you, baby. Bye."

Ring. Ring. Ring. Ring.

"Brandon, it's been five days now, five whole days and, well, this isn't funny anymore. I mean, I'm starting to worry. Call me. Okay? I love you."

Ring. Ring. Ring. Ring.

"Brandon, I called Gill. He told me he hasn't seen or heard from you either. I finally got a hold of Sean. He told me he hasn't either. What's going on? You've really got me worried now. Will you please call me? Bye."

One day Gill came knocking at his door. "Brandon? You in there, man? Julie asked me to come by and check on you. She says she's been trying to reach you for the last week. If you're in there, little brother, let one of us know. Okay? Julie's worried out of her wits about you. I'm starting to get a little concerned now myself. Give somebody a call. Okay?"

The next day, Julie came by. "Brandon? I know you're in there. I've seen the lights go on and off. And your car is still out in the parking lot. Brandon? Will you come to the door? Brandon? What's wrong, honey? Are you alright? Brandon, if you don't open the door, I'm going to Gill's place and call the police." The word *police* got his attention. The last thing he wanted was them bothering him. As she started away, he cracked the door just enough to peer out. She stopped and turned around.

"Okay, you've seen me," he said. "You satisfied?"

"Brandon?"

"You've seen me. Now will you just go away?"

"What's going on? Why haven't you answered your phone? Is something wrong? I've been really worried about you."

"I don't want to see you anymore," he said. "Okay?"

"What? You don't want to—Brandon, you're not making any sense. Open the door and let's talk." Julie moved toward the door.

"No! Don't try to come in!" Startled, Julie froze. "Just go away and leave me alone!"

"Brandon, why are you acting this way? What's happened?" A voice inside his head began to speak to him. *Get rid of her. Turn her away. You don't need her. She's white. She's evil.*

"Look, can't you understand English, white girl? I don't want you anymore!"

"What? W-What do you mean, you don't want me anymore?" Tears began to well up in her eyes.

"I mean exactly what I said," he said. "I don't want you anymore. I've got somebody else. You didn't really think you were the only one I was seeing all this time, did you? I've got other women. You're not the only one."

"You're lying," Julie said, looking as if she were on the verge of breaking down at any moment. "I don't believe you."

"White girl, don't flatter yourself. You think you're so special just because you're white, don't you?"

"Why are you talking like this, Brandon, with this white girl stuff? This doesn't sound like you."

"Look, I don't want you anymore! Okay? So, why don't you just get the hell away—" Julie fell against the wall, sobbing, her face buried in her hands. He had done what he had had to do. And he hated himself for having done it. One part of him wanted to go to her and soothe her hurt feelings, tell her he hadn't meant any of it. Another part, the part that had taken over inside his head, held him back. Brandon closed the door. Standing there at the door, he heard her, still sobbing, slowly start away. The voice in his head began to speak again. *Let her go. Let the white girl go.*

■ ■ ■

As days turned into weeks, he began to lose track of time. He no longer knew, nor cared, what day it was, for whatever day it might be would be no different from the one before or the one to come. Occasionally, he would catch a glimpse of himself in the mirror through his tired, bloodshot eyes. Each time he would see less of himself than he did the day before, like he were gradually fading away and would soon be nothing more than a mere shadow. Some days he ate; other days he didn't. When he did eat, it was usually just enough to sustain him, for he no longer had any real appetite. After awhile, his clothes began to sag on him because of the weight he was losing.

Most of his waking hours were spent curled up on his bed, lost in the sea of music that continually wafted through the apartment, as he brooded over his failed life. From time to time, Rachel Toney would cross his mind. What if she hadn't rejected him and, instead, had gone out with him? Maybe they would have started dating and he never would have gotten involved with Julie. Then maybe none of this would ever have happened. But those were far too many *what ifs* to grapple with. Strangely, however, it wasn't bitterness he felt toward Rachel, but desire. In his fantasies about her, the two of them might be strolling hand in hand along the beach, her skin radiant in the mid-day sun. Or they might be jogging through the park together. Once, they were dancing around a huge ballroom floor that had no boundaries, just the two of them.

He lost all interest in any personal grooming, allowing his normally neat and closely cropped hair to grow long and unruly and his normally clean-shaven face to become overgrown with a thick, scraggly beard. He let his apartment go in the same way as well. Dishes piled up in the sink and garbage began to overflow and stink. About the only thing he still had any interest in was listening to Miles play his horn. He felt that it was the only thing that he still had any commonality with. Yes, Miles knew of pain. He had to, for it was in every note he blew. Occasionally, he would watch TV. When he did, he would turn the volume all the way down and watch the actors in the sitcoms acting out their silly little antics. How could these people carry on like this, so carefree and lighthearted? Didn't they know of the frailty of life, that it was too serious to be toyed with? Didn't they know of the pain that was in the world, that there were many who were hurting like himself? But then he realized that most of the people in these sitcoms were white people. What did they know of pain? Yes, they could afford to laugh and joke and be merry. The whole society was designed for them. After awhile, he stopped watching TV altogether, for it had little relevance to him anymore.

He left the apartment only to get the most basic of necessities. And when he did venture out, it was usually late at night, to reduce the chance of running into Gill or Julie. Sometimes he caught the bus and rode around, looking out at the city as it slept.

One night as he was on his way to the bus stop, a faint rain falling, a car pulled up to the curb next to him. Out of the corner of his eye, he saw that it was Julie. He quickened his stride. But before he could get far, he heard the car door open and her call to him. "Brandon?" Her voice had a questioning ring to it, like she wasn't at all sure if it was really him. It froze him in his tracks, but he didn't turn around. The last thing he wanted was some kind of emotional scene with her. He wanted to just quickly walk away, but he knew that she would only follow him, dragging the whole thing out even more. "Brandon?" Julie ran to catch up to him. She approached him cautiously at first, like she was still unsure whether it was really him. Then, apparently satisfied that it was—or maybe having come to grips with his disheveled appearance—she rushed toward him, throwing her arms around him and burying her face in his shoulder. "Oh, baby," she cried, "I've missed you so much." He didn't return her embrace but, rather, stood coldly, unfeeling. She let go of him and stepped back, like she didn't know exactly what to make of him now. Because of the rain, he couldn't tell if the water streaming down her face was rain or tears. Yet he knew she was crying because he could hear the anguish in her voice.

"You remember that day that I came by your place and you said all those awful things to me? The next day I got a hold of Sean. He told me all about what happened, about you losing your job and all. He'd found out from Fran. I've been worried sick. We all have. I knew you didn't mean all those mean things you said to me that day. I knew there wasn't anyone else. Please, come home with me, baby." She waited for him to say something, but he just continued to stand there in stony silence, his eyes diverted from hers. "Okay. If you won't come home with me, will you at least let me take you wherever it is you're going?" When he still didn't respond, she reached for his arm. "Come on. Let me take you somewhere. Please? I want to help. For Christsake, you're gonna catch your death of cold out here, honey." He brushed aside her arm and, still avoiding her eyes, shook his head no. "Brandon, what has this thing done to you? What has it done to us? I love you! Look, I can see you're hurting. Is there something I should have done that I didn't do? Tell me, and I'll try to make it up to you. Will you at least talk to me? If it's a job, I can help you get another one. My father knows people who can—"

"I don't want your father's help," he said, looking at her now for the first time. "Don't you understand, Julie? It's got nothing to do with you. It's not your fault."

"I don't care if you blame me, baby. I just want… I just want us to be like we were before all this," she said, breaking into sobs.

"Go home, Julie," he said, brushing her aside and starting past. "I don't live in your world anymore. Whatever we might have once had is over."

"Brandon!" she cried out, slumping to her knees and burying her face in her hands, her sobbing muffled by the falling rain. He kept walking, not turning to look back, for he knew that if he allowed himself to go back and comfort her that he wouldn't be able to let go.

■ ■ ■

The groundhog made its annual appearance, ushering in the month of February. As always, much ado was made as to whether or not it saw its shadow. For Brandon, though, it didn't matter, for whether spring came to the world earlier or later, he knew that winter would not soon be drawing off from the private world he inhabited. About a week later, the Washington area was brought to a virtual standstill by the first major snowstorm of the season. Nearly six inches fell in some places. After several days of the white cover on the ground, the rain, helped by the rising temperatures, came and washed it all away. And then the rain seemed not to want to stop. It seemed to rain every other day. But Brandon didn't mind. As a matter of fact, he found himself looking forward to the rain, especially a hard rain, for it was as if the world was being washed and purified of all its filth. He especially liked the clean, fresh aroma of drenched soil and grass and the ozone smell after a thunderstorm that drifted in through his opened balcony door. As he'd listen to the rain pelting against the windows, he'd imagine that it was pouring down inside his head, washing away all the debris of accumulated sorrow and anguish.

During a particularly torrential downpour, he stood at his balcony door watching the rain slamming its cold, hard fists down upon the earth. This was more than cleansing, he thought. It was punishment. The rain came down with such viciousness that it distorted the shapes of things, transforming the outside world into one big, dark blur of wetness. Far off on the horizon, a blinding flash of lightning appeared, followed by the grumbling of distant thunder. Not long afterward, a bright flash of lightning lit the air just outside his balcony, followed by a deafening roar of thunder. As the lightning continued to flash and the thunder continued to roar, something told him to look down at the ground. Through the blinding, drifting rain he saw a faint stain of crimson. Though the rain beat hard against it, it couldn't wash it away. Not only could the rain not wash it away, but the stain began to grow, first into a puddle, then into a stream, and finally into a river. What was this river of crimson? It was clear that it was blood. But whose blood was it? He watched as it continued to flow from some unknown fount. But just as suddenly as it had appeared, it dried up. The storm tapered off, and the sun peeked back out from behind the clouds. Was all this some kind of a sign that his own personal deliverance might be at hand? From that point on, a questioning began in him, a deep and abiding urge to know the means of his release.

As February drew to a close, his world became even bleaker. First, his car was repossessed. Then his electricity was cut off. To stave off the bitter, bone-chilling cold of his apartment, he huddled in layers of blankets. He knew he'd be facing eviction soon. If an answer were coming, it had better come soon.

Chapter 15

While out riding the city bus to escape the chill of his apartment one Sunday morning, Brandon saw a church up on a hill off in the distance, its steeple shimmering in the cold sunlight. He thought of the preacher he'd met at the barbershop who had given him his business card. Did he still have it? He checked his wallet. It was still there. Looking at the address on the card, he wondered how far he was from the church. He got up and approached the driver.

"Excuse me, but do you know where Arledge Street is? 3482 Arledge Street."

"Arledge?" the man said. "Sure, Arledge is about three or four blocks over from where we are now. It runs the same direction we're headed now. And that address, what was it again? It sounds familiar."

"3482. It's the address of this church called Mt. Sinai Baptist."

"Yeah, okay. I knew that address sounded familiar. They have a radio broadcast I listen to sometimes on Sunday morning. You wanna go there?"

"I'd like to. But I don't know if I can get there in time, though," Brandon said, glancing at his watch. It was nearly eleven-thirty.

"If they're like most Baptist churches," the driver said, checking his own watch, "you got plenty of time to make it for the preaching and probably some of the singing, too. You can get there from here easily in ten, no more than fifteen minutes. Just get off at the stop at Kersey Avenue, which is about three or four stops from here, and walk three blocks east to Arledge. Then go north one block or so and you'll see it on your right. I hear they got a really good choir over there. And Hollings, the pastor, he's supposed to be some kinda preacher, one of the best around."

"Okay, I think I'll go."

■ ■ ■

The church was an impressive, beige-brick structure with picturesque stained glass windows. Brandon mounted the steps and entered through the double doors. As he waited in the foyer to enter the sanctuary, the rhythmic rise and fall of a fervent prayer issued from inside. Peering through the glass portals of the doors leading in, he caught sight of the man praying. He was standing behind the rostrum up in the pulpit, with people gathered down front.

"...'cause we know that you a heart fixer and a mind regulator, a burden bearer, and a heavy load sharer, that you a very present help in the time of trouble."

"*Say it!*" someone cried out.

"You know all about us, Lord. Yes, you do. So we askin' you this mornin', if it be yo' will, if you might come this way."

"*Come this way, Lord!*"

"And when you come, Lord, just have yo' own way."

"*Please, Jesus!*"

"Come like you want to. For we know, Good God A'mighty!, if you have yo' way in our lives this mornin', that everything will be alright."

"*Be a witness!*"

"That that pain somebody's got in they body, it'll be alright."

"*Be alright!*"

"That that son that's strung out on drugs and that daughter that's sellin' her body on the street, it'll be alright. That that messed up marriage, it'll be alright. That that weak, cancer-ridden body that the doctors done give up on, Good God A'mighty!, it'll be alright. That that heartache and that heartbreak, it'll be alright."

"*Have mercy, Jesus!*"

"For we know that you's a God that sits high and looks low. Yes, Lord, Good God A'mighty!"

"*Yes, Lord! Yes, Lord!*" a woman began to shout.

"We know you can do anything but fail. For whatever the condition, Lord, you just move in yo' own time, move in yo' own way. Have yo' own way right now, Good God A'mighty! Yes, we turnin' it over to you, Lord..."

When the prayer had concluded and people had started back to their seats, the doors swung open and an usher, a lady in a white uniform, invited Brandon to enter. Inside, another usher escorted him to a row near the middle of the church to one of the last available seats. The choir, which stretched across the choir loft, was dressed in colorful African robes and headdress. Many of those in the congregation, as well as some of the ministers in the pulpit, were also attired in African garb. On the back wall up over the choir loft was a black crucifix.

"We want to thank Reverend Ellis for that most fervent prayer," an elegantly dressed woman said from a podium down in front. Her comments were met with a chorus of amens from the congregation. "And we want to send out an especially warm greeting this morning to those of you in our radio listening audience who've tuned your dial our way. It's our sincere prayer that this broadcast, coming to you live and direct over radio station WLOK, will be a blessing to you. We will now be ministered to in song by the Mt. Sinai mass choir, under the most capable direction of organist and Minister of Music Mr. Darren Ables, and featuring sister Marva Mickens, singing *Can't Nobody Do Me Like Jesus*. After which time, our pastor, that anointed man of God, the Reverend David R. Hollings, will come to us breaking the bread of life." Amens went up again from the congregation.

The musicians, with the organ out in front, launched into a lively, hand-clapping selection. In addition to the organ, there was a bass guitar, piano and drums. The bass guitar player stood out because he was white. After the musicians had played their introduction, the director brought in the choir.

Can't nobody do me like Jesus.
Can't nobody do me like God.
Can't nobody do me like Jesus.
He's my friend.

The soloist, who was standing out to the side in front of her own microphone, began answering the choir as they repeated the verse.

Can't nobody (Can't nobody!) do me like Jesus.
Can't nobody (Can't nobody!) do me like God.
Can't nobody (I said can't nobody!) do me like Jesus.
He's my friend.

Picked me up (Picked me up!) and told me to run on.
Picked me up (He picked me up!) and told me to run on.
Picked me up (Picked me up!) and told me to run on.
He's my friend.

The woman, her melodious voice skillfully weaving in and around the chorus that the choir was repeating, held her head back heavenward, as if she were calling on some power greater than herself to enable her to sing. Her voice possessed a tremendous clarity and power, yet at the same time possessed the same feeling and raw emotion of the blues singer that night in Georgetown. But whereas the blues singer had been singing of an overwhelming sorrow, the woman was singing of a bright, bountiful assurance.

As the choir sang, people in the audience, galvanized by the soul-stirring singing, began to rise from their seats and join in. Then the choir broke off into the refrain, *Can't nobody do me like Jesus,* which they kept repeating, as the soloist began to answer, singing *Nobody, nobody!*

When the choir finished, amens and applause issued up throughout the sanctuary. Some waved their hands in the air; others wiped tears of joy from their eyes. One woman, tears streaming down her face, her hands lifted high in the air, shouted *"Thank you, Jesus! Thank you, Jesus!"*

Brandon now caught his first glimpse of the Reverend, as he rose and stepped to the podium. He was wearing a red and white ministerial robe, with a Kinte cloth draped around his neck. "It's good to have family!" the Reverend said. "It's good to have friends! But as much as I treasure friends, as much as I treasure family, can't nobody do me like Jesus! 'Cause one day when I was languishing on the garbage heap of life, he picked me up! And he told me, David, you run on! And I've been running on in his name ever since, sometimes stumbling, sometimes falling. But through it all, I've learned to lean and depend on his holy word. Anybody here this morning ever been picked up by the Lord, ever had your body healed by the Lord? If so, you ought to praise him!" The already revved up congregation responded even more enthusiastically, as the musicians let go with their own responses. When the praises finally subsided, Hollings continued. "It's good to see so many of you out this morning on the last Sunday of the month we set aside to celebrate Black History. Doesn't the mass choir look just splendid in their colorful attire?" He looked around admiringly at the choir. The congregation responded approvingly.

"And many of you out in the audience, as well as some of my ministers up here in the pulpit with me, are wearing your African dress. It's nothing wrong with being proud of where you come from. Some people think it's silly, foolish, running around talking about Africa and saying you're proud to be descendants of Africans. Excuse the bad English, but let me go on record as saying that ain't no sadder people than a people that ain't got no roots and don't know where they come from!" People around the church offered up amens and applause. Some stood to applaud. After waiting once again for the praise to subside, he continued, this time in a more subdued tone.

"As you know, we've been preaching all this month on some aspect of the black experience and how it relates to our faith. So, on this final Sunday of Black History Month, I want to speak to you on a subject that is quite troubling in our communities, and that's the plight of the black male. For it seems that everywhere we turn, whether it's the sociologist, the criminologist, the psychologist, the politician, or just society in general, they've all but written off the black man in America. According to them and all their statistics, we'll be all but extinct by the turn of the century. So, I've entitled this message *Black Man, Stand Up*. And I'm going to use for a text the well-known and oft-told account of Jesus' raising of Lazarus from the dead, as told in the eleventh chapter of the Gospel according to John."

The Reverend started slowly, building his sermon little by little, laying the foundation. "...Jesus was a man of color who raised another man of color, whose name was Lazarus, from the grave. The story tells us that when Jesus first heard of Lazarus' death that he told those around him, 'this sickness is not unto death, but for the glory of God, that the Son of God might be glorified...'"

With the exception of an occasional crying baby, the audience sat quietly, listening intently to the message. It didn't take long to discover that the Reverend's reputation as a gifted orator was well-deserved, as he spoke entirely without notes, weaving a beautifully crafted sermon. Hollings was not a tall man, but his presence as he spoke was so commanding that he seemed to grow taller with each passing minute. As he spoke, he would occasionally slip out a handkerchief from underneath his robe to wipe away the perspiration from his face.

And as Hollings told the story, dramatizing it so clearly that a child could understand it, he began to rise up upon the balls of his feet to make his points. The congregation, which had up to now been content to sit quietly and just listen, began to talk back to him, shouting their encouragement.

"Tell the story!"
"Preach!"
"Say it!"
"Come on up now!"

Gripping the sides of the podium, Hollings began to lean into the mike, his face mirroring every word that issued forth from his mouth. It was as if he had taken into him fire and had no choice but to spew it out or be consumed by it. People were now perched on the edges of their seats in eager anticipation, waiting to catch that fire, as he began to climax, bringing his message to a close.

"...And it says that Jesus told them to roll back the stone. And after he had prayed a brief prayer, he cried out in a loud voice, 'Lazarus, come forth!' But you see, before Lazarus could come forth, he first had to stand up. So, that's why I believe that if Martin Luther King, Jr. were here today, he'd say, 'Truth crushed to the earth will one day rise again. So, though you've been buked and scorned, know that truth will one day out. And the truth will set you free. Black man, stand up!' He'd say 'stand up, even though the forces of racism may sometimes be arrayed against you. But don't let past hurts keep you bound and cemented to hate. Ask God to help you put it behind you and go on in Jesus' name. Black man, stand up! And if Frederick Douglass were here, he'd say 'Power concedes nothing without struggle. So, though life might be a constant fight, black man, stand up!' And if Booker T. Washington were here, I believe he'd say 'Cast down your buckets where you are.' Yes, because of the color of your skin, you might have to work a little harder. You might have to struggle a little more. But just do your best. For if you do your best, and put your trust in God, you can make it. Black man, stand up!...'"

The Reverend continued to evoke the names of great black men and women throughout history. And as he did, Brandon began to feel an awakening begin inside of himself, like there was a Lazarus asleep in him and he was being stirred.

"...But none of those great leaders are with us in the flesh anymore. They are all asleep, awaiting the resurrection. But I heard that that same man named Jesus who raised Lazarus from the grave, that same man from Galilee, that same man who turned water into wine, that same man who fed the multitude, that same man that's got wonder-working power, is coming this way. And he's saying to men of every race, creed and color, but especially to black men, stand up! Black man, you're the salt of the earth. But somewhere along the way you've lost your savor. Somewhere along the way you've lost that overcoming spirit that the prophet Elijah said was like fire shut up in my bones. Somewhere along the way you've lost sight of Him who said to Moses, 'tell pharaoh that I AM THAT I AM has sent you.' Somewhere along the way, you've lost sight of Him who they called the Rock of Ages and a Rock in a Weary Land. Tell Satan to loose you from those grave clothes, those grave clothes of a self-defeatist attitude, those grave clothes of a low self-esteem, those grave clothes of irresponsibility, those grave clothes of drug and alcohol dependency, those grave clothes of depression, those grave clothes of..."

As Hollings continued to preach, men and boys of all ages began, one by one, to stand up at their seats. There was even a young man in a wheelchair who, with the help of those on either side of him, was standing up. Even up along the balcony they were standing up, one by one. And then Brandon suddenly realized that he, too, was standing up. A woman sitting next to him touched him lightly on the arm. Turning to her, he saw that she was offering him a tissue. Only then did he realize that tears were flowing from his eyes. He accepted the tissue, dabbing at the wetness. At first he felt ashamed that he was crying, until he looked around and noticed that other grown men had tears streaming down their faces. That questioning that had been screaming out inside him had suddenly been quieted. Was this the answer?

"...and every black man that's decided to stand up today, I want you to keep on standing. Stand for yourself, stand for your family, stand for your community, but most of all, I want you to stand for Jesus, not a white Jesus, not a black Jesus, but stand for the Father!"

"*Yeh!*"

"Stand for the Son!"

"*Yeh!*"

"And stand for the Holy Ghost!"

The whole church was on its feet now, as people were clapping and shouting, lifting their hands into the air as if victory were just within reach. The musicians joined in on their instruments with the congregation in answering the Reverend. Finally, Hollings brought the sermon to a close and extended the invitation.

"Now, as the choir prepares to come to us with a song of invitation, I'm opening the doors of the church." The musicians began playing softly in the background. "Come right now, man, woman, boy or girl. This is the accepted time. If you feel a change in your heart and you want to stand for something that's real, you ought to take that step. Step out on faith. Maybe you've tried just about everything else, but you want to try that man named Jesus. Come now, while the blood is still running warm through your veins, while you've got the activity of your limbs and you're clothed in your right mind. He's calling you to stand up and come forth, to come and live for Him. You can come by letter, Christian experience, or as a candidate for baptism."

Continuing his appeal, the Reverend came down out of the pulpit, along with the other ministers. "Or maybe you want to be restored into proper fellowship with God, or you just want the church to pray for you. Whatever it is, I want you, if the Spirit of God is right now speaking to your heart, whoever you are, and wherever you've come from—it doesn't matter—I want you to stand up and come give your hand to me or one of the other ministers up here. But more importantly, come give God your heart." A heavy-set man in the choir began to sing.

Come, ye disconsolate, where'er ye languish.
Come to the mercy seat, fervently kneel.
Here bring your wounded hearts.
Here tell your anguish.
Earth has no sorrow that heav'n cannot heal.

As the man sang, his deep, bass-baritone voice reverberating throughout the church, Brandon felt a soothing, calming sensation come over him, like a cooling balm spread over an open wound. At the same time, he felt a comforting voice calling to him, not a physical voice that he could hear with his ears, but nonetheless a voice that was as real as any he'd ever heard. It was saying simply, *"It's alright. It's alright. It's alright."* Suddenly, all the accumulated pain of the last few months seemed to roll away, in the same way that the heavy stone in front of Lazarus' tomb had rolled away. He felt washed and cleansed in a way that not even a thousand rains could ever have washed him.

Joy of the desolate, light of the straying,
Hope of the penitent, fadeless and pure.
Here speaks the Comforter, tenderly saying,
Earth has no sorrow that heav'n cannot cure.

Brandon gave himself over to this urging deep inside and found himself headed down the aisle to the front, where the ministers were waiting with outstretched hands. With each person who came forward, shouts of joy went up throughout the sanctuary.

"*Hallelujah!*"

"*Thank you, Jesus!*"

Down at the front, he was warmly received by one of the ministers. The Reverend, upon recognizing him, came over and embraced him. He was offered a seat there on the front row with the others. When the church clerk had gathered the necessary information from all those who had come forward, they had them stand and face the congregation. The church clerk then approached the mike.

"Reverend Hollings, we have seven who've come forward as candidates for baptism, and three who want to join on their Christian experience."

"*Amen!*"

"*Praise the Lord!*"

"*Glory!*"

"As I call your name, please step forward," the clerk said. Brandon's name was the last to be called. "Brother Brandon Northcross comes to us as a candidate for baptism."

"We finally meet again, young man," the Reverend said, taking Brandon's hand in his. "Met this young man some time ago, think it was at the barbershop, wasn't it?"

"Yes," Brandon said.

"Brandon, do you accept Christ as your personal savior?"

"Yes, I do."

"Do you believe He died on the cross for your sins and mine, was then buried in the grave and was raised on the third day with all power in heaven and earth in His hands and that He now reigns in heaven with His Father?"

"Yes, I do."

"Brethren, you've heard the confession of brother Brandon Northcross. Do I hear a motion?"

"Brother Pastor," one of the deacons said, "I move that we accept Brother Brandon Northcross as a candidate for baptism. And after completion of new member's class, be given the right hand of fellowship and be accepted as a full-fledged member, granted all rights and privileges as any other member."

"I second the motion," another deacon added. The Reverend took over again.

"It has been moved and seconded that Brother Brandon Northcross be accepted as a candidate for baptism. And after completion of new member's class, be given the right hand of fellowship and be accepted as a full-fledged member, granted all rights and privileges as any other member." All in favor indicate by saying aye." Ayes went up all over the church. "The ayes have it. Brother Northcross, I extend to you the right hand of welcome," Hollings said, shaking his hand. "The church will be in touch with you later this week on a date for your baptism."

As those who had come forward returned to their seats, Hollings launched into a spirited victory song, which the congregation and musicians immediately picked up.

Glory, glory, hallelujah, since I laid my burden down.
Glory, glory, hallelujah, since I laid my burden down.

I feel better, so much better, since I laid my burden down.
I feel better, so much better, since I laid my burden down.

■ ■ ■

On his way home, Brandon felt as if his life were beginning anew, as if the last two months had never happened. After shaving and cleaning himself up, he went by to see Gill.

"Brandon?" Gill said in astonishment, as he looked at Brandon, who was standing just outside his door. "Is that you, man?"

"Yeah, it's me, alright."

"Well, I'll be! Come on in, man," Gill said. "Make yourself at home, while I go grab this casserole out of the oven." Brandon came in and closed the door, as Gill retreated to the kitchen. "So, what wind blew you in? I didn't know if you had gone back to New Hampshire or what."

"A lot has happened," Brandon said. "A lot."

"Yeah?" Gill said, pausing to look at him again. "Well, have a seat, man. I didn't know what had happened. One day Julie came by all crying and everything. She said she finally talked to you and, in her words, you didn't want anything more to do with her. She was pretty hurt. It was all I could do just to try and calm her down."

"That wasn't really me that day, Gill," Brandon said. "I'll have to tell you about it sometimes."

"Well, hey, you can tell me all about it over dinner, if you like," Gill said. "You're just in time. You hungry?"

"Yeah."

"Well, grab a plate and pull up a chair. It'll be like old times again."

■ ■ ■

"Hello?" Julie answered the phone.

"Hello, Julie? It's me, Brandon."

"Brandon?" she said, excitedly. "Where are you? Are you okay?"

"I'm fine. I'm over at Gill's place."

"I've been worrying myself silly, wondering if something had happened to you." She paused. He wanted to say something, but he didn't know just what. Julie didn't wait for him to. "I've also been doing a lot of crying, Brandon, wondering if we'd ever get back together. Ever since that night when it was raining… and you told me it was over between us—"

"I know," he said. "I'm sorry. I didn't mean what I said that night, Julie. It wasn't really me talking, just like it wasn't really me that day when you came by my place and—"

"I know, baby. I realize that now. You don't have to explain." They were both quiet for a moment.

"Can I see you?" he said.

"When?"

"How about this evening?"

"Okay. Where?"

"You remember O'Malley's down on Connecticut, where we used to go sometimes?"

"Yeah, I remember it. You wanna meet there?"

"Yeah. Can we hook up there in, say, an hour?" Brandon said, checking his watch.

"An hour? Okay. I can come pick you up, if you want."

"No, I'll just take the train," he said. "There're a few things I want to do first."

"Okay."

"I'll see you then," he said. "Bye."

"Bye."

■ ■ ■

Julie was waiting just inside the door of O'Malley's when he arrived. She was wearing the same shade of cherry lipstick she had worn that night they'd met down in Georgetown. Memories of that evening came flooding back to him.

"Hey, baby," Julie said, throwing her arms around his neck and kissing him. He returned her kiss eagerly. Finally, they relaxed and came up for air. "Missed you."

"I missed you, too, sweet girl."

"I haven't heard that in a long time."

"What?"

"Sweet girl."

"Oh," he said, smiling.

"It's just one of the many little things about you I've missed."

"Well, you don't have to worry about missing them anymore," he said, pulling her close to him.

"Is that a promise, Brandon Northcross? Cross your heart and hope to die?"

"Cross my heart and hope to die," he said. They kissed again.

"Come on, let's go inside," she said.

■ ■ ■

"So, what's it been like for you all this time, honey?" Julie said. "I know you've been through some serious changes."

"The best way I can describe it is that it was like being down in a deep, dark hole all by yourself," he said. "You can see the light way up over your head. But you can't get to it. And there's no way to get out. I didn't care about anything, especially myself."

"People commit suicide sometimes when it gets that bad."

"It was getting to that point."

"Oh, you poor baby," she said, getting up from her bar stool and caressing him from behind.

"One time, something really strange happened," he said. "It was like something out of a dream. Only it wasn't a dream. I was wide awake."

"What happened?"

"Well, there was this really bad thunderstorm. It was raining really hard and lightning really bad. I was standing at my balcony door, when I happened to look down at the ground and saw the strangest thing. There was this, like, puddle of blood. It was small at first. But then it gradually starting getting bigger and bigger. It was as if it was coming up out of the ground or something. It kept growing and growing until it was almost like a river, a river of blood, flowing across the courtyard and out into the street. And then, just like that, it was gone."

"Wow! That *was* strange."

"It was like a vision or something," he said.

"Well, whatever it was, baby, you made it out. You were strong, Brandon."

"But it wasn't me, Julie," he said, twisting around on his stool to face her. "That's just the thing. It wasn't me. This morning, when I was out riding the bus, I ended up at this church. Something happened to me there that I can't explain. It was like I was reborn on the inside. And all my depression just went away, just like that."

"Oh, Brandon, I love you so much," she said, hugging him. "Say, I've got an idea."

"What?"

"How about we head down to the harborfront, take a walk along the river like we did that first night?"

"Okay."

■ ■ ■

They parked on one of the side streets leading down to the river. It was a cold, gray, overcast day, but there was still enough sun peeking through the clouds to light the late-evening sky with a tinge of faded gold. A gust of wind flapped their coats.

"Man, it's chilly out here," Julie said, snuggling up to Brandon. "But luckily I've got my own personal heating blanket to keep me nice and warm." He kissed her on the cheek. They continued along toward the pavilion.

"Everything looks so different from the way it did that night," Brandon said.

"Yeah, and it's so quiet, too, so peaceful," Julie said. With the exception of a few people out walking or an occasional jogger, the harborfront was almost deserted. "Oh, look, Brandon. There's the little gazebo. Let's go inside." Taking Brandon's hand, Julie led him up the steps of the gazebo. "C'mon, let's dance like we did that night."

"But we don't have any music," he said.

"We don't need any music," she said. "We can pretend."

"They began to slow dance around the gazebo, the only sound being the cry of the doves out over the water. Suddenly, Julie stopped.

"What is it, Julie? What's wrong?"

"Brandon, I'm scared," she said. "If I lost you again, I don't know if I could handle it."

"That's not gonna happen, baby," he said, pulling her to him. "Nothing's ever going to come between us again. I promise."

■ ■ ■

"Go right on in," the church secretary said. "The pastor's expecting you."

"Thank you." Brandon knocked at the door, which was slightly ajar.

"Come on in, man," the Reverend said, getting up from behind his desk to greet him. "Have a seat."

"Thanks."

Mounted on the walls of the Reverend's study were a host of diplomas, certificates and plaques. On his desk, along side a family portrait, was a wooden placard engraved with the inscription *Ye shall know the truth and the truth shall set you free.*

"So, my friend, I see you finally decided to come by and pay us a visit here at Mt. Sinai," the Reverend said. "And on top of that, you joined up with us. I can't tell you how happy I am that you did, especially a young man of your caliber. We need more positive young men like yourself in the church."

"Thank you," Brandon said. "I feel I made the right decision."

"But tell me something," the Reverend said. "When you came forward yesterday, I sensed that something had been troubling you. And you didn't look like you'd been keeping yourself up."

"That's what I wanted to talk to you about," Brandon said. For the next few minutes, he told the Reverend all about losing his job and the whole ordeal he had gone through afterwards.

"Yes, it definitely sounds like you've been through quite a lot over the last few months," the Reverend said. "And I'm glad that you seem to be on the other side of it and that you allowed that inner voice that was speaking to you to direct you to the church. And you definitely have a testimony of God's healing power, the way you say it ministered to you during yesterday's service. But I also want to raise the possibility that— because what you just described has all the characteristics of clinical depression—if at some point you find yourself slipping back into it, you might want to consider some professional treatment. We can arrange it through the church. And it'd all be handled under the strictest of confidence."

"I definitely will, Reverend. Thanks."

"Now, let's talk about your current needs," the Reverend said. "It looks like you're going to need somewhere to stay, at least until you can get back on your feet. Right now you're staying with your neighbor, Gill. Is that right?"

"Yes, but it's only for the next few days, until—" A knock came at the door. "Excuse me," the Reverend said. "Come in." The bass player at Sunday's service entered, a set of keys in his hand.

"Hey, Doc. Sorry for the interruption," the man said, handing the keys to the Reverend.

"That's okay, man," the Reverend said. "Listen, I want you to meet one of the newest members of our church family. Brandon Northcross, this is Joey Blass, that white soul brother that was kicking up all that fuss on that bass guitar yesterday."

"Nice to meet you, man," Joey said, shaking Brandon's hand. "Welcome."

"Thanks," Brandon said. "Nice to meet you, too."

"Well, gotta run, man," Joey said to the Reverend. "Family's calling. You know how it is with a new baby and all."

"How is Debra and the little one?"

"Aw, they're doing just fine, both of 'em. Did I show you the latest picture of him?"

"No, I don't think you did." Joey removed a photo from his wallet.

"Here you go," Joey said, passing the photo to the Reverend.

"Why, look at that handsome little devil," the Reverend said. "I can't believe how much he's grown. You and Debra are gonna have your hands full with him. What's his name again?"

"Donovan Lawrence," Joey said, beaming with pride.

"Well, alright then," the Reverend said. "Show it to Brandon." Joey handed the photo to Brandon.

"Nice-looking family," Brandon said. The woman in the photo was a medium-complexioned black woman; the baby was a shade or two lighter, with most of the mother's features. "I know you're proud. Is it your first?"

"Yep, first one," Joey said, slipping the photo back in his wallet. "Maybe if I'm lucky, we'll get a couple of hours of sleep tonight. Man, that little joker keeps you up."

"I remember what it was like," the Reverend said. "I remember all too well. So, I guess I'll see you Sunday, that is, if you can manage to get enough sleep between now and then."

"I don't know about that," Joey said, chuckling. "But I'll be here, well-rested or not. Take care now, Doc."

"You, too, Joey."

"And it was nice meeting you, man," Joey said to Brandon, clasping his hand.

"Nice meeting you, too." Brandon said.

When Joey was gone, Brandon asked, "How long has Joey been here at the church?"

"Joey? Joey's been here, you might say, practically all his life," the Reverend said. "You see, Joey was orphaned when he was quite young. We took him in when the first four or five orphanages they took him to wouldn't, because they didn't have room. Now, this was before I came here, mind you, and back when the church still ran an orphanage. So, Joey grew up right here in this community. And this community was just as black then as it is now, if not more so. On Sundays, with the exception of an occasional visitor, he's usually the only white person here. But he feels quite comfortable here. It's his home and the people love him like a son. We consider him, I guess you might say, one of our own."

"Well, I know one thing," Brandon said. "He can sure work out on that bass."

"Yeah, he knows what he's doing with that thing, alright. And he learned how to play it right here. He has a band. And from what I hear, they're pretty popular around the area. They're supposed to be releasing their first album pretty soon. But he loves his church. He's a regular tither. And if he's not on the road with his band, he's right here on Sundays and sometimes through the week for mid-week services. Now, as I was about to say, we need to get you situated somewhere, at least until you can get back on your feet. Let me just make a call." The Reverend picked up the phone and dialed.

"Hello, Deaconess Merriweather? David Hollings. How are you?... Good... Say, listen, do you have an extra room at your place? I've got a young man here who could use somewhere to stay for awhile...Yeah. Uh-huh. As early as tomorrow? Okay, let me ask him." He turned to Brandon. "She says you can move in tomorrow, if you like. You interested?"

"Yes. That'll work out just fine," Brandon said.

"Okay." Speaking into the phone again, the Reverend said, "He says tomorrow's fine....Okay...His name is Brandon Northcross....Thank you so much, Deaconess...You, too." He hung up. "Let me give you her address." He wrote the address on a piece of paper and handed it to Brandon. "It's easy to find."

"What's the lady's name again?"

"Deaconess Azalea Merriweather," the Reverend said. "She's a longtime member of the church, retired, who rents out rooms in her house to people trying to get back on their feet. She charges only a nominal fee. You pay whatever you can and the church picks up the rest."

"I appreciate it, Reverend."

"No problem, man. That's what we're here for, helping people get their lives back together. Now, you're gonna need some money. I don't have anything to offer you in your area in the way of employment of course. However, to put some spending money in your pocket in the meantime, there's a job driving the church van that's open. The job entails delivering groceries and prepared meals to the needy. It'd be something just until you could get something better."

"Well, I appreciate the offer," Brandon said. "But I've decided to see if I can't land another job in my field right away. With all the businesses in the Washington area, there's got to be something out there for me."

■ ■ ■

The house was an old, wood frame two-story with a big pecan tree out front. Bordering the sidewalk was a stone wall with wrought-iron ornaments jutting up from the top. Gill waited out at the car while Brandon went to the door and rang the bell. A tall black woman who looked to be in her mid sixties came to the door. The bluish-gray strands intermingled with her jet black hair added to her dignified, matronly appearance. She smiled and opened the door.

"Hello, Deaconess Merriweather?"

"Yes, and you must be Brandon," she said. "Reverend Hollings said you'd be coming by sometime this morning. Come on in." He stepped inside. "I see you've got your things out in your car. Just bring them on in. Your room is upstairs, the second door just off the stairs. As a matter of fact," she said, going over to the staircase, "I'll see if I can't get Lloyd to come give you a hand. That way it'll be a lot quicker. "Lloyd?" she called up the stairs.

In the living room, a woman in her late twenties, her hair in rollers, sat on a couch watching TV. Dressed in a housecoat, she was smoking a cigarette. Deaconess Merriweather turned to her. "Lena, have you seen Lloyd this morning?"

"I thought he was in his room," the woman said, not taking her eyes off the TV. One of the daytime soap operas was on. "But you know how Lloyd is. He have to take them sleeping pills in the middle of the night sometime to sleep, Miss Merriweather. So, he might not be up yet."

"That's right. I forgot all about that, Lena. I shouldn't be disturbing him."

"Yes, ma'am?" a man answered from the top of the stairs.

"Lloyd, honey, that's alright," the Deaconess said. "I was gonna see if you could come down and help our new roomer move his things in. But Lena reminded me that you've been taking your sleep medication. So, we'll manage. You just go on back to bed."

"No, problem," the man said. "I slept good last night, for a change. Just let me throw on some shoes and I'll be right down." While they waited for Lloyd, the Deaconess introduced him to the woman watching TV.

"Brandon, this is Lena. You've been with us now, what, about three months, Lena?"

"Yes, ma'am, just about," the woman said, looking away from the TV for the first time. "How you doing?" Her eyes were dull and listless.

"Fine," Brandon said. "It's nice to meet you." Lloyd now joined them.

"And this is Lloyd," the Deaconess said.

"Hi, I'm Brandon," he said, extending his hand to the man.

"Lloyd," the man said, shaking his hand. "That your stuff out in that station wagon?"

"Yeah. A neighbor of mine is out there waiting."

"While you all get started bringing the things in," the Deaconess said, "I'll go on up and make sure everything's in order in your room."

When they'd finally gotten all of Brandon's things moved in, Deaconess Merriweather brought each of them a cold glass of lemonade and tried to get Gill to stay for lunch.

"I'd love to, ma'am, and I appreciate the lemonade, but unfortunately I've got to get going," Gill said. "I've got a photo shoot across town."

"Well, I can certainly understand that," the Deaconess said. "Your work has to come first. But next time, you plan to stay and have a bite with us, you hear?"

"I certainly will, ma'am. You folks take care now," Gill said, heading out the door. "Be talking to you soon, man."

"See you, Gill," Brandon said. "And thanks again."

A little later, they all sat down together for lunch.

"Okay," the Deaconess said, "let us bow our heads for grace." Everyone lowered their heads. "Lord, we thank you for this food you've blessed us with for the nourishment of our bodies. And we ask that you remember those who may not be as fortunate. In Christ's name we pray, amen."

"Amen," the rest of them added.

"That's one of the things we always try to practice, saying grace before—"

"Miss Merriweather, ain't it no more chicken salad left?" Lena said, looking over the sandwiches.

"Excuse me," the Deaconess said.

"Huh?"

"I said excuse me. I was talking, Lena."

"Aw, excuse me, Miss Merriweather."

"And, no, I don't think there's anymore chicken salad. I've got to put it on my list of things to buy when I go grocery shopping."

"Would've been some left, if Lloyd, with his ol' greedy self, hadna ate it all up," Lena said.

"Girl, you oughta be shame of yo'self," Lloyd shot back. "As much as you like to eat, I'm surprised it was any left for me *to* eat up."

"Lloyd, you the one—"

"Lena? Lloyd?" the Deaconess broke in. "Let's not argue at the table, now."

"I'm sorry, Miss Merriweather," Lena said. "But Lloyd know he ate that chicken salad."

"Shh!" the Deaconess said. Lloyd made a face at Lena, who stuck out her tongue at him. "You two behave now. Okay, before we eat, why don't we tell a little about ourselves, let Brandon get to know us? I'll start. I'm a retired school teacher, taught in the public schools here in D.C. for thirty-three years. My husband and I moved into this house a year after my oldest son was born. I've got two boys. One's a doctor, lives in St. Louis. The other is an architect. He lives up in Philadelphia. When my husband passed back in '82, I decided to rent out several of the rooms to boarders, especially people trying to get back on their feet. I also give piano lessons, only part-time now, though. Okay, who wants to go next? How about you, Lena?"

"Let Lloyd go next," Lena said, bashfully, dropping her gaze to her lap.

"Okay, Lloyd, you want to go next?"

"Alright. Ah, let's see," Lloyd said, his head bowed.

"Just tell something about yourself, that's all," the Deaconess said. "Just whatever you want to share."

"Okay. My full name is Lloyd Demitrius Green. I was raised and grew up here in D.C. I got two brothers and one sister that's livin'. Two of my brothers, they dead now. My momma, she died a few years ago. I ain't never known my daddy. I'm just tryin' to get things back together." He nervously fidgeted with his napkin. "See, I been away for a couple of years."

"You was in jail," Lena said. "That's where you was away at."

"Alright, Lena," the Deaconess said. "Let Lloyd tell his own story."

"Yes, ma'am."

"Yeh, I did time," Lloyd confessed. "That's right. For stealin' cars. Before that, it was for other things, mostly little petty stuff. See, I dropped outta school when I was in the tenth grade. And since that time it seem like I done always been in some kinda trouble with the law, mostly for stealin'. But, like I said, I'm tryin' to turn things around now."

"Tell Brandon about how you're going back to school, Lloyd," the Deaconess said.

"Aw, yeah," Lloyd said, looking up for the first time. "I'm goin' to night school to get my GED."

"And we're proud of Lloyd," the Deaconess said. "He's come a long way. And he's in church now, too."

"Yeh, I'm in church now, too. That's a big difference from how it was before. I think I can make it now."

"And with God's help you can," the Deaconess said. "Okay, Lena?"

"Ma'am?"

"Your turn." Her head still bowed, Lena began.

"Well, my name is Lena Stansberry and I'm originally from the Bronx. I been down here in D.C. for 'bout the last three years. I done had some problems with drugs, mostly crack. Right now, I'm waitin' to get in a drug rehab program. I was in one before, but it didn't work out. I'm hopin' this next time, though, it'll be different. Ah, let's see," she said, toying with her bracelet. "I recently had a baby. But it was a crack baby.

The state put it in foster care. I got another child, a little boy. He just turned four. He livin' with my mother down in North Carolina. And, well, just like Lloyd said, I'm tryin' to get myself together, too."

"And we're praying for that to happen, too," the Deaconess added. "Okay, Brandon?"

"My name is Brandon Northcross. I'm from Manchester, New Hampshire. I've been living here in the D.C. area now for a little over six months. There're a lot of things I could tell you about myself, like where I went to school, my parents, and other things. But I guess the one thing I want to say is that I'm trying to get my life back together, too. I moved down here thinking things were one way, as far as people go, and I found out I'd been seeing things blindly practically all my life. I ended up going through a lot of serious changes because of it. I've never been in jail. And I've never been hooked on drugs. But I do know what it's like to be so down and feel so hopeless that you don't even want to go on living. So, I'm looking to rebound in my own way, too."

"Thank you, Brandon," the Deaconess said. "Okay, we can eat now."

Chapter 16

*B*rrrriiiiinng! *Brrrriiiiinng!* Brandon was awakened early the next morning by the loud, metallic ringing of the alarm clock next to his bed. *Brrrriiiiinng! Brrrriiiiinng!* He reached over and shut it off. With the heavy quilt pulled over him, he lay there, reluctant to abandon its warmth on this cold, winter's day. He began to think of all the things he had to do that day. First, he would go by the library to check out the job listings in the newspapers and job databases. Next, he'd spend some time working on his resume, then go by the Unemployment Office to see about filing for unemployment. Around noon he was meeting Julie for lunch. And there were still some things at his old apartment that he needed to get. Later, he was to be baptized at church. As he continued to contemplate his agenda for the day, he became aware that he was drifting off to sleep again. Tossing the covers aside, he swung his legs over the side of the bed and catapulted up.

■ ■ ■

The prayer service was just wrapping up when he arrived at church. Deacon Sanders was up front at the microphone. "The prayer and testimony portion of the service is now over and we are now going to move into the baptismal portion. Are the candidates present?" Brandon and the others who were there raised their hands. "Would you all go with Mother McGowan and Mother Childress at this time to prepare for the water?"

The candidates followed Mother McGowan and Mother Childress to the dressing rooms behind the baptismal pool, where they changed into their baptismal clothes. When they were all ready, the two old women prayed mightily for them, laying hands on them. They were then led single file out to the pool, which was up in the choir loft. Out in the sanctuary, the congregation was singing solemnly.

Take me to the water.
Take me to the water.
Take me to the water to be baptized.

The Reverend and one of the deacons, both dressed in black robes with white towels draped over their shoulders, waited in the pool. The Reverend signaled for the first candidate, a young girl. Mother McGowan helped her down the steps into the pool. The singing hushed.

"Tamara Allen, do you love the Lord?" the Reverend asked.

"Yes, sir." The Reverend raised his right hand.

"Now, my sister, in obedience to that great commandment, I baptize you in the name of the Father, the Son and the Holy Ghost. Placing his hand over the girl's nose and mouth, he dipped her back down into the water and brought her back up. The singing started again.

I love Jesus.
I love Jesus.
I love Jesus.
Yes, I do.

When it came Brandon's turn, the Reverend received him down into the pool.

"Brandon Northcross, do you love the Lord?"

"Yes, I do." With his right hand high in the air, the Reverend made his pronouncements.

"Now, my brother, in obedience to that great commandment, I baptize you in the name of the Father, the Son and the Holy Ghost."

As the Reverend took him back, the water closed in over his head. At that instance, time suddenly suspended and darkness enveloped him. Then a glimmer of light broke through. In front of him stretched a vast body of sparkling water the color of sapphire. Hovering just above the surface of the water, but off in the distance, was a pulsing white light, a light brighter than any he'd ever seen. This light was beckoning him. A warmth radiated from it, a warmth that made him feel good all over. He wanted to be with this light. Just as he started toward it, he began to hear voices behind him, familiar voices. They were calling to him. Looking back, he saw that it was his parents, his former school teachers, his childhood friends and others. They were standing back on the banks calling to him, begging him not to go, not to leave them. He didn't want to leave them, but he felt he had to. He had no other choice. He began to move toward the light, gliding just above the water, closer and closer. Just as he was about to reach out and touch it, he broke through the surface of the water. The singing began anew.

None but the righteous.
None but the righteous.
None but the righteous shall see God.

■ ■ ■

During the next few weeks, buoyed by his newfound optimism, Brandon set about the business of finding a new job. The same bright shades of hope and unlimited possibility that had colored his world back in August once again burst back upon the canvas of his life. Each morning he would get up, get the daily newspaper and go through the job listings. Then he'd go down to the Unemployment Office and search their databases, as well as those at the library. Then he'd start responding to ads, either calling prospective employers or sending out his resume. He even attended a couple of local job fairs. Through his efforts, he was able to line up a number of interviews. But, for one reason or another, nothing ever came of them. At each place that he applied, it was always the same story. If the job wasn't already filled, he either didn't have the right qualifications or he didn't have enough experience. Even when he got a positive response over the phone from an employer, telling him, 'Yes, we could definitely use someone like you,' when he showed up and they took a look at his application, it was the same thing all over again. A mistake had been made. Either the job had already been filled or they had felt the need to look at other candidates before making a decision. He would be extended the sincerest of apologies for any inconvenience their oversight had caused him.

Was racism behind it? It was quite possible, he now realized. What he *did* know was that it wasn't because CSU was giving him a bad reference. Personnel had assured him that the only information they ever gave out on an employee was the person's job title and dates of employment.

After a couple of weeks of continued rejection, discouragement began to set in. He tried to remain confident, however, that something would soon open up. But there was little that positive thinking could do about the fact that his money was again running low, even with the money his father had given him. Because of the terms of his dismissal, he had been denied unemployment benefits. And Julie had already made him one loan. He wasn't about to allow her to make him another one. Once or twice he considered taking the job at the church, just to make ends meet, but decided against it, for he was still certain that he'd find work any day now. In the meantime, he tried keeping his mind occupied by focusing on other things.

■ ■ ■

"Reverend, would you bless the food?"

"Let us bow our heads," the Reverend said. "Heavenly Father, we thank you for this food that we're now about to receive. We ask that you bless it and consecrate it so it might be nourishing to our bodies. This we ask in Jesus' name. Amen."

"Reverend, thank you for joining us for dinner," the Deaconess said. "And you, too, Julie. By the way, how'd you like the service today?"

"I loved it," Julie said. "I really did. The singing, the Reverend's preaching, everything. It was just great. I've visited white churches before, but their services were nothing like today's, especially the singing. It was so moving."

"Aw, I bet white people could sing like that if they wanted to," the Reverend said. "Don't you think so, with a little practice maybe?"

"No, Reverend," Julie said, smiling, "I don't think so, not in a million years. White people just can't sing like that."

"Deaconess Merriweather," the Reverend said, "what was the name of that church that visited us—"

"Awight, Lloyd," Lena interrupted. "Why you take the last drumstick?"

"What?" Lloyd retorted. "Ain't my fault you didn't get no drumstick this time."

"I woulda, if you hadna took all of 'em. Soon as the chicken get set out on the table, you go grab every drumstick on the plate you can get your hands—"

"Lena!" the Deaconess said.

"But, Miss Merriweather, Lloyd took the last drumstick. He always do that. He do that just so I can't get one." The Deaconess sighed heavily.

"Lloyd, will you give Lena one of your drumsticks, please?"

"Why I gotta—"

"Please? That's the only way she's gonna to be happy."

"Yes, ma'am." Begrudgingly, Lloyd forked over a drumstick to Lena's plate. "Huh, girl." Lena made a face at him. "You see that, Miss Merriweather? She made a face at me, after I done went and gave her one my drumsticks."

"I ain't made no face at him, Miss Merriweather," Lena said. "Lloyd just making stuff up, just 'cause he ain't wanna—"

"Alright!" the Deaconess said. "That's it! Now, the two of you just behave yourselves. We've got company and I'm not gonna be putting up with this foolishness. I'm sorry. Now what were you saying, Reverend?"

"Oh, no problem," the Reverend said. "I was just asking if you remembered that white church that visited us a couple of years ago, the one with the swinging choir."

"Oh, yes. I certainly do."

"Now, those were some singing white folks," the Reverend said. "I don't know where they got it from, but they had some soul in them. Yes, sirree. And they had some rhythm, too. They were rocking like some black folks up in there." The Reverend demonstrated. "Weren't they, Deaconess Merriweather?"

"Now, Reverend, I don't know if they were doing all that," the Deaconess said, laughing.

"But they had it together," the Reverend insisted.

"Maybe it was the two or three black people they had with them," the Deaconess said.

"Maybe so," the Reverend said. "But whatever it was, they were doing some singing. Back home, Julie, we call it *sanging*. And I bet their pastor was a hooper, too. What do you think, Deaconess?"

"Now, Reverend, you know you oughta quit," the Deaconess said, stifling a laugh.

"You don't know what hooping is, do you, Julie?" the Reverend asked.

"Isn't that what some black preachers do when they close out their sermons?" Brandon said.

"Yeah," the Reverend said. "That's when you sing it out. That's hooping. Now, I'm not a hooper. But we have some come through Mt. Sinai every now and then. We're having one coming up for Spring Revival, one of them old-time, country hoopers."

"I think I'd like to hear him," Julie said.

"Well, you have Brandon bring you," the Reverend said. "It'll be in April, about the last week of the month."

"I'll put it on my calendar," Julie said.

"Who was that preacher, Reverend, that tore it up last month durin' early mornin' service?" Lloyd said. "He was from Mississippi, I think."

"Oh, Lloyd, you're talking about Charles McCray," the Reverend said. "He's a preaching machine, that Charles McCray. Yeah, now he was a hooper. Deaconess Merriweather, she doesn't go in a lot for that hooping stuff, do you, Deaconess?"

"No, Reverend, you're right," she said. "I'm not a big fan of it. But if the Lord's behind it, then fine."

"Well, I'm glad Mt. Sinai's not one of those churches that was raised on hooping, 'cause like I said, I'm not a hooper."

"I've heard you hoop before, Reverend," the Deaconess said. "And you can hoop with the best of them, when you want to."

"Well, thank you, Deaconess," the Reverend said. "But I'm more of the lecturer type."

"Well, you're certainly excellent, Reverend Hollings," Julie said. "I really enjoyed your sermon today."

"Thank you, Julie," the Reverend said. "Well, we've been doing so much talking here, more talking than eating, that we'd better get going, before ol' Lloyd eats up the rest of all this good chicken."

"Yeh, you right, Reverend," Lena said. "Lloyd know he like him some chicken. While y'all been talkin', Lloyd been cleanin' up." They all laughed.

Chapter 17

The first week of April, people flocked to the Tidal Basin to view the blooming of the Cherry Blossom trees. A windy rainstorm blew through the area a few days later, covering the Basin in a sea of soft, pink petals. With the advent of spring, Brandon felt a renewed sense of optimism at his chances at landing a job. Something had to give. That something gave one day the following week when he was offered a position with a brokerage house in downtown D.C. A couple of days after interviewing with the company, they'd called and made him an offer and he'd accepted. It was arranged for him to start work that Monday afternoon. The afternoon was chosen because his new boss, Dorothy Farrell, wouldn't be in until then.

On the way up in the elevator, he checked his appearance in the mirrored doors. Yes, he'd known it'd be only a matter of time before something opened up for him. It wasn't Big Red, but it was a start. And maybe a smaller company would be better for him, anyway, give him more of a chance to stand out. In any event, he was back in the saddle. He knew the rules now and knew how to play the game. He was ready. The elevator doors opened. Well, this is it, he thought. Straight ahead, through a set of glass doors, was the receptionist.

"Good afternoon, sir," the woman said. "May I help you?"

"Yes, I'm here to see Dorothy Farrell."

"And your name?" she said, as she dialed.

"Brandon Northcross."

"Thank you." Brandon took a seat.

A few minutes later, Dorothy Farrell came out to greet him.

"Brandon?" she said, offering him her hand. "Dorothy Farrell."

"Nice to meet you," he said.

"My office is right this way," she said, leading the way. "I can't tell you how happy I am to have you joining us, Brandon. Your interview with Erin went really well, from what she told me. Actually, I don't know why she decided to wait and defer the hiring decision to me. You were by far our most impressive candidate for the position."

"I'm glad to hear that," Brandon said.

They went down a plush corridor through another set of double doors and into the inner offices. Ahead was Dorothy Farrell's office, her name on the door. In the area just outside the office was her administrative staff.

"I put the file you requested on your desk, Dorothy," the woman seated closest to the office said. "And this is a call that just came for you." She handed Dorothy Farrell a slip of paper.

"Thanks, Peggy. Oh, let me introduce you to the newest addition to the department. This is Brandon Northcross. He's going to be taking over Kelly's old position."

"Nice to meet you, Brandon," Peggy said.

"Nice to meet you, too, Peggy."

"Come in and have a seat, Brandon," Dorothy said, ushering him into her office. She offered him a chair in front of her desk and closed the door. "Okay. The first thing we're going to do to get you started is have you fill out the usual forms. After we get those out of the way, I'll show you around a bit. How's that?"

"Fine." The woman removed some forms from inside her desk and handed them to Brandon.

"What we've got here are just the standard tax withholding forms. I'm sure you're familiar with—" A knock came at the door. "Yes?" The door opened. It was Peggy, her secretary. She had a slightly worried look on her face. "What is it, Peggy?"

"I'm sorry for the interruption, Dorothy, but could I see you for a moment?"

"Can it wait a few minutes? I'm right in the middle of—" Some sort of signal from Peggy, which he didn't see, cut the woman off. "Excuse me for just a moment," Dorothy Farrell said, getting up and going to the door. "I'll be right back."

What was it about? Could it be something about him? She had left the door ajar, so he was able to peer out at them from his chair. Although he couldn't hear what Peggy was saying, he could tell by her facial expressions that whatever she was saying wasn't of a very pleasant nature. And as she spoke, she kept nodding toward the office. Whatever it was, he'd find out soon enough.

When Dorothy Farrell returned, she smiled, then closed the door and took her seat behind the desk.

"I don't really know how to tell you this," she began, nervously looking from Brandon's face to her hands, which were clasped in front of her, "but, well, it seems we're not going to be able to have you fill the position after all. You see, I didn't know it, but the job's already been filled. I was unaware that one of the other managers had already filled the slot with another candidate. That's what Peggy was just telling me. I can't tell you how sorry I am that this..." He was no longer listening to the words coming from the woman's mouth, as he sat stunned, fighting to contain the anger that was building inside him. This was like all the other rejections he had gotten, false leads that ended up taking him nowhere. Only this was worse. He had actually been hired, and then had had the job cruelly snatched from under him. Yes, she was lying. The job hadn't been filled. They just didn't want him to work there. And the only reason he could think of was that he was black. It hadn't been enough simply to deny him; they were now making sport of him, toying with him. Indignation flared in him, as he jumped to his feet.

"You're lying!" he shouted. "I don't believe a word you're saying! You don't want me to work here simply because I'm black! That's all to it!" The woman froze, as she stared at him wide-eyed. Then very slowly, and carefully, she got up and stepped behind her chair.

"Look, I think you'd better just leave, young man." The door to the office opened. It was Peggy.

"Is there a problem, Dorothy?" Brandon was standing over the desk, his eyes pinning the woman to the wall behind her.

"I'll leave," he said. "But I'm going to hire a lawyer and sue you and this company for discrimination! You can bet on that!" Snatching up his briefcase, he stormed out of the office.

■ ■ ■

Back out on the street, as he headed up the block, still boiling inside, he heard someone calling his name.

"Mr. Northcross! Mr. Northcross!" When he looked back, he saw that it was one of the women from Dorothy Farrell's administrative staff running to catch up with him.

"What do you want?" he said, tersely, when the woman drew near.

"I need to talk to you," she said. "It's about why Dorothy Farrell didn't keep you on."

"What about it?"

"It's not the way you think. It wasn't because you're black."

"Did she send you to tell me that, because she's afraid I'll make good on my threat to sue?"

"No, you've got it all wrong," the woman said, shaking her head. "She didn't send me after you. She doesn't even know I'm out here. But believe me, it's not like you think."

"Well, if race wasn't the reason, then what was?" She hesitated. "Well?"

"Okay, if you really must know, I'll tell you," she said, finally. "But if I'm ever asked about this, I'll deny it. I swear I will. Anyway, it's like this. When you came in today, Dorothy had every intention of having you fill the position."

"Yeah, I know," he said. "But they'd already hired somebody else. That's what you want me to believe, right?"

"No, please listen," she said. "What Dorothy didn't know was that your name was on a reject list. She'd been out for the past week, so she hadn't seen it when she called to offer you the job."

"What do you mean, a reject list?"

"A reject list," she said. "A black list. For some reason, you've been blacklisted."

"Blacklisted?" The word reverberated through his head like an echo.

"I don't know why or by who," the woman said. "But whoever it is, they've probably blacklisted you throughout the Washington area. Again, you didn't hear any of this from me." He opened his mouth to speak, but no words would come out. He didn't want to believe the woman, yet he knew she was telling the truth. It was Bob. Bob had blacklisted him. "Look, I have to get back before they miss me. I'm sorry." She touched him on the arm in a consoling manner, then turned and hurried away. As he stood there, a feeling of hopelessness began to overtake him.

■ ■ ■

Over the next several weeks, he began to withdraw back into his shell. During the day he would wander the streets, not returning home until late at night when he was certain everyone was already asleep. He would then leave out again early in the morning before anyone had risen. Julie left phone messages for him, but he never returned her calls. When he was home, he stayed to himself in his bedroom. All his will to fight had been drained from him. He felt so lost that even when he tried to pray, he couldn't. What was the use? He had been naive to think that he could fight against the system and win. And it wasn't just Bob. It was all those who had gone along with it, even the woman who had supposedly risked her job to inform him that he had been blacklisted. It was the whole system, the whole white system. The deck was stacked against him and always would be. Once again, thoughts of suicide began to tap at the window of his mind.

One day as he lay on his bed staring up at the ceiling, he decided that he couldn't take it anymore. There was no question anymore what he had to do, only how. After thinking about it for awhile, Brandon remembered the sleeping pills that Lloyd kept in the bathroom medicine cabinet. There'd be no pain. It would be just like falling asleep. Quietly, he went down the hall to the bathroom. Opening the medicine cabinet, he reached for the place on the shelf where he had always seen the familiar green bottle of pills. His hand froze in mid-air. It wasn't there. Frantically, he began to search for it. Then he spotted it, behind a can of shaving cream. The bottle was nearly full. He removed it and turned to lock the bathroom door. But as he did, he accidentally knocked a jar of cold cream off the sink. It made a loud thump on the floor, but didn't break. He picked it up, then sat down on the toilet seat. The face looking back at him in the floor-to-ceiling mirror was like that of a stranger.

After prying the cap off the bottle, he emptied half a dozen of the little white pills into his palm. How many would he need to take? If he took too few, he'd probably only make himself ill. He'd take them all. With a glass of water in his hand, he stared at the pills, trying to push everything from his mind except what he was about to do. Then, in one swift motion, he threw his head back and popped them into his mouth. He followed with several gulps of water. Not allowing himself time to back out, he repeated the process again and again, until he had swallowed all the pills in the bottle. There, he'd done it. All that was left was for him to wait for the pills to begin to work.

But after nearly ten minutes, nothing had happened. He could feel no effect from the pills. He started to get up. But about halfway up from the seat, he felt a hard, downward tug on his body, like a heavy anvil had suddenly been strapped to him, forcing him back down on the seat. At the same time, a powerful drowsiness overtook him, making it difficult for him to keep his eyes open. His vision began to blur and he began to lose his balance on the seat. The drinking glass slipped from his hands to the tile floor with a loud plink. No longer able to maintain his balance, he felt himself sliding forward off the seat. He could see in the mirror his image coming to meet him. Or was it the other way around? After slamming face-first into the mirror, he fell heavily to the floor, ending up on his side.

"You alright in there?" It was Lena. She knocked on the door.

"What was that noise coming from the bathroom, Lena?" the Deaconess said. "Sounded like somebody fell."

"I don't know," Lena said. "Won't nobody answer."

"Is that you in there, Brandon?" the Deaconess called through the door. Then he heard the door open. "Lord! What happened!? Did you slip and fall?" He felt her hands on him, gently rolling him over. He could barely open his eyes.

"Look, Miss Merriweather!" he heard Lena exclaim. "This Lloyd's bottle of sleeping pills. And they all gone!"

"What!? No! No!" the Deaconess screamed. "Lena, call an ambulance! Hurry, now, child!"

"Yes, ma'am." Brandon heard Lena's quick footsteps as she left the bathroom. Then he heard Lloyd's voice. Soon, he became aware that his heart beat was slowing and that a numbness was gradually spreading over his body. When he opened his mouth to speak, the muscles that controlled his speech refused to respond. Time began to slow.

"They say they on their way, Ms. Merriweather," he heard Lena say from what seemed like across the street. Everything then faded to black.

■ ■ ■

When he came to, the bright lights overhead, magnified by the white walls, assaulted his eyes. Almost immediately he became aware of a terrible, knotting pain in his stomach. It felt like his insides had been scraped raw with sandpaper. Still shielding his eyes from the light with one hand, he tried to prop himself up with the other.

"Just take it easy now, young man," the doctor said. "You've been through quite an ordeal." The man coaxed him back down to the bed. "Let's just take a look here." He pulled back one of Brandon's eyelids and shined his penlight into the eye. He did the same with the other eye.

"What day is it?" Brandon asked.

"Thursday," the doctor said, continuing to concentrate on what he was doing. There was a knock at the door, then a nurse stuck her head in. The doctor clicked off his penlight and turned to the woman.

"Yes, nurse?"

"Doctor, can he receive any visitors yet? There're some people here who want to see him. They've been waiting since this morning. I told them I'd check with you to see if it was okay."

"How many?"

"Three."

"Okay, but just for a minute."

Julie was the first one through the door, followed by the Deaconess and the Reverend.

"Hey, baby," she cried, rushing over and hugging him.

"Hey," he said, hugging her back. They embraced for a long while. Then Julie leaned back and looked at him.

"Brandon, why didn't you tell me what was going on? Why didn't you talk to somebody?" He reached up and smoothed her hair back from her face. She kissed his hand and held it to her face. "I love you."

"I'm sorry," he said. "I guess I just couldn't see any other way at the time. I realize now how stupid it was." He looked over at the Deaconess and the Reverend who were standing on the other side of the bed.

"Come on and give me a hug, too," the Deaconess said, bending over to embrace him. "I'm so happy that our prayers were answered." She released him, then scowled. "The next time you think about doing something like this, you talk to somebody. You hear? If I had my switch with me, I'd give you a good whipping, scaring us like that."

"Yes, ma'am, I think I'd help hold the young man while you tanned him a good one," the doctor said.

"Hey, man," the Reverend said, giving him a firm handshake. "I echo the Deaconess' sentiments. You scare us like this again, I'm gon give you one of them good, old-fashioned whippings like the kind my daddy used to give us out in the country when I was a boy. Ain't gon use no little switch, either. But seriously, man, we're glad that the Lord smiled on us and brought you back. While you were out of it, people from the church, as well as your friends, came by to check on you."

"Yeah, Gill and Sean dropped by, Brandon," Julie said. "Those who couldn't make it, either called or sent cards or flowers." She motioned toward a small table where a number of cards and floral arrangements were sitting.

"And Julie," the Deaconess said, "bless her heart, stayed all through the first night, and wanted to stay the second night, too. But we made her go home and get some sleep so she wouldn't be falling asleep at work."

"I…I don't know what to say," Brandon said.

"That's alright, man," the Reverend said. "You don't have to say anything. We're all human and we get weak sometimes. We just thank God that he brought you through it. That's enough in itself."

"Amen," the Deaconess said.

"Oh, by the way," the Reverend added, "we tried contacting your mother. Actually, we did reach her, but she seemed a little under the weather at the time." He knew what had happened. They had called and she had been intoxicated, probably too out of it to make sense of what they were saying.

"My mother has a drinking problem," Brandon confessed. "She sometimes goes on these binges."

"I understand," the Reverend said. "But we were able to get in touch with a family friend, a Mrs. Raphael. She says she's going to arrange to come down with your mother. They might even be getting here as early as today."

"Thanks, Reverend."

"So, Doctor," the Reverend said, "what's next on the agenda for your patient?"

"Well," the doctor said, hanging his clipboard at the end of the bed, "we've pumped him out pretty good. Right now, we've got him on Narcaine. I want to try and get that stomach back into some kind of reasonable shape before we let him go. Then with the approval of our staff psychiatrist, we ought to be able to have him out of here in three to four days. Of course, part of the treatment is that he be set up for some outpatient counseling."

"We can arrange that through the church," the Reverend said.

"That should do just fine, then," the doctor said. "As for now, I'm afraid I'm going to have to bring our little visit to an end. I want him to try to get as much rest as possible these next few days."

"We understand," the Reverend said. "Brandon, you take care now. And call me at the church or at home—you have both numbers—should you need anything."

"Same here," the Deaconess said.

"Just remember one thing, baby," Julie said, caressing his hand. "I love you." She gave him a kiss.

"Love you, too," he said.

Chapter 18

Draped across the front of the house was a big banner that read, *Welcome Home, Brandon!* Waiting out on the porch was the Deaconess, the Reverend, Gill, Lisa, Lloyd and Lena. As he and Julie started up the walkway together, Lisa ran out to meet them.

"Brandon! Brandon!" Brandon swept her up in his arms and whirled her around.

"Hey, Lisa! How's my favorite girl?"

"Fine."

Up on the porch, he was greeted warmly by everyone.

"You all make me feel like it's my birthday or something," Brandon said.

"Well, it is, in a way," the Deaconess replied. "You're starting the first day of the rest of your life today. That's how we look at it. We've even got a cake inside for you."

"And, naturally, Lisa made us get ice cream to go with it," Gill said.

"Excuse me, everybody," the Reverend said. "But, Brandon, I think there's somebody inside you might want to see, who I know wants to see you." Then he signaled for someone to come out. A tall, middle-aged black man slowly stepped out onto the porch. They stood just looking at each other for a long while, before finally rushing toward each other and embracing.

"My son," the man said, choking back tears.

"Folks, why don't we go on in and let these two do some catching up," the Reverend said, holding open the door. They all went inside, leaving Brandon and his father alone.

"Let me get a good look at you, boy," his father said, holding Brandon back from him. "The Reverend told me all about what you been through since moving down here, about you losing your job and all, and about all the prejudice you ran up against. And then this thing with the pills." The man paused for a moment, taking a deep breath to try to compose himself, before going on. "I just wish I had it to do all over again."

"But—"

"Just let me finish this," his father said. "I let your mother convince me that it was best that you not know about what we'd had to go through in our day, with segregation and all. But I can't put the blame entirely on her. I should've insisted that you know where you came from, what it'd been like for us in our day. I can't help thinking that if I'd been around these last few years for you, stuck it out, in spite of your mother's drinking… But then when I lost my job, I guess I felt like I couldn't be the man I thought I ought to be, the breadwinner and all."

"I just thought it was partly because of me that you left. I always thought it was because I couldn't be the son you wanted me to be. But I tried—"

"Don't you believe that for minute, boy," his father said. "You're the best son a father could have. I want you to know that. I've never been good at admitting when I was wrong, but I'm starting right now. It was me. I was too stubborn to see it then, that you had your own way. But I want you to know, and this is the honest-to-God truth, that I never—even when you didn't hear from me—I never stopped loving you, boy. Wherever I was, I kept a picture of you nearby at all times. Even though I didn't always say it, you've always been my pride and joy." They hugged again. His father then backed away and took out a handkerchief. "I bet this is the first time you ever seen your old man cry, huh?" he said, patting his eyes with his handkerchief.

"Yeah," Brandon replied, wiping his own eyes.

"Well, I guess we better go on in and join the others before they eat up all that cake and ice cream," his father said, with a grin.

That evening, after seeing his father off at the airport, Brandon called the Reverend to see if the job driving the church van was still available.

"Sure, man," the Reverend said, "it's still available. Deacon Williams, he's been pitching in driving it when he can, but we still need somebody full-time."

"Great. When can I start?"

■ ■ ■

The next morning, Brandon reported to the church to begin his new job. After a briefing from Mrs. Triplett, the church secretary, and taking some time to familiarize himself with a map of the area, he loaded up the van and set out on his first run. As the Reverend had explained, many of those he made deliveries to were either elderly or homebound. Others were those on some form of public assistance whose food stamps had run out.

At the end of the day, he returned the van to the church and took the keys up to the office. The office staff had left for the day, but the Reverend was still there. Brandon tapped on the open door.

"Oh, hey, man," the Reverend said. "Come on in. How'd it go today?"

"Oh, just fine, Reverend," Brandon said, stepping inside. "Didn't mean to disturb you, but I wasn't sure what to do with the van keys."

"You can just leave them with me," the Reverend said, accepting the keys. "So, have you had a chance yet to think about what you're going to do now, long-term?"

"I'm considering a couple of options," Brandon said. "One is to relocate to Atlanta where my father is. He says the job market's pretty good there. I also might go back to New Hampshire."

"Well, I think you're going about it the right way," the Reverend said. "No need to rush into anything right away. Give yourself time to recoup." A painting on the wall of the Last Supper caught Brandon's attention. "That painting fascinate you?"

"Yes, I don't think I've ever seen a picture of the Last Supper quite like it."

"You mean with black men in it?"

"Well, yeah. Just like the crucifix with the black Jesus that's up over the choir loft. Every picture I've ever seen of Jesus, he's white."

"I know," the Reverend said. "It's like that for most people. It's pretty much a shock to people at first, black people included, to see prominent figures of the bible, not to mention Jesus himself, portrayed as black."

"So, are you saying, then, that Jesus was actually black?"

"Well, I don't know if I can answer that with a definite yes or no. You got a minute?"

"Sure."

"Have a seat," the Reverend said. "I'll tell you a little about it." Brandon grabbed a chair. "Now, from what we know historically about Jesus, his lineage, his place of birth, where he lived, it's pretty much accepted among theologians and historians alike that Jesus was not of Caucasian descent. In other words, he was not a white man as we know race today. Some go so far as to say outright that he was a black man. I don't know if that can ever really be proven. But what I think is clear is that he was of mixed ancestry, what you'd call a mestizo. So, in any event, he was definitely a person of color. And that's hard for a lot of people to deal with, especially white people. They can deal with him being a Jew or that he might have been Asian. But you start saying he might have been black, and that's generally where they draw the line."

"Why do you think that is, Reverend?"

"Well, for white people to accept the idea that Jesus might have been a black man, that would mean they'd have to get beyond all the negative stereotypes that have been perpetuated about black people down through the years. And I don't believe white people, at least most of them, are quite ready to do that."

"So, Jesus probably looked more like you and me?" Brandon said, studying the painting again.

"Most likely," the Reverend said. "It's the same when it comes to the disciples. When you look at the geographical regions they came from, there's no way around the fact that many of them were people of color, too. And some of them very dark-skinned."

"In every movie I've ever seen about the bible, the only black people I ever remember seeing were slaves," Brandon said.

"The people who run Hollywood design it that way," the Reverend said. "They don't want you to know, for instance, things like the Egyptians back in biblical times would be considered black people today, and that most of the Pharaohs were black. They didn't look like Yul Brenner. And Moses probably didn't look like Charlton Heston, either. What do you think might have happened if black people years ago, I mean ordinary black people, had known this? They might not have been as patient with being treated as second-class citizens for as long as they were. That's one possibility, right?"

"Yeah. It's definitely something to think about."

"Listen, if you're interested in reading more about this," the Reverend said, "I can recommend a couple of good books on the subject. As a matter of fact, you can borrow my copies."

Brandon stayed up well into the night reading the books the Reverend had loaned him. Suddenly, a thirst for knowledge, knowledge about black people, began to spring up in him. He wanted to know everything he could about his heritage.

■ ■ ■

Every other day or so when he'd finish a book, he'd return it and borrow another. Soon, he began checking out books from the library. When he'd get off work each day, he would immediately submerge himself in his reading. The books dealt not only with black history, but other subjects, such as American and world history, political science, and anthropology. But of all his readings, he became most fascinated with the teachings of Malcolm X. He read every book he could get his hands on that had anything to do with him. He even memorized excerpts from some of his speeches. Often, when he'd return to the church in the evening, he'd sit and talk with the Reverend about what he'd read.

"I've been reading about the sit-ins back during the '60s," Brandon said, one evening. "How well do you remember them?"

"The sit-ins?" the Reverend said. "I remember them quite well. I was a part of them. I was a college student at Fisk at the time. You remember reading about the sit-ins in Greensboro, North Carolina at the Woolworth lunch counter?"

"Yeah. Wasn't this in 1960?"

"Yep, February of 1960," the Reverend said. "Well, not long after that, sit-ins started up in other places throughout the South. One of those places was Nashville, Tennessee. I was involved in those sit-ins, the ones at the lunch counters in Nashville. We were all a part of what was called the Nashville Student Movement, which was closely allied with SNCC."

"The Student Nonviolent Coordinating Committee," Brandon said.

"That's right."

"What was it like being involved in the sit-ins?"

"Well, we had to deal with a lot of harassment. That was the main thing."

"What sort of things would happen?"

"Oh, at lunch counters, we'd have stuff like sugar and ketchup poured on us, be cursed and spit on, things like that. They'd call you all kinds of names, like coon, porch monkey, spook—and nigger, too, of course. I remember one time, one ol' boy plastered me and this girl sitting next to me, Carolyn Sanderford, with a whole bottle of ketchup, just showered us with it, totally ruined my shirt. It was one of those silk shirts with the long, pointed collars that were real popular at the time. It was lime green with white trim. I didn't mind so much the ketchup on me, but not on my favorite shirt. I wanted to get up and tag that joker a good one right in the jaw when he did that. Yeah, that white boy tested my nonviolence to the max that day. Sometimes, though, it got worst, like when you'd get slapped or even punched."

"Is there one particular incident that stands out in your mind?"

"I'd say the one incident that stands out most in my mind was when this white guy spit on this girl named Arnella and called her out of her name, called her a black something. I don't remember what the term is he used, but something real derogatory. Well, Arnella, schooled in non-violence like we all were, just held her tongue, didn't say or do a thing, just took a napkin, wiped the spit off her face and just sat there. That would have probably been the end of it. But her boyfriend, this guy named Jimmy Rayford, happened to be out on the sidewalk with the rest of the crowd looking in through the window at what was going on. And Jimmy wasn't 'bout no nonviolence. No, sir. Jimmy was a bad dude, from the street. He didn't take no stuff off nobody, black or white. When that white boy spat on Arnella, Jimmy pulled out the biggest butcher knife you ever seen in your life and came in there after that rascal. Man, that white boy was turning over chairs, knocking over tables, pushing folks out the way getting out of there. Good thing Jimmy had a bad leg and couldn't run that fast, or that white boy would've been through. Jimmy had to be the craziest Negro those white folks had ever seen.

"The news photographers at the scene were all busy snapping pictures of Jimmy chasing that white boy out of the lunch counter and up the street. It was the funniest thing. The major newspaper in town ran a front-page picture the next day of Jimmy chasing that white boy, that butcher knife in his hand. The caption under the picture read, *Negro With Knife Chases White Hoodlum From Lunch Counter.* We laughed about that for the longest, man."

"I bet that was something," Brandon said.

"But like I said, desegregating that lunch counter at Woolworth is what got the whole sit-in movement going across the South. When people saw what had happened in Greensboro, they started doing it everywhere."

■ ■ ■

One day as Brandon was preparing to go out on a delivery run, the Reverend called him into his office.

"Brandon, there's an older gentleman who's a partial shut-in, a long-time member of the church, that I'd like you to be sure to get to before making your other stops. His name should already be on your delivery list." The Reverend scribbled something on a piece of paper and handed it to him. "That's his address. His name is Arthur Singleton. He lives with his daughter. I think you'll find Mr. Singleton to be a pretty interesting fellow."

"Oh? How so?"

"You'll see," the Reverend said, smiling.

Many of the homes along the man's street had no visible address marker, making it difficult for Brandon to locate the house. After driving up and down the street several times, Brandon pulled over to ask for help from two women who were passing by.

"Excuse me, but I'm looking for the home of a Mr. Arthur Singleton. The address I have for him is 1211."

"Mr. Arthur Singleton?" one of the women said, looking quizzically at the other. "You know anybody along here named Arthur Singleton, Purma?"

"Ain't never heard of nobody by that name before 'round here," she said. "And I been living on this street since I was a little girl. You sure you got the right street?"

"Yeah. It's right here," Brandon said, showing the women the address on the paper.

"What does this Mr. Arthur Singleton look like?"

"I've never met him, myself," he said. "But he's an older gentleman, a long-time member of Mt. Sinai Baptist, over on Arledge Street. He's also partially shut in, I was told. But I don't know how long—"

"I know who he talkin' 'bout now," Purma said. "He talkin' 'bout Mr. Homeland."

"Mr. Homeland?" Brandon said.

"Yeh, that's got to be who he talkin' 'bout," the other woman said. "What you do is you go to the next block, and about five or six houses from the corner you'll see it. There's a old car sittin' next to the house. It's on the right. You can't miss it."

"Thanks."

It was an old, weathered gray clapboard, more or less like all the others. The address marker was obscured by ivy that spiraled up the front of the house. A rusted-out lawn mower was parked in the yard, as if someone had been in the process of mowing the grass and had simply walked away in the middle of the job and never returned. It was just as well, for there was very little grass left in the yard to mow anyway. Brandon stepped up on the porch, which sagged and creaked under his weight. Through the screen door he could see a woman busy in the kitchen. He knocked.

"Be right there," the woman said. She wiped her hands on her apron and came to the door. She was wearing a bandanna on her head. "Yes?"

"Good afternoon. I'm here from the church to deliver some groceries to Mr. Arthur Singleton. Is this where he lives? I was also told that people around here know him as Mr. Homeland." The woman chuckled as she unfastened the screen door. "Come on in. You got the right house." He went inside. "You can put those down on the kitchen table right through there," she said, pointing to the kitchen. The inside of the house was quite neat and orderly. The living room furniture, though old, was polished to a sheen, as was the hardwood floor.

"Who's that out there, Mabel?" a man called from the back of the house.

"It's the man with the groceries from the church," Mabel answered.

"Is that Mr...." Brandon said, then hesitated.

"You can call him Mr. Homeland," Mabel said. "That's what everybody call him. You wanna meet him?"

"Well, I don't want to bother him."

"Naw, you won't be bothering him. Come on back," she said, leading him through the little, narrow hallway. "Daddy, somebody here wanna meet you."

All around the room were all sorts of African artifacts, including drums, hideous-looking masks, wooden dolls, terra-cotta figurines, and little statuettes made of bronze and stone. Seated in a rocking chair was a proud-looking, dark-skinned man with strong, broad features. There was a penetrating quality in his eyes, like he could read a person just by looking at them. A walking cane with African faces carved on it lay on the floor by his chair. On a nightstand next to him was an old bible, a pair of reading glasses, a little hand-held spray pump, and several bottles of prescription medication.

"Who you say this is?" the man said, as he studied Brandon.

"He's the new delivery man from the church," the woman said. "I'll let him tell you what his name is."

"What's yo' name, boy?"

"Brandon Northcross." The man was suddenly seized by a rough, wheezing cough. Picking up the little spray device beside him, he put it up to his mouth and pumped several times. His breathing quickly returned to normal. He looked back up at Brandon.

"Brandon, huh?"

"Yes, sir. I came by to deliver your groceries. I put them in the kitchen." The man didn't say anything, but just continued to look at him, a smile beginning on his face. "I just thought I'd come back here and meet you, since I'm going to be the one bringing your groceries now," Brandon added, unsure of whether the man was waiting to hear some further explanation, perhaps, of why he was there. The man continued to look at him.

"Boy, you been to college, ain't you?"

"Ah, yes, sir. I've been to college."

"You sound like it. Have a seat there and sit awhile."

"Thank you." Brandon took a seat in an old, straw-bottomed chair, as he continued to admire the various artifacts throughout the room.

"You like this stuff, don't you?" Mabel said.

"Yeah," Brandon said. "It's almost like being in a museum."

"Anything 'bout Africa, my daddy gets it and puts it here in this room," Mabel said. "That's why they call him Mr. Homeland." A look of pride beamed from her face. "Been collectin' these things since I was a boy, younger than you," the man said.

"Were you an art collector or something?"

"Hmmph," Mabel said, chuckling. "Daddy ain't never been no art collector or nothin' like that. He just go 'round, see stuff he want and, if people don't want it, he bring it home with him. I remember when I was a little girl, when he'd come back from bein' on the road workin', he'd almost always have some little do-dad or somethin' either from Africa or about Africa with him."

"Never had to buy none of 'em, either," Mr. Homeland said. "People just give 'em to me."

"Daddy, tell him about that little stone head—that's what I call it— that yo' grandmama give you when you was a boy. Brandon, look behind yo' chair there." Brandon pulled his chair out. Sitting in a bookcase was a terra-cotta sculptured African head. "You can pick it up." Brandon lifted it gently from the shelf. The face on the sculpture was that of a warrior with a fearless expression. It was oblong-shaped and its features were flat and blunted. Diagonal slashes ran down each cheek.

"Your grandmother gave you this?" Brandon said.

"I'm gon go back in the kitchen now. I'll let y'all talk," Mabel said, leaving the room.

"When I was just a boy, she gave it to me," Mr. Homeland said. "See, my grandmama, when we would go visit her, she would always tell us stories 'bout Africa. These was stories that her mama had tol' her. You see, my grandmama was born a slave."

"A slave?"

"That's right. She was a young girl 'round the time the slaves was freed. She tell me, my grandmama did, that her grandfather, whose name she said was Napoleon—that was his slave name—brought this with him from Africa. But that's all she ever knowed 'bout it."

"She never said where in Africa he had come from, what country?"

"Never knowed none of that, where he come from in Africa or nothin'. She just knowed that he had brought it with him."

"You said that your grandmother would tell you stories about Africa?" Brandon said, placing the head back on the shelf.

"That's right."

"Do you remember any of them?"

"Not too many of 'em," the man said. "But I do remember a few. One I used to love to hear her tell was about when her grandfather was a young warrior and they had to keep from gettin' captured by the slavers. The way he told it, the white slavers and their guides was spotted just a little ways off, moving real quietly through the jungle, trying to catch 'em by surprise. This would happen from time to time, he said. When it did, they would often have to pick up and move to stay ahead of the slavers. Now, there was women and children amongst 'em, which meant that if they had tried to all stay together, the slavers woulda probably caught 'em. So what they did was hide the women and children, putting some of 'em up in the trees. Others they hid in the tall grass. Then, just as the white men got nearly up on 'em, the young warriors took off through the jungle. The slavers, of course, gave chase. Over the next day or so they did what they called backtrackin'."

"What was backtracking?"

"Backtrackin', from the way my grandmama explained it to me, was when they would lead whoever was after 'em around in a circle. It'd be over a long distance, this circle. So, if you was chasin' 'em, unless you knowed the land, you wouldn't know you was goin' in a circle. And what would happen was, when the slavers would stop to camp down for the night, they'd slip up on 'em from behind, the warriors would. They was able to gain so much ground on 'em 'cause, whereas the white men would be stoppin' to camp down, them warriors would keep movin', almost constantly. Of course, the white men thought when they was campin' down for the night that, naturally, the warriors, they'd be campin' down, too. But they wouldn't. They could go for days without no sleep, my grandmama said. And they could run for long distances, with just a little rest here and there. The white man didn't think no man could run like that.

"So, before the white men knowed anything, the warriors would be comin' up behind 'em. You be thinkin' you the hunter, when, before you know it, you be the one that's bein' hunted. They wouldn't know what was happenin' 'til it was too late. Anyhow, they ran practically all night long. Then early the next day, before dawn, the warriors, they snuck up on the white men, who had camped down for the night and was sound asleep. They went through the camp real quiet-like and stole most of the white mens' guns and a lot of their supplies. They did this without rousin' a single one of 'em. I loved to hear the way she'd tell that story, the little details she'd put in. But I done forgot most of 'em."

"How well do you remember your grandmother?"

"I remembers her very well. She was a grand ol' lady, she was. Her name was Esther. I recall how she used to read the bible to us. I remember how when we used to go to her house, me and my brothers and sisters, how durin' the summertime she'd pick out one of them plump melons from her patch. They called 'em Jubilees. And they'd always be sweet. And we'd eat watermelon 'til we was full. Other times, she'd have hot biscuits and molasses waitin' for us." The man paused for a moment, apparently reflecting on his grandmother, before resuming. "I remember also that she used to talk about Frederick Douglass, what a great man he was. She would describe him, say he was a tall man, had a head fulla white hair, beard and all and, Lord, she say, couldn't he speak. She say couldn't nobody 'round durin' them days, black or white, hold a candle to him as a speaker."

"Did she ever see him in person?"

"Not only did she say she seen him in person, but she say she had the opportunity of meetin' him. As a matter of fact, she say she once had dinner at his house and even spent the night, her and her husband. At that time, my grandmama, she was a young woman livin' up here around D.C. with her husband, a man by the name of Calvert, Mr. Jasper E. Calvert. He was somethin' important with the black newspapers at that time. They was invited to Frederick Douglass' home, them and a group of other folks from the newspaper business. When they got there, they saw this big, white house sittin' way back on a hill. Didn't too many white folks even live like that back in them days. She say she remember sittin' there in the parlor with a group of other folks, all the men with they wives, and Frederick Douglass with his wife. I believe she say he was married to a white woman at the time. But beside the man hisself, she remembered that house. She talked 'bout it so, I swore that one day I was gon go see it for myself. But I reckon that house been tore down long since by now, though." He paused again.

"But before she died, when she gimme that there little stone head you was lookin' at, she said to me, 'Boy, always be proud of Africa, no matter what nobody say 'bout it, cause that's where you come from.' She said that to me on her dyin' bed. I'll never forget it. She was a woman ahead of her time in the way she thought 'bout things. That's why from then on, I started collectin' things that was from Africa. Even if I didn't know what it was, I could look at it and say, this is what my people made." Just then, Mabel reappeared in the doorway, a glass of water in her hand.

"Daddy, it's time for yo' medicine."

"I thought I just took that stuff," Mr. Homeland protested mildly.

"You took somethin' else, but not these," she explained, coming over and setting the glass of water on the nightstand beside him. She tapped out a couple of pills from one of the bottles into her father's hand.

"Okay, here we go," she said. "Down the hatch." Reluctantly, he popped the pills into his mouth, the taste making him wince. She then handed him the glass of water, which he turned up and drained. "Now, that wasn't so bad was it?"

"Sick of all these pills," he said. "A pill for this. A pill for that."

"Aw, don't you start fussin' again now," she said. "You know you doin' a lot better since the doctor started you on this new medicine. Your breathin' is a whole lot better."

"What that doctor know 'bout anything?"

"I don't know what he know or don't know," Mabel said. "All I know is that them new pills is helpin' you a lot and you gon keep takin' 'em, too, Mr. Homeland, so you can be 'round here to tell people 'bout Africa for another seventy-nine years," she said, in mock reprimand. Then she smiled, bent down and kissed her father on the top of his head. Affectionately, he reached up and put an arm around her. "You see, Brandon, his bark is a lot worse than his bite."

"Well, I guess I'd better be getting on," Brandon said, rising from his chair.

"Ain't you gon stay and have lunch with us?" Mr. Homeland said. With the aid of his cane, Mr. Homeland slowly rose to his feet. Even though the advanced years had robbed him of his full height, Brandon could see that he had been a towering man.

"Thank you for the invitation," he said. "But, unfortunately, I've got to get back to work."

"We understand," Mabel said.

"When you gon come have supper with us, boy?" Mr. Homeland asked.

"Well," Brandon said, caught slightly off guard, "I don't know. Is there any particular day that's convenient?"

"Just any ol' time," Mabel said. "We here all the time. Just come 'round six o'clock or so in the evenin'. We just be sittin' down to eat 'bout then."

"Okay, then. I will."

Chapter 19

"You're changing, Brandon," Julie said to him one day as they relaxed on a bench in the park.

"What do you mean, I'm changing?"

"I mean you're changing toward me. You're pulling back from me. Sometimes it feels like you're a million miles away."

"I'm not pulling back from you, Julie? Why do you think that?"

"Well, like now," she said. "Why don't you have your arm around me?"

"What?" he said. "Why is whether I have my arm around you at this very moment suddenly an issue, Julie? I put my arm around you all the time."

"Yeah, but you don't do it as much as you used to," she said. "You used to always have your arm around me no matter where we went. Or you held my hand. You don't do that now. It's almost like you don't want people to see us as a couple anymore."

"Oh, Julie, please. Don't you think you're blowing this just a little out of proportion?"

"No, Brandon, I don't. And something else. We don't go out nearly as much as we used to. It's like all you seem to want to do now is read these books. That's all you seem to be interested in. It's doing something to you, Brandon. It's doing something to us. Can't you see?"

"Julie, I don't feel any differently toward you," Brandon said. "Sure, I'm spending a lot of time reading. But it's helping me grow. It's showing me so much more than I used to be able to see." A young black woman passing by cast a stern look of disapproval their way. Brandon stiffened slightly.

"See! This is what I'm talking about," Julie said.

"What?"

"I'm talking about how when that black woman just looked at us, you flinched. You used to not care if people looked at us like that."

"I didn't flinch."

"You did, too!"

"Okay," Brandon said. "Maybe I did a little. But it's different now, Julie."

"It's different? Why all of a sudden is it different? I love you. I *thought* you loved me."

"That's not the point, Julie."

"Oh. It's not the point?" she said. "Well, excuse me. I thought it *was* the point." Angrily, she turned away from him.

"Julie, I'm sorry. I didn't mean it like that. You know that." She turned to face him.

"Brandon, do you really want to be with me?"

"What do you mean, Julie? Of course, I want to be with you. Look, I'm sorry. It's just the things I've been reading lately."

"What kinds of things?"

"You know, about how it used to be between blacks and whites. For example, did you know that as recently as twenty-five years ago there were laws that made interracial marriages illegal in some states in this country? And that's nothing. Do you know what would have happened in the Deep South not that long ago if a black man was caught sitting next to a white woman like I'm doing now?"

"Okay, Brandon," Julie said, sighing. "Okay. But that was then. What does that have to do with us right here and now? Yeah, a lot of bad stuff happened back then. But why do you have to go dredge all that up? Why can't we just live our lives and not worry about what happened twenty-five, thirty years ago? What's the point?"

"But, Julie, don't you see? In some ways, things really haven't changed that much since then. Remember those racist cops that hassled us that time?"

"Okay, two white cops hassled us," Julie said. "They were just two ignorant rednecks. Back home in Minneapolis you see interracial couples practically everywhere you go, and they're mostly black men with white women. As a matter of fact, you see interracial couples pretty much everywhere. You rarely hear about anyone harassing them."

"It's not just racism, Julie. Black people and white people, they're so far apart in this country in the way they see things."

"So, what are you saying, that all of a sudden you're not sure if you can relate to me because I'm white? Is that it?"

"No, I'm not saying that."

"Well, what *are* you saying, Brandon? I'd really like to know." She waited for Brandon to answer, but he didn't. "Look, baby," Julie said, in a much softer tone, "what does any of this black/white stuff really matter if we love each other?" She pulled him close and they kissed.

■ ■ ■

A few days later, Brandon took Mr. Homeland and Mabel up on their dinner invitation. After the meal, he and Mr. Homeland retired to the front porch.

"How long have you and Mabel been living here, Mr. Homeland?" Brandon said, as they watched the late afternoon sun sink slowly toward the horizon.

"Well, we moved here, me and my second wife, Luvenia, just a coupla years after Mabel was born. I think it was somewhere 'round '48 or '49."

"What happened to your wife? Is she still living?"

"She died back in '67, I believe it was. She was a good woman. My first wife, Carrie, though, she hurt me something awful when she runned off with this white man. He was a white man I worked for, sharecroppin' on his land, a Mr. Tyler, Mr. Ben Tyler. And he was a mean white man to work for. He made it hard on you and then when it came time to pay you, he didn't want to pay you fair. I knowed he wanted her, but I didn't think she'd leave and go off with him like she done. It broke my heart when she left, leavin' me and the children. Took me a long time to get over it." Mr. Homeland's chin sagged to his chest.

"So, where'd you live before you moved here?" Brandon asked.

"Well, we come up from this little town down in Mississippi by the name of Gunnison, Gunnison, Mississippi."

"What was it like back then, I mean, for a black person in the Deep South?"

"Well, basically, if you was a Negro—that's what they called you back then—you kept a low profile around white folks in them days."

"What do you mean?"

"Well, for instance, let's say you was walkin' along on the sidewalk and you met up with a white person comin' from the other direction. You stepped out the way to let them pass, even if that meant steppin' off into the gutter. I remember I got one of the worst whuppin's of my life from my Daddy when I didn't step off like he told me to. We was walkin' and this here white woman was comin' at us. Hmmph. My daddy knowed that if I'da kept up that kinda attitude, when I got older ain't no tellin' what trouble I'da got myself into at the hands of white folks. It was the same way in a store. When you went in the store, you always waited 'til the white folks was waited on first. Even if you was next in line, if a white person walked in, you backed up and let them go first. Then you waited 'til the man spoke to you. And you never looked him in the eye, either. You kept your head down."

"Why didn't black people patronize their own stores, if they were treated so badly? Didn't some blacks have stores and other businesses?"

"Some of 'em did. But in a small town like Gunnison, the white folks would often burn 'em out or do worse. They thought that was too uppity, a black person openin' up his own store. Or they might threaten black people with they jobs for takin' they business to a black-owned store. Naw, they didn't take too kindly to that. But all that kinda stuff, it was just things you learned to put up with if you was a Negro. It was just the way things was. You accepted it, for the most part, 'cause the last thing you wanted was to stir up white folks against you. But sometimes, even when you didn't even do nothin', they might still come after you."

"Did white people ever mess with you or anyone in your family, as far as you know, Mr. Homeland?" In the brief span of time that Mr. Homeland took to collect his thoughts, his face seemed to take on a more somber countenance.

"Well, late one night, when I was a little boy, these white men, 'bout six or seven of 'em, they come to our house and ordered us to get up and come outside. My daddy, he kept his 30.06 over in the corner. But they knew he had that rifle and that he knew how to use it, too, so they rushed in 'fo he had a chance to get to it. So they gets us all together and marches us outside. At the house at that time it was me; my two little brothers; my little sister; my older brother, Clem, who was the oldest of us children; and my older sister, Jessie. Jessie wasn't no mo' than 'bout thirteen at the time, but she was mature for her age. She had the body of a full-grown woman, Jessie did. All the white men 'round about talked about how if they ever caught her out by herself how they was gon lay her. My daddy, though, he had sent word out that if any cracker—that's what he called 'em—messed with Jessie, they was gon pay for it. Well, that didn't sit too well with some of the white men 'round in them parts, a Negro threatenin' to stand up to white folks, even if it was standin' up for his own family. So, they took Jessie, took her right there in front of us."

"You say they took her. You mean they—"

"I mean they took her. They raped her, right there on the ground and made us all watch, as every last one of them low-down crackers had her. She was cryin', beggin' and pleadin' with 'em to stop, but they just kept on. And they held they guns on us, made us watch and said they'd kill us if we tried to look away. My momma, she fainted and the rest of us kids was cryin', 'cause Jessie was cryin' so. My daddy, if it had only been him, he would've tried to do somethin'. I know he woulda. He wasn't 'fraid of no white man, or no gun neither. But he knew they would harm us kids, if he tried anything.

"When it was all over, Daddy carried po' Jessie in the house. My momma, she tended to her. But Jessie just wouldn't quit screamin'. She screamed all night long. The next mornin', my daddy, he couldn't take it no mo'. He took his 30.06 and his pistol and left, sayin' somebody was gon pay for what they had done to his daughter. My momma and Clem, they begged and pleaded with him not to go, but they couldn't stop him. We knowed what Daddy was gon do. The next day, we heard he had found and shot one of the men and the white folks was lookin' for him. They come lookin' for him at our place, but, course, he wasn't there. But they burned us out anyway. Except for the clothes on our backs, we lost practically everything we had. When they found him, he was able to get one mo' of 'em before they got to him. Then they took him and strung him up right there in front of the courthouse, sayin' it was to be a lesson to any other uppity niggers. For days, they let his body hang there, before they let us take him down and give him a decent funeral and burial."

"Was the sheriff part of the mob that strung up your father?"

"The sheriff? Not only that. He was one 'em doin' the rapin'," Mr. Homeland said. "And the preacher was, too."

"The preacher?! You mean the preacher was one of them?"

"Why sho', it wasn't nothin' for a white man—whether he was a preacher, a sheriff, or what—to force hisself on a black woman back then. They knowed wasn't hardly nothin' gon be done 'bout it. And when they wasn't forcin' 'em, they was goin' with 'em all over the place. And it didn't matter if the woman was married or not. They'd still try and go with the woman. So much of it went on that it wasn't that uncommon to see a black woman with a little white-lookin' child that was her own. Everybody, black folks and white folks alike, knowed who the real daddy was, which was usually some white man that lived 'round about. But didn't nobody say nothin' too much 'bout it, 'cause it was just the way things was then."

"What about the white women? Didn't they object to what was goin' on?"

"The white women? I suppose some of 'em minded, but, for the most part, like I say, it was just the commonly accepted thang at that time. Hmmph! A black man, if he had a good-lookin' woman, he had to always be worryin' 'bout a white man tryin' to lay with her. And if she was a real light-skinned woman, what they called a high yellow woman, then they was sho 'nuff after her. And she better not be white-lookin' enough where she could pass. Why white men would see it bein' 'bout like a black man bein' with a white woman. I knowed a black man who was married to this real pretty high yellow woman. Unless you heard her talk, you wouldna never knowed she was black. Well, this white man that lived just down the road from him took a likin' to that woman and told him that he was gon have her, one way or another, even if he had to kill him to get her. And one day he did. Shot him in broad daylight, too. And wasn't nothin' done 'bout it. But if a black man was even accused of lookin' at a white woman, much less rapin' her, he was through."

"They'd lynch him?"

"Lynch him, do anything they wanted to him. I remember—and this was in the late '50s down in Alabama—a black man could be beat up just for lookin' at a billboard with the picture of a white woman on it. That's how bad things was. And I seen with my own eyes, when I was a young man, a white mob take this black man, put him down in this hole, fill it up with kerosene and light it. Burned him alive. All because a white woman claimed he had tried to rape her. Another time, this white mob got a hold of this black boy. He couldna been no more than 'bout seventeen years old. They caught him in bed with a white woman. They took that boy and chained him between these two cars and, as God is my witness, they pulled him apart, just tore him to pieces. You could hear that boy scream like you ain't never heard nobody scream before in yo' life. It was awful. Yes, suh. Didn't nothin' get white folks mo' riled up than the idea of a black man bein' with a white woman."

"Did anything much ever go on between white women and black men back then?"

"There was white women, more'n a few, that slipped around with black men. But they was generally real careful 'bout it. Sometimes, though, white women made black men go with 'em, in secret of course. I knowed this one black fellow by the name of Frank Wilson. What happened to him was that the wife of this white man he worked for took a likin' to him. She was a nice-lookin' woman, too. She'd come to her husband's business from time to time to bring him his lunch. He owned a saw mill. Anyway, one time when she was there, she slipped Frank a note tellin' him to meet her somewhere. Well, fearin' for his job—and probably his life, too—he refused to go. But the next note he got from her she told him if he didn't meet her like she wanted him to that she'd go to her husband on him, tell him he'd tried to get fresh with her."

"What did he do?"

"Well, seein' he didn't have too much of a choice in the matter, he went along with her, until he could manage to get out from under the situation. You had white women that would do things like that."

"So, what happened to your sister?"

"Po' Jessie, she never spoke after that, never said a word to nobody. She would just sit and stare, just sit and stare. Couldn't nobody seem to reach her, the preacher from our church or nobody. It was like she just give up on livin'. Then one day, we found her in the creek out behind my aunt's house, where we had to move to. She had drowned herself."

Brandon swallowed hard.

"How do you keep from hating white people, when they've done so much wrong to you and your family, Mr. Homeland?"

"Well, I reckon I did hate white people at one time. I couldn't see no reason why I shouldna hated white people. I swore on my sister's grave that I was gon get the rest of them white men that had done her like they did. And I hated them white men, and other white folks that had done black folks wrong, done 'em wrong for such a long time. I carried that burden around with me for a long time, 'cause that's exactly what it was, a burden. 'Cause it wasn't nothin' I could do 'bout what had happened, at least nothin' that wouldna brought even mo' pain and sufferin' on my own people. But I finally decided to just let it go. I try not to dwell on what all done happened. I just believes in what the bible say: 'Vengeance is mine, saith the Lord, I shall repay.' And he shall repay, 'cause ain't no dark deed that no man do, white or black, is gon be hid from the Lord come Judgment Day. I just go on and try to live the best way I know how, treat every man the way I would want him to treat me. That's what I done tried to live by all these years."

■ ■ ■

"So, you've been reading up on the motherland, huh?" the Reverend said as he and Brandon met in his study one evening.

"Yes, mostly about the beginning of the slave trade," Brandon said.

"What are you learning?"

"Well, for one, I didn't know that before the European slave trade, that slavery had already been flourishing in Africa and in other parts of the world for quite some time. Of course, for the most part, it wasn't slavery as it came to be after the Renaissance, when the Portuguese and the Spaniards ran the slave trade and used Christianity to justify it. But I also came across something that I'm still having a hard time accepting."

"What's that?"

"Well, there's no escaping the fact that our own people helped enslave us, even from the very beginning," Brandon said. "The kings and princes sold their own people to the slave traders. I just don't understand how they could have done it." The Reverend leaned forward in his chair.

"But you need to understand something about that," the Reverend said. "The same thing's going on today, in one form or another, black people selling out other black people. And it's been happening since they brought us over here, too. And we do it in so many different ways. When we fail to support our own businesses and institutions, that's a form of selling out each other. A Jewish friend of mine once said to me, 'David, if only ten percent of black people would emulate what Jews did in this country—starting and patronizing their own businesses, pooling their resources, pulling together to support each other financially—black people could have a power base in this country within twenty years, or maybe less.' And you know what? He was right. To some degree, as a people, we still believe that old saying that the white man's ice is colder. And that more than anything is perhaps the single most lasting and damaging affect of slavery."

■ ■ ■

During his immersion into reading, Brandon still found time to visit Gill and Mr. Homeland from time to time. Mr. Homeland always had some fascinating story for him about his days as a young man traveling throughout the south looking for work. Once, Brandon arranged for Gill and Lisa to come by and meet Mr. Homeland. Lisa so attached herself to Mr. Homeland that Gill got out his video camera and shot some footage of them out on the porch and in the yard together. Something else that Brandon was able to do was move into his own place.

While making deliveries, Brandon got the chance to get to know a number of kids in the neighborhood. He would often talk to them about staying in school and keeping out of trouble. One of them was a kid named George. George was different from the others. Though very bright and well-mannered, he was rather withdrawn. He seldom hung around with the other kids, choosing, instead, to stay to himself. One day Brandon found out why.

He and George were talking when an unshaven and obviously inebriated man came staggering toward them from the park across the street. Brandon paid no attention to the man at first, as he'd become accustomed to seeing drunks coming and going in the area. With an open whiskey bottle in his hand, the man made his way over to them, calling out, "Go home, George. Go home." At first, he figured that the man was simply talking out of his head. But that was only until he saw George drop his head and turn away.

"Go home, George," the man repeated. The strong stench of alcohol rose from him as he drew along side Brandon. His eyes were fiery red. Reeling from side to side, he grabbed hold of Brandon to try to steady himself. "That's my boy, George, there. I'm his daddy," he said, punching himself in the chest with his forefinger. "I don't want him gettin' in no kinda trouble. That's why I want him at home... George? George?" George continued to ignore the man. "I know I ain't all I ought to be as a father, but I try. See, ever since I lost my job down at the factory, they don't respect me at home no more. You understand what I'm sayin'?" Brandon nodded that he did, in hopes that the man would just leave. After standing there awhile, just staring off into space, the man turned and started back the way he had come. Brandon watched as he wobbled, sometimes almost falling, through the park on his way to his next bottle.

"Hey, man, if you ever want to talk about it, I'm here," Brandon said to George. "Okay?"

"Okay," George replied.

■ ■ ■

As Brandon was leaving the church one day on the way to his car, he felt a tap on his shoulder from behind. Before he could turn to see who it was, he was grabbed roughly around the collar and shoved hard up against the chain-linked fence that boarded the church parking lot.

"What the—?!" Brandon gasped, as he spun around, ready to do battle with whoever it was. He froze, however, when he saw the long, shiny blade of steel snake out from the man's hand.

"Shut the hell up!" the man said, pressing the cold steel of the switchblade against his throat, as he quickly glanced one way then the other along the sidewalk to make sure no one was watching. He then fixed a hard glare on Brandon. The man had a crazed look in his eyes. His brute strength was evident in the vise-like grip he applied to Brandon's collar.

"Hey, listen, man," Brandon said. "If it's money you want—"

"I don't want your money." This frightened Brandon even more.

"Well, w-w-what do—

"What do I want?" man said. "I wanna tell you 'bout yourself."

"Tell me about myself?" Brandon said. He had never seen the man before in his life.

"Yeh, see I been hearing about you," the man said, "how you been feeding these young kids around here all this big talk, about how if they just get an education and play by the rules that they can make it just like the white kids. Man, what do you know about being a black man out here in the streets? You don't look like you ever had to watch your mother or father grow old before their time from doing back-breaking work, making just enough to put food on the table for their family. Naw, you probably don't know nothing about that. Do you? See, all you doing is making it harder for 'em. 'Cause I don't care what they do, the white man's gon still hold 'em back. You hear what I'm saying? So, what you telling these kids ain't nothing but a bunch of fairy tales, and it's gon get 'em hurt. See, I went to college, got my degree, thought I was on my way. But the white man still wouldn't gimme no job. Man, you hear what I'm saying? He still wouldn't gimme no job, except maybe some slave hustle paying minimum wage. That's how they do black men. But he'll give the black woman a good job. You know why? 'Cause he don't want no woman looking up to a black man, even the black man's own woman. You hear what I'm saying?"

Brandon wanted to tell the man that he did, indeed, understand. But, instead, he decided to just keep quiet, let the man get what he wanted off his chest.

"So, a black man ain't got no choice but to take what he needs," the man continued. "That's the only way he can make it. Naw, see, I don't want that blue-eyed devil giving me nothing. I *take* from him what I want." He then relaxed his grip on Brandon's collar slightly, a sly, sinister grin now spreading over his face.

"And you know something else? I take his women, too. Yeh, that's right. I like hearing them white bitches crying and begging when I'm about to put it to 'em," he said, jabbing the knife at Brandon's face for emphasis. "I tell 'em, bitch, this is for my great grandmama that your great granddaddy raped! And this is for my great granddaddy that your racist great granddaddy castrated! Yeh, that's right. I take their women, just like they took our women. You think I'm sick, don't you?" The man paused to give Brandon a chance to reply, but he said nothing. "Maybe I am," he said. "Yeh, maybe I am. But if I am, it's 'cause the white man made me this way. But before you get too righteous, I see that white girl that comes by here in that Porsche and picks you up sometime. I bet you think when y'all getting it on that you making love to her, all sweet and tender and everything. Naw, nigga, you ain't really making love to that white girl. You might think you are. But you taking it, just like me. You just don't know it. Now you think about *that!*"

The man then clicked the button on the handle of the knife and the blade disappeared as quickly as it had appeared. He released his hold on Brandon's collar and, continuing to look him in the eye, slowly backed away, before turning and casually starting away.

Brandon stood there frozen with fear, as he watched the man disappear down the street. Pulling himself together, he got in his car and left. Even when he had made it nearly home, he was still shaking from the ordeal. But it wasn't so much what had happened, the knife and all, but what the man had said at the end, about what he was actually feeling when he was intimate with Julie. Once again, those same mixed emotions about his relationship with Julie resurfaced. On the one hand, he thought better than to allow the rantings of some madman bent on revenge for some historical wrong to unsettle him. The man had no knowledge of the depth of his relationship with Julie. Yet, what the man had said continued to haunt him, to pick at his conscience.

■ ■ ■

That night when he and Julie were together, Brandon found himself looking at her and once again thinking about what the man who had accosted him had said. They had just finished dinner and Julie was loading the dishes into the dishwasher, her back to him. He was sitting at the kitchen table, just a few feet away.

"And tomorrow I've got to meet with the head of the design team, because the design has once again changed," Julie said. "I don't know why they always manage to wait until the very last minute to let me know about these changes. It drives me damn near insane sometimes. I mean, it would be so much easier if they would just…"

Who really was this girl, this white girl, he wondered, as he watched her, her words coming to him now as if from far away. He did love her. Yes, there was no doubt in his mind about that. But did his attraction to her have anything to do with the fact that she was white? Did it? No, he thought, he had never wanted her because she was a white woman. Or had he? It troubled him that doubts kept creeping back into his mind over this. Was she, as the man had claimed, merely a white woman, the prized white woman, the taboo white goddess, on whom he acted out some subconscious rape/revenge fantasy? Yes, they had rough sex sometimes. Was he, subconsciously, raping her?

"…and, if I have time, I can stop by the mall and pick up a gift for Kristen's baby shower. Oh, and did I tell you that when I was downtown the other day that I saw the most handsome double-breasted, charcoal grey suit at Macy's? I know you'd look really good in it, honey. Maybe if you're real nice to me, I'll buy it for you. I also saw the neatest loafers, with these little..." That haunting voice from earlier in the day suddenly returned. *Naw, nigga, you ain't really making love to that white girl. You might think you are. But you taking it, just like me. You just don't know it. You just don't know it. You just don't*—Julie suddenly turned around.

"Brandon, you're not listening to me, honey."

"Huh?" She came over and leaned across the table, her face just inches from his.

"I said you're not listening to me."

"I was listening," he lied.

"No you weren't," she said, coming around the table and climbing into his lap. "But that's okay, because I know what you were really thinking about." She began planting little kisses on his cheeks. "You were thinking about how you'd like to grab me, rip all my clothes off and ravish me. Now don't disappoint me. That *is* what you were thinking, isn't it?"

"How'd you know?" Brandon said, kissing her back.

■ ■ ■

A few days later, he was finally able to put the whole matter out of his mind. He even questioned whether the man was really a rapist, or just making it all up. Yet, for sometime afterwards, whenever he heard of an alleged rape by a black man in a predominately white neighborhood, he wondered if it was him.

Chapter 20

One evening as Brandon was headed up Georgia Avenue on his way home, traffic suddenly slowed to a near standstill. Car horns blared, as impatient motorists fumed behind the wheels of their cars. Curious pedestrians hurried ahead to see what was happening.

"Hey, what's going on up there?" Brandon called out to a man who was headed that way.

"I'm not sure," the man said. "They say something happened at this Korean store up the street here." Brandon pulled over to the curb and got out to see for himself.

Several blocks up, a crowd of enraged blacks was gathered out in front of a Korean grocery. They were jeering the store owners, who looked small and helpless as they peered out through the window. A Korean man brandishing a club was standing in the doorway yelling something back at them. Police stood between the man and the angry crowd. Police cruisers blocked off the street in front of the store in both directions. An ambulance, its emergency lights punctuating the sky with its crimson flickers, was parked out front. Its siren suddenly cut on and it lurched forward. But the milling crowd, which had now spilled out into the street, was making it impossible for it to move.

"You people stand back out of the way!" a cop commanded, as he and other cops tried to get people to move aside.

"What happened?" Brandon asked a woman.

"They say somebody got shot inside the store," she said. "They say it was a black girl. That's all I know."

"Clear the way!" the cop ordered the crowd. A path was finally cleared, allowing the ambulance to pull away. At the same time, the air quickly became saturated with the heavy blare of sirens, as more and more police converged on the scene. One of those just arriving jumped out with a bullhorn.

"We're ordering you to disperse now! You must disperse now!" Police in riot gear took up positions in front of the store. But it seemed that the more the police tried to disperse the crowd, the more unruly it became, with some pushing and shoving now taking place. In addition to emergency vehicles, TV news crews also began arriving. Police quickly set up barricades and began rerouting traffic onto side streets. "Unless you disperse, you will be subject to arrest!" the cop with the bullhorn warned. Fearing that things were about to get out of hand, Brandon returned to his car.

Traffic in the area was so badly snarled that it took him nearly an hour to make it home. Once there, he immediately raced inside and cut on the TV. A news reporter was reporting from the parking lot of a liquor store just down the street from the Korean store. "And as you can see behind me," the woman said, "we're in the middle of an ugly disturbance, one of the ugliest to rock the Washington area in some time…" Rioters were shown skirmishing with police, who were armed with batons and riot shields. The Korean store had been set ablaze, the front totally engulfed in flames. As fire fighters tried to extinguish the blaze, they, themselves, were being targeted with rocks and bottles. Police chased the perpetrators, arresting those they could catch and loading them into waiting police wagons. A number of rioters and police were bloodied from the confrontations. Paramedics tended to the injured at the scene. Black and Hispanic youth mugged for the news cameras, chanting, "Burn, baby, burn!"

"…Police are advising citizens to stay out of the area. A number of police cars have already been overturned, several even set afire. There, right over there, if our cameras can get a picture of it," she said as the camera panned the scene. "Right over there you can see one of them, still smoldering from having been firebombed." The cameras zoomed in on the police cruiser, its emergency lights still rotating. "Luckily, we are told, the officers inside were able to escape with only minor injury. Police are trying their best to get a handle on this before nightfall. Dozens of arrests have been made, and eight people have been admitted to area hospitals for injuries, two of them police. None of the injuries is deemed to be life-threatening.

"The whole thing is thought to have started because of the fatal shooting earlier of a sixteen-year-old black girl inside Soo Tan's grocery behind me. She was allegedly shot by one of the Korean storekeepers, a woman. Neither the identity of the victim nor that of the storekeeper is being released at this time. We are told that the girl died in route to the hospital, after valiant but futile efforts by paramedics to save her. The details at this time are still sketchy. But it appears there was some sort of dispute over shoplifting between the storekeeper and the girl. Words were exchanged between the two, according to witnesses, and the girl turned to leave. And that's when the shooting occurred, the storekeeper allegedly pulling a large-caliber handgun out from behind the counter and shooting the victim in the back of the head at very close range."

The news anchor at the station then asked, "Is there any indication at this time, Denise, if the girl was, in fact, shoplifting, or if it was—"

"Mark, sorry to interrupt you," the reporter at the scene broke in, "but I've just been joined by Police Chief Robert Clancy. Chief, can you shed any light on what led up to the shooting earlier that precipitated all this? And, also, can you share with us what your officers are doing to try to bring it under control?"

"Denise, outside of the fact that the shooting involved a dispute that arose over an allegation of shoplifting on the part of the shooting victim, I'm not at liberty to divulge any other information on the case at this time. The investigation is in progress. As to getting things under control, we think the worst is over, as we now have our people out in sufficient strength to contain whatever might flare up again. However, we want residents of the area to remain indoors unless it's absolutely necessary they venture out, because it's still dangerous out here in the streets and we don't want innocent citizens being caught up in this. We can't stress that enough."

"Thank you, Chief Clancy, for taking the time to talk with us this evening," the reporter said. The chief nodded and turned to leave. "For those of you just joining us, that was D.C. Police Chief Robert Clancy here on Georgia Avenue, where, if you haven't already heard, there was a fatal shooting earlier today of a black teenage girl, allegedly by a storekeeper here at Soo Tan's grocery. There was some sort of dispute concerning alleged shoplifting on the part of the victim, which we are told led to the tragic shooting. That is all we know at this point. But the result is the unrest you see going on. According to the chief, the police are finally getting a lid on things, but, again, as you can see behind me, there is still a lot of tension out here in the community. I think it suffices to say that it will be awhile before things really return to normal."

"Denise, has there been any word from any of the civil rights organizations or community groups in response to the events that have unfolded, either to the shooting or to the rioting?" the anchor asked.

"Yes, Mark, I can tell you that we got a chance to talk briefly with a spokesman for the CBBC, which stands for the Coalition for Brotherhood in the Business Community, who was on the scene earlier. And he said that an emergency meeting has been called for tonight at 8 pm on the campus of Howard University at Hale Hall in the university's Student Union Building to discuss the incident and to adopt a response. The meeting is open to the public and concerned citizens are invited to attend. That's at 8 pm tonight on the campus of Howard University. Mark, back to you," the woman said, sending it back to the studio anchor.

"Thank you, Denise," Mark said. "That was Denise Dornburg reporting live from—" Brandon clicked off the TV and went over and looked out his window. A thick cloud of black smoke was lifting into the air from the area of the rioting. Something, maybe just curiosity, moved him to go to the meeting that night at Howard.

■ ■ ■

The lecture hall was nearly full when Brandon arrived, even though he was fifteen minutes early. He found an empty seat toward the back. Someone passed him a flyer.

Apartheid in the Nation's Capital: The Case Against Korean Grocers

On August 2, 1989, Deanna Wilkins, a sixteen-year-old black teenager, was shot and killed by a Korean grocer at Soo Tan's Grocery over a shoplifting dispute. She was shot in the back of the head at point blank range. This brutal shooting was unprovoked, unwarranted, and unjustifiable. Although by far the most egregious, it is only the latest in a series of incidents that have been perpetrated against the black community by Korean store owners in the D.C. area.

Following are some of the complaints that have been lodged against Korean groceries by citizens in the black community within the past year:

- *Customers being short-changed when paying for their purchases. When contesting it, they are often dealt with rudely, sometimes cursed, sometimes accused of lying. Others have been threatened with having the police called on them.*
- *Customers being refused bags for their purchases when they request them.*

- *Customers having their change tossed on the counter, rather than placed in their hands. This has been reported quite often.*
- *Stale products being sold at the stores, especially meat products. These are products that are often already over-priced.*
- *Price-gouging. Goods at these stores are routinely marked up much higher than that at other stores.*
- *Allowing only a few black teenagers in the store at one time, because of the racist notion that most black youth are shoplifters.*
- *Customers being physically manhandled. In one incident, an elderly woman was pushed from the store over a dispute, causing her to fall and break her hip.*

Brothers and sisters, it's time to take a stand against these Jim Crow and apartheid-like practices that are going on every day in our communities. Join us tonight for a townhall meeting with the CBBC at 8 pm at the Student Union Building on the campus of Howard University.

Student Auxiliary of the Washington D.C. Chapter of the NAACP

As people continued to file into the auditorium, all the remaining seats were soon taken, forcing those just arriving to find a place to stand along the wall. Many of those present appeared to be college students. There was little laughing or joking, as a serious mood hung in the air. Two men seated behind Brandon discussed the shooting.

"Man, you know if that had been a white person or another Asian that had been shot, that Korean woman would be in jail right now."

"You mean they went and let her out on bail?"

"Let her out on *bail?* My brother, they didn't even arrest that woman. You hear me?"

"Didn't even arrest her?" the other man said, in disbelief. "Man, you got to be joking!"

"She ain't been arrested. She ain't been charged. *That's* what makes it so bad. All they say is that she was questioned."

"But y'all really wanna hear something wild?" another man seated nearby said. "They got the whole thing on video. The store's security camera caught it. They been showing it on the evening news. It shows this black girl starting away from the cash register for the door. Then all of a sudden this Korean woman just ups and pulls this gun out from under the counter and caps the girl in the back of the head. Just like that.

No questions asked. Just BAM! Look like it blew the back of that girl's head off, man. It was cold-blooded."

"Damn! You mean they got it on video and this woman still walking around free?"

"Okay, we're ready to commence the meeting, if we can all come to order," a man said over the PA system. Down on stage a well-dressed black man with a graying beard was seated at the table behind the mike along with an Hispanic man, another black man and two black women. A banner that read, *Coalition for Brotherhood in the Business Community (CBBC)*, was draped across the front of the table. The man at the mike rapped his gavel for order. "Please, let's come to order now." The crowd gradually toned down. People were now lining both walls of the auditorium.

"As most of you know, I'm Bernard Lipscomb, chairman of the CBBC. I and the other members have called this emergency meeting tonight, as I'm sure you are all aware, because of an unfortunate and tragic incident earlier today at one of our Korean groceries in the area, where a young lady, a customer, was fatally shot. Before we open up the floor for your comments, let me just say that we are all deeply saddened by this tragedy and we share the community's grief. I spoke earlier tonight with several of the Korean merchants, and they all expressed their regret over the incident. Also, I'm sure you'll be happy to know that we've been assured by D.C. law enforcement that a full and thorough investigation into the incident has already been launched. In fact, I was told this by Assistant Police Chief Nevels, himself. But let me also add that, while we can sympathize with your anger and your grief, we cannot condone the wanton violence and destruction of our neighborhoods that followed this evening. I cannot emphasize that strongly enough." He was met with a chorus of boos from the audience. Lipscomb pounded his gavel for quiet. "We will now open the floor for comments. Please be brief and to the point, as we want to hear from as many of you as possible within the time we have allotted."

Microphones had been placed in the middle aisle for the audience to use. People who wanted to speak were instructed to step out to the mikes and wait to be recognized. The first to be recognized was a young man near the back. "I understand all this about what the police promised to do and all, but what I want to know is what is the CBBC planning to do? I mean, y'all supposed to be representing the community. 'Cause we're tired of hearing this get-to-know-your-neighbor stuff every time we come to you with a complaint about these Korean store owners. It's always this stuff about how we need to better understand our neighbors, how we ought to try and sympathize with their difficulty in relating to us. Hey, the way I feel, these Koreans, they ought to be trying to get to know me, especially if I spend my money in their stores. I don't hear 'bout no Koreans going 'round talking 'bout trying to get to know and understand their black neighbors better!" Shouts of approval rang out through the hall. "And on top of that," the man continued, even before the crowd had quieted, "I really don't care to understand my neighbor if he gon shoot my brothers and sisters down in cold blood like what happened today! All I want is some good, old-fashioned justice! To hell with all the rest of this getting-to-know my neighbor stuff!" The crowd went wild, as the man took his seat.

"Please, let us be calm about this," Lipscomb said, pounding his gavel. "We must try to be rational. We understand your frustration. We do. Believe me, no one understands more so than I do. But we are doing everything we can to remedy this problem. What you have here—and I don't mean to sound cliché—but what you have is a cultural gap. People, *that,* more than anything, is the problem."

An Hispanic woman took her turn at the mike. "This is not the response I was looking for. I grew up in this community, and blatant acts of discrimination against black and Hispanic people have been happening in these stores for years and not once has anything concrete ever been done about it. I wonder if you and the others there on stage are really as in touch with the people in the community as you say you are. I don't even think any of you know the people in the community anymore." Her comment was met with more cheers and applause.

A black woman wearing a T-shirt with a picture emblazoned on it of a dashiki-clad Angela Davis sporting a big Afro was next to speak. "All I have to say is this. If these Korean grocers can't treat us with the respect we deserve, when we're the main ones patronizing their stores, then I think it's time to run them out of our neighborhoods! Then, maybe, they'd learn how to treat people! And that goes for anybody else that just got off the boat!" The crowd came alive once again.

A half-dozen or so others spoke, all pretty much echoing the same sentiments. A man wearing a Howard University sweat shirt then spoke. "What we're seeing here is the culmination of years and years of frustration in dealing with people who, when it's all said and done, have a fundamental disrespect for black people. It mystifies me why it has taken this long for all this anger to finally boil over. The saddest thing about it is that it had to take a young sister's senseless death to bring it about. Folks, something's gonna have to give!" The crowd became even more emboldened.

"Send them yellow midgets back home!"

"Send them back to the rice paddies!"

The chairman banged his gavel. "Look, people, I've just about had it with this Korean-bashing. A lot of you talk like you want us to run them out of the community or something. In fact, some of you have even said as much. I mean, I've sat here for I don't know how long and listened to you call them everything from rice-eaters to little yellow midgets and complain about how they don't like black folks. I just want somebody here to tell me one thing. Who do you think is going to take over these businesses if they leave? Black people? Folks, it'll never happen. What you'd end up doing is shooting yourselves in the foot. That's what you'd be doing. And I doubt very seriously if black people would support them in any appreciable numbers if they did." He was quickly met with a volley of boos and jeers.

Without even realizing it, Brandon rose from his seat and started for the microphone. Standing at the mike, he waited patiently for the fervor to subside.

"If you all don't mind, I think there's somebody at one of the mikes that wants to say something," Lipscomb said, rapping his gavel. The room quieted.

"Sir, if I may, I'd just like to briefly respond to what you just said, about blacks not being able to step in and open their own stores if the Koreans were to pull out. I beg to differ with you..." After his first couple of statements, he noticed that people began to really listen, like they were weighing his every word. "Our history in this country, contrary to what society would have us believe, says that we *can* succeed at being entrepreneurs. This idea that blacks don't have what it takes to run their own businesses somehow didn't reach the ears of our forefathers who, way back at the turn of the century, flourished as grocers, restaurateurs, caterers, bakers, and tailors. Others operated shirt factories, funeral homes, rubber good shops, cotton mills, lumber mills, and carpet factories. And it wasn't whites who kept those black-owned businesses going. It was blacks, black people supporting their own, often under the threat of reprisal from whites."

"Teach, my brother, teach!"

"Educate him, my brother!"

"And this idea that blacks won't support their own somehow didn't reach the ears of Booker T. Washington, who was instrumental in forming the Negro Business League. It failed to reach the ears of Madam C. J. Walker, who became the first black millionaire with her hair products enterprise."

"Take him to school, my brother! Take him to school!"

"Tell the story!"

"Is there anybody here who really believes that black people won't support black-owned businesses?"

"No!"

"Is there anybody here who believes that black people are that backwards?"

"No!"

"If the Koreans can do it, can't we do it?"

"Yeh!"

"If the Chinese can do it, can't we do it?"

"Yeh!"

"If other people can come here and open businesses and make it work, can't we do it?"

"Yeh!"

"Then we need to get mad."

"Yeh, get mad!"

"Get so mad that we do what we know we ought to do, knowing that we can own and run our own businesses in our own communities. And when the banks deny our people the loans they need to open those businesses, then we need to take our money out of those banks and put it in banks that value our business."

"Yeh!"

"Yes, we need to get real mad!"

"Yeh!"

"And so I say that until black people see that the wheels of justice begin to turn in this incident, and that the person who shot Deanna Wilkins be arrested and charged, if the evidence so warrants, and that these Korean merchants begin to show a willingness to improve their treatment of black people in a way that is satisfactory to us, that we get so mad that we withhold our patronage from these stores and go shop somewhere else."

"Yeh!"

"I believe this will send a strong message that black people are not going to continue to be anybody's doormat to be walked on. For us to demand anything less is to concede our rights to be treated as first-class citizens. Martin Luther King once said that a man who won't stand for something will fall for anything. I say it's time that black people took a stand!" The entire hall erupted, as people rose to their feet cheering and clapping. A chant, began somewhere down in front, was quickly taken up by the entire hall.

"Boycott! Boycott! Boycott!" Lipscomb and the others on stage nervously eyed the audience, who seemed ready to take to the streets that very minute.

"Can we please have some decorum in here, people?" Lipscomb said, banging his gavel. As the crowd continued their chant, a young man seated toward the front of the hall stepped out into the aisle and started up the steps toward Brandon. Handsomely dressed in an Italian double-breasted, navy blazer, a yellow silk kerchief peeking out of the front pocket, a yellow mock turtleneck, and a pair of off-white slacks, he came and stood beside Brandon. Turning to the crowd, he raised both hands high in the air, like a quarterback signaling to his team's fans to quiet down. People gradually hushed and took their seats. The man looked around at the crowd, then removed the microphone from its stand.

"Most of you know me. I'm Edward Cantrell III, a student right here at Howard. And I'm currently the president of the Student Auxiliary of our local chapter of the NAACP. Now, I don't know the brother who just spoke. I didn't put him up to speak. As a matter of fact, I've never even seen him before in my life. All I know is that, based on what he just said, he's talking about the kind of action we need to take on this matter."

"Damn right!"

"Tell 'em, Cantrell!"

"Let me also just say—and this is out of no disrespect to you fine people of the CBBC—but, like the rest of the brothers and sisters here tonight have said, every time something happens that involves these Korean grocers slighting black folks, y'all come to us with the same tired old line about 'let's just try to get along.' I say, like the brother earlier said, later for that brotherhood bit. And I say like my man here," he said, throwing his arm around Brandon's shoulders, "it's time to take a stand! And on that note, I move—even though I don't even know the brother's name yet, but I will—that he be made the spokesman for our protest movement—"

"Excuse me, Mr. Cantrell!" Lipscomb said, rapping his gavel.

"—under the auspices of the Student Auxiliary of the D.C. chapter of the NAACP, to lead a boycott against these racist Korean grocers!"

"And I second it!" someone hastily added.

"Cantrell, this is not your meeting, you cannot vote—"

"Alright, then," Cantrell continued, over the vehement objections of the chairman, "it has been moved and seconded that this brother become the spokesman for our movement. Everybody here in favor, say aye." An ocean of ayes reverberated throughout the hall. "Any nays, go home."

"Mr. Cantrell! Mr. Cantrell!" Lipscomb was up out of his chair now, bristling with anger, as he furiously pounded his gavel. "You are out of order. This is not your meeting. Besides, you do not have the approval from the local NAACP board to launch any such boycott."

"I don't yet, but I will by tomorrow morning. You can count on that."

"Young man, you are still out of order and—"

"So, CBBC," Cantrell interrupted again, "move over for the N—come on, y'all help me say it—the *N-A-A-C-P!*" The entire hall joined in, drowning out Lipscomb's protests.

"This meeting has not officially been adjourned!" Lipscomb shouted, hammering away with his gavel. But no one seemed to be paying him any attention, as people began to spill out into the aisle and converge on Brandon.

"Man, that was some kinda speech you just made," a man said, shaking his hand.

"Thanks."

"Let me shake your hand, too," a middle-aged woman said, coming behind the man. "We needed to hear that tonight, young man. That was nothing but the gospel you spoke. And you did it so eloquently, too. I wish my son could've been here to hear you."

"Thank you," Brandon said.

As people continued to approach him, it was like what was happening was all part of a dream. A short man with wire-framed glasses and a briefcase nudged his way between Brandon and Cantrell, who was also busy greeting people.

"Cantrell, I think we on the move now!" he said, pumping Brandon's hand. He then looked at Brandon. "Great speech. I'm looking forward to some big things happening now." Unsure of just what to say, Brandon simply smiled at the man. Then he turned to Cantrell. "Listen, ah—"

"Aw, yeah, my man," Cantrell said, shaking Brandon's hand now. "What's your name now?"

"Brandon Northcross."

"Brandon, this is Smitty, the secretary of the Student Auxiliary. His real name's Terrence Dilbert, but everybody just calls him Smitty."

"Nice to meet you," Brandon said.

"My pleasure," Smitty said, shaking Brandon's hand again. "You rocked the house tonight, my man! It's just what we needed to hear."

"It's especially what that jive-ass Lipscomb needed to hear," Cantrell said.

"For real," Smitty said. "I can't believe he said some of the stupid, ass-backward things he did. How'd he ever become chair of the CBBC, anyway?"

"Listen, guys," Brandon cut in, "I just want to say that I appreciate your thinking so highly of the little speech I gave and choosing me to be the spokesperson for your boycott, but I really don't think I'm the right person for this sort of thing. Really."

"Not the right person?" Cantrell said. "After what we heard tonight? Man, you were it tonight, brother. I mean, you sounded like Jesse Jackson or somebody up in here."

"No lie," Smitty added.

"I know," Cantrell continued. "You work during the day, right? Well, we can arrange—"

"Well, as a matter of fact, I do work during the day, but—"

"Listen, Brandon," Cantrell said. "We need you, man. The community needs you. I don't know exactly how much we can offer you in the way of salary, but if you decide to work with us, I'll personally try to see to it that it's worth your while, even if you can only work with us a few evenings out of the week. That's how bad we want you, man. Ain't that right, Smitty?"

"Yeah, that's right," Smitty said. "After word gets back about what this man did here tonight, ain't no way the board wouldn't come through."

"Well, again, guys, I'm really flattered," Brandon said. "I really am. But—"

"Tell you what," Cantrell interrupted, obviously determined not to take no for an answer. "Take one of my cards. It has the address and phone number of our chapter office on it." Cantrell removed a card from his coat pocket and handed it to Brandon. "All we ask is that you just think it over. You'd be doing a real service to the community. We know you're concerned, or you probably wouldn't have even been here tonight. So just sleep on it. If you feel like you want to help us, just give me or anyone at the office a call. Is that fair?"

"Fair enough," Brandon said.

"Okay, then," Cantrell said, clasping his hand. "Hope to hear from you soon."

"Take care," Brandon said, then headed for the exit.

■ ■ ■

That night as he and Julie lay in bed, Brandon struggled with what he should do. "I've never felt like I did tonight at that meeting," he said. "It was almost like I was someone else when I was standing up there talking. I didn't really think about it. It just happened."

"I know what I'd like to happen right now," Julie said, snuggling up close to him and massaging his chest.

"I wonder what it'd be like being involved in a protest movement," Brandon mused, as he stared up at the ceiling. "You ever wonder what it'd be like to do something like that?"

"The only movement I'm thinking about right now is here in this bed with you, baby." She began planting little kisses on his face and neck.

"No, Julie, I'm serious," he said, sitting up in bed. "You think I oughta get involved with this thing?"

"Oh, Brandon," she said, sighing. "Why go and get yourself mixed up in this stuff? This doesn't involve us. We hardly spend that much time together now as it is. And what about our plans for Europe? Brandon, why start with this thing? You don't even live in that neighborhood." He turned to her.

"But, Julie, it *does* involve us. It involves me. I can't just walk away from this. Don't you see, baby?"

"Here we go again," Julie said, turning away and pulling the covers up over her. "Brandon, I'm sorry, but I'm afraid I just don't get it."

Chapter 21

The NAACP offices were located near downtown D.C. in an old, two-story brownstone that looked like a converted church. The Student Auxiliary met upstairs. From an open doorway midway the hall, Cantrell's voice could be heard.

"See, if you notice this area over here in Northwest that I have marked, they don't have these kinds of fiscal problems, simply because the income levels are close to 70 percent higher than down here," Cantrell said. "You see what I'm saying?"

"Yeah, I see where you're coming from," someone replied.

"Okay, now watch this," Cantrell said. "I'm going to show you something." Brandon peered into the conference room to see Cantrell, Smitty and another man gathered around a big map of D.C. Cantrell was busy placing stick pins on the map to mark various locations. "Now, take this area here, which isn't far from where we are now," Cantrell continued. "If you could get the city to invest just—" Brandon tapped lightly on the door to get their attention. The three men looked around. "Well, if it isn't the man of the hour," Cantrell said. "Come on in, my man. We were just talking about you not long ago. I told Smitty I had a feeling we hadn't seen the last of you. So, how you doing, guy?" He reached out to shake Brandon's hand.

"Good," Brandon said. "And you?"

"I'm making it. Oh, I don't think you met Feldon last night, did you?"

"No, I don't think I did," Brandon said, turning toward the man.

"Feldon Metcalfe," the man said, clasping Brandon's hand. He was tall with clean-cut looks.

"Brandon Northcross."

"And you remember Smitty," Cantrell said.

"Good seeing you again," Smitty said, shaking his hand.

"Same here."

"So, you gonna come work with us, Brandon?" Cantrell said.

"Well…I thought about it," Brandon said.

"And?"

"And I decided I'd give it a shot."

"Well, alright, then!" Cantrell said, slapping him on the shoulder. "It's gon happen now!"

"Yeah, Feldon," Smitty said, "you should've heard my man last night. He fired 'em up!"

"Yeah, that's what everybody's been saying," Feldon said.

"Welcome," Smitty said, giving Brandon's hand another vigorous workout.

"Yeah, welcome, man," Feldon said. "Glad to have you." Two women entered the room, bringing their conversation with them.

"Girl, you know that's just like my mother to go sign me up for—"

"Let's hold it down now, ladies," Cantrell playfully admonished them. "There's business going on in here."

"Cantrell, what business could you all possibly be taking care of?" the shorter of the two women said. "You know no real work happens until we women get here, since you men are just so helpless without us."

"Look, I want you all to meet the newest member of our team," Cantrell said. "Yvette, Angela, this is Brandon."

"Hello," Angela said. Slender and smartly dressed, she had a cordial but business-like air about her.

"And the fast one is Yvette," Cantrell said. A hint of Asian in her features gave her a decidedly exotic look.

"He's the one that spoke last night at Howard," Smitty informed them.

"Oh, yeah?" Yvette said. "I heard about that. That was you?"

"Yeah, I guess I'm the guilty party," Brandon said.

"Guilty party, my eye," Cantrell remarked. "This man single-handedly put old Lipscomb in his place."

"It would've been worth it just to see that," Angela said.

"Well, as soon as Yow gets here, I guess we can get started," Cantrell said, looking at his watch.

"Is he coming?" Smitty asked.

"He said he was," Feldon said. "He might have gotten tied up over at the school."

"Well, while we're waiting, let's go ahead and take our seats," Cantrell said. "Sit wherever you like, Brandon." They took their seats around the big table.

"Any old business, folks?" Cantrell asked.

"Wait a minute," Feldon said. "I think I hear him." The sound of someone whistling filtered in from the hallway. A few moments later, a thin, dark-skinned man with a smooth, boyish face strolled into the room, a backpack swinging from his shoulder. He was wearing a little kente cloth hat and a long, emerald-green dashiki, embroidered with gold trim, over khaki pants.

"Hello, everybody," he said.

"What's up, Yow?" Cantrell said.

"Hey, big guy. Am I late?"

"No, we hadn't really gotten started yet."

"Oh, good news. Good news," the man said, in his distinctive, African accent. "I think I finally got the new database working. Now, I'll be able to tap into the national database."

"That's great, Yow," Cantrell said. "Yow, this is Brandon, the newest member of our team."

"Hey, nice to meet you, man," Yow said, reaching over to shake his hand.

"Same here."

"Yow's in charge of membership," Cantrell said.

"So, how's the membership drive going, Yow?" Angela asked.

"It ought to be going pretty good," Yvette said, before Yow could answer. "I hear he's over at the girls' dorms recruiting nearly every day. At that rate, half the girls at Howard ought to be members by now. Y'all know the reputation these African men have with women."

"Yeah, I've been hearing about ol' Yow," Feldon said, getting into the act, too. "He's a smooth operator with the ladies."

"Aw, c'mon now," Yow said, laughing at the good-natured ribbing. "You know I recruit just as hard with the guys."

"Sure you do, Yow," Smitty said. "Sure you do."

"We're just kidding, Brandon," Yvette said. "Yow takes his job as membership coordinator for the group very seriously. Our membership has been growing steadily since he took over the position."

"Okay, everybody," Cantrell said, "before we get down to business, why don't we go around and let Brandon know what each of us do and maybe say a little about ourselves? I'll start it off. I'm Edward Cantrell III, the group's president. I'm a senior criminal justice major at Howard. I plan to go on to law school when I graduate."

"Another shyster lawyer," Yvette said under her breath.

"I heard that," Cantrell said. "But ain't nothing shyster 'bout success. It's all about the American dream. But don't worry, Yvette. When

Feldon's got the car and I see you waiting at the bus stop in the morning, I'll stop and pick you up in my Ferrari."

"Oh, would you really, Cantrell?" Yvette said, with playful sarcasm. "That's so thoughtful of you."

"So, that's me," Cantrell said. "Oh! I almost forget. I'm a member of Theta Psi Phi fraternity. Who's next? Angela?"

"I'm Angela Hardy, vice-president of the Student Auxiliary. I'm a business major at Georgetown University. And I'm a member of Alpha Beta Rho sorority."

"By day Angela's a student and mild-mannered intern at a Fortune 500 company," Cantrell said. "By evening, she's doing her thing here with the Student Auxiliary. How long you been with the group now, Angela?"

"I've been with the group about three years now," Angela said.

"Yvette?"

"My name is Yvette Samuels."

"Soon to be Mrs. Feldon Metcalfe, right?" Cantrell said.

"Cantrell, honey, if there is an engagement to be announced—which there isn't at this time—Feldon and I will see to it that you're one of the first to know."

"Aw, I'm sorry," Cantrell said, feigning innocence. "I thought there had been an announcement."

"Sure, Cantrell," Yvette said, narrowing her eyes at Cantrell. "Anyway, I'm a journalism major at Howard. Here with the Auxiliary, I'm responsible for public relations. I've been with the organization for about two years now. And my sorority is Zeta Phi Delta."

"Yow?"

"I'm Yow Toburi. As you've already been told, I'm responsible for membership. I'm a third-year electrical engineering major at Howard. I'm originally from Nigeria. And I've been working with the Student Auxiliary now for a little over a year."

"Feldon?"

"My name's Feldon Metcalfe. I serve as the group's treasurer. I'm a pre-med major at George Washington University. My plans are to go on to medical school and one day open my own practice."

"And last, and certainly least, is Smitty," Cantrell said.

"Thank you," Smitty said. "I'm the secretary for the organization. My real name is Terrence Dilbert, but everybody just calls me Smitty. I'm a political science major at Howard. And I'm a member of Gamma Psi Gamma fraternity. And I just want to say that if there's anything I or any of us can do, don't hesitate to—"

"Yo, Smitty," Cantrell interrupted. "All you supposed to do is introduce yourself, not be the damn welcome wagon committee. This is just like a Gamma, always trying to usurp authority." Everyone broke into laughter.

"Damn right!" Smitty said. "That's because Gammas rule."

"Yeh, they rule alright," Cantrell said. "When nobody else is around." Smitty and Cantrell hurled more playful barbs at each other's fraternities, prompting more laughter.

"This is a wild bunch, Brandon," Feldon said.

"Very wild," Yow added, laughing.

A slightly hunched, silver-haired white man in his early seventies entered the room. "Hello, everyone," he said, plopping a worn, brown satchel down on the table. "Sorry I couldn't get here sooner, but I had to stay late with a client."

"You're just in time, Mr. Goldman," Cantrell said. "We had just finished introducing ourselves to our newest member. This is Brandon Northcross. He's gonna be working closely with the Auxiliary on the boycott initiative."

"Hello, Brandon," Goldman said, nodding.

"Hello," Brandon said.

"Is he the one who spoke at Howard last night?"

"He's the one," Cantrell said.

"He's some speaker, Mr. Goldman," Smitty said. "You should've heard him."

"So I hear. So I hear."

"Brandon, Mr. Goldman's an attorney," Cantrell said. "He works part-time for the NAACP as one of its legal advisors. How long have you been working with the NAACP now, Mr. Goldman?"

"Oh, for a long time, Edward, way before any of you kids in this room were even around, all the way back to the early '50s."

"That *is* a long time," Cantrell said. "Okay, everybody, let's get down to business. The boycott."

"And just how exactly do we go about planning this boycott?" Yvette asked. "I've never been part of a boycott before. Anybody else here ever been involved in one before?"

"I know I haven't," Cantrell confessed. "And that's probably true for the rest of us, right?" Everyone nodded yes. "But that's okay. That's what Mr. Goldman's here for, to show us just how to go about it. Right, Mr. Goldman?"

"Well, I'm gonna try to help you put it together," Goldman said. "But it's gonna be your plan. What I'll be providing primarily are the ground rules for conducting a successful boycott and guidance along the way, especially legal advice. And I'll certainly give you my ideas of how things should go. But the final decisions will be up to you. From what Edward and Smitty have told me—and a lot of it is still sketchy at this point—I'd say you're probably looking at a boycott that's likely to last a number of weeks before any negotiations even begin. And it could be several months before any actual agreements are reached.

"So, people, you're looking at what could likely shape up to be a somewhat lengthy ordeal," Goldman continued. "So, before we get started, the question I want to put to each of you is this: Are you sure you're prepared for that kind of a conflict, especially the mental and emotional price it's likely to exact? Because when you start threatening people's livelihood, no matter how noble your cause, things can get real nasty. Now, it's gonna take 100%, nothing less, from everybody here." Goldman then removed his coat, rolled up his sleeves and went to the white board. "Alright, then, let's begin."

For the rest of the evening and into the night, they brainstormed, tossing about ideas. They discovered that they had more questions than they had answers, and that none of them had really given that much thought to what exactly they wanted from the Korean grocers. Yes, they knew they wanted better treatment for black customers. But what else? And what exactly did better treatment mean?

Around 9:30, Goldman brought the meeting to a halt. "I think we've gotten off to a good start," he said, rolling down his sleeves. "Let's get back together tomorrow. Okay?"

"Yeah, let's do that," Cantrell said, rising from his chair and stretching. "But let me just say one thing before we adjourn. We need to get this show on the road just as soon as we can, while this incident is still fresh in people's minds. My father always said to strike while the iron is hot. We've got a chance to really make something happen in the community. People are fired up like I haven't seen them fired up in a long time."

"What Edward just said is quite true," Goldman said. "You've got the community's ear. Now's the time to act."

"So, just how long is this gonna take, putting together the plan for the boycott?" Angela asked, looking to Goldman.

"Well, today's Friday," Goldman said. "If we make good time—and that means working through the weekend—maybe we can have everything worked out by, say, this coming Monday."

"Is there anybody who can't make it this weekend?" Cantrell asked. No one said anything. "Good, then. I'll see everybody tomorrow at 10 am sharp."

■ ■ ■

Saturday morning, just as they were preparing to begin, Carla Yancy, the president of the chapter, stopped by.

"Well, hello, Ms. Yancy," Cantrell greeted her. "This is certainly a pleasant surprise."

"Hello, Edward," she said. "And hello, everyone. I was in the vicinity and just thought I'd drop in and see how things were progressing. I hear you all are off to a really good start."

"Oh, they're a bright bunch, Carla," Goldman said. "You'd think they were veterans at this."

"Well, great then. Now, I think I know just about everybody here," she said, looking around the room.

"You probably don't know Brandon," Cantrell said. "He's new."

"Brandon?" she said, going over and giving him her hand. "Nice to meet you."

"Nice to meet you, too, Ms. Yancy," Brandon said.

"Brandon's the one who spoke over at Howard the other night," Angela said.

"Yes, I heard about that speech," Carla Yancy said. "People were quite impressed by it."

"Thank you," Brandon said.

"Now, I want you all to know that, on behalf of the NAACP executive board, we are fully behind your efforts," Carla said. "And we are here to support you in any way we can. I've gotta run, now. But I'll be keeping in touch."

Once Carla Yancy had left, Goldman got things underway. "Every really successful movement has a spokesman," Goldman said, "a point man or woman around whom people gravitate. That's because people often need someone they can identify with before they can truly get inspired enough to join in. If that person resonates a certain charisma, it helps. And if on top of that he happens to be a compelling speaker, then all the better. Martin Luther King was the prime example. Brandon, everyone I've talked to who was there at Howard that night seems to agree that you have a definite flair for the oratory. Because of that, I think we oughta leave the packaging of the talks up to you. We'll all have input into the content, but you'll handle the presentation. Is that okay with everyone?"

"Fine by me," Cantrell said. The others agreed, as well.

"And is that okay with you, Brandon?" Goldman said.

"It's fine with me, if it's okay with the others," Brandon said.

"Good, then." Goldman pulled down an overhead map of D.C. "Okay, with that out of the way, if we look at the area I've indicated here,"

Goldman said, drawing a circle on the map, "it pretty much encompasses where I think we need to focus the boycott."

"Excuse me, Mr. Goldman," Brandon interrupted. "But why is that?"

"Why is *what,* Brandon?"

"Why are we limiting the scope of the boycott to just that one area?"

"Well, that's the community where the shooting occurred."

"True," Brandon said. "But again, why are we only focusing the boycott on that one area?"

"Ah, what are you getting at, Brandon?" Goldman said, a bit puzzled.

"May I?" Brandon said, getting up and indicating the pointer.

"Sure," Goldman said, handing Brandon the pointer.

"The four stores we're targeting are all down in the lower Georgia Avenue corridor, right?"

"Right," Goldman said.

"Why are we only targeting those stores, when there are Korean stores that do the same thing up here, and here, and over here, and over here?" Brandon said, indicating the various locations on the map.

"Well, like Mr. Goldman said," Angela remarked, "they're in the neighborhood where the shooting took place. Why should we be concerned about those other stores?"

"Wait a minute," Goldman said, coming back over to the map. "I see what Brandon's getting at. I don't know why I didn't see it before. For us to have any long-term impact, we've got to expand the scope of this thing. If we come down on only a few stores, the storekeepers will simply ride out the storm by falling back on their relatives who run other stores. This is good, Brandon, very good."

"That means we need to mobilize in a variety of communities simultaneously," Brandon said.

"But how are we gonna do that?" Smitty said. "There're only seven of us and you've got probably close to a dozen or more stores targeted there."

"What we do is we appoint neighborhood coordinators," Cantrell said.

"Neighborhood coordinators?" Yvette said.

"Yeah, people who have it as their responsibility to oversee the boycotts at their neighborhood stores."

"But how do we keep control over what's happening day to day?" Feldon said.

"We teach them what to do," Cantrell said. "First thing Monday morning, we get on the phones and start recruiting volunteers."

"That's a good idea, Edward, having neighborhood coordinators," Goldman said. "But at the same time that we're boycotting the stores, let's make sure that protesters are out in front of the District Building downtown every day. We've got to keep up the pressure on the District Attorney's office to bring charges against the storekeeper. Let the media show the protesters down there, so the public doesn't forget that, so far, no one's been charged with the slaying of Deanna Wilkins."

"Wow," Feldon exclaimed, "that seems like a lot of ground to be trying to cover."

"Sure it is, Feldon," Brandon said. "But we can do it if we commit ourselves."

■ ■ ■

Sunday around noon, they met for a late brunch at a nearby restaurant, then went to work. In addition to the actual planning of the boycott, Goldman brought up another issue. "Brandon, as point man for the boycott, I hope you're aware that your privacy isn't going to be what it was before. Your name and picture are going to be all over the papers. You're going to be hounded, both by reporters and by people who just have an opinion about the boycott or about you personally. And not all of these people will be supporters or admirers of yours. It can get pretty bothersome. Are you ready for that kind of attention?" Brandon thought for a moment.

"I guess I hadn't really thought about it," Brandon said. "I don't mind working with the boycott, but I don't know if I want to give up my privacy."

"I know," Angela said. "Go by a pseudonym. You know, a pen name."

"That's a great idea, Angela," Goldman said.

"Yeah, that might work," Brandon said.

"But even if he does use a phony name, what's to stop people from recognizing him anyway?" Cantrell said.

"What if he wore some kind of a disguise?" Yvette suggested.

"A disguise?" Cantrell said. "Hey, what is this, a masquerade party or something? First you want him to change his name. Now you want him to wear a disguise. Maybe we can get one of those wigs with the hair sticking straight up and he can go as Don King. How 'bout that?" They laughed

"I know," Brandon said, getting in on the fun. "How about if I grow a mustache, get my hair braided, put on some dark shades and go as Stevie Wonder?"

"That's it!" Goldman said.

"*What's* it," Brandon said. "Go as Stevie Wonder?"

"No, Brandon. Sunglasses."

"What?"

"Wear a pair of dark sunglasses," Goldman said. "No one would recognize you, at least not easily. Anybody got a pair on them?"

"Yeah, I got a pair right here," Feldon said, producing a pair from his front shirt pocket.

"Great. Let me see them," Goldman said, taking the sunglasses from Feldon. "Here. Try them on Brandon." Brandon put them on.

"See?" Goldman said. "Perfect. Now for a name. Any suggestions?"

"What name do you like, Brandon?" Smitty said.

"Maybe something with X in it," Brandon said.

"You mean like Malcolm X?" Smitty said.

"My brother, my brother," Yow said, laughing. "You're gonna be a revolutionary."

"That's it!" Brandon said.

"What's it?" Cantrell said.

"What Yow just said."

"What?" Cantrell said. *"My brother?* That's what you wanna be called?"

"No," Brandon said. "Brother X."

"Brother X," Cantrell said, thinking it over. "Yeah, I can go for that. It does have a nice ring to it."

"It'll work," Smitty said.

"Brother X?" Goldman said, extending his hand to Brandon. "It's nice to meet you."

Later that evening, Goldman finally gave his approval to their plan. "Okay, guys, I think we've put together a pretty solid plan of action. Like I said, though, these things are funny. You've heard that expression, 'the best laid plans sometimes go awry?' Well, that's never more true than with these kinds of things. But if we're lucky, we'll never have to find out if it works or not."

"What do you mean, if we're lucky we'll never have to find out if it works?" Yvette said. "You mean, after all this work, you think we oughta just scrap it?"

"No," Brandon said, "I think what Mr. Goldman is saying is that if we're lucky, the store owners will concede to our demands without us having to go through with the boycott."

"Exactly," Goldman said. "Remember, the whole aim of this is winning concessions, not boycotting."

"So, we only boycott as a last resort," Cantrell said. "If they don't give in, *then* we take action."

"But first, we threaten them," Goldman said. "We make them an offer."

"An offer they can't refuse," Smitty said.

"Hopefully," Goldman said. "We give them each a copy of the same letter, stating what our demands are. And we give them a date by which they must respond, say a week."

"And if they say no to our demands or don't respond?" Cantrell asked.

"Then we move ahead with our plan," Goldman said.

For the rest of the meeting, they discussed what they wanted included in the letter. Angela volunteered to type it up.

■ ■ ■

The next day, Angela brought in the letter she had drafted and displayed it on an overhead projector.

August 6, 1989

Dear Grocer:

We, the Student Auxiliary of the D.C. Chapter of the NAACP, are writing to request that you comply with specific demands that were deemed necessary because of a history of unfair treatment toward people of color who shop at certain Korean-owned groceries in the D.C. area. Your store is among those identified.

These problems have been ongoing for some time, but recently came to a head with the fatal shooting of Deanna Wilkins at the Soo Tan grocery on August 2, 1989. It is our belief that these demands are reasonable and long over due.

Our demands are as follows:

- *Desist from all rude and discourteous behavior toward customers.*
- *Require that any employee who deals directly with customers attend a 1-hour workshop on race-sensitivity and cultural diversity.*
- *Discontinue price gouging.*
- *Sign an agreement to invest a certain percentage of your profits back into the community in which you do business.*

- *Hire at least one person of color from the neighborhood to work in your store.*

Please respond to this letter in writing by August 14, 1989.

Respectfully,

Student Auxiliary of the NAACP

After a brief discussion and some minor revision, the group approved it.

"What we do now is we hand-deliver a copy of the letter to each of the Korean groceries that we've targeted," Goldman explained. "Not send, mind you, but hand-deliver. That way we know for certain that they've received it."

"I can get the stores further out," Cantrell said, "indicating them on the map."

"I can get the rest," Angela said.

"Okay, Angela, we'll get together on it after the meeting," Cantrell said. "Is there anything else we should make sure of when we're delivering the letters, Mr. Goldman?"

"No, just make sure you put it in their hands and, if possible, the storeowner's hand," Goldman said. "Because we don't want them coming back and saying that they never got them."

"Okay, well, I guess that's about it, then," Cantrell said.

"Oh, I almost forgot," Yvette said. "The funeral for Deanna Wilkins is tomorrow at 1 o'clock at the Morning Star Missionary Baptist Church on Rhode Island just down the street from Gaither's Funeral Home."

"Thanks, Yvette," Cantrell said. "I'm glad you reminded us of that. I'm planning on going. Who else is going?"

"I think we all should go, if possible," Brandon said.

"I agree with Brandon," Goldman said. "Not only would it be a good thing to do as a way of showing our support for the family, but it would also let the community at large know that we're concerned on a personal level."

"So, whoever can make it, let's plan to meet at the church tomorrow at, say, a quarter 'til, so we can all sit together," Cantrell said. "If anybody needs a ride, just let me know."

■ ■ ■

All of them, including Goldman, made it to the slain girl's funeral the next day. People from all over the D.C. area, luminaries as well as ordinary citizens, crammed into the small church, the crowd overflowing out into the street. Speakers were set up outside so those unable to get inside could hear the service. Even the mayor was on hand. Earlier, Angela and Cantrell carried out the plan to deliver the letters to the Korean merchants. All that was left to do now was wait.

■ ■ ■

The day after the deadline, they got back together to discuss the results. Angela took the floor. "Well, as you know, the deadline has passed, and to my knowledge we've heard from just two stores, that's two out of fourteen. One called to say 'go to hell.' The other wrote to say they'd promise to be nicer to black people in the future. I don't think this is what we had in mind."

"You mean none of the others even bothered to respond at all?" Smitty said.

"No."

"Personally, I didn't think we'd get much of a response," Goldman said. "But I did think it'd be better than this."

"Well, folks," Cantrell said, "I think it's time we let our Korean merchants know we mean business. This Monday, we kick off the boycott. In the meantime, let's get those flyers printed up announcing it. Smitty, you, Feldon and Yow get in touch with all the picketers and let them know where we want them to meet, what time, and who their coordinators will be. Yvette, make sure the black newspapers and radio stations know about it."

"What about our kickoff rally?" Angela said.

"That's right," Goldman said. "We don't want to forget about that."

"How about Sunday evening at the Howard campus outside on the mall in front of the Student Union Building?" Angela suggested.

"Excellent," Goldman said.

"Make sure the word gets out about that, too, Yvette," Cantrell said.

■ ■ ■

Sunday evening, they met at the NAACP building and rode together to the rally. A large crowd was already gathered when they arrived, and more were on their way. Many of the area's black churches had provided buses to transport the elderly and those without transportation from their various neighborhoods. Brandon and Cantrell mounted the stage, joining those already there, to the cheers of the crowd. Cantrell promptly got the rally underway.

"Greetings, my brothers and my sisters! On behalf of the Student Auxiliary of the Washington D.C. chapter of the NAACP, I welcome you to the beginning of what will undoubtedly go down in history as a time when the little people stood shoulder to shoulder and said to the mighty giants, no more! You've pushed us around enough! We're not taking it anymore! That's why tomorrow we're gonna do what?"

"Boycott!" the crowd shouted.

"I can't hear you! What did you say?" Cantrell said, cupping his hand to his ear.

"Boycott!"

"Well, alright then," Cantrell said. "We're going to start things off by asking the Reverend T. L. Leaks, pastor of the St. John AME church, if he would come and ask God's blessings on our behalf. Reverend Leaks?" Dressed in a black suit with a white clerical collar, the minister stepped to the podium.

"Let us pray. Father God in heaven, we come to you this evening asking that you consecrate what we're about to undertake, for we believe that it is both good and noble. We ask that you bless us, especially those who're going to be standing on the battle lines tomorrow. We ask that no hurt, harm or danger might befall them. And we ask that you infuse this movement with a power from on high, so that no man or woman will be able to withstand the truth on which we're standing. Now, keep us under your merciful, watchful eye, Lord, as we go about your work. Keep us prayerful and ever mindful of you. And we'll forever give you the praise and honor that you so richly deserve. Amen."

"Amen."

A number of politicians, ministers and grass roots activists gave brief speeches, interspersed with spirited selections from several local church choirs. Finally, it came time for Brandon to speak.

"It's prime time, my man," Cantrell whispered to Brandon, as he rose to introduce him. "How you doing, D.C.?" he said into the microphone. "Are you ready to go to another level?"

"Yeh!"

"You remember that fiery young man that spoke the other night, that young man that warmed our souls, fired us up, got this whole thing started?"

"Yeh!"

"I said, do you remember him?"

"Yeh!"

"Well, he's gonna come and say a few words to us this evening. Is that alright?"

"Bring him on!"

"Let him speak!"

"Alright, then," Cantrell said. "Without further ado, the man you've been waiting for, the man with the master plan, Brother X! Give it up!" The cheers and applause reverberated through the air as Brandon stepped forward. "It's all yours now, my man," Cantrell said, squeezing his hand.

"Thank you, my brother, for that rousing introduction," Brandon began. "My friends, it was little over a week ago that we met inside the building just behind us here, met for a hastily called community meeting to address an egregious wrong."

"An egregious wrong!"

"An egregious wrong that had been committed against our family."

"Yeh!"

"The unjustifiable shooting of our young sister, sixteen-year-old Deanna Wilkins, a student at Cordova High School. Before we go any further, I just want to say that our prayers are with the family of this young lady." He paused for a moment before proceeding. "Now, the circumstances surrounding Deanna Wilkins' tragic and untimely death stirred deep emotions within all of us. And from the stirring of those emotions, we, the Student Auxiliary of the NAACP, saw the need to do something to address and correct the circumstances that had led up to that incident. So, we got together, put our anger aside, put our frustrations aside, and sent out a letter to all the merchants who had been identified as having a history of ill-treatment toward people of color in the community, asking them if they might pledge to make just a few good-faith efforts to show that they've had a change of heart.

"We even said we'd be willing to work with them on these demands. We didn't ask for much. But like the Egyptians back in biblical days, they turned a deaf ear to the pleas of the people. That left us no choice but to do what we're doing now. So, when we go out tomorrow, go out there with our picket signs, let us go with the resolve and the determination that we can make a difference. As for those who have yet to enlist in our battle for justice, saying, perhaps, 'It doesn't affect me,' I'm reminded of what Dr. King once said in his letter from a Birmingham jail to the white clergy of the city who had called his actions in the city unwise and untimely. Dr. King told them that injustice anywhere is a threat to justice everywhere."

"Yeh!"

"So, though you might not be feeling the lead boot of oppression on the back of your neck today, just keep on living!"

"Just keep on living!"

"Just keep on living, and some dark clouds will hover overhead."

"Yeh!"

"Some rain will fall in your life."

"Yeh!"

"That's why we're here today. Looking out among you, I see that we've come from different walks of life. Some young, some old, some white collar, some blue collar. But one thing we all have in common is a thirst for justice. For whether we've personally been mistreated in these stores or not, we all know that it could just as well have been us. My friends, this is a pivotal point in the history of our city, the nation's capitol. As tragic as the death of Deanna Wilkins and as pressing as the need for fair treatment of people of color in these stores, this movement is bigger than that. This is a pivotal point because, as the nation's capitol, it should and must embody the ideals of this great country of ours. Those ideals are those of democracy, freedom, liberty and justice for all. These ideals are nowhere more trumpeted than through the words inscribed on the Statue of Liberty that stands tall, proud and majestic out in the New York Harbor.

"We all know those famous words, which were penned more than a hundred years ago by the poet Emma Lazarus. In her poem she talks about America saying to the world to bring to it those who are tired, poor, those who yearn to breathe free. She says send them to me. And I'll give them rest. Successive waves of European immigrants came, believing in the promise expressed through those hallowed words. But sadly, some who stepped upon these shores, and who had already been here for several centuries, were not tired until they got here."

"Say it!"

"Sadly, some who stepped foot upon these shores were not yearning to breathe free until they got here."

"Alright, now!" He was forced to pause until the applause subsided.

"These were those who had been brought to these shores to pick the cotton, to cultivate the tobacco, the rice and the sugar cane, which all helped to build this country."

"Yeh!"

"If we are true Americans—and we are—then we must not just ask, but must demand, that we be accorded the same rights as other Americans." He was interrupted again by applause.

"Yeh!"

"Only then can we truly feel like Americans."

"Yeh!"

"We've got our marching orders. We know what we've got to do. So, when we take to the streets tomorrow morning, when we go out, let us go out with the unbending determination that it's time for a change!"

"Time for a change!"

"Time for a change from injustice to justice."

"Yeh!"

"Time for a change from unfairness to fairness."

"Yeh!"

"Are you ready to help bring about that change?"

"Yeh!"

"I said are you ready to help bring about that change?"

"Yeh!"

"Well, let's make it happen then! Thank you. And God bless you." Brandon stepped away from the podium and waved to the cheering crowd. The media trained their cameras on Brandon, trying to get the best angles.

"Time for a change!" Cantrell repeated into the mike. "Thank you, Brother X, for reminding us what this is all about and why we're out here. Now, I just wanna know one thing. Just one thing. Can I count on you, starting tomorrow morning, to help make this change happen?"

"Yeh!"

"Are you ready to help make sure that change takes place?"

"Yeh!"

"I'm counting on you," Cantrell said. "We're now gonna ask our sister, gospel recording artist Beneatha Adams, if she would now come and lead us in singing a couple of stanzas of that old anthem we used to sing back during the civil rights days, that anthem that gave our people the strength to persevere against all odds, *We Shall Overcome.*" As the musicians began to play, the woman stepped to the mike.

"I want everybody to join hands cross ways with the person next to you," she said. "See, when we're holding hands this way, it gives us strength, gives us unity, for you can't fall for the hand that's holding on to yours. And now when we sing this song, I want everyone to just think back, think back over the years to a time when God brought you or someone close to you through a difficult, trying time. Think about how the Lord made a way when there was no way. Let us now blend our voices." With arms linked, out in the audience as well as up on stage, they began to sing, swaying from side to side.

We shall overcome.
We shall overcome.
We shall overcome some day.
Deep in my heart, I do believe.
We shall overcome some day.

The Lord will see us through.
The Lord will see us through.
The Lord will see us through some day.
Deep in my heart, I do believe.
We shall overcome some day.

Chapter 22

Monday morning, they put their plans into action, as picket lines went up at each of the stores they'd targeted. Brandon and Cantrell's first stop was Soo Tan's grocery, site of the shooting. Eight to nine men and women walked quietly in single file in front of the store, carrying picket signs and placards that read:

Don't shop Soo Tan's
They discriminate

Don't spend your money where
you're not appreciated

Remember Deanna Wilkins
Don't shop Soo Tan's

A bearded man with dreadlocks and wearing an LA Lakers sweat suit bellowed through a bullhorn at passersby. "Don't shop here! Send a message that black people will not be taken for granted! It's time for us to stand up, my brothers and my sisters!"

At the Blue Oyster grocery, their sixth stop, Brandon and Cantrell arrived to find one of the storekeepers engaged in a heated argument with some of the picketers.

"Why you picket my store? Why? I no treat you people bad," the Korean man said, in an almost pleading manner.

"If that was true, then we wouldn't have to be out here marching in front of your store!" one of the picketers, a woman, said. "Let me give you an example. When black people buy something in your store and you give them change, you and the rest of your family act like they've got some kinda contagious disease or something, the way you toss the money down on the counter. It's like you're afraid something's gon happen if you touch their hand by handing it to them politely."

"Politely?" the man said, with a baffled expression.

"Yeh. Politely. You know what the word politely means, don't you?"

A middle-aged Korean woman came running out from inside the store. Behind her was a young Korean man who looked like he might be her son.

"You go! You go now!" she shouted at the picketers, flailing her arms about, as if to shoo them away like chickens. When none of the picketers moved, she grabbed the sign one of the women was carrying and tried to wrestle it away from her.

"Woman, I bet you better let go this sign!" the black woman said, struggling with her.

"Hold up! Hold up!" Cantrell said, stepping between the two women.

"Tell them take signs away!" the Korean woman said, relinquishing her hold on the sign. "Tell them take signs away now!"

"Look, whether you like it or not, these picketers have a right to be out here," Brandon said. "They are operating within the law. *You* are violating the law by trying to take their signs from them."

"Who are you?" the Korean man said.

"We're with the Student Auxiliary of the NAACP," Cantrell said.

"And that's Brother X!" an angry young man said. He was among a small group of spectators that had gathered. "And you better not mess with him, either!"

"Brother X? Who Brother X?" the Korean man said.

"You mess with him, you'll find out!" one of the man's friends said.

"You brothers, let's be cool now," Brandon said.

"We got yo' back, Brother X," the man said. "We ain't gon let 'em push you 'round!"

"All of you go!" the Korean woman shouted. "Go away! You hurt business! No customers come!"

"We ain't goin' nowhere!" one of the men said. "You don't own this sidewalk!"

"Yeh. *You* git the hell out of here, bitch!" another man said.

"You don't talk to my mother like that!" the Korean woman's son shouted, shaking his finger in the man's face.

"Whatchu' gon do 'bout it!?" the man said, readying for a fight.

"Look, everybody!" Brandon said, raising his hands to try to restore order. "Just cool it! Alright? There's no reason for this." Both sides calmed down. "Now, you brothers really need to chill. The name-calling, it's unnecessary. Just be cool." Then turning back to the Korean family, he said, "Now, ma'am, now, sir, this is a peaceful boycott. These people are not here for confrontations. No one's going to try to stop anyone from entering your store to do business who wants to."

"But the signs, they—"

"They have a right to display the signs, sir," Brandon said.

"A right?" the Korean man said. "But why?" Brandon motioned for the man to step over to the side with him, away from the crowd.

"Sir, some of these people out here are very upset, very angry about what happened with the shooting of the teenage girl at the Soo Tan store. I think it would be in your best interest to take your wife and son and go back inside your store. Nothing good is going to come from you being out here confronting them. You're not gonna change their minds. If anything, you're only going to aggravate the situation."

"You Brother X? Yes?" the man asked.

"Yes, I'm Brother X."

"They listen to you. Yes?"

"Yes, I suppose they listen to me."

"Tell me. You dislike me?"

"No, I don't dislike you."

"Then why this?" the man said, gesturing toward the picketers behind him.

"Your store is being picketed because a pattern of discrimination was found to be occurring against people of color who shop there," Brandon explained.

"Discrimination?"

"Yes, discrimination," Brandon said. "When you comply with the terms stated in the letter you were given, the picketing will end."

"Letter?"

"Yes, the letter we gave you, the one from the NAACP." The man's bewilderment now turned to open hostility.

"That letter, it nothing but lies!" he shouted. "Nothing but lies!" Then he spat on the ground. "That what I think of your letter! And what I think of NAACP!" He returned to his wife and son. "Come! No honor among these people. They lie! No honor! No honor!" He stormed back toward the store with his family.

■ ■ ■

Upon arriving home that night, Brandon found a message from Julie on his answering machine.

"Brandon? It's Julie. I miss you. Give me a call. I love you. Bye." He dialed Julie's number. There was no answer, so he left a message for her.

"I got your message, Julie. I miss you, too. You won't believe how busy I've been. I'll try to call you tomorrow sometime, if I get a chance. Bye."

■ ■ ■

Brandon and Cantrell's usual routine each day would be to join the picketers outside the Soo Tan store first thing in the morning. They would then drive to the other stores to make brief appeals using a megaphone to those within earshot. They also spoke at community rallies at night, where they would try to motivate the people to stay with the boycott. At the end of each rally, an appeal would be made for people to become members of the NAACP, if they weren't already. It was all done in much the same spirit of a church revival. And, as always, one or two Black Muslims would be there, observing.

About a week into the boycott, the Student Auxiliary held its first press conference. It took place at the NAACP building. Seated at a table with Brandon and Cantrell, behind a bank of media microphones, Yvette got things started. "Hello, I'm Yvette Samuels, public relations director for the Student Auxiliary of the Washington D.C. chapter of the NAACP. On my left is Edward Cantrell III, president of the Student Auxiliary. And on my right is Brother X, principle spokesperson for the organization. Brother X will now take the first question from the lady right over there," she said, pointing to a black woman who was with one of the local TV stations.

"Sir, exactly what does the NAACP hope to accomplish through this boycott of Korean groceries?"

"What we want—and we have stated our demands explicitly in a letter we delivered more than a week ago to each merchant we're targeting—" Brandon said, holding up a copy of the letter to the cameras, "is for each merchant to: One, desist from all rude and discourteous behavior toward their customers. Two, have each employee who deals directly with customers attend a workshop on race sensitivity and cultural diversity. Three, discontinue price gouging. Four, sign an agreement to invest a certain percentage of their profits back into the communities that they do business in, which, for the most part, are black communities. And five, to hire at least one person of color from the neighborhood to work in their store."

The woman quickly followed up with another question. "The Korean store owners say that nothing is wrong, that their customers are, for the most part, contented with the goods and service they receive. Many say they have no intention of negotiating. With that kind of hard-line stance, how long is the NAACP prepared to stay with this boycott?"

"Well, first of all, let me say that we're not surprised by that kind of blatant denial coming from them," Brandon said. "As far as how long we're prepared to stay with the boycott, we're prepared to stay with it for as long as it takes to see that our demands are met." Yvette recognized another reporter.

"You call yourself Brother X. Are you a Black Muslim?"

"No, the name has no connection to the Black Muslims or to any other group," Brandon said.

"The gentlemen over here," Yvette said.

"People are already comparing you to another X, Malcolm X," a white reporter said. "You remind people of him—your oratory, your command of facts, your whole persona, one might say. What's your reaction to this comparison?"

"Well, I'm certainly flattered by such comparisons. But my knowledge and whatever oratory skills I may possess are nothing compared to that of Malcolm X. If people really knew about the man, they wouldn't be tempted to make such statements, though well-intentioned, I'm sure. I'm just the designated spokesman for this one boycott. At the same time, however, since I've studied Malcolm X's life and teachings extensively, I guess it's only natural that when I speak that I might evoke his memory at times. But I'd just like to make one thing clear. And that is, while I certainly agree with Malcolm's teachings on the black struggle in America and throughout the world for equality, I'm not an adherent of the Islamic religion. I'm Christian. I don't want anyone being mislead on that matter."

"Are you suggesting, then, that because of religious differences between yourself and Malcolm X—you being Christian, him having been Muslim—that there are things about his philosophy toward race relations between blacks and whites in America that you perhaps don't agree entirely with?" the same reporter asked.

"No, I'm not saying that at all," Brandon said. "As Malcolm often preached, blacks in America as well as those around the world have infinitely more in common, because of their shared experience of racial oppression, than they do differences because of religion."

"The lady standing by the wall," Yvette said, recognizing a different reporter.

"Brother X, just how long do you plan to try to keep your identity secret?" Brandon hesitated a moment before answering.

"Well, for as long as I can."

■ ■ ■

Following the press conference, there was a noticeable change, but not in the direction they had hoped. The Korean store owners, some of whom who earlier had given indications that they might be ready to negotiate, became even more hardened in their resistance. Phone calls also began coming in to the NAACP office from the media, trying to uncover the real identity of Brother X.

■ ■ ■

"Canty, didn't drive your dream car today, huh?" Yow said to Cantrell one evening as they were busy upstairs. "What, is it in the shop or something? Or does the girlfriend have it today, maybe?"

"Yow, what are talking about?" Cantrell said, barely looking up from what he was doing. "It's parked right out there in front of the building where I always park it. I know what you want. You want me to go look out the window so you can holler, gotcha! Right? Well, it ain't happening, at least not today, Yow." Yow went over to the window and glanced out.

"Okay, whatever you say, Canty. But I'm telling you, it ain't there." Yow headed off to his work area. Cantrell looked over at Brandon.

"Yow's up to it again." But in less than a minute, Cantrell had eased over to the window to take a peek out. "Somebody done stole my car!" Cantrell screamed. "Somebody stole my car, y'all! I parked it right out here like I always do! And now it's gone! I knew this was a bad neighborhood! I been telling Ms. Yancy this ain't a safe neighborhood!"

"Are you sure you parked it there, Cantrell?" Yvette asked, coming over and looking out the window herself.

"Am I sure!? You damn *right* I'm sure. What, you think I'm crazy or something?!"

"Okay, okay," Yvette said. "You don't have to get all bent outta shape. Just wanted to make sure."

"Maybe you should report it to the police," Yow said, bringing over the phone.

"Yeah, that's what I ought to do," Cantrell said. He took the phone from Yow. "At least somebody's thinking around here." Cantrell dialed the police. "Hello? Yes, I want to report a stolen car."

Cantrell was giving out his name and license tag number to the police when Yow, standing on the other side of the room now, said, "Hey, this looks like your car out here, Canty."

"Excuse me," Cantrell said into the phone, then placed his hand over the mouthpiece. "What did you say?" Some of the others had now joined Yow at the window.

"Yeah, this does look like your car, Cantrell, "Smitty said.

"Excuse me, but could you hold for a second?" Cantrell said into the phone, then went to the window. "Why, that *is* my car! How the hell did my car get—" That all-too-familiar look on Yow's face, the one he displayed whenever he'd duped someone, stopped Cantrell in the middle of his question. All he could do now was smile at having been taken once again.

■ ■ ■

"Brandon?" He was leaving the NAACP building one evening when he turned to see Julie waiting in her car out front.

"Oh, hi, Julie," he said through the open passenger side window. "What are you doing here?" He opened the door and got in. But when he went to give her a kiss, she leaned away. "What's wrong? I do something?"

"You do something?" she said. "How about trying did you *not* do something?"

"Oh, that's right," he said, slapping the dashboard. "I was supposed to call you back the other day. I'm sorry."

"And the day before that. Remember that, Brandon?"

"Julie, I've just been so busy. I'm sorry."

"I saw you on the news the other night. Some of my friends saw you, too. They've been calling asking me if it's really you and, if it is, why you're calling yourself this Brother X. Have you turned into some kind of radical all of a sudden, Brandon?" Feldon and Yvette, who were walking by hand-in-hand, glanced over at them. Feldon waved. But Yvette, when she got a look at Julie, abruptly turned her head away. "Are they friends of yours here at the NAACP?"

"Yeh. That's Feldon and Yvette."

"They make a really handsome couple," Julie said. "But she certainly didn't seem too pleased about seeing me. So, what's up with this Brother X thing, Brandon?"

"Brother X is just a name I'm using while I'm involved with the boycott. That's all. We thought it might help keep my identity secret, at least for awhile. I'll be just plain Brandon again as soon as the boycott's over."

"Whenever that is," Julie said offhandedly, then looked away.

"Julie, I told you I'd probably be working with the NAACP on this boycott."

"I know you did," she said, turning toward him. "But you didn't tell me you were going to be sleeping and eating it, too. Brandon, we haven't been together one night since you started with this thing. I can never get you on the phone. And you hardly ever return my calls."

"I'm sorry," he said. "It's just that this is the first time I've ever been involved in something like this. I want to give it my best, give it 100 percent."

"Well, unless my math is wrong, I guess that leaves all of about zero percent for me," Julie said.

"You know that's not what I meant, Julie."

"Can we get together Friday night?" Julie said. "Or are you maybe afraid some of your black female friends like Yvette will see you out with me?"

"C'mon, Julie. Let's not get into that again."

"Why not? I thought you enjoyed talking about bigotry and people who are bigots."

"Yvette's not a bigot, Julie, if that's what you're implying," he said.

"No? Well, what is she then?"

"Julie, you wouldn't understand. You just don't know what it's like to be black."

"Oh, so that's it, huh?" she snapped. "You're right. Maybe I don't know what it's like to be black. But let me tell you something. Your people aren't the only ones who've ever been persecuted. I'm Jewish, remember?"

"I know all about the holocaust, Julie. I know—"

"It's not just the holocaust, Brandon. See, that's the problem. People think that when Jews immigrated to America that they somehow automatically had it made, that they left all the anti-Semitism back in Europe. That's bullshit! My grandparents caught hell over here. There were quotas every way they turned, whether it was getting jobs or moving into certain neighborhoods. My parents didn't have it that much easier either. And anti-Semitism is still very much alive today. I may not get singled out in the same way you do, but it's there. I hear the comments. It's 'Jews this' and 'Jews that.' Some of the most derogatory things you can think of. And because most people don't know I'm Jewish, unless I tell them, they say these things around me. Sometimes I just wanna scream!" Julie took a deep breath and let it out slowly. "I'm sorry. I didn't mean to go off like that."

"It's okay," Brandon said, caressing her hand. "I guess I had it coming." They were both quiet for awhile.

"I don't know if I ever told you this," Julie said, "but my mother and father, when they were college students back in the '60's, they went down south one summer to participate in the Civil Right's Movement."

"They did?"

"They got to know a lot of black students and became good friends with some of them. Blacks and Jews were allies back then, fighting a common enemy. What happened to that alliance? It's definitely not there anymore, not among our generation." They sat quietly for a moment, reflecting. "So, when will I see you again?"

"I don't know, Julie. All this week and next week I've got meetings and rallies to speak at in the evening. My life's just crazy right now."

"Well, call me when you get a chance. Okay?" Julie said.

"Okay." They kissed goodbye.

■ ■ ■

That evening, Brandon gave Reverend Hollings a call. He hadn't seen or talked to him since getting involved with the boycott.

"Hollings residence."

"Hello, Reverend Hollings?"

"Speaking."

"It's Brandon. How are you? "

"Oh, hey, man. What's going on? I was just talking to the Deaconess about you. She was asking me 'isn't that Brandon on the news?' I said 'I think it is.'"

"Yeah, it's me."

"And she said 'He's going around calling himself Brother X now. When did he become a Muslim?' I said 'I didn't know he had.' So, are you a Black Muslim now, Brandon?"

"No, I haven't converted," Brandon said, with a chuckle. "It's just a thing for the boycott. That's all. Let me ask you something. Have any reporters been snooping around the church, asking about me, by any chance?"

"We've gotten several calls from the media, wanting to know if it was true that Brother X was a member of the church. I told them if they wanted to know anything about Brother X to talk to him. I figured you obviously wanted to try to remain anonymous, at least for awhile, 'cause you know it's just a matter of time before they find out your real name, right?"

"Yeah, I know they'll find out eventually," Brandon said. "But, like you said, I don't want it out just yet."

"I hear you," the Reverend said. "Well, I'll pass the word along to the Deaconess and anybody else I run into here at the church who I think would know your name."

"I'd really appreciate it, Reverend."

"No problem. So, how are you doing?"

"The boycott is coming along okay," Brandon said.

"No, I know how the boycott's going," the Reverend said. "I mean how are *you* doing?"

"Oh, I'm doing fine," Brandon said. "I feel like I'm burning the candle at both ends sometimes, though."

"Well, you take care of yourself," the Reverend said. "Try not to over-extend yourself with this thing. And be careful."

"Thanks, Reverend. I will."

"And if you need anything, just let me know."

"Thanks. I will. Bye."

Chapter 23

About three weeks into the boycott, as Goldman had warned, things began to get ugly. Hooligans, suspected of being hired by the Koreans grocers, began smashing windows and slashing van tires at the NAACP building. Placing citizen patrols around the building at night, however, soon eliminated the vandalism. But something that had not been anticipated, even by Goldman, was that the local Ku Klux Klan and skinheads began getting into the act. Their position was that the boycott was just another attempt by blacks to take over society, and that the DA's office was right in refusing to bring charges against the storekeeper. In fact, they announced plans to hold a joint march through downtown D.C. to show their support for the Korean merchants.

Tensions ran high throughout the city, as word spread that some of the rival black gangs had agreed to a truce among themselves to unite to face off with the Klan and skinheads if they marched. They promised, in their words, that blood would run in the streets of D.C.—white blood, this time. Fortunately, the march never came off. Still, there continued to be plenty of worry just over the inflammatory rhetoric that was coming from the white hate groups. An indirect consequence of it, however, was that more people began to become sensitized to the boycott, spreading it to other areas of the city to include some white-owned groceries that had also been accused of discriminatory practices toward blacks.

In the meantime, hate mail began arriving at the NAACP office. There would usually be a statement or two in the letters deriding the efforts of the organization. Then there would be something to the effect that blacks ought to go back to Africa if they weren't happy here in America, or that blacks were responsible for the deterioration of the country. Sometimes they would be addressed to the NAACP, other times to Brother X. A couple of times they were addressed to Nigger X. But in addition to the hate mail, there were many letters in support of the boycott. Some of them were even from female admirers of the phantom Brother X.

As the grocers continued to show no visible signs of giving in anytime soon, the NAACP prepared for what was shaping up to be a long, protracted battle. The Student Auxiliary began to focus some of its attention on some of the sore spots in the communities. One of the most pressing of these was the rampant drug trafficking. People in the neighborhoods had complained about the drug trafficking for years, but little had been done about it. To try to combat the problem, the Student Auxiliary decided to begin making sweeps through some of the drug-infested areas during the evenings, to try to reach some of those caught up in the drug culture.

Brandon, Cantrell, Feldon, Smitty and a half dozen or so other Student Auxiliary members made their first sweep just a few blocks over from the NAACP building, where a virtual open-air drug market flourished, with drug dealers hawking their wares all along the street.

"Everybody, listen up," Cantrell said. "Anybody looks like they're about to get bent oughta shape because of what we're trying to lay on 'em, just back off. Don't press it."

"Yeh, and keep your eyes open, too," a tall, stocky man named Pervis said. "Some of these guys out here are hooked up with these Jamaican drug posses. I grew up 'round here. I know how they operate."

"Jamaican drug posses?!" one man exclaimed.

"Some of 'em," Pervis said. "They're the worst. But all these drug gangs can be cut-throat."

"Whoa!" the man said. "I didn't know it was gon be this serious. Y'all sure y'all know what we getting into here? I mean, I wanna help and all. But I don't wanna end up getting shot in the process."

"Yeh, me either," someone else said.

"Yeh, I don't know if this was such a great idea, after all," yet another man said. "Maybe we oughta go back and study this thing some more."

"Look, are we gonna let the fact that these brothers are packing scare us off?" Brandon said. "Nobody's denying there's some risk involved in doing this. We knew that before we came out here. But are we gonna let that stop us? If we don't try to reach these brothers, then who will? Do we wanna wait until another 8-year-old gets gunned down, caught in the crossfire over a turf battle, before we do anything? Do we?" Brandon looked hard into the faces of each of them. "And it's probably not gonna be much different anywhere else we go."

"You can count on it," Pervis said.

"So, are we gonna go through with this or what?" Brandon said. No one said anything.

"Look, everybody that's in, let's see it with your hand," Cantrell said, stretching his hand out into the middle of the group.

"I'm in," Brandon said, placing his hand on top of Cantrell's.

"I'm in, too," Pervis said, slapping his big hand down on top of Brandon's. Smitty and Feldon followed suit. Then slowly, one by one, the others joined in.

"Alright then," Cantrell said. "This is what we're gonna do. We're gonna break up into two groups. One group take this side of the street. The other take the other side."

"Yo, somebody needs to stay back at the van, in case we need to make a run for it," Smitty said. "And if anything goes wrong, to be ready to beep the horn. Kinda be a lookout."

"I can do it," a man said. One of his arms was noticeably shorter than the other.

"Alright, Wyndell," Cantrell said. "You be the lookout. You see anything 'bout to go down, you toot the horn."

"And keep the motor running, too," someone added.

"Yo, can I say a word?" Pervis asked.

"Yeh, go ahead, man," Cantrell said.

"While one is talking, the others be looking out," Pervis said. "'Cause if they think we trying to interfere with their business, it could be some trouble, something we definitely don't want. But if everybody just stays cool, there shouldn't be no problem."

"Thanks, Pervis," Cantrell said. "Okay. Any questions?" No one had any questions. "Okay, then. Half of y'all go with Brandon; the other half come with me. We'll meet up at the top of the hill. Wyndell, you take the van up there, where you can see everything." Cantrell handed Wyndell the keys to the van. "If I blow this whistle here," he said, showing the man the whistle he had hanging from around his neck, "you bring the van and bring it quick. Okay?"

"I gotcha," Wyndell said.

"Okay. Let's do it."

Brandon and his group, which included Pervis, Feldon and three other men, crossed to the other side of the street, where they soon came upon a man about to commence a drug transaction. The thick, rope-like gold chain swinging from his neck glittered in the light from the street lamp as he leaned over to talk with a white man in a car with Virginia plates.

"Yo, how many rocks you want, man? They ten dollars a piece. It's some good shit, too. I don't carry nothing but the best."

"Gimme three," the man said, passing three bills to the drug dealer.

"Here you go, my nigga." He handed the goods to the man. "Enjoy. And come back when you ready for some more." The car moved on.

"Hey, my brother," Pervis called to the drug dealer, just as he was about to approach another car that had pulled over.

"Yeh," he said, looking around. "What it be like? Y'all want some good shit? I got it, the best crack you can get anywhere 'round here. For just one Hamilton, I'll give you some rock that'll rock you stone out yo' mind. What's it gon be, gentlemen? What's yo' pleasure? I might even give y'all a group rate."

"Naw, man," Pervis said. "We ain't into that."

"Aw. Okay. Well, what y'all want, some powder? Or some weed? I can hook you up with that, too. Ain't no problem. You want some acid? I got that, too. You at the we-aim-to-please, all-night drugstore. We never close. Whatever you want, we got. And if we ain't got it, we can get it."

"Naw, we ain't into drugs at all," Pervis explained. "This is Brother X. You heard of Brother X?"

"Brother X?" the man said, looking Brandon over. "Naw, my nigga, I ain't down with it. But check it out. I love you, but I ain't got time to jaw with you right now. It's cash money to be made tonight. That's the only reason I'm out here." The man started away.

"Can we talk to you for just a second?" Brandon said to the man. "Just for a second?"

"Look, man," one of the man's acquaintances said, coming over, his hand inside his jacket. Another man was with him who also appeared to be packing. Both were tough looking. "Just step. Okay?"

"We don't want any trouble," Brandon said, his hands raised, palms outward. "We're not here to interfere with your business. We just want to talk to you for a minute. Just give us a minute. That's all we ask. Just a minute of your time." The man thought for a moment.

"Awight," he said. "A minute. Then you step. Awight?"

"That's cool," Brandon said. "All we want is for you to think about what you're doing out here. Think about how you're hurting your own people by what you're doing. Think about the fact that these drugs you're selling are poison, poison piped into your community, probably by well-to-do white men, to poison the minds and bodies of mostly black people. They'd never allow this to go on in white communities. Think about that. And the little money you're making, it's a drop in the bucket to what the man's pulling down. And with little of the risk you're running."

"They're using you," Pervis put in. "Matter of fact, they're pimping you. That's really what they're doing. Open your eyes, my brothers. Open your eyes and see the light."

"Man, what you talkin' 'bout, somebody pimpin' me?" one of the men said. "Ain't nobody pimpin' me. I'm makin' cash money."

"Is that money more important than your pride?" Brandon said.

"More important than my *pride?*" the man said, looking at Brandon strangely.

"Yeah. Is it more important than your pride, more important than your self-respect?"

"Look, man, I don't know what you talkin' 'bout," the man said. "Anyway, yo' minute is up. Bye." The two who were packing started away. The first man stayed.

"How is me bein' out here makin' money mean I ain't got no pride?" the man asked. "Explain to me that?"

"You're selling out, selling out yourself, selling out your people," Brandon said.

"*I'm* sellin' out?" the man said. "Can you tell me where I can pull down this kinda loot in one night?" He fished out a fat wad of bills from his pocket.

"No, I can't tell you that," Brandon said. "But I can tell you how you can get a job doing an honest day's work for an honest day's pay, one where you don't have to worry every day about getting arrested and going to prison or, worse, getting shot. And at the end of the day you'd still have your dignity. Well, we'll leave you alone now. Thanks for your time. Let's go," Brandon said to the others. They started away.

"I ain't no sellout!" the man protested. "I got my dignity. I'm just tryin' to make it just like you!"

"Aw, forget that ol' square-ass shit them niggas talkin'," one of the other drug dealers said. "Ain't nobody tryin' to hear that noise."

"I ain't no sellout!" the man yelled again in Brandon's direction. "Awight?!"

Further up the street, they approached others who were dealing. Though most weren't receptive to what they had to say, some were. Cantrell and his group fared about the same.

From time to time, they repeated the sweeps through the neighborhoods that were most besieged by the illicit trade.

■ ■ ■

"Yes, who is it?" Brandon said, answering the knock at his door one night. It was unusual for anyone to drop by without first calling. There was another knock. He cut the volume on the TV all the way down.

"Who is it?" He waited, but, again, there was no response. He got up and went to the door. With the heavy security chain still in place, he cracked the door just enough to peer out. Two black faces peered back at him. The dark suits and trademark bowties told him they were Black Muslims. One was about average height and build. The other was taller and mean looking, a long scar down his left cheek. Brandon eyed the men uneasily. He knew that his constant talk of Malcolm X might be controversial with the Nation, though he never said anything, one way or the other, about the group itself. "Yes, what can I do for you?"

"As-Salaam-Alaikum, Brother X," the shorter of the two men greeted him. Brandon recognized it as the Muslim greeting in Arabic for 'Peace be unto you.'

"Wa-Alaikum-Salaam," he replied.

"May we come in?" What did they want? Should he let them inside? If they wanted to do him harm, they certainly could have done so by now. They obviously knew where he lived.

"Yes, of course." He unchained the door. "Please, come in."

"Thank you." They stepped inside. "You speak very authoritatively on El-Hajj Malik El-Shabazz," the man said, as he admired the painting on the wall of Malcolm X.

"He was a great black leader," Brandon said.

"That he was."

"Would you like to have a seat?"

"Thank you," the man said. "But we didn't come to stay. In fact, we apologize for dropping in on you like this. Allow me to introduce myself. I'm Brother Carl X and this is Brother Phineas. We're from Temple number 8. We wanted very much to meet you."

"Oh?"

"As I'm sure you've noticed, we've usually had someone at each of your speeches as an observer. We know you've not said anything that might be damaging to the Nation and we appreciate this. El-Shabazz, as I'm sure you know, ended as a controversial figure with the Nation and, consequently, the Nation has no official position on him. However, that does not preclude our privately recognizing the tremendous contributions that he made to the black struggle in America and throughout the world. We've also been monitoring the progress of the boycott and we're impressed by what we've seen so far. Where once there was apathy amongst the people, there is now activism. We applaud you and your organization for that."

"Thank you," Brandon said.

"We're more sophisticated in our doctrine now, as I'm sure you're aware," Brother Carl X said, as he moved casually about the room. "We now recognize that the struggle of our people must cross religious bounds. For whether Christian or Muslim, we are all oppressed by the same forces. Having said that, we're here to offer you our protective services."

"Protective services?" Brandon said, surprised by the mere suggestion. "Well, I appreciate the offer, but I hardly think I'm going to be needing a bodyguard, if that's what you had in mind."

"You may not think so, my brother, but our surveillance tells us differently," the man said, coming to stand back in front of Brandon. "There may have already been one attempt on your life that you probably to this day know nothing of."

"Attempt on my life?" Brandon said, clearly stunned now. "What do you mean?"

"Brother Phineas?" Brother Carl X said, drawing the other man into the conversation.

"Do you remember a few days ago when you were leaving the NAACP building heading for your car and you found the hood up?" Brother Phineas said.

"Yes, I remember it," Brandon said. "Why?"

"You probably thought somebody was just trying to steal your battery, didn't you?"

"Well, yeah," he said, vaguely recalling the incident. "I guess I did."

"Think again, my brother," Brother Phineas said. "One of our men came across someone who was doing something under your hood. Our man chased after him but couldn't catch him. We're pretty sure it wasn't your battery he was after. In making his getaway, he dropped a timing device."

"A timing device?" Brandon said, puzzled.

"Yeah. It's what they use to detonate explosives with." A chill raced up Brandon's spine.

"Well," Brother Carl X said, checking his watch, "we've taken up enough of your time tonight. Here's a number you can reach us at, anytime of the day or night." He passed a business card to Brandon. "If you need us, don't hesitate to call." The two men started for the door.

"Thank you," Brandon said. "I will." He let them out.

A timing device for a bomb? Was his life really in danger? Who could possibly feel threatened enough by him to want to harm him? It didn't add up.

■ ■ ■

"Hey, Brandon?" Cantrell called to him, as he passed his office one evening.

"What's up?"

"Come on in, man," Cantrell said. "I want to run something by you for a second, something I've been meaning to talk to you about."

"Sure." Brandon grabbed a chair next to Cantrell's desk.

"Why don't you close the door there," Cantrell said. Brandon swiveled around and pushed the door close.

"So, what's happening?"

"Well…it's about you and Julie," Cantrell said, then hesitated, like he was unsure of just how exactly to proceed. "Some of the sisters, they're talking…about you and Julie. You know how the sisters are, I mean, about the interracial thing and all." Brandon reared back in his chair, took a deep breath, and slowly exhaled.

"Yeah, I'm afraid I do."

"They've seen the two of you together a number of times," Cantrell said. "So, they know something's going on. Now, personally, I don't have a problem with it, first of all, because it's none of my business one way or the other. Secondly, if the truth be known, there're more than a few sisters that are doing the cross-over, too. They just tend to be more undercover with it than we are."

"So, I suppose they're accusing me of talking black and sleeping white, huh?" Brandon said, recalling Yvette's reaction upon seeing him with Julie that day.

"Something like that," Cantrell said. "But tell me, what really is the deal between you and Julie? I mean, is it serious? She definitely seems like a sharp lady, like she's got it all together. And not too many women, black or white, can compete with her in the looks department, in my opinion."

"Yeah, I'd say it was serious," Brandon said. "I really care about her a lot. She's really special to me. But…"

"But what?"

"Well, as much as I'm into Julie—and I really am into her—sometimes it's like we're so far apart, like we see things so differently now."

"It's the black/white thing, isn't it?"

"Yeah."

"Does she know how you feel, I mean, these doubts you obviously have about the future of the relationship?"

"It's come up before."

"Did you know she calls here for you from time to time?"

"Yeah, I knew." They were both quiet for a moment.

"If you want my advice," Cantrell said, "it sounds to me like you need to sit down with her and express to her these reservations you have, tell her how you feel."

"That's the problem," Brandon said. "I don't really know how I feel. One part of me says it's not gonna work. But another part of me couldn't bear the thought of being without her."

"Well, I guess it's like that sometimes," Cantrell said. "But whatever you decide, man, just make sure you do what's right for you, not what's right for somebody else."

"Thanks, Cantrell," Brandon said.

■ ■ ■

Brandon and George arrived around noon to pick up Mr. Homeland and Mabel. Brandon had mentioned to them a few days earlier that he'd be coming by to take them somewhere special, but he wouldn't tell them where. He had invited George along because he thought it'd be a good learning experience for him. Of all the boys Brandon had gotten to know in the community while making his deliveries, George was the only one he'd managed to keep in touch with. In fact, they had become rather close.

"He tell you where he taking us?" Mr. Homeland asked Mabel, as she helped him into the car.

"Daddy, like I said before we left the house, Brandon ain't told me no mo' about it than he told you. He say it's a surprise. So, I guess we'll just have to wait and find out."

"Surprise, huh?" Mr. Homeland said.

"You'll find out soon enough, Mr. Homeland," Brandon said, glancing over at him and smiling, as they pulled away from the house.

"You know, don't you, boy?" Mr. Homeland said, looking around at George, who was riding in the back with Mabel.

"You're not gonna get it out of George, either, Mr. Homeland," Brandon said. "I told him not to say."

The big house was perched high atop a hill, at the height of about a five- to six-story building. Turning into the visitors' entrance, Brandon started up the steep, curving drive toward the house. Towering oaks and elms shaded portions of the sprawling lawn surrounding the mansion. A gardener was busy tending one of the many flower gardens. As they continued up the drive, recognition of where they were finally dawned on Mr. Homeland.

"This Mr. Frederick Douglass house," he said, excitedly. "I remember how Esther described it. Said it wasn't no house like it she ever seen before."

"Is that where we at, Brandon, Frederick Douglass house?" Mabel asked.

"Yeah, this is it."

As they were about to take the last cross drive leading up to the house, Mr. Homeland said, "Don't go all the way up, boy. Pull up right there in the front. I wanna walk up."

"Daddy, you know you ought not be tryin' to climb all them steps," Mabel said.

"I know what I can do," he said. "Pull up right here, boy." Brandon stopped at the bottom of the last flight of steps.

"Lord, you gon' be the death of me yet," Mabel said, with a sigh, knowing it was futile to argue with her father. Brandon got out and went around to help Mr. Homeland out.

Slowly, Mr. Homeland climbed each of the dozen or so steps. When he reached the top, he just stood there, taking in the house. It was a large, white-brick colonial with four giant alabaster pillars across the front. The second story of the house had a big, three-sided bay window that opened out onto a roof balcony. Red brick chimneys rose up out of the house at either end. A giant oak cast one half of the mansion in deep shade, while the other half glistened under the bright, noontime sun. An aura of serenity and almost reverence exuded from the house. A white woman in a security guard uniform emerged through the front door.

"Hi! Y'all here for the tour?" She had a friendly, southern accent.

"Yes, I'm the one who called earlier," Brandon said, as he helped Mr. Homeland up onto the porch.

"Alright," she said. "Y'all just take your time there. We're in no hurry."

"This just like my grandmama, Esther, said it was," Mr. Homeland said, running his hand up and down one of the thick columns, as he surveyed the porch. "She say she sat right out here on the porch, her, her husband, Mr. Douglass and his wife, just sittin' and talkin'."

"I can see this house holds special memories for you, sir," the woman said. "Why don't we go on in?" She held the door for them. "You're probably gonna see many more things inside, sir, that your grandmother may have said she saw during her visit here. By the way, my name is Brenda. And if you have any questions as we go along, don't hesitate to stop me."

Stepping into the house was like stepping back into time. Except for the wallpapering and a few other items, everything they were seeing—the furniture, appliances, pictures, and so on—was original, according to Brenda. Downstairs were oil paintings of Douglass and his family, including his first wife, Anna, and his second wife, Helen. There was even one of Harriet Tubman. Various rooms were so faithfully re-created that one almost expected Frederick Douglass to walk into the room at any moment. Certain places in the house would bring back memories to Mr. Homeland of something his grandmother had told him. One such place was the women's guest room, where his grandmother was to have slept.

"Now, this is where Frederick Douglass is supposed to have come during the evenings, when he wanted to unwind," Brenda said, as they stepped through the great French doors out onto the balcony. "From here he would watch the steamboats as they traveled along the river out there."

"That the Anacostia River out there?" Mr. Homeland asked.

"Yes, sir. That's the Anacostia River."

"I remember Esther say she sat here on the balcony and looked out on the Anacostia River. Said what a beautiful sight it was to see."

"Here, would you like to take a seat in one of these rockers?" Brenda said, positioning one of the rocking chairs around toward Mr. Homeland. Mr. Homeland took a seat.

"Never thought I'd ever see this day," Mr. Homeland said, misty-eyed, as he gazed out at the Anacostia.

Chapter 24

Although there were some defections as the boycott now entered its second month, the general feeling in the organization was that, overall, things were going well. However, there was concern that, unless something happened soon, the tide of defectors would soon begin to grow, as people became increasingly weary of the boycott. To help prevent this from happening, they kept up the neighborhood rallies.

And as the boycott stretched on, Brandon's contact with Julie grew less and less. It wasn't that he didn't think of her, because she crossed his mind often. But instead of picking up the phone and calling her, he would push her from his mind by immersing himself deeper into his work with the boycott. As soon as the boycott was over, he told himself, he'd get back together with her and things would be as they were before. But how would he explain to her why he had virtually estranged himself from her? He wasn't even sure he could explain it to himself. His way of dealing with it was just to not deal with it at all.

One evening as Brandon and several others were dining on the outdoor patio of a restaurant near Georgetown, he happened to spot Julie coming out of a boutique across the street. She was with two other women. He hurried over to greet her.

"Julie!" She stopped and looked around.

"Brandon?"

"Hi," he said, catching up with her.

"Hi," Julie said. "Look, you guys go ahead," she said to her friends. "I'll just be a minute." The two women continued on.

"You look nice," Brandon said.

"Thank you," Julie said. "So do you. You've changed a little, though. The mustache. That part of your new Brother X image?"

"No, not really. It's just something I'm trying." They stood there for a while in awkward silence, before Brandon spoke up. "I was across the street with some friends, when I happened to look up and see you."

"Oh, I see," Julie said, checking her watch.

"Julie, I miss you," he blurted out.

"Look, Brandon, I really have to go. Okay?" she said, looking away, as she looped the straps of her bag up over her shoulder.

"Didn't you hear what I said? I said—"

"I heard what you said," Julie said, looking him in the eye now. "But, Brandon, I tried calling you. I left messages for you. But never once did I hear from you. Not once. It's been weeks now. Weeks. Then one day you see me out, purely by accident, and you tell me that you miss me? Man," she said, shaking her head, "I don't know what you want anymore. I mean, I'm not even sure *you* know what you want anymore. But whatever it is, I think it's clear it doesn't include me."

"Julie, I'm sorry. But—and I know this is no excuse—but suddenly, with this boycott thing. Well, it just…I don't know… All I know is not a day passed that I didn't think of you, think about us." He reached out and took her hand in his. "Julie, I don't want to lose you. You mean too much to me." Looking at him out of a deep hurt, she gently disengaged her hand from his.

"Look," she said, "I've got to get home and finish packing. I'm leaving in the morning for New York."

"How long will you be gone?"

"A couple of weeks. I'll be there working on a contract."

"Will you call me?"

"I don't know."

"Well, will you at least call me when you get back?" She thought about it. "Please?"

"Okay," she said. "I'll call you when I get back. That's the best I can do. But I'm not making any promises."

"Julie, I—" he started to say, as he reached out for her.

"No…don't," she said, backing away. "Look, I've got to go. My friends are waiting." He watched as she hurried away.

■ ■ ■

The next day, not long after getting home, Brandon received a phone call from Mabel.

"Hello?"

"Brandon? This is Mabel."

"Oh, hello, Mabel. How are you? Everything okay?"

"It's Daddy. He took ill this morning. We had to rush him to the hospital."

"What happened? Is he alright?"

"He's pretty sick," she said. "I'm gonna try to get back out to see him this evening."

"What hospital is he in?"

"St. Joseph's. By the way, he asked about you."

"He did? Well, I'll definitely try to get by to see him first thing in the morning. Do you know what the visiting hours at the hospital are?"

"I think it's from nine to eight at night," she said. "But you can call and they'll tell you exactly. It's room 314, the East Wing." He jotted down the information.

"Okay, I've got it," he said. "You take care. And if you make it by this evening, tell Mr. Homeland I'll be by to see him in the morning." It must have been a pretty bad asthma attack this time, he thought, as he hung up.

■ ■ ■

The following morning, as he was preparing to leave to go visit Mr. Homeland, Cantrell phoned. He was calling an emergency meeting of the Student Auxiliary to address some problems that had suddenly arisen with the boycott. Carla Yancy as well as Goldman would be there. Brandon decided that he had to attend.

The meeting ended up running into the late afternoon. When it finally ended, Brandon headed straight for the hospital.

■ ■ ■

"Can you tell me how to get to the East Wing?" Brandon asked the woman at the information desk at St. Joseph's.

"Sure. Go down this hallway to the end. Take a right. And you'll see the sign directing you to the East Wing."

"Thank you."

To his surprise, the room was empty. He must have the wrong room, he thought. He checked the piece of paper he'd scribbled the room number on. No, it was the right room.

"Excuse me," he said to a passing nurse, "but I'm looking for a patient, a Mr. Arthur Singleton. I was told he was here in room 314."

"I'm sorry, but you'll have to check at the desk, sir," she said. "I'm just coming on duty."

At the main desk, the nurse was on the phone and two other people were already waiting to talk to her. Mr. Homeland had probably already been discharged and Mabel had taken him home, he decided. He'd go by the house.

■ ■ ■

When Brandon arrived, he found the house strangely quiet. He knocked at the door. No one answered. Funny, he thought, that no one was home. He knocked again. Still there was no answer. He decided to go next door to see if the neighbors might know what was going on. But just as he was about to step off the porch, a taxi pulled up to the curb and Mabel got out.

"Mabel, I just got back from the hospital," he said, going to meet her. "I'd planned to get by earlier, but I was in—"

"Brandon, Daddy passed this afternoon," she said, plainly.

"What?"

"This afternoon at the hospital."

"He *passed?*" For a moment he felt as though all the breath had suddenly been sucked out of him.

"It was the cancer, the doctors say."

"Cancer? I didn't know Mr. Homeland had cancer."

"Had it for the longest," she said. "They had told us some time ago it had reached the point where wasn't nothin' else they could do for him." Brandon buried his face in his hands.

"Something told me I should've made it by the hospital this morning like I'd planned to," he muttered.

"This mornin' he got real sick. I tried to call you at home to tell you, but you was gone. I left a message."

"I haven't been back home all day," he said.

"Anyway, I hadn't too long been home from havin' just got back from the hospital this mornin', when Ida, this girl I know that's a nurse there, called sayin' I better come quick, 'cause Daddy had took a sudden turn for the worse, that he couldn't get his breath. So, I runned down to the store and got Mr. Bilbo. He locked up the store and we rushed to the hospital. When we got there, the doctors was tryin' all they could to get Daddy to breathe. But I could see right then he wasn't gon make it. He died not too much longer after me and Mr. Bilbo got there."

"I never knew he had cancer," Brandon said, wiping the tears from his eyes.

"Daddy wouldn't let folk know 'bout a lot of stuff that was ailin' him," Mabel said. "He believed in keepin' it to hisself. That's how he was."

Brandon stood there stunned, trying to come to grips with what had happened.

"Is there anything I can do?" he said finally. "Do you need anything?"

"I'm okay," Mabel said. "All the funeral arrangements and everything been made. It's gon be at Mt. Sinai this Monday at 11 o'clock, with the wake Sunday night at 6 o'clock at Edwards and Sons Funeral Home over on Martin Luther King. The funeral home car suppose to be by here to pick up the family Monday 'bout a quarter to eleven. You can meet here and ride over with us, if you want to. Daddy woulda wanted you with the family."

"Thanks, Mabel. I will."

■ ■ ■

The opened casket, surrounded by a host of wreaths and flowers, sat at the front of the church. As the organist played softly in the background, people went up to pay their last respects. Deaconess Merriweather, Lloyd, Mr. Bilbo, Gill and Lisa were among the many who had come. Finally, the funeral directors came and closed the casket. The ministers, led by Reverend Hollings, now entered the pulpit. After a selection from the chair, one of the associate ministers stepped to the podium. "We will now be led in prayer by the Reverend Coleman Brown, pastor of the New Salem Missionary Baptist Church."

"May we bow our heads in prayer," Reverend Brown began. "God of Abraham, Isaac and Jacob, the author and finisher of our faith, we come to you today saying, thank you, Dear Master. Thank you for the celebration of life that we are here to partake in. We thank you that, though death has stealed into our midst, that we can yet say with blessed assurance, all is well within our souls. But we realize, Dear Master, that none of us know how long we have to stay here. We're just travelers passing through. So, Father, as we go about commemorating the life of your faithful servant, who is now at rest from the troubles of this life, we pray that you might yet in the midst of our grief pour out a portion of your Holy Spirit, so that we who remain might be convicted to live more holy lives, until that time when we, too, must stick our swords in the sands of time and study war no more. And when it becomes yours to call and ours to answer, meet us somewhere in a dying hour, Lord, and grant us a place in thy kingdom, a place where the wicked shall cease from troubling and the weary shall be at rest. And we'll forever give your name to praise. We ask these blessings in the glorious and mighty name of Jesus. Amen."

"*Amen.*"

After the reading of the scripture, there was another selection from the choir. Then it was time for the tributes. Reverend Ellis gave the last one. Standing behind the podium and looking out over the congregation, Reverend Ellis began. "Well, when they asked me to say a few words about Arthur Singleton, I had to think about it for awhile as far as what I'd say. 'Cause there's so much I could say. But more than anything, Arthur Singleton was a Christian. And he was a friend. I been knowin' Arthur since he moved to the area, way back in the late '40s. We worked down at Bruce Lumber Yard together for a number of years. And we became close friends over the years. I could always count on him. And I never knowed him to lie 'bout nothin'. He was just down to earth. I remembers the time, very well, when I took sick and couldn't work. Me and my wife, we had six mouths to feed. But, outside of a little money my wife could bring in from washin', we didn't have hardly nothin' to buy food with.

"I don't know how Arthur found out about it—'cause I didn't really wanna be advertisin' my problems around—but every week, he'd come and leave a big sack of groceries at my doorstep. He'd come way over from where he lived at, all the way over to where we lived at to bring them groceries. I remembers the first time he done it. Ruby come in sayin', 'honey, somebody done left a sack of groceries at our door.' I said, 'did you see who it was left 'em?' She said 'it was some man drivin' a ol' gray-colored Chevy.' I said 'that was Arthur Singleton, couldn't have been nobody else.'

"It took me the better part of two months before I could get back on my feet and work again. And you know, never in that whole time did my family ever have to go without food on the table. Soon as I got some money in my pocket, I went to Arthur and I said, 'I appreciate what you done done for me and my family. Now, I wanna settle with you, pay you what I owe you.' He said to me—and I'll never forget it—he said, 'Ellis— that's what he called me—you don't have to pay me. You don't owe me anything. God, he'll pay me. I'm just glad to be able to do somethin' for somebody.' And, you know, that was the kinda person he was. So, Arthur Singleton was somebody special to me, you see. I'll miss him. But I know he's somewhere up yonder singin'! I know it! I feel it down in my soul! Thank you, Jesus!"

Next on program was a musical selection. Three women all dressed in white gathered at the front around a single microphone. The one in the middle leaned forward. "I just want to say that I been knowin' Mr. Homeland since I was a little girl, grew up with his daughter, Mabel, over there. He was a good man and we gon all miss him a lot. But right now we just wanna try to do this little song in his honor. They tell me it was one of his favorites." Then, with no accompaniment, and each with an arm folded behind her back, they began to sing in three-part harmony.

I've seen the lightning flashing
And heard the thunder roll
I've felt sin's breakers dashing
Which tried to conquer my soul

I've heard the voice of my Savior
He bid me still fight on
He promised never to leave me
Never to leave me alone

No, never alone
No, never alone
He promised never to leave me
Never to leave me alone

Up until then, the service had been mostly free of any displays of emotion. But as the women continued to belt out the song in their raw, untrained but melodious voices, people began to let out their feelings. *"Amens"* and *"Yes, Lords"* rose throughout the sanctuary. The ushers had to go attend to several people who became overcome with emotion. After three verses of the song, the women took their seats. It was now time for the eulogy.

Hollings stepped to the podium. "If you knew Arthur Washington Singleton, better known to many of us as Mr. Homeland, even if you only met him briefly during his sojourn through this life, then you know why we're celebrating today like we are!" The congregation responded enthusiastically. "Even though some of us may be weeping, we're not here today to cry tears of sadness, but to cry tears of joy, because our dear brother is home at last. Yes, we're going to miss him, and we feel a deep void because of his passing, but we come today to say *Thank you, Jesus!* that you allowed him to pass our way. We say *Thank you!* that you let him touch us with his love, touch us with his wisdom, and touch us with his life. I just wanna know one thing. Did he touch anybody here?"

"Oh, yes he did!" came resounding from all over the church.

"You know how he got that name, Homeland? He got that name because he dared to believe that, even back before it became fashionable, that there was something he ought to be proud of about his homeland,

Africa. Yes, he loved America, even back when America didn't love him. But he loved his homeland, Africa, too. But the thing that stood out most about Mr. Homeland, even more than his love for Africa, was that he was genuine, he was real. With Mr. Homeland, what you saw was exactly what you got. He was the real thing. I'm not gonna even take a text for my sermon today. Ushers, you may take your seats. I'm not gonna be long. I'm just gonna tell you what I knew about the man, let his life speak for itself.

"You remember Caleb, back in the Old Testament, the son of Jephunneh the Kenezite, back there with old Joshua. You recall when Moses sent out the twelve from the various tribes to go over and spy out the Promised Land, and how they all came back and all of them, except for Caleb and Joshua, murmured against going over, how Caleb, along with Joshua, was the only one to stand up? What did he tell the people? He told them, 'Let us go up at once, and possess it; for we are well able to overcome it.'

"Well, in a sense, Mr. Homeland was to me what Caleb was to Moses. Let me tell you what I mean. See, when I first came to this church, I was a young man, just out of seminary, had never pastored before. We weren't in this big, beautiful sanctuary we're in now. Those of you who were around then remember that we had outgrown the old building. It was old, the roof was leaky, and it was literally falling apart at the seams. We needed a new building. So, I proposed that we look into building a new church. So, we put together an expansion committee to search out some bids on what it would take to build this new church. They came back with the figures and they looked good on paper. I just thought for sure that they were gonna support it before the people. I just knew that we were gonna be building that new church. I was walking by faith.

"But when the business meeting came around that week, and they got up and made their recommendations to the church, all of a sudden they were singing a different tune. They were saying that they didn't know if we should do it. One by one, they stood up and denounced the plan, saying it was foolhardy, that it was ill-advised, and that it was gonna put the church in financial ruins. I couldn't believe what I was hearing, as I sat by and watched. They even suggested that I was trying to run some kinda scam on the church to put money in my own pocket. People that I thought were with me, turned out to be against me.

"About that time, Mr. Homeland stood up. He was a tall man, so when he stood you couldn't miss him. He turned to the people and said, as best I can remember, 'If I hadna been here to hear this with my own ears, I wouldna believed it. Here, this man's trying to lead us into something that's an improvement, something we been needing for a long time, and y'all talking against him like this. You oughta be ashamed of yourselves. Not only that, but you even talking against him personally, saying that he ain't spiritual enough, that he's even trying to rob the church, that maybe it was a mistake bringing him here to begin with.' Then Homeland said something to the effect of 'I heard about the report that came back. But it ain't the one I'm hearing tonight. I don't know what's gotten into some of y'all, especially some of you deacons here, but you better search yourselves. Those of you that's backstabbing and backbiting against this man, you oughta fall down on your knees and pray to the Lord, ask Him to search you and root out that evil spirit that done got hold of you, 'cause it ain't nothing but the devil. You know this here man. You know what he's done since he been here. Are we gon support him? Or are we gon turn our backs on him?' Then Homeland said, 'I say that when we take this vote, that we vote with the faith that God, himself, has put this man here in our midst to be our shepherd. Don't let a evil spirit get in this place and turn us around from what we know is right!'

"Let me tell you that when Mr. Homeland sat down from serving up that tongue-lashing, you couldn't here hardly a peep from them old devils. The church voted. And they voted for the proposal to build the new church. And we've been growing and adding ministries ever since!"

"Hallelujah!"

"Thank you, Jesus!"

"That's why I say Mr. Homeland was my Caleb. He didn't mind taking a stand for what he believed in. He wasn't afraid to swim against the tide. He wasn't afraid to go it alone, because he knew, I believe, that like the bible says, they that be for us are more than they that be against us. God and me make a majority. No, he didn't mind standing for righteousness. Not only that, but I saw the man endure pain. I saw him many a time, when he was hurting in his body, here at mid-week bible study and prayer meeting. He was a soldier. He'd stand up and testify— even though he was racked with pain—about the goodness of the Lord. And if there was anything he could do for you, he didn't hesitate to do it. If ever there was a life worth emulating, it was that of Arthur Washington Singleton. As the old folks used to say out in the country when they were out in the fields picking, he's reached the end of his row and his bag is full. And now he's calling to the rest of us, come on!"

"Yeh!"

"Come on and live for Jesus! Because only what you do for Christ will last!

"Yeh!"

"Come on! Get on board that Old Ship of Zion!
"Yeh!"

"Come on! I heard it's landed many a thousand!"
"Yeh!"

"Come on! I heard it landed Paul and Silas!"
"Yeh!"

"Come on! I heard it's a good ship, that Old Ship of Zion!"
"Yeh!"

"I'm glad I've got my ticket to ride!"
"Yeh!"

"I wanna know, have you got your ticket?"
"Yeh!"

"I wanna know, when he calls, will you be ready?"
"Yeh!"

By the time Hollings finished, the atmosphere had been transformed into that of a Sunday morning worship service. Finally, it came time for the recessional. The flower bearers came and gathered up the flowers and wreaths.

"May we all stand," the Reverend said. With the congregation standing, the choir began to sing.

Time is filled with swift transition
Naught of earth unmoved can stand
Build your hopes on things eternal
Hold to God's unchanging hand

As the choir sang, the Reverend, reading from the scriptures, led the ministers out of the pulpit. *"Man that is born of a woman is of few days, and full of trouble. He cometh forth like a flower, and is cut down. He fleeth also as a shadow, and continueth not..."* At the same time, the funeral directors began to slowly push the casket up the carpeted aisle. Following behind the casket was the Reverend and the other ministers, then the flower bearers, then the family, row by row. As the coffin passed, some reached out to touch it for the last time. *"...For there is hope of a tree, if it be cut down, that it will sprout again, and that the tender branch thereof will not cease. Though the root thereof wax old in the earth, and the stock thereof die in the ground..."*

At the front door, Brandon joined with the other pallbearers to carry the casket down the steps to the waiting hearse. Once all the cars in the entourage had lined up, the police motorcycle escorts, their blue lights whipping the bright air, led them away from the church.

As Brandon rode in back of the funeral home limousine, bound for the cemetery, something Mr. Homeland had once said to him when they were talking about death came back to him now. *'Ain't no fear in dyin' if yo' soul is at peace within you.'*

Chapter 25

As Brandon browsed the pictures along the wall upstairs at the NAACP building, killing time until the others arrived, Yow passed by on his way to the mail room with the day's mail.

"Anything for me today, Yow?" Brandon asked.

"Oh, hello, my brother," Yow said, stopping and retracing his steps. "Didn't think you were here yet." Yow handed him several letters. Brandon sorted through them just to see who they were from. Among them was an envelope with no return address. Like the others, it was addressed to Brother X. He held it up to the light to see if he could make out the writing inside. The letter was scented with perfume. "Another letter from one of your secret admirers, Brother X?" Yow remarked. "You're becoming quite popular with the ladies, it seems." It was not unusual for Brandon to get letters that smelled of perfume from female admirers. But the lack of a return address made him a little suspicious. "Well, aren't you at least going to open it, to see who the mystery lady is? Or maybe you already know who she is." Brandon handed the envelope back to Yow.

"There's no return address on it," Brandon said. "You know our policy. Toss it."

"I can't believe this," Yow said. "You mean you're really not going to open it?"

"That's right, Yow. I'm not going to open it."

"Well, okay," Yow said, shrugging his shoulders and starting for the mail room. Just at the doorway, he stopped and turned back to Brandon. "But if you won't open it, I guess I have no other choice but to call in master detective Toburi to get to the bottom of this most baffling mystery."

"Have it your way, Yow," Brandon said, focusing his attention again on the pictures. He glanced at his watch. The others should be arriving soon, he thought. *BOOM!* An earthquake-like jolt slammed Brandon hard up against the wall, as the whole building, it seemed, shuddered in a violent spasm. The sound of shattering glass was all around, as pictures, vases, and light fixtures smashed to the floor. Dazed, Brandon struggled to his feet. He touched his hand to his forehead and felt a wet stickiness. Taking his hand away, he saw that it was blood. Panicked footsteps raced up the stairs toward him.

"What the hell was that?!" Cantrell shouted.

"Sounded like a bomb!" Feldon said.

"You alright, man?!" Cantrell said to Brandon.

"I'm alright," Brandon said, still stunned, as he held his forehead.

"Here," Feldon said, putting a handkerchief in Brandon's hand. "Hold this to your head."

"I don't know what it was," Brandon said, pressing the handkerchief to his forehead. "But it sounded like it came from the mail room. Yow just went in there with the mail."

"Come on!" Cantrell said, leading the way.

When they reached the mailroom, they froze. Windows had been blown out, furniture overturned, and books and papers strewn everywhere. But there was no sign of Yow.

"Yow!" Cantrell called out. "You in here? No time for playing games now."

"Yow!" Brandon shouted.

"Maybe he didn't come in here after all," Feldon said. "Maybe he went back downstairs."

"There's one of his sandals!" Brandon said, a sickening feeling coming over him.

"Yow!" Cantrell said.

"Look!" Feldon said, pointing. A foot was sticking out from under an overturned bookcase.

"What happened?" Yvette said, arriving along with some of the others.

"Quick! Give me a hand with this, Feldon!" Cantrell said, grabbing one end of the bookcase. Carefully, Cantrell and Feldon lifted it from Yow's body.

"Oh, my God!" Yvette screamed. The horrible sight before them made Cantrell and Feldon almost drop the bookcase. Yow's whole body was a mangled, bloody mess. One of his hands appeared to have been nearly blown off. And he was hemorrhaging badly.

"Somebody call an ambulance!" Cantrell shouted, as panic ensued in the room. "Call an ambulance!"

■ ■ ■

The door opened and the doctor, still in his surgical gown, entered the waiting room where the Student Auxiliary and other NAACP officials had been sequestered from the media.

"Hello, my name is Doctor Carney. I've come to brief you on Yow Toburi's condition." They immediately began to pepper the man with questions.

"How is he, doctor?"

"Is he gonna be alright?"

"How bad was he hurt?"

"He's gonna make it," the man assured them. "That much we feel confident of. I know you've been waiting patiently for word on your friend's condition, so let me just lay it out for you. Mr. Toburi sustained a concussion," he said, reading from his clipboard, "various internal injuries, including damage to his small intestines, spleen, and his right lung. He also sustained third-degree burns to his face and upper body, a perforated ear drum, along with a host of lacerations and abrasions. And he lost two fingers on his left hand."

"Thank God," Yvette said, drawing closer to Feldon, who had his arms around her. "It could've been worse."

"Well," the doctor said, dropping his clipboard to his side, "we most certainly do have a lot to be thankful for, indeed. But, unfortunately, it was worst. He lost both eyes in the blast."

"*What!*"

"*Oh, no!*"

"We knew going in that one eye was beyond saving," the doctor said. "But we thought we had a chance with the other one. But once we got in, we found there was just too much damage to the nerve endings to save it. I'm sorry. He's just come out of surgery and he's resting in his room. He's not going to be able to receive any visitors, though, probably until tomorrow this time, at the earliest."

■ ■ ■

When they reached Brandon's apartment, a number of reporters were camped out in front.

"Man, do these people ever leave you alone?" Brandon said, as he, Cantrell and Smitty headed toward them.

"Hey, it's their job. Come on," Cantrell said, leading the way up the walkway. "You just gotta know how to play hard ball with them."

"Aren't you Edward Cantrell, president of the Student Auxiliary of the NAACP?" a reporter asked, as he and the other reporters descending on them. "And aren't you Brother X?"

"Yep. Right on both counts," Cantrell said, pressing through the reporters. "But at this time, we really don't have anything to say. So, if you good people would excuse us." Brandon unlocked the door to his place.

"Brother X? Brother X?" a reporter called out. "Can you at least confirm that—" The door slammed shut, cutting off the rest of the reporter's question.

"Just go away, please," Brandon said, his back pressed against the door.

"Maybe they'll get tired and leave after awhile," Smitty said.

"Don't count on it," Cantrell said.

"Hey, you guys have a seat," Brandon said. "I'm gonna get me a beer. Can I get you guys one, too?"

"Yeah, I'll take a cold one," Smitty said.

"Man, after today, I could down a whole keg," Cantrell said. Brandon returned with their beers.

"Damn!" Smitty said, shaking his head. "I knew we got hate mail and all, but I never thought anybody would be crazy enough to actually do something like this. It's like that terrorist shit you hear about over in the Middle East."

"Just goes to show you," Cantrell said. "It's some crazy people over here, too. But I got a strange feeling that this bombing wasn't just about the boycott. It was more than that."

"Whadaya mean, Cantrell?" Smitty said.

"I think I know what Cantrell's getting at," Brandon said. "Drugs."

"That's exactly what I'm getting at," Cantrell said. "The folks that run the drugs into our neighborhoods can't be too happy about what we've been doing. You can bank on that. Since we started those sweeps through the community, drug sells have been dropping off, and for the first time in years." They sat for a moment, sipping their beers, contemplating what they had just stumbled upon. "One thing's for sure, though, Brandon," Cantrell said. "That bomb wasn't meant for nobody but you, my man. Look, why don't you lay low for awhile? Go visit your family or something. Just get away from here. We can handle things."

"Yeah, I agree, Brandon," Smitty said. "Because you don't know when somebody'll try something like this again. If they tried it once, they'll try it again."

"I appreciate you guys' concern," Brandon said. "I really do. But that's exactly what they want, to silence us, just when we're about to make a difference in the community. I've got ways of protecting myself. You'll see. I'll be alright."

"Well, I hope so," Cantrell said, taking a swallow of his beer.

"Hey, turn on the TV," Smitty said. "There's got to be something on the news about it."

"Yeah, cut it on, Brandon," Cantrell said. Brandon picked up the remote and clicked on the TV. A news reporter was reporting from an overpass above the interstate.

"...earlier today, on this stretch of the beltway near the Pennsylvania Avenue overpass where I'm standing now. There were reports of young blacks pelting passing cars with rocks and other objects. Luckily, no serious injuries to any motorists were reported. The most serious of the incidents reported was of several white riders of the metro train being roughed up by roving gangs of black youth. Police seem to think that it, too, was in retaliation for the bombing, as witnesses recounted hearing some of the youth shouting 'this is for Brother X,' as they kicked one man down the steps of the station. All of those attacked were treated for bruises and other minor injuries at the scene."

"Wait a minute," Brandon said. "Why were they saying 'this is for Brother X'? I wasn't the one that was—"

"Hold up," Cantrell said. "Let's check it out." They listened again to the reporter.

"...to the work of community leaders who quickly mobilized and fanned out through the black community, particularly to predicted hot spots, to squelch rumors that Brother X had been the one injured, and maybe even killed, in the bomb explosion that rocked the NAACP..."

"They thought it was me," Brandon said.

"Yeah, and they thought you'd been killed, too," Smitty added.

"Sorry to have to interrupt you, Stewart," the anchorwoman back in the studio broke in, "but we are now going to take you live to the College Park campus of the University of Maryland for this late-breaking story." A scene from the campus flashed onto the screen. Fires could be seen burning in the background, as mobs of black and white students battled each other. Police were trying to break up some of the skirmishes, but seemed badly outnumbered. Some were even retreating. The cameras showed a reporter in the foreground, shielded partially from the melee taking place behind him by his news van.

"Jim, can you hear me?" the station anchor said.

"Yes, Connie. As you can see behind me, we are in the midst of—and I don't know what else to call it but what it is—and that's a race riot. It is very scary out here. Groups of black and white students are going at each other with fists, bricks, bottles, sticks and anything they can manage to get their hands on. It all started out in front of one of the dorms, from what we've been told, when a group of white students allegedly joked that they had been the ones who had sent the letter bomb to the NAACP building earlier today. A group of black students overheard it and took offense to it. Some heated words were exchanged between the two parties, leading to some fist fights. And it seems to have escalated from there. And escalate it did. At least one dorm and an administration building have been set afire. There have even been some unconfirmed reports of sniper fire. Someone with a rifle was reported to be firing out of one of the top floor windows of one of the dorms. This has not been confirmed, however, let me make clear. I can confirm this, however, that in one incident, a young black man was kicked and badly beaten by a group of whites, who then doused him with some kind of liquid, possibly gasoline. But before the mob could do anything further, the young black man was rescued by several other white students, who heroically rushed to his defense, risking their own personal safety to save him. Connie, it is just plain unbelievable some of the things we've witnessed out here this evening."

"Jim, what are university officials saying about the disturbance? Is it something that caught them completely off guard?"

"No one from the university is saying anything publicly at this point, Connie. I expect some sort of official statement will be forthcoming. But while no one, I don't think, could have predicted that something of this magnitude would happen, it is no secret that racial tensions have been running high for the last couple of years at the school now, after several highly publicized racial incidents between black and white students, especially black and Jewish students. Many I've spoken to in the community thought it was just a matter of time before something like this happened, though not on quite this large a scale, that it was just a tinderbox waiting for the right spark. And that spark seems to have ignited this evening, Connie."

"What are the police saying about their ability to get this under control? It looks like pure chaos out there."

"Connie, the police moved in at one time to try to break things up, but had to pull back when things heated up and they came under attack themselves. They now admit that they severely underestimated the size of the disturbance. So they're pulling back for now, with plans to come back with a much larger show of force. They fear that the worst may be yet to come, if they aren't able to get a handle on things by nightfall."

"Jim, just in your opinion, based on what you're seeing out there, do you think the police are going to be able to quell this thing with this larger show of force, as they put it?"

"Connie, I hate to be a pessimist, especially in a situation as grave as this, but, personally, from what I'm seeing out here—and you and the viewers can see it for yourselves—I find it very doubtful that the police alone are going to be able to contain this thing. It's just building and spiraling more and more out of control by the minute. For instance, just over to my right here—if our cameras can get it—another building is now on fire." The camera showed flames licking out of the top floor windows of the building. "But just to try to put things into perspective out here, I remember the Kent State riot back in the '70's and other campus riots, but I don't recall anything that quite compares to this. So, I think they're going to eventually have to call in the National Guard to quell this thing, and the sooner the better." Just then there was what sounded like a gunshot.

"What was that, Jim? Sounded like a gunshot."

"Connie, what you heard was tear gas being fired into the courtyard behind us. You can see the white fog that's spreading over the ground. Other canisters of tear gas are also being fired, as you can hear. Police had said that they might have to use tear gas to try to disperse the crowd, before moving in on them. In fact, you can see them, what must be a hundred or so police, outfitted in gas masks and full riot gear. They're now beginning to advance on the students. But I can tell you, Connie, that the police are still severely outnumbered and—" Suddenly, there was a clunk and the picture from the campus went out of focus.

"Jim? Jim? Can you hear me, Jim?"

"Yes, Connie," the man said, a few moments later, as the picture came back into focus. "What happened was a brick just hit one of our cameras."

"Is the camera crew alright?"

"What?"

"Is the camera crew okay?"

"They're okay, but we're going to have to find a safer place to set up, because rocks and bottles are now increasingly flying in our vicinity."

"Okay, Jim. You guys seek a safer location. And we'll try to get back to you later."

"Okay, Connie." The picture then went back to the studio and the anchorwoman.

"Again, that was Jim Summers reporting live from the College Park campus of the University of Maryland, where heavy rioting is going on between black and white students. The whole thing, we are told, was precipitated by—" Brandon clicked off the set.

"Man, can you believe this?" Smitty said. "They're actually rioting over at Maryland!"

"If anything," Cantrell said, "you'd have thought this would be going down out in the street, not on a college campus. Man, this is the '60's all over again."

■ ■ ■

"Brother Carl X speaking."

"Brother Carl X?" Brandon said into the phone. "This is Brother X. Did you hear about what happened today, about the bombing?"

"Yes, I did," Brother Carl X said. "And I wish I could say I was surprised, but I can't. Were you hurt at all?"

"Except for a small cut on my forehead, no, I wasn't," Brandon said. "But a co-worker was. It was a letter bomb, the police say, and he apparently opened it and it blew up in his face. He lost both eyes."

"Very sorry to hear about your co-worker, very sorry. But I'm happy to know that you were not seriously injured."

"Thanks."

"You think you might now want to avail yourself of our services?" Brother Carl X said. "The offer still stands."

"Yes, I think so," Brandon said.

"Good. We can ill afford for another strong voice in our community to be silenced through violence. Just as soon as I get off the phone, I'm sending over someone to guard your place tonight. And I'll be in touch with you first thing tomorrow about the security arrangements we'll be putting in place for you, my brother."

"Thanks, Brother Carl X. I really appreciate it."

"No problem. As-Salaam-Alaikum."

"Wa-Alaikum-Salaam," Brandon said.

Almost as soon as Brandon put the receiver down, the phone rang.

"Hello?"

"Brandon?"

"Julie. Where are you? Are you back in town?"

"No, I'm still in New York. Listen, are you alright? They said on the news that there was this big explosion at the NAACP building today, that it was some kind of letter bomb."

"Yeah. I'm okay. But Yow got hurt pretty bad. He lost both eyes."

"Oh, no!"

"He apparently opened it and it blew up in his face," Brandon said. "I was across the hall when it happened and he was in the mail room. We just got back from the hospital where they rushed him to."

"How's he doing?"

"Well, they wouldn't let anyone in to see him. But the doctors say he's stable. He's got some other injuries. But none of them are thought to be life-threatening."

"That's good," Julie said. "So, you sure you're okay?"

"Yeah, I'm okay. I've got a little cut above my eye from when the blast knocked me up against the wall. But, other than that, I'm okay. My nerves are still a little shot, though."

"I can imagine," Julie said. "Well, I just wanted to see if you were okay. I'll let you go. Bye."

"Wait," Brandon said.

"What?" Julie said. Brandon hesitated. He wanted to ask if she had given any thought to them getting back together when she got back in town, tell her how much he'd missed her. But for some reason he couldn't.

"Nothing," he said. "Listen, thanks for calling. And take care."

"You, too." A pregnant silence filled the line. Julie finally broke it. "Bye."

"Bye." Another long interval passed before one of them actually hung up.

Chapter 26

The rioting at the university lasted for two whole days before the National Guard could finally bring it under control. Six people were killed, dozens of others injured, many of them seriously. Early estimates of the amount of damage to the campus ranged in the millions. No one even began to try to estimate the damage that had been done to the relationships between blacks and whites at the school.

It was several days before they were finally able to get in to see Yow. His condition had been upgraded from critical to serious. The bombing made the whole boycott personal for Brandon now. Before, it had just been something he was doing out of a sense of civic duty. Never had he really considered that he might be seriously injured or even killed working with the boycott. Now, that reality hit him squarely in the face like a heavy fist. The NAACP joined with the school in setting up a fund to help defray some of Yow's medical expenses and to pay for his parents to travel from Nigeria to take him back home. It was unclear, at the moment, what Yow's plans would be for the future. The NAACP building, because of its sturdy design, had escaped any serious structural damage. Only that part of the building where the blast had actually occurred had really been affected.

A predominately white, non-denominational bible study group at the University of Maryland got together with similar groups at other area colleges and held a candlelight prayer vigil on the Maryland University campus the following night. There were no speeches, only prayers. It was held out in front of the Black Student Center, which had been heavily damaged by the rioting. Brandon and other Student Auxiliary members attended.

The inability of the police to arrest anyone for the bombing only intensified the black community's frustration. As many blacks saw it, the fact that no arrests were forthcoming was further indication that their lives were not valued very highly. There was widespread concern that if the DA's office continued to refuse to take action in the slaying of Deanna Wilkins, that the black gangs would make good on their earlier threat to unite to jointly attack Koreans and whites.

Brandon and Cantrell seized upon the opportunity to set up a meeting with the mayor and his top aides to discuss the situation, to see what could be done to further pressure the DA's office into action. They met that Monday. At the meeting, it was agreed that a noontime march and rally would be held on Friday of that same week. The staging area for the march would be in front of the District Building on Pennsylvania Avenue. From there, they would march to the District Courthouse over on Constitution Avenue.

For the remainder of the week, the Auxiliary worked feverishly to make all the necessary arrangements for the march. With the help of the black media, the event was publicized throughout the Washington area. From feedback they received, a sizable crowd was expected. Security was increased and everyone was on the alert, as several bomb threats were phoned in anonymously to the NAACP offices. There were no incidents, however.

One unforeseen consequence of the rioting was that whites, both college students and young professionals, began calling the NAACP office to volunteer to help with the boycott. The issue was raised at one of the meetings of the Student Auxiliary.

"I guess you've all heard that we've been getting calls from some white college students and others wanting to join with us in working with the boycott," Cantrell said. "Personally, I have reservations about it. How do the rest of you feel?"

"I think there's a role for whites to play," Smitty said. "I'm just concerned that if they get involved that it might weaken our efforts somehow. I mean, I'm concerned that blacks in the community might begin to wonder whether we're compromising on our positions."

"And why do they want to help now?" Yvette said. "They never wanted to help before?"

"Yeah. That's right," someone said. "Plus, all the real work has already been done."

"What do you think, Brandon?" Cantrell said. Brandon thought for a moment.

"Well, I think if they want to help, we ought to welcome them aboard," Brandon said. "Let's not forget that by presenting a multi-racial front, it can only strengthen our position. While the boycott is about securing fair treatment for blacks and other people of color, it's also bigger than just that. It's about fairness for all people. As far as them waiting until now to offer their help, well, I guess it's better late than never."

"What about you, Angela?" Cantrell said. "What do you think?"

"I think Brandon's right," Angela said. "And they're not asking to take over the boycott, only to help. We could certainly use them on the picket lines and to help with the rallies. We need all the able-bodied people we can get." They took a vote on the matter and voted not only to allow whites to participate but to welcome them at the strategy sessions as well.

In addition to whites, a number of young black professional also volunteered to work with the Student Auxiliary on the boycott. One of them was Chelsea Hazeltine, a bright, young, attractive bank loan officer, daughter of a prominent Washington-area dentist.

"Drats!" Chelsea said, stomping her foot on the tile floor of the breakroom one evening. The drink machine had once again rejected her dollar.

"For some reason, it doesn't seem to like your money," Brandon said. She turned to see him standing a few feet away, smiling.

"Oh, hi," she said. "I've just about had it with this stupid machine."

"Here, let me try," Brandon said, taking the dollar bill from her. "Sometimes you have to sort of mash it up a little before this machine will take it." He crumpled it into a ball, then flattened it out again. "Now, let's try it." Brandon reinserted the bill into the machine. This time the machine took it. *Bing!*

"Well, thank you very much," Chelsea said, making her selection. The canned drink slid down the chute. "And to show my appreciation, can I offer to buy you a pop, too?" Brandon glanced at his watch.

"Sure. Why not." After getting his soda, Brandon joined Chelsea at one of the tables.

"I'm Chelsea Hazeltine," she said, offering him her hand.

"Hi. I'm—"

"Brandon Northcross," Chelsea said. "Also known as Brother X." They shook hands.

"Yes. Hopefully, better known as Brother X. What else do you know about me?"

"Well, I also know that you have an MBA from Dartmouth, that you used to work as a marketing research analyst at CSU, and that you're originally from New Hampshire."

"Well, I see you've certainly done your homework."

"You might say I make it my business to know about people I find interesting," she said, smiling.

"Well, I'm certainly flattered to be among that select group," he said. "But you really find someone as ordinary as me interesting?"

"Whether you know it or not, you've become something of a folk hero," Chelsea said, holding up a copy of the Washington Post with Brandon's picture on the front.

"So I have," Brandon said, taking a look at the picture. "Tell me, with those shades on, can you tell it's me?"

"Not really."

"Good."

"I take it that getting involved with the boycott wasn't something you'd really been planning on doing."

"That would be a fair statement," Brandon said. "It sort of found me, you might say."

"So, how *did* you get involved with it?"

"Well, I went to the community meeting held by the CBBC to discuss the shooting of Deanna Wilkins at the Student Union at Howard the night of all the rioting. I got up to say a few words and ended up giving a little impromptu speech. It just sort of happened. And, well, one thing led to another. And here I am. Brother X."

"I've heard you speak on several occasions," she said. "And neither time did you use any notes. But you related so much information. You're very gifted."

"Well, thanks," he said. "I don't know about being gifted and all. But as far as being able to recall facts, I read a lot. And when you read a lot, I guess things have a tendency to stick in your mind."

"I read somewhere that most people use only 5 to 10 percent of their brain's capacity, and that if they could tap into more of that capacity, they could more than quadruple their ability to remember."

"Interesting," he said. "Did it say how to go about tapping into the rest of that 90 to 95 percent?"

"No, but I suppose in the case of memory, it would help if one focused on whatever it was they wanted to remember," Chelsea said. "Would you agree?"

"Yeah, I would agree." Chelsea leaned forward just slightly.

"And people tend to focus on things that they find of interest. Right?"

"I would agree with that, too."

"And speaking of focusing," she said, toying with her gold necklace, "you definitely seem to be the type of person who seems to know how to put his mind to something and stay focused on it."

"I try to be," he said.

"So, no distractions for you right now? Like a social life, for instance?"

"Well, unfortunately, I don't have time for much of one at the moment," Brandon said. "This boycott is just too all-consuming." He stole a glance at his watch. "Well, looks like it's time to get back to work." He stood up.

"Oh, yeah, me, too," Chelsea said, rising from her chair.

"It's been real nice talking," Brandon said.

"Same here."

■ ■ ■

That Friday, Brandon and the other Student Auxiliary officers met at the NAACP building. From there they, along with a contingent of Nation bodyguards, left in a caravan for the rally. When they reached the District Building, a sizable crowd had already formed out front. Police barricades were up, blocking off the parade route they would take. A contingent of motorcycle cops waited near the entrance. As they headed down the ramp of the District Building to its underground garage, flashbulbs from press cameras exploded all around them. Once inside the garage, they took an elevator up to the main lobby, where everyone, except for Brandon, Cantrell and two of the bodyguards, got off. On the eighth floor they were ushered into a private lounge to await the start of the rally. The bodyguards waited out in the hall.

From the window overlooking the mall, Brandon looked down on the crowd, which was swelling by the moment.

"Well, how you feel, man?" Cantrell said, joining him, a cup of coffee in his hand.

"A little nervous, to tell the truth," Brandon said. "There're a lot of people out there."

"Yeah, they're out there," Cantrell said, looking out at the growing mass. "And it's probably gonna be a lot more, too, by the time we get to the courthouse. But just remember, you don't need to tell them anything you haven't told them already. Yeah, they're looking for a big speech and all from you, but the essence of what you've got to tell them is basically what you've been telling them all along. You agree?"

"Yeah, I agree," Brandon said, wondering if what he'd been telling them up to now had really, in fact, been what they had needed to hear. A knock came at the door and one of the mayor's aides stuck his head inside.

"You guys ready?"

"Yeah, we're ready," Cantrell said.

"Good," the man replied. "The mayor's waiting."

Once the mayor's security chief had given them a short briefing, they all took the elevator down to the lobby. When they emerged through the doors leading outside, they were met with cheers. The mayor, being the consummate politician, waved heartily to the crowd, as did Brandon. Moving out in front of the marchers, they joined other notables, assembling about a dozen abreast. Positioned immediately in front of them was a complement of Nation bodyguards, with another group forming a protective shield behind them. With the police escort leading the way, the march got underway. People lining the parade route cheered as they went by. Some leaned out of the windows of office buildings, waving and displaying banners in support of the rally and the boycott.

"Hey, homeboy! Homeboy!" Brandon kept hearing over the din of the crowd. Glancing over toward the sidewalk, he spotted Redding, who was keeping pace with the marchers.

"Redding!" he yelled back, waving.

"Stop by the club sometime!"

"I will!"

"And stay black!" Redding shouted, thrusting a fist high into the air.

A chant began from within the ranks of the marchers.

"We want justice now! We want justice now!"

When they arrived at the courthouse, Brandon and the other dignitaries mounted the platform. A sea of faces surrounded the stage on all sides. Throughout the crowd were signs reading, *"No Justice, No Peace"* and *"Black Life Is Valuable, Too."* Just as Cantrell had predicted, the crowd seemed to have nearly tripled in size from what it had been earlier. A feeling of tense anticipation hung in the air, like an electrical charge just waiting to explode into a shock wave of thunder. Cantrell took his place at the podium.

"What's up, D.C.?" Cantrell said. "How you feel? You feel alright?"

"Yeh! "

"I said do you feel alright?"

"Yeh! "

"We're going to get things started with a word of prayer from Elder Roger Stubblefield, pastor of the Temple Church of God in Christ. Elder

Stubblefield?" A little man with silver-flecked hair, a crucifix depending from around his neck, came forward.

"May we bow our heads. Heavenly Father, we come beseeching your throne of grace today, bowed with humility and awed by your omnipotence. We know that we've come this far only because of your divine goodness and your undying love for sin-sick humanity. We ask that you look down on our endeavors here today and bless us in such a way that we can bring about the change in our brothers' and sisters' hearts that needs to take place here in this great city of ours. Inspire us, Lord, and consecrate us with your Holy Spirit. Then endow us with power from on high. For if we're endowed with just a portion of your miracle-working power, we can say to yonder mountain, mountain, be thou removed and be thou cast into the sea. For the bible says that you can open doors that no man can shut. And you can close doors that no man can open. Finally, Lord, let our efforts today be not in vain, but let them be as bread cast upon the proverbial waters, that in due time they may return multiplied sevenfold. We ask it all in your precious and mighty name. Amen."

"Amen."

"Thank you, Elder Stubblefield," Cantrell said. "We're now gonna ask Carla Yancy, president of the D.C. branch of the NAACP, to come and say a word to us." Carla Yancy stepped to the mike.

"Thank you, Edward. Hello, D.C!"

"Hello!"

"As I look out at all of you, from all over D.C. and surrounding areas, it warms my heart to know that we're finally coming together as one. People, this is beautiful." The crowd applauded. "I'm encouraged when I see people concerned enough about what's going on in our communities to take off from their jobs and come out to show their support. By just being here you're sending a message loud and clear to the courthouse all the way to the White House that the citizens of the District of Columbia can no longer and will no longer be taken for granted." She was interrupted by applause again. "Whether we're granted statehood this year, next year, or never, we're sending out the message loud and clear that we mean business. And our business today is to see to it that the meanness that we've been subjected to in our communities from certain merchants is brought to an end. And that this practice of the judicial system looking the other way when black people are victimized is also brought to an end!" She paused for the applause before continuing.

"Yeh!"

"Say it, Carla!"

"People, if we want things to change, we've got to demand that things change. And the only way to do that is to do what we're doing today, standing shoulder to shoulder united. Let me also say that I've been just overwhelmed by the outpouring of support for the NAACP these last few months. Membership is at an all-time high, and contributions have been generous. I challenge you to keep up that support, and not just wait until we have a crisis. And support our other organizations in the community that are attempting to serve the people. Thank you." Cheers and applause rang out. Cantrell hugged Carla Yancy as he came back to the podium.

"Thank you, Ms. Yancy. I now wanna bring—what?" Cantrell turned to hear what someone behind him was trying to tell him. "Rudy? Rudy's here?" Cantrell said into the mike, as he looked out into the crowd. "Where you at, Rudy?" A little freckled-faced man down front was frantically waving his hands about. He was dressed in a red shirt with long, pointed collars, a yellow vest and a green derby with a long, red feather sticking up from the side and a pair of brogans. Those around him were laughing. "Come on up here, Rudy. Come on up." The man made his way up onto the stage, where he went over and shook hands with the mayor and others before joining Cantrell. The crowd cheered him.

"Yeh, Rudy!"

"Rudy!"

"Rudy ain't on program—he never is—but he always manages somehow to get on program," Cantrell said. "Rudy, for those of you who might not know, is always at community-related events. If it's something to do with the black community, something positive, he's usually there. So, we're gonna ask him to say a few words to us. Come on, Rudy, say a quick word to the people. Just a quick word, now."

"Hello, everybody!" Rudy said.

"Hey, Rudy!"

"Y'all know I laugh and clown a lot, that I can clown with the best of 'em. But why we here today, folks, is for serious business, serious business. What happened to that young girl gettin' shot down in that store like she was shouldna happened to a dog. You hear me?"

"Say it, Rudy!"

"I'm tellin' you, it burned me up, when I heard what happened, and then saw it played back on TV. We need to stand up, people. Don't shop at these stores that's treatin' our people wrong. Have some pride in yourself. When I sell my hot dogs down there on the corner of 15th and Connecticut, I tries to treat people right, treat 'em with respect, treat 'em the way I'd want to be treated. If somebody ain't treatin' you right, don't spend yo' money with 'em!"

"*Yeh!*"

"And tell yo' friends not to spend they money with 'em! That's all I got to say. Can I do my little dance now, Cantrell?"

"No dancing this time, Rudy," Cantrell said, playfully shooing Rudy off the stage. "Let's hear it for Rudy, ladies and gentleman!" The crowd cheered as Rudy stepped down from the stage. "Alright, folks, we're gonna switch gears a little now and bring on the man who has led this great city of ours for a number of years, who stood for us back when the iron boot of oppression was planted firmly on our necks. He marched with us, he sat in with us, he protested with us, he even went to jail with us. He's our champion. I'm talking about the Honorable Hubert Raines, mayor of the District of Columbia! Mayor Raines!" Cheers rang out as the mayor took his place at the podium.

"First, let me say that as mayor of this great city, I commend each of you for joining with us today to help keep this city a great place to live, a place where people of all races, religions and nationalities can live and work together in harmony, side by side. Give yourselves a hand." Applause issued forth from the crowd.

"Let me begin by saying that we're facing some frightening times, people, when a person can be shot down in cold blood by a merchant simply because of a shoplifting dispute. It's frightening times, people, when the legal system is so biased that it refuses to even arrest the merchant who—as evidenced on video tape—clearly committed this injustice. I want to know how long we can take this abuse of power. I want to know how long we can simply stand by and idly watch the wheels of justice, not just turning at a snail's pace for our people, but not turning at all. However, I want to make it clear that it's the judicial system that we're protesting against, not the Korean people. We are an inclusive city. There's room for everybody." The crowd responded with applause.

"When I was elected mayor, I was elected to be mayor not just for black people, not just for white people, not just for this group of people, or for that group of people, but for *all* people. That's why I'm determined to see this thing through." He was forced to pause once again for applause. "When the leaders of the Student Auxiliary approached my office about staging this rally, I told them that they could count on my full support. I've seen the kind of injustice that prompted this boycott. I had hoped that these kinds of things were in the past. But it seems that racial intolerance still lingers in this country. As you know, I've devoted much of my adult life to eradicating it as well as other forms of injustice. So, I'm not about to stop now. I don't know about you, but I've come too far to turn back now!"

"Yeh!"

"We've made too much progress, climbed too many mountains, to turn back now. But if we're gonna make it over, we've got to somehow learn to live together, to get along with each other."

"Yeh!"

"Come on!"

"For as the late Dr. King would often say, either we learn to live together as brothers, or we all die as fools. I want to know, are you devoted to seeing this thing through?"

"Yeh!"

"Together, can we do it?"

"Yeh!"

"Together, can't we bring about a change?"

"Yeh!"

"Alright, then. And now, I ask that you welcome to the podium a young man who's won the heart of our great city through his vigilant work with the Student Auxiliary of our local chapter of the NAACP, in trying to right some of the wrongs in our communities. I bring to you Brother X!" Brandon rose and headed for the podium. A chant started up from somewhere in the crowd.

"X, X, X!"

At the same time, two Nation bodyguards came and flanked him on either side. The other bodyguards spread out down along the front of the stage, facing the crowd. A big sign near the back of the crowd read, *"What Would Malcolm Say?"* While they were still chanting, Brandon began.

"My brothers and my sisters, I hope that that X you're chanting is for Malcolm X, and not Brother X. 'Cause I'm just a follower, like you. Malcolm was the leader." The chanting started anew. He waited until the crowd quieted before continuing.

"We've come here today, some of us taking off from our jobs to be here, to send a message to the DA's office that we're not going to accept having black people's lives counted of less value than that of others. When Deanna Wilkins was gunned down in cold blood, shot in the back of the head over an accusation of shoplifting, that was our sister, our daughter being gunned down. That's right. That could have been any one of our loved ones, murdered in cold blood."

"Make it plain, Brother X!"

"You telling it right!"

"Now, we're not asking that the laws be rewritten for us. All we're asking is that we be written into the laws. That's all we ask." A roar went up from the crowd, as the chant *"X, X, X!"* started back up. Brandon began to feel a kind of bonding taking place between himself and the crowd, in the same way he had when he had spoken at the meeting that night at Howard. It was as if their energy was beaming up to him and his down to them. And not only could he hear and see them, but he could feel them, and they, in turn, could feel him. He waited again for the chanting to die down, then continued.

"You see, the law is only as good as the application of it—the equitable application of it. In this case, it is not a matter of the unjustness of the law, but simply of its application. When a law—any law—is applied unequally, applied indiscriminately, it loses its credibility in the eyes of the people that it is used against. What I'm saying simply is that if it's wrong for a black person to take the life of a person of another race, then it ought to be equally wrong for a person of another race to take the life of a black person."

"Yeh!"

"Say it!"

"When our judicial system sits down on us, it's time for us to stand up to it!"

"Yeh!"

When truth, itself, seems compromised by those in power, those without power must lift their voices as one, and restore truth to its rightful place." He waited for the applause to end. "Now, there are those who said that this boycott was a bad idea, that all it would do is drive a wedge between the races, bring out the bad in those whites and Asians of ill will, and alienate those whites and Asians of goodwill. They point to the recent bombing, where one of the officers of the Student Auxiliary, Yow Toburi, was very seriously injured, as proof that they were right.

"And furthermore, they said that this boycott was simply doomed to failure from the very beginning, that this simply wasn't the time for it. They said that the failure of the boycott would just embarrass the black community, reveal our internal weaknesses. But I want to tell you today, my friends, that sometimes there comes a time when you must put the popularity polls aside and press ahead with what you believe deep down inside is the right course. And even if you fail, it is much better that you tried, tried with all your heart, than that you never had the courage of your convictions to have ever tried at all. I'm reminded of the words of Martin Luther King in his *Letter from a Birmingham Jail,* when he said, 'right defeated is stronger than evil triumphant!' I'd rather it be said, when this is all over, that we were a people who decided that this was something worth standing up for. I'd rather it be said, years from now, that we were a people who didn't mind tasting the bitter cup of defeat, in the hope that it would make victory just that much sweeter in the future. If we give up now, if we give in to the pressures, both from within and without, then we will have failed not just ourselves, but we will have failed the very essence of who we are as a people. We will have failed our ancestors. If Frederick Douglass were here today, could we look him in the eye and tell him, I don't think we can go on. It's too hard. It's too dangerous. We're giving up?"

"*No!*"

"Could we say it to Harriet Tubman?"

"*No!*"

"How about Sojourner Truth?"

"*No!*"

"How about Nat Turner?"

"*No!*"

"How about John Brown?"

"*No!*"

"How about Booker T. Washington?"

"*No!*"

"How about Marcus Garvey?"

"*No!*"

"How about Malcolm X?"

"*No!*"

"How about Martin Luther King?"

"*No!*"

"No?"

"*No!*"

"Well, then, let us resolve with unbending determination to press on!"

"*Yeh!*"

"Press on with the assurance that, no matter what obstacles come our way, God is with us. Bombs cannot defeat us, for we've got something stronger than any bomb, or any physical force, and that is spiritual force. And with this spiritual force we intend to keep on fighting, to see this boycott through. And we intend to keep on pressuring the DA until he wakes up and does the right thing, even if it means that we have to come down here every day for the next year. For we are determined, in the words of Malcolm, to gain our God-given rights as men and women in this city, at this point in history, *by any means necessary!*"

The crowd went crazy, their cheers and applause rolling up to him on the warm air like thundering waves, overlapping one another, and showing no sign of subsiding. Though he had more to say, as he looked out over the ecstatic crowd, he knew that he had already done what he'd set out to do. Those on stage, as well, were on their feet applauding wildly. Cantrell was the first one over to him.

"My man! My man!" he said, hugging him gleefully, as if he'd just scored the winning basket for their team.

"Brother X?" the mayor said, the next to embrace him. "You did it!"

"Thanks, Mr. Mayor."

"Great speech!" someone else said, pumping his hand.

Descending the platform, Brandon was mobbed by people trying to congratulate him. Flashbulbs lit up the air, as news photographers jockeyed for position to try to get a good shot of him and reporters thrust their microphones at him.

"Brother X, there have been reports that more and more people are crossing the picket lines at the stores," a reporter said. "Do you think your speech is going to turn that around?"

"Well, I really hadn't heard that there were that many people crossing the picket lines," Brandon said. "But I will say that I certainly hope my speech, as well as the others today, will help inspire the community to stick it out."

"Brother X, did it shake you up when you learned that the letter bomb that exploded at the NAACP office, injuring one of your co-workers, was actually intended for you?"

"Well, certainly it did. I think it would shake up anybody. But what disturbed me even more was to know that there are people out there who would stoop to such viciousness."

"Brother X?"

"Brother X?"

"That's all. Thank you," Brandon said, trying to move away. But reporters continued to pursue him.

"Brother X?"

"Brother X?"

"Sorry, but no more questions," Cantrell said, as he and the Nation bodyguards hustled Brandon away.

Chapter 27

Reaction to the rally and to Brandon's speech in particular was mainly positive. Within a few days, however, much of the excitement that had been generated by the rally had subsided. And when there was no immediate response from the DA's office or the Korean grocers, certain leaders in the black community who had never really supported the boycott to begin with began to speak out against it. They claimed that the continued resistance by the merchants to the NAACP's demands was proof that the boycott had failed and that, furthermore, it had been ill-advised from the very beginning. Some, who would have turned a deaf ear to such talk before, now began to turn their backs on the boycott. To try to stem the tide of defectors, the Student Auxiliary canvassed the neighborhoods day and night, urging people to continue to honor the boycott. They had only so much impact, however, for with each passing day more and more people crossed the picket lines. Although the overall number of defectors was still small, if it continued, it would soon sound the death knell for the boycott.

But of even greater concern now were rumors that the black gangs had already put in place plans to carry out their threatened attack in just over a week. The gangs would give the boycott until then to produce results. If nothing happened by then, the war was on, as they put it. In addition, many young blacks, who before had supported the boycott, now spoke in favor of the action being proposed by the gangs. To their way of thinking, the system had failed them, so they had no other option but violent confrontation.

Then late one evening, with only a couple of days left until the gangs' imposed deadline, as Brandon and the others were all upstairs in the conference room working on a new strategy, Smitty raced into room, his eyes lit up like he'd just won the lottery. "Quick, everybody! I just got a call! The Korean merchants just called a press conference! It's supposed to be on right now! Come on!" Everyone dropped what they were doing and rushed down the hall to the TV. Smitty cut it on as they all crowded around. A Korean man, seated at a table in front of a bank of microphones, was reading from a prepared statement.

"...has been a very grueling and demanding ordeal for our stores, as well as for the community. We seek nothing but to serve the community to the best of our abilities, with the finest service and highest quality in goods at low, affordable prices. This has always been, and will continue to be, our aim. Nevertheless, to put this whole unfortunate episode behind us, we are conceding to all demands put forth by the NAACP." The reaction was spontaneous, as they began high-fiving and hugging each other.

"Yeah!"

"It's over!"

"Wait a minute, everyone!" Angela said, as a reporter came into the picture. They quieted down.

"... word just in that the DA's office is reconsidering its decision not to prosecute the storekeeper who fatally shot Deanna Wilkins, the young black woman whose death sparked the boycott back in..."

"We did it!" Smitty yelled. "It's over!"

"Where's that champagne we been chilling for the last month?" Cantrell said.

"I'll go get it," someone said, hurrying from the room.

"Break it out and bring some glasses, too," Cantrell said. "This is cause for some good, old-fashioned celebratin', folks!"

The champagne flowed freely, as they toasted their success. Someone put on some hard-driving dance music and people took to the floor.

"Well, my man," Cantrell said to Brandon, as they clinked their glasses together. "We pulled it off."

"Yep. We did it," Brandon said. "I just wish Yow could be here with us."

"Yeah, I really miss the little guy," Cantrell said, pausing a moment to reflect. "We all do."

"Hey, let's keep the party going, man," Smitty said, coming over and thrusting out his glass for a refill.

"Now, damnit, Smitty, don't go gettin' drunk," Cantrell chided, as he refilled Smitty's glass. "'Cause you know you ain't used to no real champagne. This ain't none of that ol' cheap-ass ripple y'all drank out in the country where you from."

"Cantrell, get the hell outta here," Smitty said, laughing, before heading back out to the dance floor.

"Oh, by the way, Brandon," Cantrell said, "has Ms. Yancy talked with you yet?"

"No. What about?"

"Well, Colin Delaney, president of Delaney and Associates, the largest black-owned marketing firm in the area, saw your resume and wants to talk to you about a management position with his company," Cantrell said.

"Really?"

"Yeah," Cantrell said.

"Well, alright, then!" Brandon said, giving Cantrell a high-five.

"Give Ms. Yancy a call this evening," Cantrell said. "She's been trying to reach you all day."

"Yeah, I will," Brandon said. "Thanks for the news."

"Hey, if anybody deserves it, you do, man."

"Thanks."

"Are you guys just gonna stand over here in the corner talking, or are you gonna ask a lady to dance?" Angela said, striking a sassy pose in front of them, her hands on her hips.

"Girl, you ain't said nothin' but a word," Cantrell said, setting his glass down and taking Angela's hand. "I'm gon show you some real dancing."

Some of the newer Student Auxiliary members who had been working downstairs appeared at the door.

"Hey, what's with the party, guys?" one of them asked.

"You mean you all haven't heard?" Yvette said.

"Heard what?"

"The boycott's over!" Smitty shouted. "We won!"

"Y'all come on in!" Cantrell said. "Join the party. There's plenty champagne. And pizza's on the way." They wasted no time joining in the festivities. Brandon spotted Chelsea and went over to greet her.

"Chelsea."

"Oh, hi, Brandon! Congratulations!" She gave him a big hug. Suddenly, it was like he was seeing her for the very first time. Maybe it was the softness of her hazel eyes. Or maybe it was the way her pouting lips parted when she smiled. Or perhaps it was the contrast of her lustrous, jet black hair against her smooth, golden-brown skin. Whatever it was, the attraction was apparently mutual, as she held his gaze.

"C'mon, let's dance," Brandon said, reaching for her hand. Squeezing in among the other couples, they quickly found their groove. As they danced, Brandon began to feel some of the same emotions he had felt when dancing with Julie that night down in Georgetown. The twinkle he saw in Chelsea's eyes told him that she felt something, too. But did she? He decided to find out. It was just a little peck on the cheek. She blushed. Then she kissed him back, on the lips. It was now his turn to blush.

"Hey, Brother X," Pervis said, playfully nudging Brandon with his elbow, "quit hogging this pretty woman all to yourself, man. Let me get just one dance with her."

"Be my guest, Pervis," Brandon said, good-naturedly stepping aside.

As Brandon looked on at the celebration, he thought of Julie. She hadn't called as she'd said she would. But neither had he tried calling her. For the first time, he forced himself to face up to the painful reality that it was over between them, and actually had been for some time. But he still cared about her and probably always would. And no matter what happened now between him and Chelsea, nothing could ever change what Julie had meant to him. Catching his eye, Chelsea waved. He smiled and waved back, then left the room to find a phone.

"Hello?" Julie answered. He was about to say something when an idea popped into his head. What if he surprised her with flowers and didn't even let her know he was coming? It'd be a classy way of saying goodbye, of closing one chapter of his life before beginning another. Then he'd return to the celebration and to Chelsea. "Hello?" He'd be back before anyone even missed him. Gently, he hung up the receiver. There was only one problem. He didn't have his car with him, as his bodyguard was still chauffeuring him everywhere. After thinking for a moment, he came up with a solution. Returning to the lounge, he went up to Smitty, who was working out hard on the dance floor.

"Smitty."

"Hey, what's up, my man?" Smitty said, giving Brandon a high-five. "Man, I still can't believe it's over!"

"Yeah, me either," Brandon said. "But listen, Smitty, I need to ask a favor."

"Just name it."

"I need to borrow your car. I want to make a little run." He knew that Smitty probably didn't need his car, because he often left it parked overnight at the NAACP building.

"Hey, no sweat," Smitty said, digging into his pocket for his keys. "But I thought your bodyguard was still driving you around."

"Well, actually, he is," Brandon said. "But I need to take care of a little personal business. You know."

"Yeah, sure, man," Smitty said. "No problem." Smitty handed over his keys. "Just be careful, though. Alright?"

"I will," he said. "Thanks."

Brandon's bodyguard was reclining in a chair near the front door reading a newspaper. He was able to avoid him by ducking out through a side door.

Unlocking the door, Brandon scooted behind the wheel of the big Buick. It was an old car with plenty of miles on it, but it was dependable, according to Smitty. Brandon cranked it up and headed for a nearby florist. There he bought a half-dozen red roses, Julie's favorite. Exiting the shop, he heard the grumbling of thunder in the sky from over in the direction he would be heading. Dark clouds were forming and rain seemed imminent. He got back in the car and started on his way.

By the time Brandon took the exit off the interstate for Julie's place, the sky had darkened and a steady rain was falling. He turned on the windshield wipers. They made a hard, grating noise against the windshield, as they fanned back and forth. He wondered what Julie would think when she opened the door and saw him standing there with roses. What if she had company over? He reminded himself that he was going there to say goodbye and wish her well, not to pay her a visit. His mind wandered back to the evening he and Julie had met outside work. It seemed like only yesterday. An object in his rear view mirror interrupted his musings. It was the dark, shadowy form of a car. It was following close behind him, its headlights dimmed. Studying the outline of the car closer, he was finally able to make it out. It was a police cruiser. The incident with the two racists cops clicked in his mind with a disturbing abruptness, as he remembered the cop's warning: *'Boy, you got off easy tonight. Next time you might not be so lucky. You can count on that!'* Was it the same cops behind him now? Fear began to gnaw at his insides.

Conscious now of his surroundings, Brandon noticed that the stretch of road he was on had no street lights and was bordered on both sides by nothing but dense foliage. Not a house was in sight. It also dawned on him that he had missed his turn somewhere back along the way, as the road he was now on didn't look at all familiar to him.

Suddenly, the lights on the cruiser flashed on. Brandon pulled over onto the shoulder. Glancing in his mirror, all he could see was the bright, swirling gale of lights and the stabbing headlights. Then he heard the car doors slam and saw the figure of a cop emerge from the glare. As the man drew nearer, Brandon's worst fears were realized. It was Manny, the same cop from before. Brandon tensed as he prepared to face him. The cop motioned for him to roll down his window. He complied.

"Well, look who we got here," the cop said. "Remember me, boy?" He had his baton out and was striking it in the palm of his hand in a menacing manner. "I knew it'd be just a matter of time before you and me met up again. So, just cut the engine and step on out here." Brandon hesitated, as he tried to decide what to do. "And I mean right now!" the cop yelled, slamming the baton down hard across the roof of the car.

In that split second, Brandon decided that if he were going to try to make a run for it, then it had better be now, as it was clear what the cop had in mind for him. Reaching for the gear shifter, Brandon quickly threw the car back into gear and punched the accelerator, sending the Buick barreling down the rain-slicked road.

His heart pounding, Brandon pushed the big V8 engine for all it was worth, as he tried to gather his wits about him. Where was he? What road was he on? He didn't even know what direction he was headed. But he had to get away. It was no telling what they'd do to him now. The police car came into view in his mirror. And it was gaining on him, too. Maybe he could turn off somewhere and ditch them. But there were no turnoffs. Then on a hill up ahead, through the trees, he saw some lights. As he drew closer, he saw that the lights were those of a convenience store. Yes! If he could make it there, where there were people, maybe he'd have a chance. With witnesses, they'd be forced to think twice before doing anything to him. Maybe they'd leave him alone.

WHAM! The police car rammed him hard from behind, causing him to nearly lose control. But the weight of the big car kept it from going off the road. WHAM! It rammed him again. This time the car skidded over on to the shoulder, but somehow he was able to get it back onto the road surface. Then before he knew it, he was upon it, the road leading up to the store. This might be his only chance. Slamming on the brakes, he cut the wheel hard to make the turn. But the combination of speed and wet road conditions sent the car skidding sideways, then into a spin. He fought to regain control, but the next thing he knew he was plunging down a steep, pitch black embankment. It happened so fast that all Brandon could do was ride the brake and grip the steering wheel. A fraction of a second was all he had to brace himself for the clump of trees looming just a head. Instinctively, he threw up his arms to shield his face. After caroming off a number of trees, the Buick finally came to a rest against a large oak, the impact hurling him into the windshield, dazing him.

By the time he was able to clear his head, the cops—who were now joined by several other cops—were shining their flashlights down into the dark gully, trying to locate him. Both of the car's headlights had been smashed.

"Quick, get that spotlight over here!" one of them said. He had to get out and make a run for the store before they spotted him! That was his only hope. But when he tried opening his door, he found that it had jammed. Frantically, he threw his shoulder into it. Still it wouldn't budge. He tried rolling down the window. But it too was jammed. And he couldn't get out through the other door, because it was smashed up against the tree. He was trapped!

"There he is!" one of the cops said, as the bright cone of light found him. He had to somehow get out of the car and fast! But how? The window! Kick it out! Leaning back, he kicked at the window again, and again, until, finally, it shattered. Wasting no time, Brandon squeezed himself out through the opening, careful to avoid the jagged edges of the broken glass, then took off in the direction of the convenience store. He ran as fast as he could, but it was uphill and the smooth leather soles of his shoes worked against him, causing him to repeatedly slip and slide over the wet, muddy ground. Looking back to see how close the cops were to him, he tripped over a vine and fell. In the process, his pants leg snagged on a thorn bush. Damn! He struggled to get free. But by the time he was able to free himself, they were nearly upon him. It was too late to try to run. Seeing a thick tree limb laying nearby, he picked it up to defend himself.

"So, you wanna play a little hardball, huh?" Manny said, coming at him, his baton poised for action.

Seeing an opening, Brandon swung the limb with all his might, catching Manny across the bridge of his nose. The blow sent the cop to the ground in a heap. Grabbing his face, Manny let out a sharp, pained yelp, as he writhed on the ground. One of the other cops came at him now, his night stick raised. Brandon swung at the man, but missed, as the cop ducked under the limb. At the same time, the cop swung his night stick, connecting flush across Brandon's wrist, causing him to drop the limb. Grabbing his wrist, Brandon tried to run. But the other cops moved in, raining down a volley of blows, staggering him, and finally sending him to his knees. Brandon managed, somehow, to struggle back to his feet, but quickly went back down again under the heavy barrage of blows from the cops' batons. To protect himself, he curled up into a fetal position, his arms around his head.

"You're gonna get it now, nigger!" Manny said, as he and the other cops began to beat him mercilessly all along his body, from his ankles to his head. Soon, Brandon's entire body was nothing but a throbbing, aching mass of fire. Blood began to stream from his mouth and nose, mixing with the rain. His eyes nearly swollen shut, he winced at each blow.

Several times he heard Neil yell, "That's enough, Manny! That's enough! Back off! You gon kill him! You gon beat him to death!" But the blows kept coming.

Finally, the beating ceased, as he heard Neil shout, "You went too far this time, Manny! You went too damn far!"

"He ain't moving," a cop said, crouching over Brandon.

"Come on!" Neil said. "We got to get him to a hospital!"

"It might be too late for that," the cop said. "I'm not getting much of a pulse."

"Goddamnit, Manny! You done killed him! How am I gon cover for this? If you had just backed off when I told you to, he'd still be alive!"

"Damnit, Neil, it was me the nigger waylaid in the face with that goddamn limb! Not you!"

"But you didn't have to go and kill him! What am I supposed to say in my report now? It'll look like I didn't have control of the scene as the commanding officer!"

"Just say what happened," another cop said, "that he attacked us with that tree limb and that it was justifiable use of force to subdue him. That's all. And remember, he did try to run from us."

"Well…that's true," Neil said.

"And another thing," the cop added. "It's better if he dies here, than we take him to the hospital and …"

As the cops' voices and the crackling of their radios began to fade in his ears, Brandon felt himself become lighter and lighter. His last thoughts were of the roses back inside the car and the peaceful sound of the falling rain around him. And in the midst of the roses, the light bloomed.